KT-164-509

Madge Swindells was born and educated in England. As a teenager, she emigrated with her parents to South Africa where she studied archaeology and anthropology at Cape Town University. The author of numerous novels, her work has been translated into nine languages and has reached bestseller lists across the world. She currently lives in Kent.

RIPPLES ON A POND

The well-heeled village of Temple Minnis presents a façade as smooth and calm as its deep, dark lake. But all is not as it seems. Simon Shepherd's marriage is a sham, his daughter running wild. When he awakes one night to the smell of woodsmoke, his fury at the thought of tramps, gypsies or immigrants on his land is fierce — until he sees the exotic and intriguing Bela who has taken refuge there. But Temple Minnis has a darker secret to hide. Thirty years before, the villagers conspired to plan and conceal a murder, but only their dying local novelist, Melissa, suffers from pangs of conscience. As the villagers face up to the past, love turns to fury and tragedy . . .

Books by Madge Swindells
Published by The House of Ulverscroft:

THE CORSICAN WOMAN
SUMMER HARVEST
SHADOWS ON THE SNOW
SONG OF THE WIND
SNAKES AND LADDERS
SUNSTROKE
WINNERS AND LOSERS
TWISTED THINGS

MADGE SWINDELLS

RIPPLES ON A POND

Complete and Unabridged

CHARNWOOD
Leicester

First published in Great Britain in 2005 by
Allison & Busby Limited
London

First Charnwood Edition
published 2005
by arrangement with
Allison & Busby Limited
London

The moral right of the author has been asserted

British Library CIP Data

Swindells, Madge
   Ripples on a pond.—Large print ed.—
Charnwood library series
   1. Murder—Tanzania—Fiction 2. Women
novelists —Fiction 3. Tanzania—Fiction
   4. Detective and mystery stories
   5. Large type books
   I. Title
   823.9′14 [F]

   ISBN 1–84617–086–9

Published by
F. A. Thorpe (Publishing)
Anstey, Leicestershire

Set by Words & Graphics Ltd.
Anstey, Leicestershire
Printed and bound in Great Britain by
T. J. International Ltd., Padstow, Cornwall

This book is printed on acid-free paper

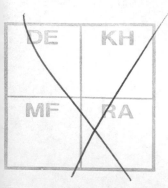

Foreword

Frost touches the north downs and the grass burns brown. The year has reached its nemesis, debts have been paid and all that is left is the grieving.

Looking back in anguish at the year that engulfed and almost destroyed his world, Simon would pinpoint the night that Bela came back as the start of his trauma. That was the precise moment the pendulum turned. At the time he'd had no idea who she was. That was the crazy part of the story. And she had no inkling of what led her to shelter in his wood on that brittle-cold, January night.

'It looked safe,' she told him months later.

Was it his own uneasy conscience drawing her to him to purge his crime? Mystics speak of a force which strives to create an equilibrium in the human psyche. They call it *karma* in the east, a Sanskrit word which translates to action-reaction. The precision with which the balance is restored is frightening for those who ignore their debts, for once disturbed the pendulum swings back . . . action-reaction! But for Simon that knowledge came much later.

Prologue

The woman turned and walked slowly towards him and for a moment of misplaced optimism Simon thought that she had changed her mind and forgiven him, but then he looked into her eyes and saw that he might lose her. She had judged him, found him guilty and accepted her loss, perhaps even welcomed it.

'I've told you how it was,' he said, with a catch in his voice. 'Now that you know, we must move on.'

She shook her head and looked away.

He was as sad for Bela as for himself. For a moment he almost lost his resolve. But how could he tell her the truth? How could she live with that knowledge? She was so young. He ached to fold her in his arms, but if he did he would weaken. Give her time, he thought. Eventually she would come to terms with what he had told her and she would forgive him.

Simon watched her, loving the sight of her and longing to comfort her, while she fumbled in her bag. Moments later he was amazed to see that she was holding a revolver. She looked absurd and he wanted to laugh. Perhaps he did. He half rose, dazed with disbelief, as the muzzle swung towards him.

'No! Bela! For God's sake . . . '

3

He felt incapable of movement as he saw her finger tighten on the trigger. There was no pain as he spun around, only a total loss of balance. The report exploded in his ears as he fell back onto the floor.

As if in a dream he saw Bela leaning over him and felt her tears splashing his face. The gun was pointing towards him, her mouth was open, but her eyes were closed as she fired again and again.

His mind wandered. He seemed to be watching from a great distance.

He had heard that a dying man might see his entire life passing in a series of images, but for Simon his life only began when he met Bela in the woods, in the moonlight, on a frosty winter's night.

PART 1

Winter, January 20, 2001

Stripped of its leaves,
Bereft and frozen,
The willow feels the sap rising.

1

Midnight! A strong east wind was soughing around the eaves, billowing the curtains so that the draught blew on Simon's face disturbing his sensuous dream. He drew the duvet closer around his neck, snuggling in, seeking a few more moments of illusion although the memory had slipped away. It was early January and the manic cries of mating foxes rang in the hills. After eighteen years of meagre sex he still yearned for passionate lust, but lately that hope was dwindling.

Simon kicked back the duvet and got up to close the window. The sky was midnight blue and the uncaring moon, like a golden scythe, sliced through the flimsy clouds and hurled them aside. Beyond the farmhouse, the sloe-black wood disturbed him with its brooding malevolence. As a fresh gust of wind brushed his face he caught the faintest whiff of wood smoke. Strange! He scanned the barns, but there was no sign of a fire, but the scent came again and he sighed, knowing he'd have to check the barns.

Drawn to his wife, he crept to the buffer zone between their virtuous beds where the alarm clock stood guard, ticking away their lives. Laura was breathing heavily, one hand thrown across the duvet, her blonde hair spread over the pillow, her breasts exposed teasingly through the dark blue chiffon nightdress. Fortyish, but still alluring. Simon had always coveted beauty and the sheer white sheen of her skin filled him with wild longing.

He pulled on the old corduroy trousers he wore to tend the sheep and a thick, tattered sweater. Taking the torch, he crept downstairs. Passing through to the scullery, he took his anorak from the peg on the wall and put on his old boots. He left by the back door, ignoring his dog, Sam, who was whining in the glassed-in porch. It was well below freezing and he fumbled in his pocket for a scarf, winding it round his neck, enjoying the sting of the crisp air on his cheeks.

Taking the footpath across the kitchen garden to the orchard, he hurried down a steep ice-slippery slope towards the stables and outhouses. Beyond the yard, the sties gleamed white in the moonlight. He breathed in deeply, enjoying the many scents that made up his world, manure, hay, the sweet-sour reek of the dairy and the warm stench of his sows. And smoke! No mistake! Dauntless, his dappled mare, whinnied and stamped, tossing her head until he paused to rub her cheeks. The pigs grunted and blundered around disturbing the roosting doves who took off clapping their wings in panic. Leaving the yard, Simon took the path bordering the ancient cemetery and hurried along the path into the woods.

The earth lay stupefied as if by hypothermia. He listened, but heard nothing, so he moved on. Groves of ash and chestnut trees obscured the pale moonlight and a thick screen of hawthorn, crab apple and dogwood tore at his face and clothes. In the still night air the crunch of his boots was like gunshots.

Reaching the river, he thought he heard a low voice warbling in a minor key. The sound stopped abruptly and all he could hear was the restless sifting of dead leaves raked by the wind. He caught a glimpse of flames flickering through the branches and he swore. Who were they? Tramps, or gypsies, or part of the growing cult of feckless, restless nomads. More likely they were 'illegals' hiding from the authorities. The world's flotsam and jetsam were trickling into Britain, changing the fabric of English life and now they were on his land, but not for long.

As he clambered down the steep bank, he was panting with fury. These immigrants were symptomatic of the entire malaise that was destroying a cherished way of life. He searched around for a stout stick before stepping into the river and wading thigh-deep through icy water.

He was sweating despite the cold as he clawed his way up slippery slopes. Before him the ground fell away to a clearing where an old cart had lain rotting for years. He used to play on it when he was a boy, but now it was burning. Sparks spiralled and a large pot propped on four stones was hissing and steaming, filling the glade with a tantalising smell. They'd stolen a lamb or a fowl. Tightening his lips he prepared for a fight, but the clearing was deserted except for a 4x4 camper parked under an old oak.

Striding towards the fire, he tripped headlong over the cart's iron axle and took a nose-dive into the mud. He heard a child screaming and a soft, whispered reply. Moments later he felt someone tugging at his shoulder. A smell of intimate, musky perfume enveloped him, black hair fell around his face and a voice murmured: 'Are you hurt?'

Public school English, Simon noticed, feeling confused. He stood up, swearing softly, feeling bemused by the blurred image of a woman in a sari. When he'd blinked a few times and wiped the damp earth out of his eyes, he saw her face and almost gasped. Something about her touched Pandora's Box and a mass of emotions and buried memories surged into his mind: hands that were velvety-soft to touch, with plump, tapered fingers, laughing eyes and mobile lips that were forever teasing him.

Shaking off forbidden images he stared too intimately. She looked so pallid in the moonlight, her skin like alabaster, her eyes seemed huge, larger than life, and her lips too full and shapely. It was a trick of the light, of course, yet from her clothes he deduced that she was at least partly Indian. She reminded him of those absurdly naïve, but heavily sexual Indian movies shown late at night on TV. Swollen pouting lips, exotic, kohled eyes, black hair falling in waves over her shoulders. Even the brooding pensiveness that was all about her spelled heady sexual undertones. Her pallid complexion contrasted strangely with her exotic features.

Clinging to his arm, she pushed him towards a canvas chair and then stood back to examine him, her eyes warm and caring.

10

'Did you hurt yourself?'

'I'm fine, thanks.'

A child began to cry fitfully without much confidence of being heard, it seemed to Simon, and the sound moved him.

'Sit there, please. I won't be long.' She turned away.

Simon had intended to tip the stew over the fire to put out the flames, but now, disarmed and defeated, he watched his chicken breaking up in the boiling water, surrounded with onions, tomatoes, carrots and rice. A sprig of rosemary floated on top. A nice touch, he thought sullenly. He made a mental note of the camper's registration number in case of further theft. Glancing around, he saw a wooden chest containing a few cooking utensils, two folding chairs and a camping table. Not the usual gypsy paraphernalia. He knew he ought to tell her to leave at once, but he was snared by curiosity and her amazing beauty. Wet through and unable to stop shivering, he settled down to wait.

He heard branches cracking. When the woman emerged from the shadows he saw a toddler sitting astride her right hip. With her other hand, she clutched a small girl of four or five years who was staring longingly at the steaming pot, while chattering in what sounded like Arabic. The children were so thin. The toddler's nose was running, there were sores around his mouth and his hair was damp. All the world's woes seemed mirrored in the little girl's eyes. He felt disappointed in their mother.

'Your child needs a doctor.'

'He has been very ill, but he's recovering.'

He guessed they were on the run, keeping their heads down, stealing a little and gleaning any odd jobs that came their way.

'Who are you? What are you doing here?' she asked, neatly reversing their roles.

'I saw the fire. The stew smells good.' He smiled at the simmering pot, hoping to overcome her embarrassment at stealing his chicken, but she misunderstood and her eyes glittered with compassion.

'Oh!' The soft implosion of breath came like a sigh through parted lips. 'You are hungry. You will share our food of course. There's enough for four.'

Did she think he was a fugitive on the run? Simon had inherited his mother's black hair and dark skin, along with her green eyes, although his were more khaki than green. Had his fall, together with his old farm clothes, completed the picture of someone down on his luck?

'The food is ready. I'm sorry there's no bread.' She shrugged as she ladled vegetables onto a tin plate. Simon pulled himself together.

'I'm not hungry, thank you.'

'But I insist. Of course you are hungry. There's no need to be shy.'

She handed him a plate containing an onion, a leg, a few vegetables and half a potato. He sat on a fallen log feeling out of touch with reality and trying to still his guilt with the thought that it was his chicken anyway. The older child wolfed down her food fast with the deep appreciation of true hunger, but the woman had to coax the

12

toddler who was whining feverishly.

Simon began to prod and pry, telling her of a distant visit to the Middle East and his admiration for the architecture of old Iraq, then he described the wild mountains near Sarajevo where he had skied, even mentioning a scuba diving trip to Turkey. She parried neatly and all he learned was that she had travelled extensively. When she announced that she was tired, he stood up.

'Thank you for the food. Perhaps I should introduce myself. My name is Shepherd . . . Simon Shepherd. I farm here.'

She shuddered, looking shocked and scared, her mouth half open, as second by second her composure drained into the bracken.

'What is it? What's wrong?' He reached towards her, but she stepped back making an obvious effort to pull herself together.

'Nothing. I must explain. I was too tired to drive on, so I pulled in here. I'm trespassing on your land. I'm sorry.'

He frowned at her. 'Stay as long as you wish. There's plenty of room. But will you be all right?' She was trembling, he noticed, yet some indefinable quality she possessed quelled pity and demanded respect.

'Of course. There are no bombs or guns here.'

'So who are you?' he persisted. 'Where are you going?'

'My name is Bela Shah and I'm on my way home.' She held out her hand. It was an obvious dismissal.

Simon said goodnight and turned away,

13

unwilling to leave, but knowing that he must. Who were they really and where did they come from? Shah was a Muslim name. The children could be Arabs, but she, with her pallid skin and huge glittering eyes, looked entirely unique. He could find no resemblance between the woman and the children and from the older child's behaviour he guessed that they weren't hers. She might be an economic migrant who had entered the country illegally, yet her voice didn't fit this scenario. So why were the children so terrified? And why had she looked so alarmed when he told her his name? He was sure that he had never seen her before, yet he was plagued with a strange sense of recognition. It was as if he'd known her well a long time ago.

Unanswered questions engrossed him as he walked back to his house. Intrigued and unable to let go, Simon packed a hamper of food. That would do for tonight, but the thought of all the tomorrows looming up made him pause halfway out of the door. The enormity of what he was taking on was daunting.

Feeling embarrassed at his unsubtle philan-thropy, Simon hurried back to the camper. What madness had led him to say she could stay? He would be drawn into her conspiracy and God knows he hated anything underhand. The glade was still and dark when he returned. Bela was asleep, it seemed, so he put the box on the roof of the camper, well away from foxes and badgers, and went home.

Next morning, the sun rose on fields covered with deep frost under a silvery sky. After

14

supervising milking, he doggedly counted every fowl, but to his surprise, none were missing. Guilt sent him hurrying through the woods with a full milk churn and a shoulder of lamb, but a pile of drenched, charred wood, a forgotten sandal, and his lingering regrets, were the only reminders of his guests for the night.

PART 2

Spring, March 21 – June 20.

Alone,
The timorous puma flees the dawn,
Leaving a sense of loss.

2

Simon woke before dawn to the sound of frantic cries from the sheep on the hillside and Sam's frenzied barking. He stumbled out of bed, grabbed his gear and his gun and set off with his dog.

It was a cold March morning and still pitch dark by the time he had climbed to the perimeter of his fallow land, where a tangle of pristine trees and undergrowth covered the chalk. Pointless to creep. Every step crunched like crackers through the thick hoar frost. He paused to examine the spoor by torchlight. Sam was shaking with tension.

'Quiet!' he muttered to his growling dog. As he suspected, the mysterious 'big cat' which had been terrorising livestock on neighbouring farms, had moved on to his land. Ten minutes later, a sudden snarl brought Simon to a halt. They could both smell the musky, sour odour that was altogether foreign. The beast was crouched in the blackthorn thicket, dense and dark and thick with thorns, not four metres away. His heart hammered with excitement. This was not the first time he had followed the big cat's trail, but always on neighbouring farms, and he'd never been so close. Leaning against a rock, Simon forced himself to wait.

After ten minutes Simon's hands were almost numb, so he eased the rifle under his arm and flexed his fingers, kneading them back to life. Sam edged towards him and pressed himself against his legs. He could feel the dog's shuddering fear.

A deep snarl sent a jolt of adrenaline surging through his veins as Simon took aim. He had half a mind to pepper the bush with shots, but once wounded the beast would take off into the hills and he would have to follow its trail, which might take days. He aimed his torch beam into the impenetrable tangle of brambles and nettles and caught a glimpse of two yellow eyes gleaming, while the menacing rumble increased in intensity. Behind him, Sam whined and shook, cowed by the loss of a lamb.

'Stay, Sam,' he whispered. His dog would die to protect the flock, but this unknown threat that crept out of the night terrified him. To Simon, the cat typified the unwelcome foreign influx that threatened all aspects of amiable English life, but one that he could deal with, he thought furiously, as again his finger tightened on the trigger.

He waited, feeling vaguely oppressed by the passivity of his strategy and longing to attack, but knowing he must not.

⋆ ⋆ ⋆

The eastern horizon glowed soft oyster grey, but as yet not a glimmer penetrated the woods. Soon the cat would have to flee in daylight, a moving target over the stony hilltop beyond the copse. There was a contract out on the beast's life and

20

an easy rivalry existed amongst local farmers as to who would kill it first and win the prize money. They had all lost lambs, even half-grown sheep and legends of the big cat's power and origins were rife in this peaceful community, but no one had seen it. A puma escaped from Bekesbourne's zoo, some guessed, or a leopard set loose as a cub. They had all examined its spoor, pads as big as saucers causing deep indentations in muddy trails. Sixty kilos, his neighbour reckoned. Simon had scoffed at the idea, but now he wasn't so sure.

With an unwelcome lurch of spunk his dog raced straight into the thicket, barking heroically. Yelps, snarls and savage spitting sent Simon lunging forward. Sam was being slaughtered, but before he could get there the dog soared in a high arc, yelping before it hit the ground. He caught a glimpse of yellow eyes glinting as something big and black rocketed past him and fled to the hills. Amazement dulled his mind and moments were lost before he fired three shots and heard the soft whack of the bullets against the leafy loam. Then he turned his attention to Sam who was badly mauled and looking agonised at his humiliation.

'You daft dog.' He stroked the quivering collie, trying to calm it as he examined the wounds, feeling that he was somehow to blame. 'Silly Sam. You should have waited. Come on. Get up. You can walk, can't you? You've had a narrow escape, my boy. That'll teach you.'

As he left the woods, the first whorls of misty mauve lit the trees and a tide of shadow retreated swiftly over the hills and valleys. A vague luminous glow spread over the chalk downs and Simon felt the chilling north wind stir and spring to life as evanescent glimpses of the retreating moon shone between racing clouds. He set off for home, glancing at Sam who was limping, but seemed to be coping. The dog was well-trained and should have obeyed instructions.

Despite the promises he had made to himself, Simon could not resist searching the woods beside the river for signs of smoke, but they remained dark and still. Then Bela came to him out of his cheating memory, her eyes glowing with admiration, her skin flawless, her hair and silk burkha wafting and shimmering in the soft breeze. There was nothing subtle about memory, Simon decided, images were hyperbolised for better or worse. He trudged on, feeling disappointed.

★   ★   ★

Cresting the next hill he could see their village, Temple Minnis, half-hidden in morning mists. Simon paused and looked back. Sam was swaying on his feet. He'd have to carry him. Taking his mobile, he called James Evans, their vet, to ask him to come in early and as usual James agreed. He was a good friend.

Lifting the dog, Simon took a short cut across a field. From the next hilltop, he could see his gaunt, stone homestead called Redhill. It had been built by a local trader, Johannes Shepherd, onto the salvaged east wing of a twelfth century monastery, torched in 1530 when the Catholic monasteries were destroyed on the orders of Henry VIII. The Shepherds had farmed here ever since, patiently adding to their acreage as the opportunities arose. To the south, banks of crocuses, snowdrops and budding daffodils framed the farmhouse. To the east, fields of grain alternated with fallow grazing land where his prize British Milksheep roamed over the hillside.

In terms of history, the Shepherds were newcomers to these parts. Stone Age clans fought and hunted here before the last Ice Age, their heroic bones enriching the fertile soil. Their flint spears, knives, scrapers and burins lay in Simon's fields. Then snow and ice reclaimed the land.

Later, hardy tribesmen returned across the marshy straits from the great plains of the Continent, settled, fought and spread across this land of haunting beauty, with its mists and gentle rain, its lingering summer twilight, its fertile, long-suffering soil, its pristine forests and pure, swift-flowing rivers. Their women walked tall beside them and fought with their men. Occasional glimpses of their legendary heroes shone through the baffling mists of pre-history. Then Celts came, bringing their Gods with them and when they raced naked to battle in their chariots, their skins adorned with woad tattoos, their hair streaming in the wind, long spears held high, Morrigan, their ferocious Goddess of war, was right beside them.

They walked in fear of Flidais, the seductive

huntress who could tempt them into the primeval woods and drain them of their vital fluids. They worshipped Cernunnos, the horned God of animals, but they held in highest affection, Epona, the horse-Goddess, who rode sidesaddle and punished those who harmed their horses. The Celts had a deep love of animals and above all their horses. The Celts were still here, Simon knew, hidden deep in English genes and the land was still full of their magic.

According to family history, a ruined Celtic chapel dedicated to Ana, Goddess of the earth and its fruitfulness, the most ancient and important of all Celtic deities, lay beneath the ancient monastery. As a boy Simon used to fancy he saw her in the swirls of mist racing up from the Channel, her half-naked body covered in tattoos, her wild red hair hanging to her waist.

★   ★   ★

Soon Simon was striding past his flock, savouring the scent of the thick damp wool.

He reached the yard, passing a line of ducks waddling past the orchard towards the dam. It was not yet seven, but the dairy had been scrubbed and hosed by his new assistant, Sarah Jones. She looked anxious as she hurried towards him, wiping her wet hands on her trousers.

She stopped short. 'Oh God! What happened?' She leaned forward to stroke the collie, quivering in Sam's arms.

'It's for real after all . . . that so-called big cat . . . It looks like a puma. Sam needs stitching.

24

I'm rushing off to the vet. Look after everything. I won't be long.'

'Did you kill it?'

'I missed.'

She looked up. 'Mum wants to see you . . . if possible, this evening . . . that's if you don't mind . . . there's a problem.'

She spoke in staccato phrases between sniffs and wheezes. Sarah had recently quit a good job at the local semi-conductor plant because of asthma and allergies. She was a strong, swarthy young brunette with a passion for horses and muscles like a blacksmith. She lived with her mother and siblings in neighbouring Newtown, which lay below the line. Simon liked and trusted her, but he failed to hide his irritation. Sarah noticed and her cheeks turned crimson.

'She can't help it. There's something that's not right. We thought of asking the police, but reckon they'd take Jules away.' Her soft brown eyes kept shying sidelong like a nervous horse.

'Your brother?'

Sarah nodded, close to tears.

'He's in trouble, is he?'

'We don't honestly know, do we.'

'Don't worry. We'll sort it out.' Simon was irked by what he guessed would be a request for money.

'Mum's on shiftwork . . . so let's say around eight.'

Why me, for God sake? And so late. Feeling unfairly imposed upon he turned away.

3

By seven p.m. Simon was running late for his appointment. He sped back from the village considering his satisfactory day. His prize-winning and favourite Friesian cow, Candida, had produced a pretty bull calf . . . milky-eyed with long black lashes, the winter crops were flourishing and egg production had increased, although one of his fowls was missing. This was his daughter's fault, he decided. At seventeen, Ana campaigned ferociously on behalf of every living creature. Belonging to a dozen different movements, she'd turned their home into a battleground, forcing Simon to abandon his costly hen batteries and replace them with free range camps. Unfairly, Simon had thought when he finally capitulated. At six p.m., Evans, their vet, had called to say that Sam was ready to leave although he looked like a patchwork quilt. Adding: 'Nothing that time and antibiotics won't heal.'

Simon had raced to the village, cursing the narrow streets blocked with 4 x 4s, and busy shoppers. He could remember when there was only a huddle of stone cottages gathered around the church, hidden by a dense grove of chestnut trees. In those days the locals depended upon the farms for their livelihoods, but the Seventies brought the village into the London commuter belt. Cottages were revamped and offered for sale at exorbitant prices and before long the locals, now mainly professionals, grew rhubarb and beans, drove their kids to gymkhanas, chose their trout at the new trout farm and played golf and tennis at the local sports club. Parking in a loading zone, Simon had hurried to the surgery, but James had insisted on hearing every last detail of their hunting fiasco, so now he was late.

Mrs Jones hadn't arrived, he noticed as he swung into the courtyard. Sam's bruises had stiffened and he could hardly move, so Simon carried him to his basket in the glassed-in porch. With luck he'd manage to grab a bite to eat.

Feeling vaguely irritated he hurried through the house switching on lights and the gas fire in the lounge. The room was large and arty, refurbished to Laura's taste with brightly-coloured settees, piles of cushions and three appalling modern paintings on the walls. The kitchen gleamed falsely with copper pots and painted pottery, all useless because he couldn't remember Laura cooking a meal there. Mrs Watson came daily from the village to clean and cook, otherwise they heated pre-cooked meals. Laura, an interior decorator, was full of contradictions and their warm and loving home was only an illusion.

A hand-written note from Ana lay beside the telephone. She had gone to see a movie with friends. Simon switched on the tape and heard the usual message from his wife: 'Hi darling, something's cropped up. A client insists we close the deal over drinks after work. He's tied up for

27

the rest of the day. See you later. I'll try not to be too late.'

He swallowed a sigh and pulled himself together. Laura had refurbished their cottage in the village, which she used as a business base, but lately she practically lived there. It was lonely and sad to have drifted so far apart. Years back Laura used to accuse him of being unable to show his feelings, but nowadays they only exchanged small talk. Feeling resigned to another lonely evening, he went out to the porch to feed Sam.

Limping badly, the dog examined the food and slunk back to his basket. Simon stroked the dog's head. 'Beaten by a cat, eh. You'd best sleep it off.'

Treating himself to a glass of dry red wine, Simon rifled the fridge and found some smoked ham and made himself a sandwich. While he munched he could not keep his mind off the coming encounter. He felt that something disturbing awaited him. Domestic confessions were his Achilles' Heel. Perhaps that was why his marriage had foundered. They had never once 'had it out', that beautiful American phrase that seemed to fix everything on the other side of the Atlantic, but was seldom resorted to in his household.

At that moment the car drew up in the yard and Sam barked feebly. 'Tch!' He took a large bite, shoved his half-eaten sandwich into the fridge, drained his glass and swilled and swallowed the mix, before hurrying to the front door.

Mrs Jones had come alone and she was groping in the boot. His glance was snared by the length and shapeliness of her legs. She retrieved a coat and bag and smoothed her clinging wool skirt, a contrived gesture. She was sexy in a blowzy way, but it seemed to Simon that all women were appealing nowadays, perhaps because his libido had been troubling him for some time. Not that it mattered. She was also blonde and he wondered at Sarah's swarthiness.

'Mr Shepherd,' she called out, smiling and waving in the manner of an old friend. At that moment Simon realised that he didn't like Mrs Jones. Why did he make these split-second assessments of people? He knew he was at fault and he usually over-compensated with friendliness to prove himself wrong, but invariably he found he'd been right all the time. Smug, self-opinionated and shallow, he decided, hating himself for being so uncharitable. Simon squared his shoulders and wished she'd get it over with as she walked past him into the living room and sat down, making a big deal out of crossing her legs.

'I'm so sorry to bother you. I know so few people here . . . ' She prattled on and eventually reached her problem. 'The vicar keeps him late, you see . . . '

As she said those words, Simon's skin began to prickle all over. Embarrassment did this to him. At that moment he would have done anything to be elsewhere.

'He's always late home after choir practice and sometimes Jules goes round to help clean up, or so he says. Suddenly he's got all this money. Says he won the cash playing cards at school. He's only twelve. I don't know what to do. How can someone like me go against the vicar?' She shrugged helplessly. 'You establishment types are better placed to confront him. I'm sure your friends wouldn't want the media to get hold of this. I don't want to lose my kid, but something has to be done. I'm scared to go to the police. As for that welfare crowd . . . ' She gave a long, loud sniff. 'Sarah said you'd help us.'

'She did? Well, perhaps I should talk to your son,' he ventured gently.

'You won't get anywhere with him. You must go in there and get him out.'

He grimaced and took a deep breath. How could she, a stranger, come here and try to push him into something so shameful?

'Certainly not,' he said with more vehemence that he had intended. 'You can't expect me to walk in and accuse the vicar of . . . well . . . of anything. After all, I only have your word for it. You could be mistaken, Mrs Jones.'

She stood up looking deadly. 'Then I'll go the police,' she threatened. 'I have to stop it now . . . at once. Jules is there and he won't be back until after nine, or later. So what's going on? You tell me.' She sounded coarse and Simon flushed.

'Calm down. Hang on. You say Jules is there now?'

'He's always there long after the others have left. If I tell Alan, that's my ex, there'll be murder.'

'Perhaps he would be your better choice . . . '

30

'We don't live together. I'm scared of what he'll do to the vicar . . . him and his friends, that is.'

Simon could picture the lynching party moving up from Newtown into their village. The image propelled him to his feet.

'All right then. Let's go.'

★ ★ ★

Simon drove rapidly towards Temple Minnis, but as they drew closer he became even more reluctant. Why had he believed this horrible woman? Simon hadn't been to church for some time. Not since Ana's christening, he remembered, but the new vicar sometimes called on routine canvassing trips. He usually accepted a glass of sherry, a small donation and a few words of encouragement. Simon tried to remember what he looked like, but knew only that he was young, pallid and wore large spectacles that kept slipping down.

'I expect Jules is waiting for you at home wondering where you are.'

'Huh!' She lifted her head disdainfully and peered down her nose at her hands. Glancing sidelong, Simon noticed that her teeth slanted backwards. Her resemblance to a rodent set him shuddering as he parked outside the vicarage.

'That's his bicycle, isn't it. So he's there, isn't he.'

Her voice grated unpleasantly in Simon's ear, propelling him out of the car.

'You will wait here.' His voice squashed any argument.

The door was unlocked. Grotesque shadows barred the way, but he could see a dim, flickering light in the distance. He heard the sound of someone groaning softly and he almost called out, but changed his mind. Something was seriously wrong. Why was it so dark and so quiet? He stumbled forward, wondering what on earth he was going to say.

Pushing open the door, he blinked and tried to make sense of a scene lit only by candlelight. The boy was kneeling. That was all right surely. The vicar's eyes were raised, revealing inner ecstasy. So far so good. But it wasn't communion bread that filled the boy's mouth.

A feeling of sick outrage paralysed him momentarily. Then confusion fled and fury took over. 'My God! No!' Simon exploded. 'My God!'

The boy jumped and whipped round, while the vicar screamed with pain and bent double, cradling his chewed member with both hands, his eyes bright with tears.

'Oh God,' the vicar echoed fatuously. Then skinny white shanks dashed for the door.

As the boy turned to flee, Simon caught a glimpse of a face that was exquisitely moulded, but his expression caught at Simon's throat. He was beautiful and depraved and he was smiling secretively. He glanced up at him as a whore might and Simon, who felt appalled, stumbled back and collided with the door. Puck might have looked so, or a debauched, malevolent angel. He grabbed the boy's elbow and pushed

32

him outside and down the lavender-edged, cobbled path to his mother.

'Wait,' he growled.

'What the hell is going on in there?' Her eyes examined him with pitiless curiosity. Inexplicably, Simon felt a deep, pervasive guilt.

'Ask him,' he began.

'We were praying,' the boy whined.

She glanced suspiciously at each in turn.

Racing back, Simon found the vicar weeping softly by his bedroom window.

Simon spun him around by his arm, smashing him hard against the wall with a crash. As he ripped off his clerical collar, he was gasping with the effort of holding back. He had a sickening fear that he might kill him.

'You're no vicar. Never.' Panting with suppressed anger, he grabbed the telephone receiver and hauled the vicar towards it. 'Call your superior,' he muttered, shaking him. 'Who is he?'

Crimson-faced, the vicar shook his head.

'What d'you prefer, a lynching party or a quick exit? Explain to the bishop and get the hell out of this town before I kill you.'

The young man dialled a number and mumbled tearfully into the receiver. He didn't seem to be making much sense. Simon took it from him and poured out the details.

'Get this bastard out of here before dawn or take the consequences. I can't guarantee his safety once the word 'paedophile' gets round the village.'

'Don't say anything,' an insidious, anonymous

voice whispered. 'Leave it to us. We'll hold an internal inquiry. There's no need . . . ' Simon dropped the receiver and rushed outside craving fresh, clean air.

'Let's go.' Lifting the boy's bicycle into the back, Simon drove to the farm in grim silence. Mrs Jones had no questions. She was crying quietly as she cradled her son in her arms. He saw them into their car, feeling relieved to see the back of them.

'Now what?' he said aloud. Should he call the police or social workers? David would know. Feeling badly contaminated, he drove to his friend's home.

4

'This is a police matter? To hell with the bad publicity.'

As chairman of the local property company which virtually ran the village, David Fergus should be in on this problem, Simon had reasoned, but now he wasn't so sure. It was an hour later and Simon had recovered sufficiently to appear remote and derisive. He had even displayed a touch of humour when describing the scene, and he had entirely concealed his freefall into a tide of disgust and mindless fury. The bottle of single malt he was sharing had helped. So had the roaring fire and the oak panelled study with its comfortable black leather armchairs.

Towering head and shoulders above ordinary mortals, David exuded enough confidence to swing any board assembly to his way of thinking. With the death of his father in the Eighties, David had joined the peerage and the role suited him.

'Madness to let it become public knowledge,' David argued. 'I'll contact the head of the Diocese.'

'I already did.'

'Good! The church doesn't need this kind of publicity anymore than we do. It wouldn't do house sales much good and share prices would fall.'

'The boy needs counselling, and what about his mother?' Simon queried. 'She'll get it out of him sooner or later. Besides . . . ' He broke off, unable to find the words to express his contempt of David's one-dimensional world governed by the share price index.

David flashed his boardroom smile. 'Leave it to me. I'll fix Mum with the carrot and stick approach and we'll pay for a shrink. If the vicar's not gone by daybreak, we'll move him out.'

'Under what pretence?'

'Let's say a breakdown caused by overwork.'

Simon laughed briefly and grimly and gave in with bad grace. 'That's preposterous. His total congregation numbers a few old ladies.'

David winked while his fingers fumbled in a silver cigar box. 'No one goes, so no one knows.' He shrugged, scribbled a note on a pad and tossed it aside. Someone else would deal with it. That was his way. Simon watched and envied his friend's ability to switch off as he turned his attention to his cigar.

'Listen Simon, I've been practically wiped out by Lloyds, as I'm sure you've heard, and I'm trying to whip up sales fast. Take a look at this.' He slid the artwork for a new brochure across the low table.

'*This corner of a foreign field will stay forever English,*' danced before Simon's eyes in scarlet italics against a green field peppered with poppies.

'You can't . . . ' Simon murmured. 'It's farcical, or worse, offensive, in fact, and bad taste. Besides, it's not true. I mean to say, look at this appalling business tonight. The England we knew has gone.' He flipped the brochure onto the table.

'Nonsense. We had a dream and we hung on to it. We won.'

But who paid? Simon fought off a memory of Angela's pallid face and the way she had looked when he dragged her to the surface of the dark, ice-bound lake. He remembered his dawning horror as he fought to revive her and failed. A dream! My God! Shock and anguish had brought on pneumonia and by morning he was hospitalised. The pneumonia passed, but his guilt never would. He felt amazed that David could still think of their past actions as 'winning'. Incensed at David's insensitivity he stood up to go. 'Leave it to the copywriters. You pay them enough.'

'Hang on, Simon. Something's cropped up.' David pushed the bottle towards Simon. 'Help yourself. You're going to need it.'

'No more, thanks.'

David paced the room, his hands in his pockets. He turned abruptly, swaying forward onto the balls of his feet and back again in a rocking motion. He hadn't changed much over the years, Simon decided. Perhaps slightly heavier, but his hair was still blond and his skin tanned to a crisp bronze. Maybe his fine grey eyes looked a trifle more calculating. At forty-six he still wore tweeds, grey flannels and fancy waistcoats over white silk shirts, just as he always had, and this particular rocking motion reminded Simon of past tricky encounters.

David was searching for the right opening.

'Don't waste time pussy-footing your way around the problem. It's me, Simon.'

'Okay. Sorry. Here goes. Your daughter and a gang of hoodlums waylaid the hunt this morning outside my home, yelling abuse and spraying the hunters with paint. Unfortunately my horse got most of it. I had to call the vet. I told him to bill you.'

'Thanks. Funny the vet didn't tell me.' Hot sorrow was burning somewhere at the back of Simon's eyes as he struggled to conceal his shock.

'I asked Evans not to and naturally I didn't call the police. I should have. For God's sake try to control Ana. I had three sure buyers and guess what? They changed their minds. Of course they were very suave and sorry. They said they hoped to get away from London's tensions and they didn't need ours.'

'It won't happen again. Of course I'll pay. I'm sorry. More sorry than I can say? How many were there?'

'About eight yobs and Ana. She seemed to be in charge. I'd actually invited her to join the hunt. That's how she got the timing right. I had no idea . . . ' He broke off scowling.

'And your horse?' Simon knew how David treasured his spirited Arab mare.

'It didn't do her much good. We had to scrub her flank with a special solvent and then wash it off with detergent. It burned and she kicked the stable hand, so he's off sick for a week.

'Look Simon.' David clamped his hand on

Simon's shoulder. 'We go back a long way. We've helped each other through far more serious scrapes. Don't take it so seriously. She's only sixteen.'

'Seventeen,' Simon mumbled.

'Send her to boarding school.'

'I can't. She's passed her A-levels.' He didn't add 'with honours' since it didn't seem appropriate.

'What about a gap-year doing something useful in the Third World. It might teach her some sense.'

'It's worth a try.' David was letting him down lightly. Simon knew how much he needed those sales.

Arguing with Ana was a harrowing experience since she countered censure with contempt and never pulled her punches. Inspired by her own sense of rightness, he'd never known her to give in. Well this time she'd have to. He left feeling heavy-hearted, knowing he would have to wait up for his daughter and lay down the law.

5

It had been a long day. Simon was tired and his head felt bleary from too much scotch. He dozed off and woke, stiff with cold, wondering if Ana and Laura had returned and left him sleeping. A quick glance out of the window assured him that there were no cars and it was almost midnight. So where were they? Disaster images flooded his mind. He fought them off and sat at his desk fighting his anxiety.

His mind veered round to Bela, as it often did. By now he knew where she lived. He had memorised the camper's registration number and it had taken him no more than two telephone calls to a friend at the council to discover the name and address of the owner, a Ms Bela Shah, as she had told him. No clue here as to her marital status or her nationality. Since then he had struggled to erase the memory of a woman seen only by moonlight. He was still trying.

It was after midnight when Ana opened the front door and crept across the hall towards the staircase. To tiptoe wearing four-inch heels requires the poise of a ballet dancer, he realised, watching his daughter lose her balance. She caught hold of the banister and bent over to wrench off her shoes. Straightening, she pushed back her mass of dark curls revealing her delicate profile, a hand-me-down from her mother. The rest of her was her own: a pointed chin, an oval face with thick dark brows and soft brown eyes that were gazing anxiously upstairs, searching for a light. There were no lights and she looked relieved.

She was seventeen, but looked at least twenty-two in her scanty top, billowing silky pants and a black silk jacket covered in sequins. The jacket was Laura's and he wondered if she knew that Ana had borrowed it. Even from this distance he could smell wine on her breath.

'You don't have to creep. Your mother's not home and I'm still up.'

She spun round. 'I wasn't creeping,' she threw at him. 'Where's Mum?'

'Working.'

'So why are you still awake and sitting in the dark?'

'I was waiting for you. Come and sit down. Thanks for leaving a note. So they serve drinks at cinemas nowadays.'

'Don't be snide. It doesn't suit you. We went to the pub after the show.'

'You're underage, it's forbidden and you're well past your curfew.'

'Stop riding me, Dad. I'm tired.'

'You're not the only one who's tired,' he snorted. 'It's about time you listened to reason. Breaking the law may be fashionable, but it's wrong.' Already on the defensive and he'd hardly begun. Damn!

'Everyone does it.' Ana rapidly changed her tactics. 'Poor old spaceman lost in time and space. You're fifty years behind the rest of us.'

41

She kissed the top of his head.

'Stop it, Ana. Sit over there. We have to talk.' He pushed her away.

'I'm tired, Dad,' she whined, reverting to the child within.

'Tough. You may not buy drinks in pubs . . . '

'I didn't. I only drank them.'

'Don't split hairs. And you're forbidden to associate with the riffraff you were keeping company with this morning, or to annoy my friends, or to embarrass me by making a fool of yourself and you're specially forbidden to be cruel to animals. You of all people! I'm ashamed of you.'

That last salvo should put her in her place, he reckoned.

Mouth open, she walked backwards, clearly shocked, but recovering fast.

'So says Farmer Giles on the way to the abattoir,' she jeered savagely, while flushing with shame. 'Listen here, Dad, my conscience is my concern, isn't it. Blood sports are degrading for all of us. A bad reflection on our society, so I *will* protest any time I feel like it and you can't stop me.'

'Oh can't I. Do as you're told or you'll lose your considerable inheritance.'

'Oh please! Is that the best you can do?' She bent down and put on her shoes as if drawing strength from the added four inches.

'Why are you doing this, Ana? You've had a good Christian upbringing . . . '

'You certainly shoved your illusions down my throat with my vitamin syrup.' Her cheeks had blanched, a sure sign she was losing her temper.

'What are you talking about?'

'I'm talking about the load of crap you pumped into me. I never got to know the real you. D'you know why? Because you're like a hermit crab hiding inside a caricature of an stiff-upper-lip Englishman. You even look the part: fit, upright and square-shouldered, like you've just come back from running the Empire.

She was leering at him. How else could he describe that horrible smile. He shrugged off the hurt. 'Sorry I can't be a fat slob for you. Let's get back to the point of the conversation, your disgusting behaviour. Your allowance is cancelled until the vet's bill is covered. If you don't like the rules, live elsewhere and earn your keep.'

In the appalling silence that followed, his daughter's expression changed from fury to shocked misery. Too bad! She wasn't the only one who was hurt.

'Sometimes I despise you,' she said softly. 'You play lip-service to a world that's decaying from the inside out. One day you might even find the real you behind your silly facade, if there is one.'

Her words were voiced with all the fervour his hot-headed daughter could muster.

'What's going on?' They both turned to see Laura standing in the doorway putting her key into her bag. She looked tired and pallid. Sooty shadows round her eyes reminded Simon of how she used to look after making love a century or so ago. Simon got up to kiss her, but she stepped aside to shut the door.

They scowled sidelong at each other.

'Ana's behaved like a fool. She's got in with a bad crowd, but she won't listen to reason.'

'Won't she?' Laura's ennui echoed in her voice, but she came to life with a spark of anger. 'I didn't say you could wear my new jacket.'

'Sorry Mum. I couldn't find anything suitable.' She took it off humbly and handed it to her mother who snatched it and ran upstairs.

'Good night,' Laura mumbled from the landing.

'Listen, Dad.' Ana's eyes were over bright. 'I don't care if you disinherit me. Money means nothing to me.' She fled, but inexplicably burst into tears halfway upstairs.

As her door slammed, a vast persuasive sadness stole through Simon. He felt a stranger in his own home. Thoughts of following his daughter faded when he heard her key turn.

★   ★   ★

Trembling violently, Laura slammed the bedroom door shut and stood leaning against it. A shard of regret pierced her mind and the pain was almost physical. Laura longed to be loved, but she knew that no one had ever truly loved her, certainly not her parents, nor her daughter. What a baffling girl Ana was, so full of wild and devious passions for every living creature? Not her genes and certainly not Simon's. He was made of stone, yet once he had lusted after a woman enough to kill. He thought she didn't know.

Laura went through her bedtime routine,

cleaning off make-up with a special lotion, followed by a cold water splash, patting serum into her face and neck, followed by the vitamin night cream, dabbing it off around her eyes and mouth, smoothing the lip ointment around her lips, brushing her hair until it gleamed and taking her pills. A glass of cold water wasn't enough to swallow all the pills needed for her health and beauty routine. She refilled the glass and reached the end at last: anti-oxides, B-vitamins to cope with her incredible tension, replacement hormones, calcium. She was longing for a shower, but she had to be feigning sleep, by the time Simon came to bed.

Wishing that she had the courage to leave him, Laura got into bed and switched off the light. Gently lowering her head onto her sculpted foam rubber beauty pillow, designed to prevent her skin from creasing and lining during the night, she closed her eyes and allowed her mind to roam free. Like a wild horse it set off joyfully into rich textures of silk, cotton and shot satin. She sighed as one brilliant design after the next flashed into her mind. One day she would paint them, she promised herself as she fell into a deep sleep.

* * *

Ana was filled with guilt. She'd been avoiding her father for weeks in case a misplaced word led her to blurt out the truth. And she almost had. Dad was so full of denial, seeing his world as he wanted it to be. She should know. She was the unwilling observer of Mother's frightful affair and quite honestly she wished she were dead. Truly! The anguish was more than she could bear.

Ana admired her mother for her beauty and her incredible talent which she seldom used. Mother despised the decor she created for David's upmarket homes. 'Chintzy, ostentatious and full of clutter,' she'd confided once. 'That's what they want and that's what they get.' She was a perfect bitch to Dad, but he adored her, perhaps for her pedigree. Everything on the farm had a pedigree, even Sam.

Now where was Sam? A jolt of anxiety banished Ana's introspection. Sam always greeted her when she came home. Taking her torch, she opened the door a crack and saw that the house was in darkness. Perhaps he'd been left outside. Reaching for her coat and boots, she crept down to the porch.

'Sam! Where are you boy?' The dog whined from his basket.

'Oh Sam, darling Sam. Who did this to you?' She knelt beside the mournful dog and gently fingered the patchwork of stitches that covered his chest and back. Dad hadn't told her, which showed how angry he was. Switching off the torch, she moved to the couch, patted the cushion and felt the dog's hot nose on her cheeks. She had to lift him up, but moments later Sam was snuggling beside her. She wound her arms around the dog's neck as her thoughts turned uneasily to her problem.

In the perfect quiet of the night she wondered

how to tell Dad that she was not going to university. She wanted to get a job, join the real world and live on her own.

★ ★ ★

Simon, who had gone outside to cool off, sat day-dreaming on an old stone bench in the kitchen garden, hardly noticing the cold as he gazed into the melting amber eyes of the mysterious woman who had strayed into his wood, but vanished before morning. He dozed off and woke to find himself freezing and for a moment he was unable to work out where he was or why. Then he remembered the fight and his daughter's contempt became a physical ache in his gut. If this was what they called 'having it out' he could live without it. He tried to rationalise his hurt. All families had problems with teenagers, but Simon was honest enough to admit that his daughter didn't admire him. Yet he did his duty to his family. In times of crisis he'd be ready to serve his country, if called upon to do so, as his father and grandfather, Tom, had done, and so many Shepherds before them. A chest full of medals gathered dust in the attic to prove it.

More than patriotism, he acknowledged a pride in his culture. He had a quiet acceptance of the rightness of the way he and his kind thought and acted. He'd never analysed being English, but he could identify it with each of his senses: the scent of new mown grass and May blossom, knowing what was cricket and what

47

wasn't, the sound of a brass band, the taste of kippers, sweet-cured bacon and roast beef with horseradish, icy cheeks on a winter's day. What was wrong with that? As for spoonfeeding myths to his daughter, her education had been left to her school, a Christian school naturally, and bloody expensive, too.

Ana was a silly girl, but she'd got under his skin and he couldn't throw off a sense of betrayal. Was she right? Was there nothing of himself he could call his own? He knew he was over-reacting, but that disgusting scene with the vicar had left him feeling deeply troubled although he wasn't sure why. It was like looking into a familiar mirror and finding it wasn't there. Just a blank wall. Something had gone forever. He shivered.

The moon had risen and the kitchen garden looked unfamiliar in its cold white light. He had the strangest feeling that he'd woken into an alien culture. It was as if the leprechauns of childhood stories had snatched his world away and left a changeling planet in its place. What if Ana were right and all his views and traditions had reached their sell-by date and were putrefying around him? What would be left of him? Precious little, he thought. Here he sat, an intelligent, aggressive primate, trying to make something special out of very little as he hurtled through space on the edge of a dying planet. Strange that the behaviour of a devious vicar and his cagey superior should have shaken him so much. But this was nonsense. He stood up and shuddered.

Hurrying inside he switched on the porch light. There lay his unyielding daughter with her arms around Sam's neck, her mouth slightly open and her hair spread over the pillow. She was little more than a child so what gave her the right to be so sure of her opinions? Ana had no emotional restraints: she loved and hated lavishly, while he, on the other hand, couldn't break through his self-imposed barriers. They'd been around too long. He hurried upstairs to fetch a blanket and crept back to cover her gently. Sam hadn't moved a muscle. He was trying to pretend he wasn't there.

6

'Why are we waiting? It's past lunchtime.
Shouldn't we eat?' Simon's mother complained
for the third time in as many minutes. Her bright
green eyes sparkled for every occasion, with
malicious humour when shooting verbal darts,
with sexual innuendoes when she fancied
someone, or with joy at the prospect of a party or
a drink. It was a drink she needed right now, not
the lunch, Simon realised. He glanced at his
watch. Five past one. Compassion surfaced.

'How about some wine while you wait,
Mother?'

'I thought you'd never ask. Even better, make
it a gin and tonic, and forget 'mother' for
goodness sake.'

At Ana's birth, Mother had decided that she
was never going to be a granny. From then on
she would be known by her name, Mae. Laura
shot him a look of annoyance as he opened the
cabinet.

'Sorry. We're out of gin,' he lied, pouring a
glass of dry white wine. 'Cheers!'

'We're waiting for Gordon. He's Simon's
friend since school days,' Laura explained to
Mae, as if she were a fractious child.

'I know who Gordon is, or should be. The
thing is . . . ' She stared pointedly at Laura. 'Do
you?'

The women of his family were limbering up

50

earlier than usual. Clearly Mother had scored although he couldn't think how. Laura fled to the kitchen and Ana was flushing.

Soon Mae was happily sipping her wine. It gave him a chance to study her. She was looking drawn, yet at sixty-six she had decades ahead of her, according to the latest life expectancy tables. Forty percent of the villagers were over fifty, financially secure and with time on their hands. They organised outings, parties, bridge tournaments and amateur dramatics in the church hall. In their spare time they ganged up in groups to drink themselves into a stupor, so her problem couldn't be loneliness.

'Did you put my flowers in water?' she asked.

'Yes. Would you like to go down now, rather than later?'

Aggressive, ever-anxious and impelled to keep on the move, Mother glanced at her watch. 'If you think there's time, let's go.' She drained her glass.

Simon glanced inquiringly at Laura.

'Why not? Gordon's late and Meli and David aren't coming. Her headache's worse.'

'Oh, that's sad. Did you bring your boots, Mae?'

'Of course.'

They set off in the wild March wind, under soaring spirals of gulls intent on surfing the thermals. It was cold, but Mae was determined, despite the ten minute, muddy walk to the old family cemetery beyond the dam. This was her weekly triumph. After his father's death, Mother had taken the first flight to Bermuda and

51

embarked on a costly legal fight to retrieve her husband's mortal remains and possessions from his mistress. She'd won and flown his corpse back to the farm, which Father had hated so much, where she'd buried his remains in the old cemetery amongst the medieval corpses.

The sky was darkening and there was a light drizzle in the wind as they trudged down the last slope. Simon never knew what to say to his mother, so he left her at the cemetery gate and walked back to the dam, where he sat on a stone to wait.

Mae hadn't been much of a mother, but there were extenuating circumstances. As an only child, reared in a boarding school, she knew nothing about homes and families. How could she? Tom, Mae's father, was a deep-sea salvage diver. He and his wife, Agnes, had no home of their own, but stayed in a serious of hotels, where Mae sometimes joined them in the school holidays.

Following their example, she married Simon's handsome, charming father, Captain Pat Shepherd, and together they travelled the world, surveying strategic coastlines for naval intelligence and leaving the farm to be run by a negligent foreman.

Simon remembered being driven to school and abandoned in the headmaster's office, when he was five.

'See you in a few weeks' time, darling,' his tall, brown-haired, greeneyed, gorgeous mother had whispered in his ear, enveloping him in her subtle perfume. He had believed her, spending hours peering through the railings of the school gates at passing cars, each one of which might be bringing his mother, but they always swept past with a whoosh that he felt, rather than heard, in the pit of his stomach. It was three years before he saw his mother next. She was unrecognisable, seemingly shorter, plumper, red-haired and a stranger. After that he was flown out to Singapore at twelve, to find a blonde dumpling who spoke with a curious accent and spent most of her time having drinks with her female friends.

And so on, until his father took early retirement due to skin cancer and returned for a brief stay at the farm, before leaving Mae to join his mistress in Bermuda. After his father's death ten years ago, Mae had sold her apartment in Spain and returned to England for good. Lately Simon was expected to pretend that they had shared a bond through the years, as if linked by a psychic umbilical cord. Mother demanded no less.

★　★　★

Ana was running towards them. 'Lunch is ready,' she called. Simon had intended to talk sternly to his mother about her drinking, but suddenly there was no time. Ana took Mae's hand and for a moment they stood side by side, gazing at the ducks dabbling on the dam.

'Wouldn't I like one of them trussed up in the oven.' Mae swallowed noisily.

'Really, Mae . . . how could you? They're our

pets.' Ana pulled a face at her and ran back to the house.

'It's good to see them enjoying the day,' Simon said warily.

She snorted. 'They're ducks, aren't they. I like folk who call a spade a spade. You earn your living breeding animals for slaughter. Why pretend otherwise? That's why your father hated farming.' She sniffed loudly.

Over the years, Pat Shepherd, deceased, had undergone a metamorphosis from sinner to saint.

'I had to choose, you see, you or Pat. I was young and in love . . . besides, your father thought boarding school would be good for you.'

'At five?'

'What's the difference?'

It was the first time that Simon had realised his mother's conscience bothered her. Why now, he wondered? Why not then? She and Pat were well-matched. Both were products of the British boarding school system which bred statesmen, artists, heroes and inventors, but did little to create lovers and home-makers.

'I wish things had been different, Mae. I would have liked to have known you both better. You and Dad. Lately I wish I knew myself better.'

'Your father said that just before he left me.' Mae sounded bitter and impatient. 'Pat thought he'd find himself in Bermuda, but he was only snatching at youth. I've seen pictures of him with that woman. He looked ridiculous.'

All roads led back to Father, in his mother's mind. There was no time for anyone else, least of

54

all foolish imaginings from her son.

Simon switched off. With luck he'd be out of the house by three. Surreptitiously he glanced towards the trees, but there was no smoke and the woods were silent.

★ ★ ★

Sunday lunch was more like an inquisition, when past sins were laid out on a plate, garnished with bitter herbs, peppered with sarcasm and served with roast beef and Yorkshire pudding, or so it seemed to Ana. Today, Gordon had been invited to add a little sauce to the meal. How could her bloody mother do that?

Dad had no idea his friend was screwing Mum. She wasn't suppose to know either, but an unexpected visit to Mum's work one evening to borrow some cash, had caught them at it. She'd tiptoed out pretty fast, not wanting to face up to the embarrassment that would follow disclosure.

Dad and Gordon went back to boarding school days when Gordon was always being picked on because he was a scholarship boy. Dad hated bullying, so naturally he'd protected him. More fool Dad! Nowadays Gordon was raking in the profits as David's architect. He was Dad's age, but he looked ten years younger with his slim figure, slanting brown eyes and puckish features.

'How's the farm going?' Gordon asked.

'Not bad at all. We're about to reap the rewards of twenty years' grind. The ewes are worth their weight in gold. I'll be able to sell more than a hundred as prime breeding stock in a few months' time.' Dad glanced around proudly, but no one seemed impressed. 'They're going on show . . . '

Mum interrupted him with a brittle smile. 'By the way, Simon, that sandal you've been at such pains to wash and polish isn't mine. Sweet of you to bother, but surely you know I wouldn't wear anything that gaudy. Where did you find it?'

Dad flushed crimson. Had he blindly imagined that cleaning and hiding a woman's shoe in the gun room was his secret? Mum had told her about it, and probably Mae, too. Naturally Gordon noticed.

'So the lady lost her slipper.' Gordon frowned and looked genuinely amused as if the idea that Dad might stray was utterly preposterous. Perhaps it was, Ana admitted, with a pang of compassion.

'It's a boring story. You don't want to hear about it.'

'Yes, we do,' Mum argued. 'Everyone's fascinated.'

'It happened weeks ago. A woman travelling in a camper with two small children, parked in the woods below the cemetery. She needed a break from driving and the children were hungry, so she lit a fire. I smelled the smoke in the night and went to investigate. End of story! Except . . . ' He frowned at Gordon. 'I had the strangest feeling that she knew me. The next morning I happened to see the shoe.'

'You went looking for her?' Ana smirked at her plate.

56

'To check that the fire was out.'

'And that was when Sir Galahad found the shoe and decided to clean it up and polish it,' Mum parried.

This snippet had been specially saved for lunch, Ana realised.

'So what was she like, Dad?'

'I assumed she was down on her luck. I felt sorry because she had two small children who looked half-starved, so I took down some provisions. An illegal, I suppose. But still, I'm not sure. Her English was perfect, although the children were clearly speaking Arabic, or something similar.'

'But what did she look like, Dad?'

'Don't ask, because he wouldn't notice.' Mum's voice was vibrant with malice. 'Not even if he saw a naked harem girl.'

Dad was losing his temper, in his own quiet way.

'She was part Indian, I suppose, and the most beautiful woman I've ever seen. Exquisite and sexy, a rare combination.'

'Did you really take her food, Dad? That doesn't sound like you. I always thought you were a bit of a racist,' Ana said, spearing her carrots viciously. She couldn't help wondering if just a tiny piece of meat would ruin her vegetarian status. It smelled delicious, but then her conscience took over.

'What strange ideas you have about me, Ana.'

Mae drained her wine and cast a greedy eye towards the bottle on the sideboard. 'Lovely wine,' she hinted.

Gordon leaped up and filled her glass while Dad sighed. He was too damned polite to warn Gordon, but now her grandmother would go through her usual routine of snide remarks, vitriolic aggression followed by paranoia and then someone would have to drive her home exactly when she felt like going, which might be in the middle of lunch.

A vast, uneasy quiet invaded the room.

Mae emptied her plate and eyed the roast hungrily. 'That is what I call a roast,' she said. 'Not those miserable slithers of meat you find on the supermarket shelves. Some people are lucky. I love meat, but I can't afford it.'

'Help your grandmother, please,' Dad told her. As Ana went to the sideboard she heard Dad say: 'You have a good income and you don't pay rent, Mother. If you spent less on . . . '

'Mae,' Mum said quickly. 'If you need extra cash why not rent a room? Simon has just threatened to turn Ana out of the house, so I'd be glad to pay you.'

Ana's felt her cheeks burn scarlet as she sat down. Dad shot an accusing glance at her and she felt absolutely miserable.

'So what's all this about, Simon?' Mae snapped.

Dad got up and put his plate on the sideboard. He'd hardly eaten anything. 'Ana was presented with a choice,' he began slowly. 'Clearly she's made up her mind. If she prefers spraying David's horses with green paint, with a crowd of riffraff, to staying home and receiving a good education then . . . ' He shrugged.

58

Mum's bow lips were drawn into a taut line. Poisoned arrows would be loosed any minute. 'Why didn't someone tell me?' She glanced angrily at Gordon who pushed his black locks off his forehead and managed a shaky laugh.

'Water under the bridge, Sweetie. David's got over his temper at the cancellations and Simon's paying the vet's bill.'

'Typical of you to keep quiet about it,' Mum snarled at Ana. 'What happened exactly?'

'It wasn't intended. It's like this . . .' Ana tried to explain while Mae finished eating.

Mrs Watson, flushed and trim in a new floral dress, her Jamaican skin gleaming, cleared the sideboard and brought in a trifle with an air of supercilious amusement. She shot a sympathetic glance at Dad and winked at him. Dad was too startled to respond. Ana ploughed on. She felt she'd never come to the end.

'For goodness sake shut up about it,' Mae interrupted her. 'You're making too much of it . . . all of you. Ana made a mistake and got a lecture, but of course she's too arrogant to be told off. Simon spoils her.'

Laura's eyes flashed towards her mother-in-law. 'The only thing he spoils are his damned livestock.'

Dad turned to Gordon. 'Don't you want a turn at darting the bull?'

'Thank God men have cricket,' Gordon mumbled into his glass.

Mum heard him. 'Oh, for heaven's sake.'

That was the moment when Mae demanded to be driven home immediately.

Dad stood up. 'I'll take you, Mother,' he offered, looking pleased to escape.

'If you don't like the rules, Laura, don't play the game,' Ana distinctly heard Gordon whisper to Mum as Dad left the room. Did screwing give Gordon the right to chastise her mother? She felt torn in half, but whose side should she take . . . Dad's because he was the trusting victim, or Mum's because she had the guts to reach out for passion? She never wanted to make the choice, which was why she was leaving.

7

Was he missing out on some vital ingredient, Simon wondered as he went outside to drive the car to the door? There must be a reason why his wife and daughter resorted to such unscrupulous sniping. He must find a way to ban Sunday lunches.

'Some people can't see their noses in front of their faces,' Mae snarled as they drove through the farm gate and turned towards the retirement village.

Simon felt his irritation rising. 'Give me a break, Mae. I've had enough for one day.' God knows what she was talking about, but it didn't take a genius to see that he and Laura weren't exactly turtle doves.

'Have it your own way.' Mae turned away from him, but her rigid stance revealed her fury. He dropped her at her cottage after a short and mercifully silent drive.

Simon couldn't help remembering how Bela Shah's eyes had shone with kindness. She had shown him more warmth that night than he had received from Laura in a decade. Finally it was his need for a better image that led him to make a hurried U-turn at Redhill's gate and speed back to the village.

Passing the church and the shops he went on past the railway bridge and turned towards Newtown, but as he neared his destination, he began to worry. Why had that lovely woman spent the night hiding in his woods when her home was only five minutes away? And why was she travelling with children that weren't hers?

She had to be smuggling children into the country. A baby farmer! Dishonesty in a woman was something Simon abhorred. But maybe he was being unjustly suspicious. What the hell was he doing here? he asked himself, yet he couldn't bear to turn back.

Moments later he drew up in front of a shabby villa. He rang the bell hesitantly and saw a curtain move in a neighbour's house. What if her husband opened the door? He shouldn't have come. She couldn't possibly be as intriguingly beautiful as he had imagined when he saw her in the moonlight.

He was staring at the shoe and searching for something smart to say about it when the door swung open. He was confronted by a dark-skinned man with big ears, a large nose and huge, suspicious eyes. In his slippers and braces, he was very obviously very much at home.

'Mr Shah?' he asked, appalled and disappointed.

'The name's Puri.'

A well-remembered voice called from the shadows: 'It's all right, Mr Puri. I know Mr Shepherd.'

The passage behind resembled a rabbit warren. Fortunately Mr Puri bolted into one of the doorways and the woman he had seen only by moonlight took on shape and form and became even lovelier than before, despite her scruffy jeans and jersey, but by daylight she looked so vulnerable. A brief glance assured him that there were no rings on her delicate fingers.

She was gazing from him to the sandal and back again with a curious smile.

'Did you lose a slipper, Mrs Shah?' he asked facetiously. 'If it fits you get to marry the Prince.'

The moment he said it he realised he was making a fool of himself. She wasn't reared on European fairy stories and anyway wouldn't share the same sense of humour. Besides it wasn't funny.

She gazed at him smilingly. 'My prince is already married, Mr Shepherd. Please call me Bela. Come in.'

Once again her eyes shone with admiration and Simon felt himself flushing. As he walked inside and shut the front door behind him he had the strangest feeling that he was shutting out his family, which was bloody silly.

She walked with the poise and grace of a gazelle, he noticed, following her down a dark passageway towards the sound of music. She beckoned him into a large room that smelled vaguely of spices and perfume. A complete absence of bright cushions, modern art or Persian carpets cheered him. Instead the wood was polished and a white rug lay in the centre. The room faced on to a backyard crowded with leafy plants looking vaguely tropical. Despite the cold, the French window lay open. She stood kneading the shoe with her hand, as if far away. Then she pulled herself together.

'It looks new. How did you manage that? I've

searched everywhere. Fortunately I kept the other one. I'll have to give it to you to clean so they'll match.'

As she rambled on, a strange sense of *déjà vu* brought a sense of unreality to Simon.

'I dried it, that's all.' He wasn't going to tell her about the trouble he'd taken to restore the sandal to its present glossy state.

'The children were playing with my clothes and . . . Well, it doesn't matter, but it has brought you here and that's important. I'd better shut the door. I do the gardening for the family . . . they don't have time . . . and they give me dinner in return.'

He sank into a roomy, faded blue settee.

'I was surprised to find that you lived nearby and . . . ' He broke off, wondering why he had revealed his suspicions so crudely.

'And you wondered why I was hiding in your wood at night when I could so easily have driven home.'

'Well, to be honest . . . yes.'

She frowned and didn't answer as she walked into the tiny kitchen annex, returning shortly afterwards with two glasses of orange juice.

'You never came back,' he persisted. 'I thought that you might. Thanks.'

As she bent forward her musky perfume and the scent of her hair enveloped him. It was strangely exciting. Sensations long since buried began to surface. Gazing up he caught a sidelong glimpse of her perfect profile and her long, graceful neck.

'Why should I?'

'Surely you knew that I would worry about you?'

'So you set out to find me.'

'That was the easy part. I had memorised the registration number of your camper.'

'And the hard part?'

'Finding the courage to come. How are your children?' he went on, trying to change the subject.

'The children are fine, but they aren't mine. I was taking them home.'

'Oh! I admit I guessed as much.' He broke off wondering why he was ruining his chances before they even got to play the game.

'Why don't you say what's on your mind?' Her large brown eyes were staring at her glass, but he sensed her mounting anger.

'It has nothing to do with me.'

'They have recovered. They have a good home. They are loved. Does that satisfy you?' She stared at him with astonishing intensity as if daring him to challenge her.

His suspicions were becoming more disturbing by the moment.

'I'm sorry. I didn't come to spy on you.' He forced the words out, wondering if she would pick up the distaste in his voice.

'So why did you come? Oh, of course, to return the shoe.' Now she was glowing with temper.

'We seem to have got off on the wrong foot. I'm sorry. I'll go.' He stood up reluctantly. 'The real reason was so simple. I was longing to see you again.'

'Oh! No, wait. You deserve the truth, Mr

Shepherd . . . Simon . . . listen to me. I need to talk about it . . . perhaps I need a verdict.'

She reached out, caught hold of his wrist and pulled him back to the settee and sat beside him. Her hands were very cold and she was biting her lip. He leaned back cautiously, feeling uncomfortable.

'We learned . . . that is, my family learned . . . that my cousin and her husband had been killed in Afghanistan and that their two children, Karim, who is only two years old, and Hadia, who is almost five, had been placed in state care. My aunt applied for permission to bring them home, she is their nearest relative, but we were told that the children don't qualify for admittance, since they are not being persecuted. We decided that the children must be found and brought back to Britain, legal or not.

'I was the obvious choice to go. I taught English at the University in Kabul, I hold a Pakistani passport and Afghan residence rights, I know the city well, I have friends there and I speak Pashto. Being a woman I would be able to travel across Europe with the two children without inciting suspicion. To cut a long story short, I found the children and brought them back. When we neared England the ferry was delayed by fog and I was too tired to drive through the night. I couldn't bring them here, so I parked in your wood, although at the time . . . ' She broke off and shrugged.

'I have the feeling that the journey wasn't quite that simple,' he said, trying to disguise his irritation. The tide of foreigners finding their way into Britain was something he abhorred.

She leaned back and closed her eyes and described in detail the incredible sadness of travelling from one orphanage to the next asking endless questions, inspecting and questioning hundreds of lost children with their lack of documentation, and the final hurt was abandoning those who were not their relatives. She made it seem so real: the smell of urine and vomit, the damaged buildings, the lack of medical supplies and trained staff, the destroyed records that made her task seem near impossible, the exhaustion of travelling from town to village in the nightmare aftermath of the war, and above all the sad, abandoned, unloved children.

He watched her and noted how she lifted her chin when she smiled and how her eyes crinkled when she talked of those she had left behind and how often she had to hold back her tears when she described the children's neglect.

'I would have brought them all if I could,' she was saying softly. 'Finally I was satisfied that I had found the right children, but I had to beg and bribe officials for permission to take them to their nearest relatives, so when the papers were signed we left at once in case they changed their minds.'

Simon had to avert his eyes from her sexy arms and graceful hands and the way her breasts quivered under her jersey, while she was telling her story. Bela was a brave and lovely woman.

'I'm glad you succeeded,' he said, wondering at himself since he knew that he meant it. He reached out in an impulsive gesture of friendship and took her hands in both of his. Gazing into her eyes he felt desire spurt like red hot lava from a near-extinct volcano. He was acutely aware of her perfume and the warmth of her body as he moved too close to her and hung on to her hands. What was he doing, for God's sake? 'Oh, Bela,' he murmured. He pulled himself together fast.

'That night in the woods . . . well, to put it bluntly, I could see what you thought. Yet you brought us a box of provisions and that simple act meant a lot to me. You are a very kind man, Simon. I'm so glad you took the trouble to find me.'

'I shouldn't have come, but I was worried about you.'

It wasn't entirely truthful, but it would do. Anxious to avoid the consequences of staying a moment longer, Simon left too hurriedly after mumbled good-byes.

As he drove, he couldn't stop thinking of Bela. He had tuned in on her aloneness and her need for someone she could trust. And he was curious. How come a beautiful girl like Bela was available? Guilt and desire were evenly matched as he neared home. He'd desired her since the night he found her in his woods. Lately she even haunted his dreams. Towards Laura he felt only a vague resentment, but binding him to her was a strong allegiance to his marriage vows and a highly developed moral code. He liked his life to run on well-oiled, signposted tracks. After some soul-searching, he decided not to see Bela again. To do otherwise would be asking for trouble.

8

The weather changed in the night. Bela heard the wind start up and then the rain drumming on the roof and windowpanes. She heard the Puri's cat crying at the window, and she got up to let her in. Fragments of old images were burping at random into her mind as she tried to reject unpalatable memories: like Simon fighting the ambulance men, while two policemen ran to hold him back. Of course, he had seen her before, but how could he remember a child of eight watching silently by the lake? She went back to bed and lay there shivering, longing to sleep, but sleep evaded her.

It wasn't only Simon who had brought on her gloom. Yesterday evening she had received a letter from her Kashmiri lawyer, sent by special messenger, stating that her father was searching for her and she must see him immediately. Eventually she fell into a restless sleep and woke at seven with a headache.

She got up feeling bleary-eyed and pulled up the blinds. The downpour had passed, leaving a light, misty drizzle that trickled down the window and fell in light drops from the branches of the shrubs. She sighed and prepared herself for yet another excursion into the past.

Home! As Bela parked in the driveway of her old home, the dusk air moved across the garden bringing its own sense of melancholy. The

69

branches of the trees were still bare and the old leaves lay rotting. The garden was neglected and the curtains were drawn, as if their house were ashamed to look her in the eyes.

Seven years ago she had flown to relatives living in a small village near Sopur, in Kashmir, for a month's holiday, or so she had been led to believe. She was trapped there for years and this was the first time she had ventured back to her home. Bela had sworn never to speak to her father, but her lawyer seemed to think it was vital that she did.

No one knew that she was the daughter of George Irving, managing director of Irving Industries, chairman of Irving Consolidated Holdings, betrayer of his own child, hypocrite, liar, and cheat. She used her married name of Shah and she earned her modest living working as a part-time translator in an asylum seeker's aid centre while researching for her Ph.D. She boarded with the Puris and tried to be like them, for her mother's sake.

Her mother, Anjana, was a Kashmiri Muslim, who could trace her roots back to the sixteenth century, but Bela was a hybrid, an alien, belonging to no one, always longing for a niche, but fitting nowhere. There was no country, language, class or religion that she could truly call her own. She was a nothing, but it hadn't always been like that.

Once they had been a loving, united family, but that was in another lifetime and remembering it hurt. She was a spoiled brat, her father's darling, clever, determined and precocious. Her mother's death brought about a change so dramatic that she could never relive the past without inducing psychosomatic headaches, followed by fits of depression. And now, as she gazed at her old home, the past surged in on her.

★ ★ ★

Her mother is house-hunting the easy way, paging through *Country Life* on a chaise longue in Grannie's Finchley garden. No one in the world has a mother as lovely as hers. Bela, aged seven, watches her adoringly, loving her long, delicate hands and her beautiful eyes that are always laughing. Mother comes across a house that appeals to her and calls them to see. Bela ogles at the pictures and tries to imagine them living there.

'*Four miles from the sea, two miles from the motorway, within easy reach of London, this charming, Queen Anne listed home is set amongst groves of oaks with a river, an orchard, ten rooms and a conservatory,*' her mother reads.

'Room for expansion,' Father whispers. The look he gives their mother catches her attention. They make an appointment and she counts the hours until they get there.

It's love at first sight for Mother, so Bela swings in the garden while Father haggles about price with the agent. Two months before, her father had put his partner in charge of their factory in Kashmir and followed his wife to England where he plans to set up another plant. Despite her mother's reassurances, Bela is anxious about going to an English school and she misses her friends.

A happy year follows, but then her mother dies. Her death is something that Bela, who is eight, thrusts deep down in a bog at the bottom of her mind. It is beyond recall. On the day of her funeral, Father sends home for Fatima, who is charged with running the house and bringing up Bela as a good Muslim. Over the years her hatred of this interloper strengthens to such an extent that every day brings new conflicts.

★ ★ ★

Fatima always won. The day she slept in father's bed was the day she gained all the power.

'Father!'

There was no reply, but through the open, sliding doors she saw a woman standing on the balcony and she flinched.

'You!' Fatima murmured. 'So you're back.'

'As you see,' Bela replied with studied indifference.

She looks exactly like a witch, Bela thought, watching the woman's expression as she left hurriedly.

'You've come, at last,' a familiar voice said. 'It's about time.'

She half-turned and frowned as her father appeared in the doorway. Immaculately dressed and groomed, as always, his aftershave created a pampered aura around him. He was still vigorous and handsome with hard, inquisitive eyes, but his hair was grey and his face lined. She quickly calculated. He was sixty-five, but he didn't look it. You could still see a trace of the buccaneering, blond-haired, blue-eyed youth who had angered his family by marrying an Indian heiress. His roots were Scottish, but he was born and bred in Kashmir and in a way he was as mixed-up as his daughter.

'You're lovelier than ever, Bela. Isn't she, Fatima?' he called over his shoulder to the shadow lurking in the doorway behind him.

Bela shrugged.

'I wrote to you often, but you never replied.' His voice was thick with sanctimonious self-pity. 'I wanted to express my grief about the cholera epidemic.'

'One of the many enriching experiences we miss in this country you dislike so much.'

'There's no need to be sarcastic, Bela. How do you think I felt? Of course you could never accept that I had chosen the best course for you.'

'Do you still believe that? After all that happened.'

'Yes, I do. We can't envisage acts of God.'

'Your sense of denial borders on madness, Father.' She was filled with violent disgust.

'Don't be rude to your father, Bela,' came the dry whisper from behind him.

'This has nothing to do with you, Fatima. Don't you have some household duties to attend to?'

Fatima gasped noisily.

'That's unforgivable, Bela.' Her father's voice was like a well-oiled, top of the range, car engine, but he was looking distraught and there was unease in his eyes. She could see that the roles of servant and master had been reversed. He turned and placed a hand on Fatima's shoulder. 'Perhaps it would be better . . .'

Fatima shrugged and stalked out like an offended cat.

'So all these years you've been bottling up this anger. Do you feel great now? Or maybe just a little bit sad and mean?'

'I don't want to talk about it.' Her voice was tense. She forced herself to relax.

'I heard about what you did in Afghanistan. The children are settling down well and recovering. You're a brave girl and I'm proud of you.' Father blew his nose vigorously before wiping his eyes. 'I'm sorry to have to break the bad news to you, Bela. The fact is, Omar, your husband, passed away in Sopur a week ago after suffering a heart attack.'

Bela flinched and walked away, hiding her face. She didn't want to remember that part of her life. 'He divorced me years ago. Omar means nothing to me.'

'No . . . evidently he never divorced you. Didn't you take the trouble to find out?'

'Why should I? I never felt married to him, so it was immaterial to me. Let's just stick to business details, shall we?' Bela said.

'Very well. You have inherited his entire estate and as you know his assets were considerable. I have to fly out to Srinagar and sort things out. I need your *power of attorney* to act on your behalf. My lawyer should be here any minute now. He's late, as usual. He's bringing the papers

74

for you to sign. Then we can get this over and done with.' He sounded confident, but she could see how much his hands were shaking.

'Is that all? Is that why you insisted that I came here today? You could have told me on the telephone.' Bela wondered just how blunt she should be, until she remembered her frantic call home and Father's refusal to speak to her.

'You were wasting your time, Father. I'll contact Omar's lawyer and sort things out. I don't need you to run my affairs. Once, long ago, you showed me that you were a liar and a cheat. You had no mercy. I'd be a fool to trust you again.'

Father turned pale. She could see how much his hands were shaking as he struggled to pull himself together.

'Don't be a fool. You have no business training and there's a great deal at stake. There's any number of business decisions to be made. Think of the plant here. Sales are down, workers are being laid off and I have to raise a great deal of finance fast. I was about to contact Omar and ask him to double his investment. I'm sure that he would have said yes. After all, we are . . . were . . . partners. This is what he would have wished.'

She picked up her coat and handbag. 'No Father. Don't waste your time. I won't let you benefit from what you did to me.'

She owed him nothing. At that moment the lawyer arrived, which gave her the chance to leave without another argument.

9

It began to rain as Bela reached the motorway. She sat hunched forward, peering through the misty windscreen, listening to the monotonous chug, chug, chug, of the windscreen wiper, a beat that brought on the blues. The sound was uniquely bonded with her own disaster. Bela searched back, trying to understand how she had missed all the signs and failed to see the danger until it was too late. Worst of all was the betrayal. However many times she tried to forget, the past kept gatecrashing the present.

★   ★   ★

Studying Middle-Eastern languages at London University, Bela struggles to find a link between her mother's traditional ways and modern life in the West. It isn't easy co-existing as a Muslim woman in a secular society, yet she is proud to be part of the new, vital Indo-European scene. She hopes that she has a spiritual message to impart to fellow students. At the end of her first year she and a group of friends establish an Islam Awareness Club.

'Defying self-interest is one of the keystones of our faith,' she says, in her first informal talk to fellow students. 'At home we learn about the joy of giving and the empowerment that comes from self-discipline and loving.'

She has just turned twenty when she gains her BA, but lately her career has been overshadowed by her all-consuming love for the handsome, witty, athletic Jason Thornton, a junior English lecturer. Naively she imagines that Father and Fatima will be pleased that they plan to marry, but as yet Bela is unaware of Fatima's treachery.

'I've been charged with bringing you up as your late mother would have wished. I'd be failing in my duty if I did less. Your mother was Muslim, and this is what she would want.'

Time and again, these words settle all arguments. It is pointless for Bela to remind her that she has been educated in an English public school with a strong Christian bias, that her father is Scottish and an atheist, even though he was third generation born in Kashmir. It's what Fatima wants that counts now and Fatima wants her gone.

'Spend a month in Sopur with our wider family.'

Father gives her that wide-eyed, quirky stare, half-smiling, half-rueful, which she's always loved.

'It's up to you to work out what you'll lose by choosing a Western-style, nuclear family and giving up your mother's ways. Then make your decision.'

This Machiavellian bluff sends her to Heathrow in the pouring rain. Father has one hand on Jason's shoulder and they are smiling as they wave at her.

So she makes the most of her time, exploring the countryside like a tourist, taking hundreds of snapshots, visiting ruins, buying books on local traditions, talking to the villagers, but they are smiling at her, not with her. They all know. Only she is the fool. The next three weeks are branded in her memory. She will never be able to forget.

★ ★ ★

Her holiday is nearly over. Soon it will be time to return to London, marry Jason and settle down to study for her Masters. So she stands in the bedroom, sorting her pictures into albums, making notes and wishing away the next few days. Suddenly she longing for Jason, picturing him, needing his touch, his hands on her body, urging her on. The holiday has lingered over-long. Sheer frustration has set in. Two weeks would have been more than enough.

Aunt Sofia, her mother's cousin, is a weirdo, to say the least. The house is full of whispered conversations, doors that slam in her face, secret visitors at midnight. Sofia's two sons laugh at Bela behind her back. They seem to be sharing in some family secret which amuses them. At breakfast they were openly sneering at her. She decides to stay in her room and read for the rest of the day and pleads a headache.

The next morning, Sofia develops a sudden urge to shop and begs Bela for help. Most of the things she buys are for Bela: silk underwear, flimsy dresses, and glittering sandals. Sweet of her to think about her coming marriage to Jason. Bela unwinds and tries to make friends.

'Honestly Sofia, I'll never get the chance to

wear these things in England. You don't understand what the climate's like.' She doesn't wish to offend her, but she's been spoiled and she prefers designer clothes and tailored styles. Nevertheless, she thanks Sofia profusely. She'll dispose of most of the gear later.

'Bela, darling.' Sofia's voice is sugary, but her eyes are glittering with fright. Why is she so afraid? Her aunt follows her to her room. That's strange. She never does that. Bela tries to ignore a sense of impending trouble.

'I have good news, my dearest Bela,' Sofia says, sitting on the bed. 'You are to be married. Your father and I have secured a most advantageous match.'

Her stomach lurches. 'Don't be silly. Ah! You're joking, of course. For a moment you caught me.' She's desperately trying to stay cool.

'No. It's not a joke.' Sofia's eyes reveal her anxiety.

Bela leaps for a suitcase which she has stowed on top of the wardrobe. 'You're mad. Insane! I won't hear another word of this nonsense. Anyway, I'm leaving . . . today. I've made up my mind. I have friends in Srinagar . . . as a matter of fact they're expecting me . . . '

Sofia knows she is lying. She smiles sympathetically.

'Don't you want to hear about your bridegroom? His family and your family are financially linked and of course they are distant relatives, too.'

'Listen Sofia. I'm already engaged . . . to

someone I love. You're wasting your breath.'

The first suitcase is full. She could get more in if she took more care. Who cares. She rams it shut and grabs the next one.

Her aunt is rubbing her hands together. She takes out a cloth to wipe her brow. She's sweating and the smell permeates the room. Bela goes to the window, which is kept shuttered for coolness in the heat of the day. The heavy wooden shutters are barred on the outside and she can't force them open.

'How dare you . . . how dare you do this.'

'Listen to me, Bela. This marriage will combine both family fortunes.' Sofia is pleading with her.

'Forget it, Sofia. This is crazy talk. I'm not marrying anyone.'

Her aunt thrusts some photographs into her hand, but she tears them up without glancing at them.

'How dare you . . . how dare you!' Fear seems to have whipped away the words she ought to use. Where's her brain gone? Her lips are taut and her mouth is dry. Only her hands are slippery wet. Sofia can't be serious, but these things happen. How many stories hasn't she heard of women lured back to Kashmir and Pakistan, only to be forcibly married. But not her, surely. Her father's Scottish. She has a degree. This couldn't be happening to her. But Fatima hates her and Fatima calls the shots.

'Just contact my father, please and you'll realise how silly you're being.'

'Would you like to read your father's letter?'

Sheets of writing paper are flickering in front of her face.

Bela puts her hands over her eyes and sneers: 'Lies, lies and more lies.'

'I'll read it to you . . .

'Dearest Sofia, Fatima and I believe that it is high time Bela was happily married and integrated into Kashmiri life.' Her aunt falters over the words. 'Fatima's task has not been easy as she tried to envisage what my late wife would have wanted over the years. As you know, I intend to retire to Kashmir and it is my dearest wish that I should live out my old age with my daughter and my grandchildren around me. I have received a letter from . . .''

'No . . . no . . . he can't . . . ' Horrified screams echo around the house. They're hers, she realises. The neighbours must hear. They might call the police. Oh God! Somebody help me. All the strange pieces of this nightmare scenario start to slot into place. She lies on the bed and calls for help.

Sofia runs out, slamming the door behind her. Bela thrusts her fist into her mouth and listens in shock to the key turn. How on earth has the key got onto the outside of the door. Obviously this has been carefully planned. Even luring her to Kashmir was part of a careful plan. What sort of a fool was she not to suspect.

She goes berserk, kicking out at anything and smashing her fists against the door. Oh you fool . . . you cretin.

'Pull yourself together, Bela. Self-abuse isn't going to get you out of here.'

Sofia, with her Third World nature, has forgotten about her mobile phone. It's hard to dial with her rubbery, shaking fingers. A hated voice answers 'Hello'.

'I want to speak to my father, Fatima.'

'He doesn't want to speak to you, Bela. Not right now, but he left a message for you. He says: 'Your mother's ways are better. You've had everything you wanted, a first class education, clothes, holidays, now it's pay-back time. You must return to your roots and traditions . . . ''

'What roots! I'm not anything.' She's shouting again.

'Well, don't blame me. I did my best. Your father wants his grandchildren brought up as your mother was. He has always loved Kashmir and its people. He intends to retire there.'

'Fuck him! Fuck him! I won't. D'you hear me. I'm coming back . . . ' The line goes dead and she sits on the bed and tries to control her sobbing.

Jason will help her. He is in France on a bicycle tour, which is exactly where she should be, if only she hadn't listened to her traitorous father. Tears brim over as she dials.

She hears his voice. 'Thank God! Oh darling, I need help. You won't believe . . . '

She gets no further. 'Listen, Bela. I'm so sorry for you, but your father's read me the riot act. He'll disinherit you if we go ahead. It seems that you've been 'promised', and if you renege on the deal, it will lead to a vendetta. Can you believe it? I checked out the statistics. People are getting murdered here in England because of cancelled weddings in Pakistan. You people have . . . '

The phrase '*you people*' hurts the most. She switches off and lies immobile on the bed, sick with grief, unable to move.

★   ★   ★

Later, feeling like a whipped child, she calls the police station and tells them she's a British national and she's been kidnapped. They promise to call and they do. She screams through the shutters and kicks the door. They are talking . . . and talking. At last the police car leaves and she lies sobbing on the bed.

It is dark. Physical problems take precedence. Namely hunger, thirst and an urgent need to visit the bathroom. Then she has an idea and hunts for her passport, but it has vanished, together with her return flight. She wonders who searched her room while she was out with Sofia.

Her call is answered at once by Sofia's son, who has been left on guard outside her room. She pulls on the sari that Sofia bought her, hides her bag and veil under it and emerges into the dimly lit passage. Sneering with pleasure, the boy lets her into the bathroom and she locks the door.

She'll make it, she reckons, as she climbs out of the window and wobbles from one ledge to the next. She doesn't care if she falls and breaks her neck and that makes her brave. She has enough cash to reach Srinagar where the British

Embassy can replace her passport and get her home. Placing a veil over her head, she sets off for the station.

It takes half an hour to walk there, but who cares. She buys a ticket and hides in the woman's toilet to wait for the train which is due to arrive at dawn. She stares at the dirty tiles and tries to think of a better place to hide. Footsteps are approaching. Men's footsteps! She tries to keep very still, holds her breath, lifts her feet, prays, but they can see the door is shut and bolted. There's nothing she can do about that.

How can dawn ever come if the seconds won't pass? They hang around like moths on a summer night, fluttering around her face, telling her all is lost. She should find another hiding place, but she can hear voices and smell tobacco smoke coming from right outside the entrance.

The train will soon arrive. She has an idea and she examines the window. It's not impossible! Dirty maybe, but who cares. Wiggling through the small outlet, she wades through long grass to the road, walks back to the station and sweeps in through the main entrance. Flicking her ticket, she boards the train. She can't stop shaking as she cowers in the corner of a full carriage.

She's made it. There's a faint tinge of grey in the Eastern sky. The train must leave soon.

The whistle blows and the noise and the smell of the puffing steam is like music as they move forward with an unearthly clatter . . . only to grind to a noisy halt. Three policemen are crossing the platform to board the train.

It doesn't take them long to find her and she is

quickly ushered to a police car and thrust into the back seat. The eldest, reeking with garlic and flashing his gold teeth, speaks to her kindly in English: 'You must think of the good of the family and put selfishness away. Obey your father's wishes, my dear.'

His concern leads her to beg. 'Please, help me . . . I've been kidnapped. I'm English. They've even stolen my passport. Take me into custody and call the British Embassy. I know they'll help me to get home.'

His eyes became stern. 'Your father, in his wisdom, has decided that our traditional ways are best. Your Aunt Sofia showed me his letter when we called. He is your guardian. How can I go against him?'

Dawn, crimson with shame, emerges from its weepy grey. Three children are sleeping in a doorway. Soon they will be begging for food. No one answers their prayers. Nonetheless, she keeps praying and hoping . . . waiting for something, or someone, to save her, but when they swing in sight of her aunt's garden she dies a little.

The house has come alive with tubs of flowers, fairy lights, tables set with cutlery and someone is putting up a bandstand. 'Oh God!' Fear grips her as two policemen push her towards the house. Urine trickles down her legs and she breaks out in a cold sweat. She's going to pass out. She's trapped.

Someone helps her to her room. Her cousin brings her a glass of orange juice. She's dying of thirst and she gulps the juice, draining the glass.

Shortly after that she begins to feels strange. Something is horribly wrong, but she can't remember what it is. She doesn't even know who she is. She wonders why she's being bathed and dressed in these strange, shimmering clothes. She wastes her last intelligent thought trying to remember the proper name of the rape drug.

★ ★ ★

The sound of a police siren brought her back to reality. 'I'm sorry. I was fleeing from the past,' she told him. 'I was remembering something so bad.'

'It pays to keep your mind on your driving, Madam.'

The traffic officer was courteous, but firm. She may argue her case in court, but not with him. She waited patiently while he wrote the ticket, feeling vaguely grateful that he had rescued her from the past. Remembering hurt too much. She must forget what happened for once and for all.

10

Simon's ploy to terminate Laura's Sunday lunches came to him in a flash while having a pint with Harry at his pub.

'Laura and I need to get out more. We don't see enough of our friends and that includes you and Shirley. Regular Sunday lunches here would be the perfect solution.'

'Solution to what?'

Harry looked warily at him. Lately he had grown into a caricature of a publican. Large, rotund and ruddy, he carried the aura of his wealth like a Chelsea Pensioner carries his medals: humbly, proudly, hardly able to remember how or why they were his.

'I just told you. Consider it booked. One o'clock, Sunday, for eight.'

'Going Dutch, are we?'

'Wake up, Harry! I'm hosting lunch.' Was paranoia an occupational hazard of businessmen, Simon wondered, remembering the Harry he used to know.

Harry looked relieved. 'Look forward to it. Barring staff emergencies we'll be with you. Choose your table.'

Simon followed Harry through a panelled archway to the former hotel dining room, which was now a series of semi-private, beautifully decorated annexes. God knows how Laura had achieved this effect. It was part of her professional magic.

'How about that table overlooking the river?'

'Fine.' Harry's voice took on an intimate murmur. 'Listen, Simon, I have to tell you about a girl I know. A glossy, sexy beast. I met her at cricket last summer. It's the real thing. Love at first sight. She's driving me crazy.'

Harry's unwanted confidences made Simon uneasy, remembering Bela and his nightly dreams. He left as soon as he could.

★ ★ ★

On Sunday, when they were sitting around the table by the window at Harry's Place, Simon realised why their old gang seldom got together nowadays. A sense of unease ran around the group. History was the incalculable element, the forgotten danger, an overlooked, unexploded time-bomb ticking away underground. Jointly and severally they had condoned a crime and they were still accessaries.

Gordon had arrived before them. He was checking a sheaf of draughtsman's plans, but when he saw them, he stood up and put his work away.

'Where's Ana?' he asked.

'She's not coming.'

'Perhaps she's getting us back for Sunday,' he declared as if he were one of the family. He practically was.

A hush fell over the noisy room and Simon looked round to see Melissa and David poised in the doorway. Was it David's extraordinary height and breadth or his personality that assured him of a dramatic entrance? Their Granada tans were still glowing, but Melissa had lost weight and she looked drawn. She'd been striking in her early twenties, but a malignant brain tumour had taken hold. She was dying, David had told Harry last week. Melissa, a successful romance author, didn't believe in marriage, but they'd lived together for the past nine years.

'Laura, Sweetie!' David grabbed Laura in a bearlike hug and sat beside her, so Simon settled Melissa beside him in the seat he'd reserved for Ana.

As usual, the conversation touched on the pros and cons of closer financial ties with the EU. David scowled around the table. 'Believe me, the most frightful item on the agenda is the survival of our business freedom. We'll be stuffed.'

'So's the duck,' Harry said, arriving with his notebook. 'Recommended.'

'I'll have the duck, Harry, thanks.'

No one spoke as they studied the menu.

'Come on you guys. I haven't got all day.'

'I'll have lamb chops,' Gordon looked up and managed a grin. 'English, are they?

'What worries me is that globalisation will knock all our policies into Never-Never land,' he went on without a pause.

There was a sudden uproar from a nearby table where soccer fans from Newtown were toasting the morning's win.

David scowled at them. 'Newtown sods! Thank God we managed to keep this riffraff from our backyards.'

That was when Simon seemed to hear the

time-bomb ticking deep inside his soul. Meli stood up, excused herself and walked towards the toilets, but moments later Simon saw her leaning over the railing, gazing moodily at the river. She looked stricken, but David was smiling as he refilled their glasses, blissfully unaware of his gaff in digging up their past crime.

Shirley came rushing towards them, drying her hands on a paper towel.

'Tell me quickly before Harry returns. What happened?' She gazed around expectantly. 'You know what I mean . . . with the vicar.' Her voice dropped to a conspiratorial whisper. 'I *have* to know. Harry's as tight as a drum. Come on, Simon. Tell me!' She placed a playful paw on his shoulder and shook him.

Simon gazed into her candid blue eyes and shook his head. 'Sorry, Shirls!'

'You won't get a thing out of Simon,' Laura said, 'but Gordon might tell you. If not, I will later.'

Shirley glanced appealingly at Gordon, but he ignored her. She only stopped nagging when her husband joined them. He pulled out a chair and sat down.

'Any luck finding a vicar yet, David?' Harry asked.

'I'll give you the bad news first.' David scowled at their unresponsive faces. 'We have a problem. The Church of England is skint, mainly because of their short-sighted property speculations in the Eighties. Bishops are losing their chauffeurs and gardeners and vicars are in short supply.'

'Get to the point,' Harry grumbled.

'That is the point.'

'Everything boils down to money nowadays. So what's the good news?' Shirley asked.

'Believe it or not, foreign vicars are filling the gaps. They hope, and I quote, 'to bring the Brits to faith'.'

'What's the difference?' Harry asked.

'Well, most of them come from the Third World.'

'Is he black?' Laura asked.

'I didn't hear that,' David said pompously. 'Listen, you lot. The property company has underwritten church costs. Our vicar will get the vicarage, a char, central heating and all mod cons, plus a modest salary. And he gets to keep the collection plate.'

'A few coins from seven pensioners,' Shirley chortled.

'That's up to him,' David said smugly. 'I think we should make a point of attending morning service next Sunday to show our moral support.'

'Why do we need a vicar?' Melissa asked.

David sighed. 'Sometimes you can be extraordinarily short-sighted, Meli. It's all part of ye olde village scene. We need a vicar-on-ice. Someone who looks the part: beaming, kindly, harmless and middleaged. An up-market country village must be set up for births, marriages and funerals . . . '

The sentence was cut short as David glanced surreptitiously towards Melissa. 'Don't worry about it. It's in hand,' he added more firmly.

91

Laura flushed and an awkward silence fell about the table.

'It's all right,' Melissa cried out, without any warning. 'We can talk about IT, in capital letters. This terribly unmentionable thing! Otherwise I can't bear to be with you all. It's not the same. You must see that, all of you. This no-go area seems to overshadow every conversation.'

Her eyes, haggard with pain lately, moved from one to the other with a touch of pleading. Moments later she was looking desperate in the face of their stubborn refusal to answer.

'I'll take you home, Meli. You're overwrought.' David's hand patted hers, but she shrugged him off.

'Being English is so . . . well . . . false. Death is *infra dig*. The only respectable way to die is to get into *The Times* obituaries. I feel like an alien because I don't fit in.' She paused, but no one spoke. 'You're my friends, so I want you to know that it's all right to talk about death and if someone says the word 'funeral' by mistake, you don't have to die of embarrassment.'

She looked around anxiously, her voice growing shrill and desperate. 'Oh Shit! This isn't working.' She was appealing to Laura, of all people.

Suddenly his wife was crouching beside her. 'How's it going, Meli?' she asked gently, her eyes dewy with compassion.

'The specialist gave me six months. That's the latest forecast, and I've never missed a deadline in my life.' She was the only one who grinned at her quip.

Simon longed to say something helpful. 'Specialists can make mistakes, too,' he ventured, but no one listened.

'And the headaches?' Laura asked.

'Sometimes unbearable, but often mercifully absent, like today.' She smiled unexpectedly for the first time.

Laura took hold of her hand.

'Six months. You must do something wonderful. Go somewhere you've always wanted to go to. If you need a travelling companion I'll go with you. I can pay my way.' She shot a questioning glance at Simon who nodded uncomfortably.

'I'll see,' Meli stammered.

'The Seychelles. The African bush. Tibet. Your choice.'

'Come on, Laura, this goes beyond the bounds of polite conversation,' Simon said.

'Okay, let's have some polite conversation. Let's talk about money like you usually do.'

From then on their conversation hung around the business of making and losing money. David had narrowly survived a massive pay-out to Lloyds and needed to sell a few more country homes fast. Gordon and Harry were his partners in the property company. Simon had sold his shares, but he controlled the only roof slates permissible, which were mined from a quarry on his farm. Laura took charge of the interior decorating, which was passed on from Gordon, the company's architect. In diverse ways they were all in it together.

'Come on, you guys. Let's get a few thoughts on the problem.'

A cool frenzy seemed to take over as ideas were flung into the think tank. Only Meli and Laura stayed in a huddle talking about life and fiction.

'But Laura, you can't ape life in fiction,' Simon overheard Meli say. 'Fiction's an art form, it gives us style and meaning. Every character has a role to play and a goal to reach, but life . . . well, let's face it, life is a meaningless jumble of events without sense or reason. People pass like ships in the night and we move from one anti-climax to the next until . . . poof!' She shrugged. 'I feel I should create a proper ending to my life, like a novel. Something moving, or amazing.'

Simon stopped eavesdropping. Melissa's tragedy was affecting him badly. He longed to comfort her, but he couldn't find the words. Back in their student days they'd had something going for almost a year, but he'd split when he met Angela and fell under the spell of her beauty. Meli had taken it badly and gone overseas for a few years. Forbidden memories.

He joined the think tank. At half-past two, Meli said she was tired, so Gordon offered to drive her home and the two of them left. The lunch party broke up soon afterwards.

11

*Melissa listens to the sounds of the night
... frogs croaking ... an owl's cry ... wind
through branches ... a dog barks far away and
she can hear cars passing on a distant motorway.
She can see nothing but dark shadows. She peers
through the gloom. There is a gate ... rusty
... creaking ... a high flint wall is looming up
through the shadows ... and she is walking
... no, no, she is creeping towards the wall,
forcing her mind to forge a path ... pushing the
gate open ... hearing the creak ... Is that all
she can hear? She gasps as fantastic shadows
dance around her from moonbeams tangling
with moving branches. The scene is coming to
life. Touch ... Scent ... Come on, Melissa.
Try harder! Damp grass ... Yes, that's it. The
scent of damp grass and the vague perfume of
decaying flowers and leaves. And something else.
Someone is moving towards her. Unease tingles
her spine like an electric shock. She hears a twig
snap close by from a careless footstep.
Unexpectedly, a hand clutches her shoulder.*

'Aaaagh!' Her screams echoed around the
house.

'Jesus! Are you crazy, or what?'

Reality intruded as Melissa spun round and
saw David leap away from her.

'What the fuck's the matter with you,
Melissa?'

'Oh! Oh God!' Fury surged as her imagined paragraphs melted like a dream.

'How many times must I beg you not to creep up on me when I'm writing? You don't understand what it's like. I was there. I was that desperate mother searching for her missing child, right there, in that horrible cemetery . . . that poor little child was buried under the turf. Oh God! I feel sick. It took me half an hour to meditate myself into the scene. Wasted! Damn you, David.'

'For God's sake! I can't take all this arty-crafty nonsense. You know perfectly well who and where you are: you're sitting in your office trying to write a second-rate novel. Stop acting like a big deal.'

She felt shocked by his cruelty, but then she understood. She'd let him down. He used to worship her, but her health had failed and so had her career. David hated failures. She reached out to comfort him, but he avoided her hand.

'Listen, David, if the scene isn't real to me, how can it ever be real to readers? You must understand.'

But he couldn't, or wouldn't. Besides, that wasn't the problem at all.

'Okay, I'm sorry.' David's voice throbbed with tension as he peered over her shoulder at the screen. 'I thought you'd put this one to bed.'

'Yes, but the publishers sent it back . . . again. 'Well-written but not enough fear', they wrote. I frightened myself half to death writing it. Now I have to do it again. I hate this market. There's only one emotion . . . fear.'

'What does it matter what you write as long as it sells?' David flung himself on the settee. 'Honestly, Meli, a professional like you should be able to write anything.'

Years back she'd been faced with a choice: David or her art and she'd chosen David and written for the money he needed, but that market was gone now, superseded by videos. She'd made a fortune with her first six books in the days when romance, plus a get rich-quick-drama, had been a big draw. She'd financed David's first property venture. It hadn't been easy for him, but he'd put a brave face on the indignity of being Melissa Marlowe's lover to everyone except their closest friends. He'd been a smart business manager, too, until the crunch came.

'I heard what you said at the pub yesterday. Six months! Is that true?'

She watched his sunstreaked hair glinting in the light like a halo. He was as fit and youthful as when she met him, but not as desirable. She saw the passion in his brute force, the energy and sex appeal, but she could never forgive him for his growing indifference, although she had never truly loved him. If it weren't so damned ridiculous she'd leave him.

'Melissa! Is it true?' he repeated.

'No.'

'So why did you lie?'

She shrugged. 'They don't know exactly,' she temporised. 'It's all so melodramatic.'

'And the headaches?'

'New pills. Stronger ones.' Should she tell him

the truth? Or would he go to pieces?

'We have two months.' The words seem to break out of their own accord and were instantly regretted. 'Or something like that. That's what the specialist said, but they can't know exactly. Will you be all right?' she asked, watching him carefully.

It was at that precise moment that she caught his flicker of relief. A split-second later it was gone and David's blue eyes, wide and guileless as ever, were locked with hers. His hands reached out and grasped hers. 'I'm so sorry.'

Frozen with disbelief, she could not answer. Eventually she turned away and frowned at the screen, as if this other bad novel that she was forced to live through could suddenly appear, ripe for sub-editing. On second thoughts it needed a total rewrite, a new theme and a happy ending. Or at the very least, lashings of grief. Was she paranoiac? What did she expect from her lover? Sackcloth and ashes? This was England after all, home of the stiff-upper-lip cult. But David had cried bitterly when his favourite horse broke its neck.

A bitter taste surged into her mouth. She swallowed noisily and saw him turn away looking repulsed.

'David, listen! Something frightens me and I must speak out. I feel it's a punishment for what we did. We ought to tell the truth. We ought to find out which one of us is the killer. I never told you this,' she hurried on. 'Years back I drafted a novel around the '85 incident. I wrote a few chapters. Thirteen, to be precise.

I'm thinking of finishing it.'

'For God's sake, Melissa,' David exploded with pent-up fury. 'Are you mad? It was an accident. Don't inflict your morbid imaginings on me. For eighteen years you've never said a word about it and now, suddenly, you come out with this crazy idea. Can't you see the tumour's affecting your reason?'

'I don't think so. To tell the truth I sent the unfinished manuscript to my publishers with a synopsis and they're interested. They want to see a few more chapters.'

'That's bloody outrageous. I'll get an injunction and prevent it from being published.'

'You'd be wasting time and money. Their lawyers checked that out pretty carefully.'

David forced a smile. 'I was joking of course. You never stop to consider your actions. The incident's dead and buried. Raking up the past can only harm us. So think about it. And don't bring up dying in public again. Try to keep up some pretense of normality.'

'Isn't dying normal?'

'For fuck's sake!'

He walked out, slamming the door and she heard him hurry along the corridor and pick up the telephone. He spoke softly into it, which was strange since he normally bellowed. Minutes later she heard the garage door open and David's BMW burst out with a surge of power, wheels squealing as he took the drive too fast. She was left with a sense of deep loneliness. How could she face this awful thing alone?

She'd been so obsessed by her own tragedy,

99

she hadn't bothered to think much of David's feelings during the past year. There had been tests and more tests. A search for second and third opinions, including a trip to the States to see a specialist who thought that the tumour might be operable. This was followed by nights of sleeplessness when a panel of experts had decided it was too far gone. She'd leaned so heavily on David. Could she really blame him for wanting it over and done with? *Yes*, a mutinous voice screamed.

The telephone was ringing. Melissa reached for the receiver. 'Hello.'

'Melissa, this is Doug. I've just heard the news. David called. I'm sorry. More sorry than I can say.'

So why had he called his lawyer? It was an effort to reply. 'It has been coming for a long time,' she said eventually.

'Does that lessen the blow? Listen, David asked me to call you. He thinks you'd be happier in a hospice . . . '

'I'm revising an old novel. I have a deadline I can't ignore.'

'Forget the novel. You don't have to worry about a damn thing, Melissa. Your will's in order, everything's tied up.'

'I'm worried about David. Lloyds almost cleaned him out and his investments aren't doing too well . . . '

The realisation that she was using David's business debacle to avoid facing her own tragedy hit home with breath taking clarity.

'So what's new? He always survives.'

'I'm not going to a hospice and that's final.'

Feeling faint, she replaced the receiver without saying goodbye.

It was ludicrous to want someone to care, she thought, as she walked out of the French windows and down towards the lake. The trees were budding, cherry blossom had burst into flower and all around her was freshness and renewal. Every living thing was bursting with life. She was out of tune with the planet. It was a time of renewal, not death. If she had to die, she should have waited until autumn.

She was frightened and her bitter spite, which never left her, was making her feel even sicker. Why her? She was still young. How could this happen? It was like watching a snuff movie and she had the star role. In two months' time, she would be terminated. Her body would be dumped in a hole and left to rot like so much garbage, her powerful, discerning mind vapourised. Just like that! And all because of a lusty foetus growing in her brain. She'd seen it on X-rays. It looked like a mushroom, but it was growing into the Angel of Death.

The ducks were dabbling in the reeds and she watched them for a while, but soon she was mulling over her hurt. She knew she hadn't imagined David's relief. He wanted her dead and buried and out of his life. Shock turned to a sullen ache in her gut. She wanted to hit back, but she couldn't think how. But what if I don't die? What if I live?

The thought was enthralling, but unrealistic. After all, the specialists had tried everything.

101

★ ★ ★

Ten miles away, David drew up on a hill overlooking Simon's land and gazed at the farmhouse in the distance. He and Simon had been mates ever since he could remember. Lately they'd lost much of the bond they'd shared because they lived in different worlds. For David, paper shuffling was his game, making a quick buck by using his wits. The tension brought floods of adrenaline surging into his bloodstream and lately everything else had become a bloody bore. Right now he was being squeezed on all sides, but he'd survive and make another million. He could always rely on his quick wits.

Simon, on the other hand, liked his route mapped out in total detail before he'd move a muscle. If he were facing danger there was no one David would rather have at his back than Simon. When things got rough you could count on him to do whatever had to be done. As he had done eighteen years ago. Like a Greek tragedy, they'd been drawn inescapably into actions which were loathsome. It was make or break for each of them and they'd got away with it. The past was well and truly buried, but it had to stay that way. Hadn't they been through enough hell?

Back there, in her office, Meli had looked so smug he'd had to get out fast before he lost his temper. Meli could be damned obstinate, he mused uneasily. Perhaps she'd die before she finished it. The idea was strangely seductive.

* * *

The telephone rang startling Melissa out of her chapter. Damn! She should have pulled out the plug. Reluctantly she reached for the receiver.

'Hi.'

'Shirley here. Sorry to break in on the muse, Meli. Our new vicar is sitting in the restaurant eating Toad in the Hole and guzzling a lager. When he's finished he's coming up to you.'

'How d'you know?'

'He told the waitress. His Licensing Service was held this morning. You should have been there.'

'Oh! Damn. Of course, I forgot. I'll plead a headache. Were you there?'

'Yes. So was Gordon, who'd roped in most of our senior citizens from the retirement home and the school kids, so it wasn't too bad. Harry dodged it. The bastard! And David. After the service they sat the vicar in a chair like a throne, handed him the key to the church and then he rang the bell nine times to tell the parish he had taken possession. He told us he'd spent the last few years driving through untouched areas of Africa in a clapped out 4-track preaching to primitive tribesmen. If you can believe him, he's fought off lions and crocs, lived off the land and been all over Africa. He should be able to cope with the locals.'

'Really? I'm not so sure. We're too worldly to be bothered with clichéd phrases and too busy to spare the time. What's he really like?'

'Naive, but good-looking. Plus, he's jet black

and huge. Willful, I would say.'

'Oh hell! Thanks for the warning. I'd better sort out the timetable. Give me a break. Make him wait for his coffee. Thanks Shirls. Be seeing you.'

★ ★ ★

One interruption was bad enough. Two signalled the end of inspiration. She might as well pack up work. Meli saved and filed off and then took another look at the thirteen chapters she'd begun so long ago. The publishers thought the story had possibilities. Her eyes skimmed the Preface:

Temple Minnis wasn't always the upmarket, snobbish green-belt Eden it has become nowadays. I remember the single, untarred street, the church and a handful of stone cottages huddled around it when I was a student in the mid-seventies. That was before the hard drinking, hard living old squire, Ebenezer Fergus fell off his horse and died of his injuries within hours. His son, David, took over and our village never looked back as we threw ourselves compulsively into the 'greedy eighties'. Wealth and status became a must and we fought, colluded and cheated in the tragic pursuit of our ambitions. And that wasn't all. Dare I say it? We murdered. Facing disaster, we reached out to our animus for strength and we won.

So there we were, rich, spoiled, and obsessed with our privileged lifestyles. So why couldn't we hang on to happiness? What is that elusive voice

104

deep inside us all that brings doubt and disillusion and creates our personal tragedies? What makes us judge and jury of our own behaviour?

That was a bit OTT, she thought distastefully, but she'd been younger then.

If she finished this novel she'd be thrust into a confrontation with almost everyone in the village, but was that such a bad thing? They'd all been avoiding her since the news about her tumour leaked. No one cared. Quite honestly, she was longing to hit back at everyone and that included David and Simon.

Could she bring herself to exhume the eighteen-year old past? Every clod of earth would stink of greed, betrayal and blunders. But it wasn't only greed that had motivated them all. They had longed to hold back change. Temple Minnis, with its twelfth-century church, the scenic trails through woods and fields, the trout fishing, the lake for boating, fields of poppies and views sloping away towards the misty Channel, was an English paradise. Something worth fighting for.

12

Those looks! They zoomed straight in like daggers and there he sat, as exposed as a newborn baby, yanked from all that was warm and familiar, tossed into a cold, dark, damp place. Dark looks, dark mutters, dark clouds. Oh shit! A snail hauled from its shell couldn't feel worse than he.

Matthew Luze glanced at his watch and wondered why the coffee was taking so long. He felt exhausted after the long, draining ceremony and a pub lunch had done nothing to improve his mood. Had they never seen a black vicar before? Did they think he was something from outer space.

Harry's Place had been easy to find: 'a plush hotel with a pub, built beside a lake', the decrepit old verger had told him, wavering an arthritic finger vaguely uphill. Beyond the lake was the kind of home you seldom saw in Africa, large, gracious and covered in creeper. He guessed this was his destination. He remembered something similar built in Tanzania by a home-sick German planter. Termites had destroyed the house, booze and mosquitoes got the planter. Within five years, both were vanquished.

He stood up and went to the till at the end of the bar.

'I'll skip coffee, if you don't mind, I must be getting along.'

A small handsome woman with china-blue eyes and bulging boobs looked him over and smiled, revealing large irregular teeth.

'I'm Shirley Young and you're the new vicar. I was at the service this morning. Welcome.' She held out her hand and shook his.

'Matthew Luze. Thanks for being there. Oh man, was I scared.'

'After all those lions?'

'Yeah, well, they're predictable, which is more than we are.' He pocketed his change and winked. 'Be seeing you.'

* * *

Ten minutes later, he reached the other side of the lake, parked and stood gazing up in admiration at the fine lines of the house. He had a letter of introduction to David Fergus and he had to collect a list of forthcoming church engagements. Squaring his shoulders he reminded himself that wealth and mere possessions were not what counted. Yeah, so who are you kidding, Matt? Feeling woefully inadequate to cope with this new, tough world, he jogged up the steps and knocked several times on the door. When he'd finished bruising his knuckles he noticed the bell discreetly placed beside him. Fuck!

The grey-haired woman who opened the door ogled him sternly, but he smiled warmly in return, beamed friendship towards her and held out his hand.

The grim lines tightened. 'Come in, Vicar. You

can sit there.' She pointed to a carved bench near the door. 'Ms Marlowe is in her study. I'll tell her you're here.'

He pulled back his hand, walked inside and made a conscious effort to open up to the feel of the place. Was it really so foreign? Before long his head began to ache unbearably while despair, fear and guilt surged into his mind. He was astonished by the experience. Whose vibes was he picking up? Turning to the bookcase, he saw several rows of books by the same author, Melissa Marlowe. *Through the Long, Hot Summer. The Lighthouse Keeper's Daughter.* There were about eleven books in total, in various editions. Taking one, he flipped open the cover and studied the author's picture. 'Melissa Marlowe lives in Temple Minnis,' he read. As the housekeeper approached, he thrust the book back.

'Come this way Vicar?' Her strong emphasis on the last word was a like a kick in the butt.

'Just call me Matt. That will do.'

Her contempt was like icy water dashed in his face.

He followed her along the corridor to a large, airy room that overlooked a garden full of spring flowers, but his total attention was riveted on the woman sitting behind a desk. Hair like flames, eyes like glittering emeralds, while shadows, dark as snakes, coiled under her eyes. Her skin was drained and dry like the winter plains back home but still she was lovely. The smell of death was all about her and he knew at once that he'd picked up her sensations. Luze was astonished by her resemblance to Miss Rose-Innes, his mission school teacher from long ago. Joining her classes at the age of five, when she was fresh out from England, he had fallen in love with all the passion a little black boy was capable of and his love had never dimmed as she slowly succumbed to the tropics, the color draining from her skin and her hair.

Unlike his teacher, who had relied on her faith, this woeful woman was tangled up in her own tragedy like a moth caught in a web. Unable to reach out, she was terrified of suffering and she feared her coming death. Compassion surged and he longed to help her.

★   ★   ★

From her chair behind her computer, Melissa gazed at the vicar and tried to pull herself together. His height was amazing. Part Masai, perhaps. Would that explain his sooty-black skin. When she'd got used to Luze towering over her desk, she found his unblinking stare to be even more disturbing. He was wearing a black suit shiny with age, a black shirt and clerical collar and a heavy gold chain. His hands were long and graceful and adorned with a multitude of large, flashy rings. He was muscular and beautiful, in a savage sort of way. His proud, distended nostrils, sullen mouth and wide, fierce eyes, reminded Melissa of a wild black stallion she had once seen on the movies. Early forties, she guessed. Sexy! She pulled herself together fast.

'Sit down please, Reverend Luze. I hope you

will be happy here. What made you decide to come to England?'

His eyes locked with hers as he sank into the chair. 'A Baptist minister visited Tanga and told us about the religious decay here. The British gave us our inheritance when they came to Africa as missionaries. Now we are like the grandchildren coming home to help the grandparents.'

She'd read that somewhere. How trite! Yet his voice was perfect. Deep and resonant, it would carry well and impress the congregation.

'Is that original?' she challenged him. 'It sounds so familiar.'

'Okay, I guess it was borrowed.' Luze sighed. 'In my teens I was trained to become the sangoma of my tribe. In other words, my tribesmen's spiritual and physical healer.'

'But that's a witchdoctor, isn't it? Does the Bishop know?' She laughed and looked embarrassed.

'I don't think that's so ridiculous. I escaped to the First World to find out who I am . . . a Christian preacher? Oh, don't worry, I have all the qualifications and the experience. I was ordained in Dar Es Salaam. Or a Zen Buddhist monk? I spent years in a desert monastery. Or my tribe's sangoma? That was the hardest training of all? Or maybe a healer?'

'Why are you telling me this? I mean . . . should you?'

'You might need me?'

Melissa frowned and glanced away. She was having a bad day, obviously it showed. Perhaps she'd take one of her stronger pills when he left and lie down for a while.

'I feel I should explain that the town is strangely divided,' she began cautiously. 'Two-thirds of the villagers live and work in an area we call Newtown, which is situated in a valley beside a semiconductor factory. About half of the factory's workers are Indians, mainly Muslims, the rest are pretty mixed, I believe, and consequently both of our Temple Minnis communities prefer to keep apart. Only the railway separates them from us, but you have to take a long detour to drive from one part of town to the other. It's what we call 'below the line'. Quite honestly, I don't think these people would feel at home in the Temple Minnis church. The previous vicar gave two entirely different Sunday services for the two communities. He used to make use of a dance hall in Newtown's main street. We hope that you will do the same.'

Luze scowled at her, remote and disapproving. 'These people!' he snorted. 'The church was half-empty this morning. What are you saying . . . that you've got some sort of apartheid going on here?'

'Don't judge us until you've been here for a while. For Temple Minnis it was a very good turnout. You'll soon get the hang of things. It's best to fit in, don't you think? Here's your schedule of church events for the coming season. We shall give you plenty of notice of forthcoming events, such as marriages and christenings . . . '

His eyes were gleaming with compassion. Hating pity, she nodded fiercely at him.

111

'Our telephone number is in the file,' she hurried on. 'If you need anything, please don't hesitate to call. I hope you will be happy here. If you'll excuse me, I must get back to work.' She nodded curtly and turned to her computer and after a few seconds she heard the door close softly.

★ ★ ★

Luze walked out in a daze. He longed to help Melissa, but knew he must not. He was amazed that she was still working, but he sensed that this was helping her to cope. Walking past the lake towards his car, Luze paused and swore under his breath. Filled with dismay, he turned away, shielding his eyes with his hands. He felt deeply shocked by his vision. It was the last thing in the world he had expected, or wanted, to see.

'Leave me. Go back to where you belong,' he whispered through lips that had suddenly dried. He had quit Africa to leave his primitive past behind him. Why would they never let him alone? A woman . . . dark-skinned . . . beautiful and Indian, he assumed, from the sari she was wearing, was emerging from a long tunnel of mist, which gave the impression that she was walking on water. Upset by the plea in her eyes, he hesitated. He knew, without knowing how, that she had died here in shocking circumstances. Ignoring her, he strode back to his car and sat behind the wheel, cursing. He'd turned his back on his past, but he could never avoid his intuitive visions. Some people called it a gift, but to Luze it was a curse. 'Not my problem,' he muttered. '*Sio Tatizo Langu.*' I'm not here to solve their ancient murders. Besides, I've put all that behind me.

★　★　★

A donkey . . . a skillful wrecker by the look of things . . . had got into the garden that lay between the church and the gaunt flint vicarage, built behind a grove of budding ash trees. Luze unlocked the vicarage door and walked inside, blinking in the dusty gloom. The small windows were closed, the rooms cluttered and wherever he walked the dust rose in a cloud making him sneeze repeatedly. Throwing open the windows, he sighed and went upstairs. It was April 1, spring surely, but bitterly cold. The view was claustrophobic, the landscape cluttered with trees, hedges and houses, with clouds resting on the chimney pots. He tried to imagine himself back home, the sun scorching his shoulders, the air moist like a ripe paw-paw and twice as fragrant, African starlings and weaver birds squabbling in the bushes and cicadas making their cacophonous din. And space! Glorious space wherever you looked.

He felt so alienated. The people he'd met here bore no resemblance to the English and German colonials he had grown up with in Kenya and Tanzania, and who, from their ranchlike homes amongst acres of sisal and copra, had dispensed animal care, rough justice and indiscriminate philanthropy.

113

He was getting morbid. He decided to go and stock the fridge and look around the area. By the time he returned, a strange, ethereal light was loitering in the garden, pale and almost shadowless. This was twilight, he'd learned. He had no experience of twilight. Back home the sun fell like a flaming orb and minutes later it was dark, but there was little point in hankering for home, he reminded himself.

Luze was an honest man and he had to admit that he found the prospect of preaching to this bunch of high-tech, arrogant villagers intimidating. As for the lovely Melissa Marlowe, he could imagine how she would ridicule him if he told her there was a force that could cure her more effectively than any medicine.

But that was the past. Luze had firmly turned his back on his primitive talents. Healing Melissa was out of the question and his psychic gifts were about to be returned to sender.

13

It was Saturday morning and Bela was working on her thesis when she heard a minibus draw up outside. Someone knocked on her door. The Puri's youngest daughter, Shasta, burst in and hugged her boisterously. She was fifteen and beautiful, like her mother, with glowing eyes and glossy black hair. She caught sight of herself in Bela's long mirror and paused, smiling at her blue silk tunic and matching trousers

'Come on, Bela. Hurry up. We're going shopping. Mum wants to find something to wear at the party on Saturday.'

A party? That was news to her.

'I really have to work, Shasta. Next time.'

Shasta's expression changed to sullen disappointment. She ran back to the minibus. More footsteps sounded on the stairs and Mrs Puri walked in while Shasta hung around in the doorway.

'Do come, Bela. Don't be shy. Our family get together and go window shopping on a Saturday morning. We'll have coffee and cake somewhere nice, and buy a few things.'

Eventually Bela gave in. 'But we'll go Dutch, Mrs Puri,' she insisted. 'You have enough on your plate.' Rashid Puri, a supervisor at the Newtown semiconductor plant, had been laid off recently. This filled her with guilt, although there was nothing she could do about it.

'Bela, my dear, you look delicious,' Mr Puri said.

Bela smothered her smirk. The truth was, with his outsized nose and ears, he stuck out like a dog rose in a flower show amongst these beautiful people. No one who had seen old Peter Sellers' classics would ever be able to take him seriously. He could have been the model upon whom Sellers had fashioned his wit. Add to that his muddled idioms and bad choice of words and he was a one-man walking comedy show. She wanted to turn away, but he targeted her with his soft, endearing gaze and made a point of helping her up the step.

Somehow they fitted into the minibus. Mrs Puri linked arms with her and beamed proudly. There was a moment when she turned towards Bela, her black hair loosened and falling around her neck, her eyes glistening with love, her face so patient and humble, but lovely, too, and precisely then, in that split-second, Bela caught a glimpse of the strength and joy of self denial. The moment passed and the feeling was lost. Mrs Puri worked all hours, but she never looked tired. Sometimes when the wind blew her silk trousers against her legs, Bela caught a glimpse of her muscled calves, thighs and buttocks.

Aunt Dohra, opposite, was as plump and still as a Persian cat, her kohled eyes narrowed with pleasure, her small hands clasped together. Shireen, their married daughter, was a serious girl who had supposedly married well, although Bela reckoned her husband, Dr Hassan Khan, an economist, was far too old for her. Auntie

116

Naomi, a rare beauty and her daughter, Sari, together with Mr Puri's two ugly sisters, were squashed together at the back. Mr Puri was driving them to Canterbury and meeting them later. Armed with shopping lists, their faces as bright as their credit cards, they were intent on having a lovely day.

The air in the mini-bus became moist and warm and filled with amazing scents: perfume, soap, scented hair, laundry-fresh clothes, and a tang of mothballs from the ugly sisters. The mini-bus bounced and swayed, the windows misted over, Bela sank into a stupor and had the strangest sensation that their auras were blending. Like colours left overlong in the washing machine, they were mixing and matching and merging . . . chug, chug, chug . . . and they would all tumble out into the car park as one and the same. Would that be so bad, she wondered? At least she'd know who and what she was.

In a way she loved them because they were just as her mother must have been and she stayed with them to renew her links with her Muslim roots. Could she ever be like Mrs Puri? She'd tried before and failed, but circumstances had been against her. The Puri's had married for love. Mr Puri never tired of telling her how he had set off for Britain to start and new life. Alisha's parents, tired of waiting for him to succeed, had arranged for her to marry one of their neighbour's sons, but she refused. When the pressure became intolerable, she and her brother left home at night without telling anyone

117

and travelled across Europe to reach Britain three months later. By the time she found Papa she'd lost 15 kilos and she had pneumonia, but she recovered and they were married.

What if she grew like them? Bela knew she didn't look like them. She looked Spanish, she'd been told, or Iranian. But looks didn't count. Nevertheless, she knew she was flawed because she wanted far more than running a home . . . she wanted the best of both worlds.

'What is it, dear?' Mrs Puri asked, smiling benevolently.

'Nothing. We're almost there.' She fumbled for her bag, smiled a brittle, false smile and felt like a traitor.

Mrs Puri patted her arm, the van drew up and they climbed out.

★　★　★

Clumsy with packages, they emerged at noon from a department store. When Bela caught sight of Simon on the pavement, the skies and streets lightened as if the sun had come out, but it hadn't. Her face flushed deep rose, her eyes pricked with tears and she became acutely aware of her old jeans, her scruffy jersey and her lack of make-up. Simon looked his usual sensuous, stern and highly desirable self.

'Oh, no,' she murmured. Shasta giggled.

Just let him pass me by. He mustn't notice me. I'm looking a fright. She shrunk back into the doorway hoping he'd pass without seeing her, but he stopped dead in his tracks and grasped

Mr Puri's hand as if they were old friends.

'Well, hello. We meet again. How's Bela?'

He was introduced laboriously to the entire family while she hid behind a glitzy pillar. Bela swore under her breath. Why should I hide? We said goodbye and it sounded like forever. She strode out.

'Simon, how are you keeping?' Then she stopped short, taken aback by her physical reaction to him. Her nipples were hardening under her jersey and she knew that it showed. He looked at her moodily, as if he disliked her. She hated that look. She'd seen it so often . . . predatory . . . all-male. She scowled back.

The Puri's looked disturbed. They seemed to have drawn apart, an invisible barrier was being erected and there she was, exposed on the pavement with Simon, who appeared to be speechless.

'We were on the way to the car park,' she told him.

He found his voice. 'So how about you all having lunch with me?'

'There are too many of us,' Mrs Puri said disapprovingly.

'Not at all. We'll find a large table.'

'We don't have time,' Mr Puri said, looking anxious.

'I'm sorry. Then would you mind if I split your party? That's if Bela agrees. I have to buy my daughter a present and I could do with some female guidance. I'll see her safely home.'

Bela was still thinking about it when Simon took her arm firmly. Other than a street brawl, there wasn't much she could do about it.

'See you later, Bela,' Shasta called.

'Do you always take over like that?'

'I wanted to talk to you. Besides, you need feeding up. Look at you. There's nothing of you.' He guided her through ancient alleyways into a café with tables overlooking the river.

She felt appeased by the discovery of this unexpected hideaway.

'This is so beautiful, Simon. You'd swear you were deep in the country.' She watched the weepy mist spread its luminous glow over the clear, trickling water, the trees were flaunting their spring buds, while birds trilled and warbled, staking their territorial claims.

'You're looking particularly lovely . . . and young. Without make-up you look like a teenager. Makes me realise what a fool I'm being. I came looking for you this morning. I actually called at your home first, but you'd left. The neighbours told me you'd gone shopping in Canterbury. I wanted to see you. I wanted to say I'm sorry for what happened last time.'

'Nothing happened.'

'I was rude.'

'You were straightforward.'

'But not truthful. I can't stop thinking about you and worrying about you.'

'I'm quite capable of looking after myself.'

'Clearly you are. Yet you send out vibes that say the opposite.'

'What do the vibes say?' She couldn't help smiling.

'They say . . . here's a girl who's lost. She

120

doesn't know who or what she is or which way to go. I'd like to be the finder, but alas, I'm married and I'm not about to take on the role of a middle-aged married man chasing after a girl half his age and telling her that he's lonely and his wife doesn't understand him. The trouble is, I'd like to, but I know I won't.'

'How did we get so serious, so fast?'

'I'm just trying to explain why I left so abruptly last time.'

'But this time you came looking for me.'

'I missed you.'

'But you still love your wife.' It was a statement, not a question.

'Of course. I love my daughter, too, and I'm not about to destroy their home. At the same time . . . the truth is . . . I wondered what you would say to a rather boring platonic friendship?'

'I love boring friendships.'

'Well then. I don't have much experience . . . not of this sort of thing. I've been married forever and our friends have always been couples, but . . . for starters I'd like to introduce you to my family. On Sunday, we're having lunch at our local. Why don't you come?'

Was he for real? He couldn't be that naive surely. She watched him anxiously. Perhaps he was using her to teach his wife a lesson. He really thought they'd hit it off. But then, why shouldn't they?'

'Maybe one day.' She couldn't help smiling.

'Don't laugh at me. So tell me about your life. What you do all day? Where do you work?'

'You first.'

121

Why couldn't people take you at face value? Bela wondered, resigned for a boring hour or so, while she learned about his wife and daughter and their many disagreements. She was about to become his psychiatrist, or maybe he needed moral support for their latest clash. Whatever!

After the first yawn she felt a gulp of pleasure when he described the sun rising over the Channel on a fine day, the two-acre slope of daffodils in full bloom around the house, the badgers who sneaked into the porch to steal the dog's biscuits, the otters in the lake and the way the wild geese returned to his lake in the woods, year after year, circling overhead before dropping like stones. As he talked on she began to understand Simon and his intense feel for all living creatures, including his livestock. He didn't once mention his family.

In turn, she told him about her research for her Ph.D, trying not to get too excited or carried away. She was tracing the origins of Greek and Mesopotamian words in Sanskrit, showing how ancient man had spread from the valley of the Euphrates into India. She explained how she loved and also hated her work at the Migrant Help Centre. Loved it because she was doing something worthwhile to help people, hated it because she could never do enough, funds were short and the people were frightened and lonely. At five, after lunch and then tea, she said she must go because she had several hours of studying to finish before morning.

'By the way,' Simon said when he dropped her outside the Puri's home. 'There's something that

122

puzzles me so much. I can't get it out of my mind. That night when I met you in the woods. You seemed to know me, or my name. You were so startled and obviously badly affected. I've tried to work out when or where I might have met you. I'm sure I would remember.'

'No! You're quite mistaken. I felt embarrassed. That's all. I must go. Goodbye.'

She got out of the car and hurried inside, closing the door firmly behind her, without a wave. Simon was left standing on the pavement wondering how on earth he had managed to ruin a perfectly lovely afternoon.

14

Ana objected to being forced to go to church. She felt unfairly saddled with her parents' hypocrisy as she followed them into the small, draughty church with its whitewashed walls and stained glass windows splashed with crimson gore. Following her mother's example, she knelt to say her private prayer: 'God, get me out of this absurd rigmarole.' Not that she believed in God, but it was comforting to imagine an old man sitting in the clouds, answering prayers if you begged long and hard enough.

Moments later she slipped back onto the hard pew and glanced at her watch. Nine-thirty a.m.! Three hours of boredom lay ahead and it was all about business. She wanted to puke. She'd voiced her objections at breakfast this morning and at least Mother had been straightforward, delivering a blunt message:

'You'll come because David needs us to be there and he gives me all his work.'

'You hate decorating his houses.'

'True, but I like the money. That coat you're always borrowing cost . . . '

'Okay, okay,' Ana pursed her lips wishing she'd never seen the bloody coat. Not if it meant Mum had to toady to that creep, David.

Dad had been more duplicitous. 'What could be more natural than going to church together? Besides, it's only polite to welcome the new vicar. I don't know what that damned, expensive school taught you. Anarchy perhaps! Don't think I don't know you fed the pigeons in Trafalgar Square, quite apart from spraying horses and all your other devious activities. It's about time you learned to obey the laws of the land and do as you are told.'

'That's what war criminals say when they're brought to trial,' she'd flung at him. 'But Dad,' she'd queried. 'How do you see God?' She badly needed answers. 'D'you truly believe in heaven and hell? Virgin births and resurrections? Devils with horns and tridents? All that?' She was trying to sort out her own muddled impressions of life and afterlife and find answers to the age-old question of why she was born and exactly what she was supposed to do with her life.

'I leave that sort of thing to the vicars. They're the experts. That's what they're here for.'

'Apart from screwing choir boys.'

Dad glared at her with frightening intensity. 'One bad egg doesn't affect Christianity. There are good and bad in every profession.'

She could tell by Dad's face that it was time to shut up, but still she persisted.

'So you believe everything implicitly?'

Doubt shone in Dad's eyes, but the moment passed.

'It's part of being English. That's what I am, a perfectly ordinary English person. You should try it, Ana. Leave religion to the church. It saves all the turmoil you're going through and leaves you free to get on with your life.'

'Top marks for footwork, Dad.'

Agonising over God wasn't the beginning and end of her problems. She worried about Britain, too. She was determined to fight against the things she detested, like cruelty to animals. One of these days she'd graduate to the human species because there was no doubt in her mind that Britain wasn't a kind country. Not any more. That's if it ever had been. Take the tramps on London's streets. The media were full of trite assurances that there were shelters for everyone, it was part of the general hypocrisy she met on all sides. The real truth was that the free shelters were full and the others charged seven pounds a night, plus the tube fare to get there. Not everyone could cope with high-tech living.

She'd first met up with hypocrisy at school. Intensely establishment, the staff cared only for presenting a good face to the world while their pupils almost froze to death in the sick bay. They'd been deprived of a balanced diet, while hypocritical shit was shovelled down their throats, like the unique advantage of being British. Looking back she'd often thought she should have run away, but that wasn't part of her make-up. School had left her with violent feelings towards any kind of establishment. Footsteps were clicking on the cold, flagged floor behind them. She turned and waved as Melissa, David and Gordon dabbed holy water on their foreheads. Gordon looked harassed as he gazed at his watch. Glancing around, Ana nodded towards the eight pensioners who made up most of the remaining congregation. There was Mae, sitting all alone near the back with a face like thunder. So she'd been press ganged into coming, too. Ana beckoned to her to join them, but Mae shook her head, pointed at her watch and shrugged.

'He's late! Not a very good start.' Mae's stage whisper was heard by the entire congregation.

★ ★ ★

Into the brooding silence interspersed with low mutterings of private prayers came the crunch of footsteps on gravel. A long, thin shadow fell down the aisle to the pulpit. Turning in shock, the congregants were flabbergasted as the vicar paused in the porch.

Well, he couldn't be that tall, nor that black, Ana decided, but as the vicar hurried down the aisle in a strange, jogging step, a quick glance assured her that he was. Not the normal black as in plain chocolate, or even mahogany, but black, as in chimneys, she thought. In fact, so black his skin absorbed the light like a black hole, so there was nothing left for reflections or lustre. The radiant whites of his immense eyes were equally disconcerting. He was loose-limbed like a colt and very beautiful. Her eyes lingered on his white polonecked shirt worn with a black dogcollar, and black stretch jeans, revealing a muscled torso and buttocks. Psychedelic trainers, three heavy gold chains and rings like knuckledusters completed the picture of a New Orleans jazz musician.

He paused by the pulpit and turned. 'I'm Matthew Luze, the new vicar here, as most of you know, and I'd prefer to be called Matt,' he announced.

'Oh!' Ana mastered her shock fast enough to murmur. 'Welcome,' against the low mumble of astonishment.

The busybodies from the retirement home looked shattered and Mae was fumbling for her hip flask: 'For my nerves.' Ana heard her stage whisper.

The vicar climbed the three steps to the pulpit and turned to the congregation, his long fingers pressed firmly together, his ardent eyes glowing with zeal.

'Hi folks. Unless you were present at Wednesday's service, I guess it's the first time you've seen someone like me here . . . an African preacher. I'll admit that mud huts and market squares are more my style. I hope you'll come to the vicarage after the service for cheese and wine, so that I can get to know you all personally.'

He looked savage, but his voice shocked Ana. There was hardly a trace of Africa there. Yet he didn't sound English, perhaps because he had no accent at all.

Ana craned her neck to enjoy David's astonishment, ignoring her mother's irate dig in the ribs.

'Stop it, Mum,' she mouthed. 'You're hurting.'
'Tch!'

Matt heard. His eyes sought hers and he winked. Wow! He was definitely cool. This was going to be a little less tedious than she'd expected.

'We have some bad news.' He glanced at his notes. 'Mrs Montrose, who normally plays the piano at our services has flu. Can anyone take over?'

Ana was about to volunteer when Mum kicked her ankle.

'Okay, so you'll have to make do with me until she's better,' the vicar said.

He's really nervous, Ana noted as he whipped out a handkerchief to wipe his forehead. He stepped down to the piano.

'We'll start off with my favourite hymn, *The Year's at the Spring*. It was taught to me years back by my mission school teacher in Tanga. Does everyone have a programme? Good,' he said to the dumbstruck congregation. 'Of course it's in your hymn books, too, but I expect most of you know it by heart.'

His voice was like treacle, thick, black, syrupy treacle, but after a couple of lines he broke off and turned round.

'This is not a solo performance. You all have to sing along. Don't you folks know that? Isn't that what you do here? Singing creates togetherness. Where I come from there's only one word for both singing and dancing. That's because we live for music and we really can't sing without dancing, or dance without singing. So if any of you feel like dancing around in the aisles, feel free. Come on Granny. Put that flask away. Singing's better for you.'

A titter of dismay ran around the pews, but the old ladies joined in half-heartedly as Matt played it again and harmonised with his beautiful voice. Laughing inwardly, Ana went along with the glint in his black eyes and sang her heart out until the hymn came to an end.

'Well, that was okay for starters. We need to get a choir together. It will give courage to the rest of the congregation. It's early days, but volunteers would be welcome.' He glanced nervously at the pulpit, Ana noticed, before mounting the steps.

'My dear friends, today we're going to talk about love. 'God said: *In any way that men love me in that same way they find my love; for many are the paths of men, but they all in the end come to me.*

'That beautiful quote comes from the *Bhagavad Gita*, known to Hindus as the Song of God. Loving God means loving every living creature and ourselves and it is the primary teaching of almost every religion, Christianity, too, emphasises that all you need is love, or to quote 1 Corinthians, Chapter 13, Verse 2: *though I have the gift of prophecy, and understand all mysteries, and all knowledge: and though I have all faith, so that I could remove mountains, and have not love, I am nothing.*'

As Luze scanned the congregation, he had to fight against his growing depression. He'd meditated half the night to produce his sermon, but he sensed that no one was truly listening. The beautiful Melissa Marlowe, sitting in the front row on the right, had a glazed look in her eyes. She was obsessed with illness and her personal misery. Her husband was surreptitiously fingering a calculator and the

130

black-haired man beside him was leaning back with his eyes closed. Not the type to waste time, so he was probably thinking about his work. There was a handful of old people, who might be present merely for social reasons, for they clearly weren't listening. The woman with the hip flask took another surreptitious sip, and the young girl with her parents in front were at odds with each other. There was something else that bothered him. It was guilt, but why? Wherever he went here, he seemed to come up against it.

Noting their expressions of resignation he sensed the centuries of Church oppression which had made them feel less than human and his anger surged. Labelled 'sinners' for so long, how could he convince them that they nurtured Godliness. But he would try to show them, starting now, he vowed.

'When you stand alone in the countryside and you feel a wave of love for our planet, or for the trees and birds, you can be sure that God is loving you. God says: '*Believe in yourselves, love God and all living creatures.*' My friends, that's the beginning and end of it. There's nothing else worth saying.'

As he glanced at their doubtful, puzzled faces, a surge of compassion caught him unaware. Was there some reason he'd been propelled to this unlikely spot, apart from his own salvation? He shut his eyes and in the silence he vowed not to sell them short. For as long as he was here he would be their sangoma.

15

Sleepy eyes and bored faces surrounded him. They'd heard these words before. Luze was feeling desperate. How could he convey the exciting, vibrant role that each one was playing out over millions of years and millions of lives, from the very dawn of life, to today's quest to conquer space and unravel the secrets of creation? Ahead of them was the limitless future, taking humanity to the far reaches of the universe. But without love only chaos would be created. He longed to impart his joy in loving. He needed to try harder.

'My friends. You possibly think that global warming and the threat of a nuclear war are humanity's main problems. I've got news for you. There is a problem far more vital. Sometimes I feel overwhelmed by the responsibility we carry and the extraordinary power of our minds.

'Mankind and God are locked in a relationship of mutual dependence. God needs our love. That will shock you, but I promise that it's true. Everywhere that man exists would dissolve into chaos if we don't recycle God's love. Love is the binding of every natural law. It is the glue of our universe. God is a force . . . a force of love, so don't be a black hole.'

This information came to him time and again in his deepest meditations. Could they possibly understand him? Mere words could never replace enlightenment. How could he help them to *know*?

'God created life to make love real, but the traffic of love can't be only one-way. Energy and love are beamed into us and we must love in return. That's a commandment, or a plea. So if you can't love God, or all living creatures, pick on one person or animal and love that one passionately, unconditionally and irrevocably and in that way you'll do your bit to recycle love.

'We, and all living creatures, share the Cosmic Nature to the limits of our brain capacities. We understand God's love of beauty, His passion for music and nature, His compulsion to create, His intense, unconditional love of humanity and all life, because we feel all this, too. No doubt there's so much more that we don't understand, but deep down we know that love and creativity from the kernel of our souls.'

He raised his voice against the vague mutterings of annoyance and hurried on, hoping to counter their antagonism with his passion.

'How many of you consider yourselves to be Christians?'

If he had clouted them out of their pews they could not have looked more shocked. They had come out of habit or duty . . . the slow shuffle of resentful people doing their duty against all reason . . . and they did not want to be yanked out of their passive role. He could sense the dull edge of their anger. They were unused to anger. They were a passive people, ruled by their intellect, they believed in the Church of England

133

as a necessary British institution, but little else. They didn't want to hear his message. Grumbling, some of them slowly raised their hands.

'Loving is an art which few people acquire. Like all arts, loving requires constant practice, discipline, passion and a desire to succeed. Living on a planet where so much hatred exists between races, religions and countries, it is vital that those who can love, should help to redress the balance. That's our job.

'When you love you're merging with God and opening yourselves to inspiration. You become vibrant and fired with energy.'

He could sense the worshippers' annoyance that he had strayed from traditional Christian dogma, but all faiths had evolved from the same spring, Luze reassured himself. His congregation could benefit from his years of training in most of them.

'You Western people brought Christianity to East Africa in the late nineteenth century, which you imposed upon us. But it was all theory. The theory of love. You never realised that practically-speaking we had always loved each other. Now African missionaries are coming back to you, bringing you the second half of your lesson in love. The practical part, the loving togetherness of a people.

'The Bible (1 John, Chapter 3, Verse 18) reads: *Let us not love in word . . . but in deed and in truth*. So if you have your heads full of Christian teaching, but you don't love all living creatures, you're kidding yourselves that you're on the right path.

'People think it's easy to love if only there was someone who deserved their love. Well, it doesn't work like that. Don't think about being loved. Think about giving love freely.'

When Luze gazed around, he sensed the bewilderment of his congregation. 'All I'm saying is, over the forthcoming weeks, we'll learn to practice what we preach.

'We'll forget about the concept of original sin. That's nonsense. We are all truly special and deeply loved by God because we are one with God. Everyone, everywhere. We share God's consciousness. We can start off by loving our neighbours. I have a plan to get the Newtown locals here so we can become a real community.'

Luze faltered and looked around. Something he'd said had really annoyed them. He wondered what it was. Shafts of pure resentment were zooming his way. He decided to bring the sermon to a close.

'We'll end the service with the hymn, '*All Things Bright and Beautiful*,' and I hope you'll join me in the vicarage afterwards.'

Luze played as they sang the last hymn and then they filed out, hovering in groups on the pavement to discuss the scandalous vicar who had dared to quote foreign scriptures to them and who threatened to bring the Newtown locals here. Only two pensioners joined Luze for a glass of wine, Ana learned later. Not even Gran went. Ana felt furious with herself for giving in and joining her parents for yet another boring pub lunch.

Luze was feeling depressed after the failure of his sermon. Later that evening he recovered sufficiently to go outside and gaze hopefully along the main street of Temple Minnis. The only signs of life were the cows in the field opposite. He stifled a howl of rage. Every extremity seemed to be burning with cold and his ears hurt so much he thought he had frostbite. Icy dew soaked his shoes and the air was so humid he might drown. He longed for Africa, but right now anywhere hot would do. In Tanga the earth would be belching back the sun's heat it had stored all day, the air wafting the sweet scent of tobacco flowers, jasmine, orange blossom and frangipani. Talented amateur bands would be belting out the latest hits in every street, and young and old would be dancing, or sitting around outside, arguing about the latest political outrages, or entertaining their friends with wickedly funny gossip.

So few people had attended his service and those that came had looked as hard and uninviting as the wooden pews. Except the young girl in the front row, who was full of fun, but just a kid. His thoughts turned to Melissa Marlowe. She was something else. He whispered her name, savouring the consonants: *Melissa*. He'd been touched by her sadness, her tragic eyes and her fear of death, all of which he had read in her aura. And then there was her beauty. He'd been fretting about her since he set eyes on her.

Someone was playing the piano and the sound drifted in the wind. A female voice began to sing along and then another joined in. At the sound of music he almost burst into tears. Tomorrow he would buy a radio and a CD player, he promised himself. He didn't know the song, but he felt drawn to the singers. The sound seemed to be coming from the village pub, so why not go there. He couldn't bear to remain alone in the vicarage for the rest of his two-year stint here.

Hurrying inside, he agonised over what he should wear, eventually choosing a Mandela-style black and yellow shirt which he wore over a black sweater and elasticized black trousers which he'd bought on a trip to Zanzibar. He combed his hair straight up and pondered on the advisability of shaving his skull, which was the fashion. He'd tried it once, but it seemed to accentuate the muscles in his thick neck and shoulders and made his eyes look at bit like ET. Not bad, he thought, admiring his gold chains and rings. Brushing the fluff off his shoulders, together with doubts and insecurity, he walked into the cold night air.

16

Simon returned from locking the dairy to find Laura's car parked outside the front door, which meant she was going out again ... and for the fifth night running. They must 'have it out', he decided. There was no love in their home, he grieved, remembering Luze's sermon, and he sensed he was to blame.

He knew that his friendship with Bela was running out of control. It was like a fever, raging more fiercely in the midnight hours, but always there, playing havoc with his concentration: a sudden glimpse of silken thighs, her shapely alabaster neck, eyes that wooed and flattered him, would set him off daydreaming. He had seen Bela three times in the past week and on the last occasion, in the heat of the moment, he had folded her in his arms. He'd come to his senses in time, thank God. He'd been through all this. Done it all, wept enough tears to fill a tidy dam. Never again! No thanks. Lust wasn't a good enough reason to ruin a family. Nothing was.

He went in search of Laura and saw her emerging from the bathroom wrapped in a thick white gown.

'Hi! You need a haircut.' She frowned at him. 'You're beginning to look like an ageing gypsy.' She perched in front of the dressing table with a round brush in one hand and a hairdryer in the other. Crossing her legs, the gown fell open revealing her luscious thighs. Fire flared in his loins.

'Laura, we have to talk. What the hell d'you think you're doing, out on business night after night? This is supposed to be a marriage.'

'Is it?' Her large, beautiful eyes looked him over contemptuously while she deftly twirled the handle of the brush. The brush rose and fell, winding and unwinding a strand of hair while the dryer blasted it.

'Switch that damned thing off.'

'I can't hear a word you're saying.'

'Switch it off,' he mouthed.

She did. The dry strand was deftly pinned on top of her head and she selected another. Moments later the brush was whizzing up and down and the hairdryer was switched to maximum heat and noise. He bent swiftly and pulled out the plug.

Laura turned towards him, her face alien and unresponsive. 'I'm late,' she said quietly.

'We have to talk Laura.'

'Not now. Don't be so bloody selfish. If you want to discuss something make a time.'

'You mean I should make an appointment . . . to speak to my wife?' He felt he was lurching along the lip of unreality. 'Are you mad? We can't carry on like this, Laura. Perhaps we need a marriage counsellor.'

Simon watched her mouth set like an inverted horseshoe, while her eyes signalled impatience. That was about the only feeling he ever got out of her.

'Perhaps I'm clutching at straws.' He wanted to add: I still love you, but he couldn't say the words. Instead he leaned forward to stroke her hair.

'Don't touch me. Just keep away. You're acting crazy. A marriage councillor,' she scoffed, selecting another strand of hair. Moments later the brush was whirling up and down and the hairdryer was blasting him out of the bedroom.

Disappointment sent him fleeing from the house, his foot hard down on the accelerator as he made for the pub. Laura had loved him once until Angela came into their lives.

★   ★   ★

The room was crowded and everyone was shouting above the hum of conversation and loud singing coming from a group gathered around the piano. It was warm, the lights were dim and Simon was glad he had come. Harry, wearing a bow tie, a fancy waistcoat and a smug smile to match, was leaning over the bar. He and Gordon had their heads together. Everyone knew David had been arrested and released, but hardly anyone knew why. Gossip was Harry's stock in trade and he was enjoying his advantage. Simon joined the group at the bar with a murmured 'Hi.'

' . . . a bloody great swipe across the back with his horsewhip,' Harry was saying. 'There's always been a public footpath cutting through David's wood, but back in the Eighties he claimed it was a private path. There are signs saying *Keep Out* all over the place. Well, two nights ago, after he'd had a couple of drinks, he came across this bloke who claimed to be recording birdsong. Not a very likely story, let's face it. He said he worked at Newtown, but that was a lie. He was a reporter and his photographer was hiding behind a tree. Someone local gave them the lead, that's for sure.'

'What a bloody fool,' Simon grumbled.

'David's on the booze again,' Harry added.

'He has his reasons,' Gordon said. 'He's in trouble and the tension's getting to him.'

'But should we talk about it?' Simon queried.

Harry shrugged and Gordon took over.

'Remember when David wanted to form a consortium of Lloyds' names and he nagged us to join?'

'I'll never forget.'

Simon remembered the summer of '88 all too well. David had made his pile, but he wanted more and still more. He'd spent weeks extolling the virtues of easy money with virtually no risk.

'Did you go in with him?' he asked Gordon.

'No. Neither did Harry. We didn't have the spare cash.'

'Same here.'

'Last year David had to pay up,' Gordon continued. 'You know how it goes. You're liable jointly and severally. His partners paid some and promptly went into liquidation. Millions were involved, but David didn't have enough cash so he hit on a scam. Now listen to this . . . it's pretty smart.' He smirked at them, making the most of the limelight.

'One of his property companies bought a near-defunct Welsh coal mine with a couple of fields thrown in. It had been in the red for years, but David claimed it was a good industrial site.'

'I can't see broadcasting this can help him . . . ' Simon began.

'It'll soon be common knowledge,' Harry interrupted, pursing his lips and looking pompous.

Gordon shrugged and went on. 'The coal mine had a very old and wealthy pension fund and their cash was invested in low-yield, bluechip investments. David reinvested the funds and guess what he bought?'

Simon shrugged. He knew the story and he felt contaminated, yet he'd done his best to talk his friend out of it.

'His own failing shares. Years back he bought heavily into Irving's local semiconductor factory. Now they're on the skids. So . . . he got his PR agency to rustle up a massive publicity campaign which pushed up share prices. David realised almost a million for his shares and paid off Lloyds.'

Simon tasted bile as he listened to the grotesque moves.

'So David should be laughing all the way to the bank,' came a comment from behind him.

'But that's not the end of the story.' Gordon leaned forward and spoke in hushed whispers. 'After the deal, the share price fell dramatically, so the Welsh miners got in a firm of independent auditors who soon found out that David had taken over their pension fund investments. Now there's a threat of fraud charges unless David refunds the cash.' Simon felt concerned. His friend was making silly mistakes due to panic.

'Thank God I'm a farmer,' he muttered. 'So why the gloom?' he asked Harry. 'Does this appalling mess affect you?'

'In a way if affects all of us. The shares were owned by our original property company. Let's face it, we don't want the '85 business dragged up. It's dead and buried and let's hope it stays that way.'

The three men stared uneasily at each other. Their sudden, pervasive quiet was more eloquent than words.

'I sold out years back,' Simon said eventually.

'I didn't,' Gordon said. 'Harry has a few, I believe. We're still directors.'

Harry nodded.

'Where's Shirley? Simon asked.

'We had a bust up. I didn't come home last night.' Harry looked shamefaced.

'It's not worth it, Harry,' Gordon urged him.

'Maybe, but Gloria turns me on and Shirley doesn't. It's like comparing caviar to warmed up old stew.'

Harry broke off as the pub became strangely quiet. Their new vicar stood framed in the doorway looking ridiculous in his jazzy African outfit with gold chains slung around his neck, his hair standing on end like a fall-guy from a comic strip.

Simon waved a greeting and turned back to Harry who swore quietly. 'Regular weirdo! David's latest idiocy. He should have waited

143

instead of grabbing a missionary. David's cracking up, but we can't write him off. Not yet. He'll come up with some clever scam.' Harry winked. 'Someone wants me. See you guys.'

After Harry left Simon felt too depressed to say anything.

'I heard you gave a talk favouring inoculating livestock for foot and mouth,' Gordon tossed into the silence.

'Yes. That's right. But I was wasting time. We're dancing to the EU's tune.'

Gordon glanced at his watch. 'Got to go. See you, Simon.'

What am I doing here? Simon wondered. He used to think that he and his kind were the backbone of the British nation, but his friends were greedy and immoral, his wife alienated, his daughter rude and unruly, intent on demolishing her world, and Melissa, who had never done anyone any harm, was dying.

Ever since his tiff with Ana he'd been unable to stop scrutinising himself and his peers, trying to decide whether or not he still believed in his myths and heroes, or in himself. He no longer knew what it was to be British. The Church had forgotten the Christian message and was suffocating in its dogma and the entire governing establishment had thrown strength aside in favour of spin, but spin was like a virus, forever devouring its hosts. A moral Ebola gripped the land. So who in England had the nerve to seek the Golden Fleece and lead the country back to some semblance of sanity and truthfulness?

17

Deeply engrossed in his gloomy introspection, Simon was only vaguely aware of the vicar's conversation with two smartly-dressed young women who were on their own. He moved on to the group gathered around the piano and stood around, drink in hand, looking bemused, while the old tunes with their poignant memories, hung in the night air like a reassuring promise. Eventually Simon waved him over and for a while they chatted about the lack of interest in church affairs, but the vicar looked troubled.

'I feel a little out of place. I seem to embarrass everyone.' Luze gazed around mournfully.

'As you can see, the locals are pretty conservative. You're different.'

'I'm not going to ape the English. I'm an African.' There was a trace of defiance in his voice.

'It will take you a while to get to know folks around here. Organise a few more church socials, visit people, ask for volunteers and get to know them.'

He wanted to say something more comforting to calm the vicar's ruffled feelings, but nothing came to mind.

Everything about him is larger than life, Simon thought examining his dark, scowling brows, huge eyes flashing with resentment, lips sullenly down turned. He was proud, fiery and inflexible, not at all what David had wanted for the village, yet Simon felt drawn by his charisma. He envied Luze, he realised. He was so damned natural and so full of passion.

'I didn't see you in church last Sunday. Did my previous sermon frighten you away?'

'Not at all. I don't spend much time in church, but your first sermon went down well. I haven't heard of any complaints.'

'Perhaps you don't remember much about it,' Luze prodded, looking ferocious.

Simon tried to remember the few phrases he had heard between his detailed planning to increase his grazing by twenty per cent.

'Love,' he came up with, much to his relief. 'It was about love. Of course you have to realise that not everyone believes in love. I don't. What is it, this strange emanation of yours? Can you touch it, or smell it? No, of course not. It's something dreamed up by romantic novelists to make lust seem more acceptable.'

'You're kidding me, of course.' Luze beamed a hopeful smile.

Simon scowled at him. 'No. I understand duty, loyalty, friendship, or maybe you mean affection?'

'I mean love. Love's like electricity. Look what happens when you switch on the Big Top. Lights whirl, music starts, the funfair comes to life, people laugh and start dancing. Just think of all the electricity of the whole world, all the computers, all their know-how, the lights, the heat, the pylons, the nuclear plants. So there's all that electricity, a whole world full of it, but we

146

don't know much about it, only what we use. Love's like that . . . a largely unknown force. So don't downgrade love, because you can't. You can't squash it or flatten it. You can't even touch it, but one of these days it's going to touch you.'

'That sounds like a threat,' Simon said flippantly. 'Look here, Luze, I get up at 5 a.m. for milking, I feed the cows, plough the land, clean out the barns, buy the feed, plant the seed, I earn my keep, provide for my family, keep Redhill in peak condition and that takes some doing, believe you me. I give the odd lecture, attend meetings, keep up with research, innoculate my herds. I lead a full life. Don't talk to me about love. Tell me about duty! That's what life's all about. This is the age of specialisation, don't you know. I leave love and praying and that sort of claptrap to you guys. You do it for us, so we can get on with our lives. That's how we do things here in England.'

'If that's the way you want it. So where are the real people?' The vicar's voice was vibrant with sudden amusement.

'Real people?'

'Shop assistants, farm workers, artisans.'

'Perhaps the high prices keep them away. There's a couple of pubs in Newtown and a recreation hall, a disco, a selection of Indian restaurants, a coffee bar, bowling alley, a modest sports stadium.' He saw a gleam of derision in the vicar's eyes and realised he was over-stating his case.

'I was warned about a self-imposed apartheid here.'

'No, not really. It's a long story.'

'I feel I ought to know it.'

'Okay. Can I get you a drink?' Simon asked.

'Thanks. Brandy on the rocks, please.'

'Cheers.' Simon said when he returned.

'Cheers.'

Apartheid! Was that what people thought? Simon decided to make an effort to explain.

'Temple Minnis was once a small community servicing the surrounding farms, but when Ebenezer Fergus died in the early Eighties, his son, David formed a property company. His friend, Gordon, a newly qualified architect, joined him, as we all did in the beginning, but later some of us sold out. I suppose we were trying to hold back change, but I think Temple Minnis became wealthier than anyone had intended.'

'So the dream worked.'

'Sort of. We got Newtown dumped on our boundaries, but it could have been worse. Water under the bridge.'

Simon broke off and drained his glass. It was time to go, he decided. 'I'll drop you there if you like. I'm leaving and I have nothing much to do.'

Luze looked extraordinarily pleased with the offer.

Simon said his goodbyes and walked out of the pub into the freezing night air. As the singing died away, the crunch of their footsteps on icy tarmac sounded like gunshots. He breathed in deeply, loving the winter scents: the faint drift of wood smoke, the sweet-sour stench of damp earth, a vague tang of ozone. The whisky had

148

numbed the pain of his defeat on home ground. He felt invigorated and almost happy.

Luze was shivering violently under his gleaming jacket.

'There's a shop in Newtown that sells anoraks for next to nothing. You'd better treat yourself or you'll catch pneumonia. My car's parked by the lake. It's not far to walk.'

'This cold, and this place, it's . . . Well, let's just say it's very strange to me. The closeness of everything. I mean, just take your roads, winding willy-nilly all over the place. We have straight roads that go on for hundreds of miles.'

Willy-nilly? Simon pondered on Luze's old-fashioned choice of words and his curious, private-school vowels. Mission school upbringing, he decided, feeling pleased with his deductions.

'You have to remember that our countryside has remained unchanged for centuries. In places you can still see the sub-rectangular Celtic fields and terraced strip-boundaries. If you're interested I can show you round some time. In daylight of course.'

'Well, thanks. I'll take you up on that. The Celts have long since disappeared I guess?'

'Depends which way you look at it. 'Scratch an Englishman and you'll find a Celt'. That's not original, I read it somewhere and it's very true. The Celts went underground, into our genes, emerging from time to time to dance around the Maypole and deck the yew tree. My farmhand, Sarah Jones, still bows three times to the new moon and turns her money over. She has a phobic fear of the Evil Eye that would slap her back to size at the first sign of wealth or pride. Here we are.' Simon pulled his keys out of his pocket and unlocked the 4-track.

★ ★ ★

Luze was not listening to Simon. Three paces behind, he was shivering violently as he experienced fear and death and icy waters closing over his head. He saw a signpost rising out of a field of snow, ghostly and ephemeral, swaying in mist that he knew was only in his mind. He blinked several times and blanked his mind to the images. Taking a deep breath, he hurried towards the truck.

'Tell me, Simon. Does that lake have a history? Did someone die there? A woman in a sari perhaps?'

He watched Simon turn pale, while his eyes narrowed with temper. 'You've been reading old newspaper reports, I suppose. There was a nasty accident years ago, in fact it was the winter of '85. A woman drowned. What made you ask?'

He shrugged. 'Ghosts perhaps. The lake looks so natural. It's hard to believe that it's manmade.

'Good God, Luze! There's always been a lake here.' Simon's voice croaked with tension.

'No offence.' Luze tried to calm him down. 'I saw a field covered in snow which was used as a parking lot . . . Something evil happened right here. Pure, premeditated evil.'

'You sly bastard. What the hell are you playing at?'

150

Simon looked stunned. Luze could sense his new friend's guilt and his rising aggression. He was about to be punched.

'I think I deserve an explanation,' Simon said stiffly.

Luze wondered if Simon would believe him. 'That's how I saw it, but I don't always see things exactly as they are, or were. You see, I'm a medium. I think that's what the English call people like me.'

'Bullshit!' Simon said stiffly. 'You're lying.'

'No. Believe me, I'm not.' He got into the 4-track and tried to ignore the cold. He decided to let Simon do the talking from now on. The man was too close to losing control.

* * *

Simon felt prickles running up and down his spine and the strangest sensation of hairs rising along his arms and the back of his neck. He'd never felt that before. He was acutely reminded of the millions of years of evolution that hung around in his genes. Why was the damn story cropping up time and again after all these years? They'd all thought it was forgotten.

'The locals won't be very impressed at your snooping and sniping.' Simon spoke mildly as his inherent good manners took over.

'Sniping? You mean like a guy with a rifle? I saw what I saw. Please believe me. It's an inherited ability. I'm sorry if I upset you, but I meant no harm. Let's forget it.' He gazed intently at Simon with a touch of pleading.

'Okay.' Simon decided to play the whole affair down. Luze looked honest and sincerely puzzled.

He got in the car, started the engine and drove slowly towards the road. But no, he thought. I can't believe his silly story. The bastard has been checking old newspaper reports, or listening to gossip. His best bet would be to show disinterest. He braked at the main road and turned towards the railway line. Seen from the distance, the village lights seemed festive and the busy conglomeration of shops, arcades, and homes, looked rich and inviting. It was a dream village, created and built to Gordon's specifications, looking exactly as they had planned back in the Eighties, and they'd all done well out of it.

Soon the lights were left behind and they were driving past low stone walls and moonlit hills and valleys. About fifteen miles along the railway track they turned right and drove for a mile, and then left at a level crossing and left again to drive back along the other side of the line.

'Why doesn't someone build a bridge over the tracks?' Luze asked.

'The council made a couple of attempts to buy land for a connecting road, but local farmers weren't keen on selling. No one seemed to care, so things stayed as they were,' Simon explained. The real truth was, farmers, homeowners and shopkeepers had got together to block the plan.

'Well, here we are,' Simon said. 'Newtown!'

Neon lights flashed from a cinema on the corner announcing three new movies. Above them, Brad Pitt lounged in Technicolor, blown up to double lifesize, a super modern deity

152

showering promises on passers-by. A fish and chips take-away rubbed shoulders with a curry and rice emporium, next door was an icecream parlour and a pet shop where tiny, dazed puppies blinked myopically at passers-by. A long, dark arcade of gambling machines led to a throbbing dark hole, like the entrance to a monster's belly and from its throat came groans and grunts of rap music throbbing its heavy beat through powerful loudspeakers. Crowds of youths with shaved heads and girls with miniskirts and leather jackets hung around in groups shouting at each other. It sounded like insults, but everyone was grinning.

'Are these the real people you were looking for?'

He tried, but failed, to erase the sarcasm from his voice as he parked at the curbside. Moments later his stomach lurched as he caught sight of his daughter with her arm around a tall, sallow man in his late twenties, looking more like a peddler than a beautiful hulk, dressed in the habitual immigrant's uniform of a black leather jacket over a black tracksuit. His stomach contracted. Who the hell had she picked up this time? Luze was forgotten as he jumped out of the car.

'Ana,' he called sternly. 'Get in the car.'

'Oh, hi Dad. Don't worry. I have a lift.' She lurched unsteadily and Simon had the impression she'd drunk too much. 'I'll be home soon. We're going for coffee.' She turned her back on him, a deliberate message that he should get lost.

'This will do nicely,' Luze said. 'Thanks for the

lift. Be seeing you.' Looking embarrassed, he got out of the 4-track.

Simon watched him hesitate and then enter the Indian restaurant. When Simon looked back, Ana and her friend had disappeared. Presumably they had gone into the disco. He stood around feeling foolish and inadequate. Ana was developing a taste for ruffians. He'd have plenty to say to her in the morning, but he didn't want to shame his daughter by making a scene and hauling her out of the disco. He had no right to do that, but at the same time, he couldn't bring himself to drive home and leave her here.

It was too cold to wait in the truck. He looked around and saw a pub across the road. *The Red Lion!* Bloody original, he thought as he parked in a nearby bay and locked the doors. Fumbling for a notepad, he tore off a sheet and wrote: '*If you want me I'm in the pub opposite,*' which he tucked into the windscreen. He looked at his watch and frowned. Nine-thirty! Surely it couldn't be that early? What on earth was he going to do with himself for the next two hours?

The pub was almost empty, which surprised him. He found a comfortable leather chair by the fire, ordered a pint of lager and leaned back with his eyes closed trying to make sense out of his conversation with Luze. What an incredible weirdo the man was. He wasn't sure whether or not to believe him.

18

Ana was vividly conscious of her surroundings, the strobe lights, the beat, the warmth and togetherness; like crowding back into a whale's womb, all these wiggling fishes, jam-packed together, about to be spilled out into the cold world. The thought amused her and she began to laugh. The incessant beat of the band was part of her, a heart beat, hugely amplified, and she was surfing the music like a wave, riding high, feeling a surge of joy as she writhed to its vague Arabian undertones.

'You're really something.'

The words jarred. The moment was spoiled. She remembered clutching her new friend, Frano, in his friend's car, but that was about all. She'd fought her way out of that silly mistake.

Remembering hauled her down from her high. Dad's expression had got through to her. Until then she'd felt she was looking great in a flimsy black miniskirt with a frilled, irregular hemline, a crimson, see-through mini-blouse leaving her midriff bare and falling off one shoulder, revealing one black bra strap. It was the look that counted and it came straight from the latest Parisian fashion shows. Dad had no fashion sense, but he'd look so ashamed. What did he want her to wear . . . a black cocktail dress from the Seventies? Dad was weird. But still. Surely he hadn't noticed that she'd had too much to drink.

This was the direct result of a nasty fight with Frano, and all because some unknown, crazy guy had slipped her an Ecstasy pill in the pub in Canterbury.

Frano's disapproval had come as a shock. 'You don't need to drink,' he'd said, taking her glass away.

'Fuck off, Frano. You don't own me. You don't even know me.'

She'd got up and swaggered to the bar to order another. What else could she do? And another. She knew she was drinking too much, but who cared. She could drink any boy her age under the table. Then an unknown guy at the bar gave her an Ecstasy pill. She never took drugs. She was laughing . . . about to hand the tablet back . . . when big mouth sidled up from behind her and had the monumental cheek to forbid her to swallow it. She'd thrown it in her mouth and washed it down with the rest of her alcopop. She didn't propose to let any man take charge of her life. 'This is England, not Croatia,' she'd snarled.

Frano had hung around looking sad, but he was reasonably good company, considering he'd been tortured. Everyone knew. He couldn't stop talking about it. He'd be perfectly normal for an hour or so, if you ignored his shaking hands and the tic in his eyes, and then something would set his teeth chattering and out would come the whole story, same as last time and the time before. They didn't like the things he painted, so they'd tied him down and given him shocks and he'd lacerated his tongue when his teeth clenched involuntarily. The awful thing was,

156

most of the male immigrants in the South-East had been tortured. The world sucked.

The Croat was hanging on to her arm, gazing at her as if she were some sort of an icon. He caught hold of her and pulled her against him so she could feel every part of his hard body. Big boned, but no flesh, his clothes hung on him like a coat hanger and his penis stuck out like a peg.

'How did I ever get to be so lucky?'

Who the fuck does he think he is? Christ! What am I doing with him? She longed to tell him to get lost, but how could she when the poor bastard had been tortured? What a sodding, awful world we live in. The minutes passed tortuously and her high became an impressive low.

'Look here, got to go. Got to be back before eleven, or Father will be after you.'

He followed her outside. 'Give me your phone number, Ana.'

'I'll call you.'

She made a show of taking his number and tucking it into her purse. She'd never call.

She burst into noisy tears in the taxi: for Dad, who hadn't realised what was happening to his world, for Frano, the Croatian, lisping and broken and deeply wounded in his pride, for the torturers and the torturees of this world because they were human and she was human and the connection was unbearable.

The taxi driver leaned back to slide the glass open and spoke over his shoulder. 'You want to talk about it? I've got three daughters, all older

157

than you. Married now. One of them has a kid on the way.'

She tried to explain. 'There's something wrong with me. It's like I've lost my emotional skin. I don't even know whose pain is making me cry. Sometimes I wish I didn't feel so much. It must be great to be a psychopath. Just think of all those tears you'd never have to shed.'

'Here we are. Out you get. Two pounds will cover it. Go easy on the booze, Miss, and give up drugs or you'll find yourself in the nuthouse. I'll throw that in for free.'

Scowling, she got out of the car. 'Everyone's trying to tell me my fucking business.'

★ ★ ★

'Cheers,' he called, as she trudged along the dark driveway, beside the orchard wall, towards their house. She couldn't stay angry for long on such a lovely April night. Bright and moonless, the Milky Way seemed like a white haze wrapped around the planet. She was tingling all over and the sensation was exhilarating and tinged with joy. Sometimes she got the strangest impression that some nebulous, living, super intelligence was wrapping itself around her, trying to tell her something, like the force in Star Wars.

19

Simon woke with a start and walked across the tired, dusty saloon bar knowing he was behaving like an over-protective fool. All the same, he decided to sit it out until closing time. He ordered a coffee and settled back to wait.

What was it Luze had said? '*I saw a field covered in snow which was used as a parking lot. Something evil happened right here . . . pure, premeditated evil*'. Was Luze telling the truth? Was the lake haunted? Premeditated evil! Dead right, Luze. I've got to hand it to you.

Simon had been only too grateful for the Coroner's verdict of accidental death. He'd accepted his reprieve, but that hadn't lessened his grief or his guilt.

Forbidden memories zoomed in like bats on a summer evening. He would never forget watching George Irving, late and harassed, limping up the steps to the conference centre clutching his daughter's hand, leaving his wife, Angela, to park the car. Alarm turned to dread when he saw Angela drive the car towards the snow-covered ice.

Then he was running, shouting, screaming: 'Angela! Stop! You're on the lake. The ice won't hold. Stop! For God's sake stop! Stop.'

He ran behind the car, scattering the snow, skidding and slithering as he heard the first ominous cracks booming like thunder. Grief

159

brought mayhem to his frantic, panic-stricken mind. This can't be happening. Not to Angela. Not to her. Dear God, don't let it happen. 'Stop, for Christ's sake!' As he gained on the car, he saw a gleam of white fur and black hair falling over it.

A gigantic splinter of ice broke off and veered steeply at a ninety-degree angle. He heard a whoosh and for split-second of manic disbelief, watched the car lift in the air, tilt and race forward into the hole. Black water closed over the car which seemed to wobble and float for a few moments before sinking out of sight.

Simon forced himself forward on leaden legs. Scrambling on his hands and knees he slithered to the edge and dived into the water nearly passing out with shock at the icy temperature. Taking a deep breath, he fought to get down, acutely aware of the stygian lake closing over his head. Fighting off panic, he kicked out with all his strength. How deep was it? He couldn't be sure. Hang on. Keep going. Got to reach the car. Kick harder.

His hands touched something smooth. He gripped hold of a ledge, fighting against his own buoyancy. His lungs were bursting, but if he gave up now she would die. He couldn't see a damn thing. Just inky blackness. He bent his arms, pulling himself down. The window was slightly open. He felt for the door handle and forced the door open. It took time and there was no time left. He touched warm flesh, fumbled for an arm, tugged at the body dragging it out. He was blacking out. Got to get air. Hang on! Hang on!

160

Wrapping his arm around her waist, he kicked his way towards the surface.

She was so limp, so easy to manoeuvre, but it seemed to take forever. He broke through gasping for breath. Moments later he was breathing air into her lungs. Panting! Taking huge, rasping breaths. Intent on blowing his life force into her pliant body. She was so still, so lifeless.

Someone had pushed a dinghy over the ice and they were paddling towards him. He thrust her into David's arms and felt himself being hauled over the side. Flinging himself over Angela, he tried to force his breath into her lungs, sobbing hoarsely as he gasped for air.

He was still trying to revive her when the ambulance arrived. Shirley wrapped a blanket around him as he stood there shaking and crying, watching the woman he loved being lifted onto the stretcher.

Harry and David caught hold of him and dragged him toward the hotel.

God help me! I don't want to remember. Not again! But he was fate's hostage, forced to watch endless replays of his past crimes.

* * *

His guilt begins and ends with Angela. She is his dream of sexual ecstasy, his forbidden love, his nemesis, his passion and his fulfillment.

The first time he saw Angela he thought he'd walked clean out of reality into an Arabian Nights dream. She had been persuaded to give an exhibition of Kashmiri dancing in the Town Hall, as part of International Youth Week. He hadn't wanted to go, but Melissa had persuaded him to come along, since she had to write a piece about it, and they had a date for a pub supper later.

A young girl in a burkha ran onto the stage and stopped short, obviously confused by the catcalls and whistles of approval. She ran back and the music stopped. Next the manager came on stage and explained that if they wanted to see her dance, they'd better damn well shut up. Out she came again to the taped, but sensuous Eastern wail of tambourines, drums and pipes. She began to move her body as sinuously as a snake, her delicate hands plucking the air, her body like a shimmer of heat in the noon desert. Her eyes, demurely downcast, seemed to glint with suppressed sexuality. There is nothing more desirable than the female form concealed behind layers of silk, Simon discovered.

The more he watched, the more he ached for her. At some stage he simply stood up and went backstage to find her. Melissa's existence was quite forgotten.

From then on his life became entirely focused on this beautiful Kashmiri girl, who was studying to be a librarian. Sweet and loyal, she offered unconditional love, which he repaid with moods, possessiveness and fits of jealous temper. He couldn't handle his emotions. He was running out of control. And then, after two years together, suddenly and inexplicably, she left. He never forgot her and then one day . . .

162

* ★ ★ ★

Noon in mid-summer. The smell of hay and cattle and pigs is everywhere. Every part of his skin exudes the telltale odours mingled with the stench of his own sweat as he mucks out the cowsheds. He works for an hour before standing naked under the cold, outside shower and scrubbing himself with a brush and carbolic soap. It's never enough and Laura always complains. Seven months pregnant, every smell makes Laura sick, but worst of all is the smell of her husband, so he's got in the habit of eating with the family at Redhill. Pat and Mae are in London, so he and Tom share a pre-cooked, microwaved curry and rice with salad. His mouth is full when the telephone rings.

'Hello.' He almost chokes on the word.

'Simon. Simon Shepherd. Is that . . . '

'Christ! Where are you? In England?'

'Canterbury. I'm in the car park by the old archway. It's called Riding Gate.'

'I know it. Wait there. I'll be twenty minutes.'

He runs to his car and races along the motorway. Nine years, he's thinking . . . Has she changed? Have I changed?

He sees her standing by her car as he drives in and parks. He hurries towards her. Catching hold of her hand, he pulls her close. 'Why? Why did you do it? I nearly went out of my mind.'

'I sent you a message.'

'Don't lie.'

She looks shocked. Then she sighs. 'It has taken so long to get back to you.'

163

'Come. Get in the car. We can talk later. We have some catching up to do.'

'Where can we go?'

She rests her head on his shoulder and pulls his hand to her mouth. Her scent, her profile, her beautiful hair, everything is familiar to him. Nothing has changed.

'This smell . . . it takes me back . . . in Kashmir, whenever I smelled hay or cows, I longed for you.'

He needs to erase the empty years. They stop at the first hotel they see, book in and pay for the night, but they are both aware that they have only a few hours.

'Would you die for me? Would you kill for me?' she wants to know.

★ ★ ★

Wintertime: they are still making love, but nowadays Simon's tenderness is false. It's all he can do not to batter Angela, he's so fired with aggression. A deep, dark emotion is surging out of some unfathomable part of his mind. It terrifies him.

Must he confront such perilous thoughts? He clutches his lover too tightly. 'I can't take any more of this,' he mutters.

'Of what?' Languid with sex, Angela turns and runs her fingers through his hair.

How can he tell her of his evil desires?

'You going back to him, sleeping with him, night after night. It has got to stop. I'll go crazy. Or perhaps you're hooked on living dangerously

164

and having it off with two different men. I can't live like this . . . I feel I might . . . most times I find myself imagining him dead. Sometimes I feel like killing the bastard.'

There! He's said it.

'Don't.' She places her forefinger on his lips. 'What else can we do?'

'Marry me.'

'We're already married. But we could have . . . once . . . when we were both free. If we were free I would marry you.'

'Oh God.' He groans with misery. 'Don't start that again. Why did you leave? You should have waited for me. Surely you knew that I adored you. I'd have done anything . . . anything at all for you. Even now.'

'Sh! Hold me, Simon. I don't want to think about the past.'

Simon has rented a cottage not far from where Angela lives. It's perfect, being remote and secluded, with a shed to hide their cars. They meet there almost every morning when her daughter is at school. The farm is suffering, Tom and Laura are getting suspicious, but he can't keep away from his obsessive love.

'You didn't come . . . you were faking,' he accuses her.

'No. I wasn't faking, but I'm tired. It's tough living like this . . . two lives instead of one.'

'Saving it for him?' he sneers.

'Look here!'

She sits up in bed and as the sheet fell away he is reminded of her absolute perfection. Nine years later and she's still perfect. She couldn't

165

have breast fed her child. The thought diminishes her in his eyes.

'We can't carry on like this, Simon. You're torturing both of us. You've got to pull yourself together or I'll have to stop coming here.'

He climbs out of bed. 'I must go. Tomorrow . . . ? No. I'm in London tomorrow. Then there's the dinner. Oh God! I can't bear it.'

'Simon, I swear to you, I had no part in George's bid to buy Redhill.'

'Don't worry. It's going to be all right.'

He can't tell her. A careless word could ruin his revenge. Love and trust should be synonymous, he decides, but for some reason it isn't.

★　★　★

Simon was propelled back to the present by the barman, who was calling for last orders. He glanced at his watch. Almost eleven. He felt exhausted and depressed as he walked to the bar. 'What time does the disco close?' He asked the barman.

'That one opposite?'

'Yes.'

'Goes on all night, mate. Terrible racket.'

He went outside and hung around the 4-track, wondering what to do. He felt depressed by his memories and the cheaply built buildings. Litter drifting in the badly-lit street only intensified his gloom. He could hear the loud percussion beat echoing through the drab arcade. Strobe lights flashed from the open doorway. To Simon, it was a vision of hell. Retrieving his mobile from the

4-track, he called home.

'Yes, Ana's back and no doubt she's asleep, as I was,' Laura told him icily.

Simon was full of misgivings as he got into the driver's seat. Ana was in with a rough mob and he knew he must have it out with her, but lately she was remote and hostile and he sensed they were on a collision course. Past attempts to guide her flashed through his mind, a kaleidoscope of dashed hopes and disappointments.

20

Home was lonelier than a desert island. After a few moments of indecision, Simon rang Bela's number. She sounded alarmed.

'Simon here. I'm sorry, Bela. I know I shouldn't have called. I need to talk to you, if it's at all possible. I'm here in Newtown. Is it too late? Were you asleep?'

'No. Is something wrong? Are you all right?'

'Yes. Sort of.'

'I can't let you in here, we might wake the family. I'll join you.'

'I'm in a pub. It's called the Red Lion . . . opposite the disco.'

'No, not there. Four blocks along, moving north, there's an all-night coffee bar. There are tables outside under a big striped awning. I can't remember its name, but you can't miss it.'

'Okay, I'll see you there.'

Five minutes later he stood in the doorway, blinking in the garish neon lights as he gazed at the tubular steel tables, the gleaming, chrome bar and bright murals of desert scenes on the wall. The café was filled with the heady scent of foreign tobacco, strong coffee and the sound of male voices talking animatedly. A woman's voice wailing in a minor key via a loudspeaker was the only indication that the female sex existed. He'd have preferred the scruffy pub.

Simon secured the last two stools at the

counter and ordered two coffees. Only Turkish was available. No wonder the pub was run down. This was a Muslim neighbourhood.

Bela arrived ten minutes later, wrapped in a khaki raincoat with a blue scarf tied around her head. She still managed to look sexy, but God knows how in that outfit. 'You're so pale. What is it? What happened?' she asked, perching on an uncomfortable stool.

'Nothing's happened. Look! There's a table coming empty in the corner. Let's go.'

'But I can see something's wrong,' she argued, when they had sat down. 'What is it?'

Her amber eyes, gleaming in the neon lights, scanned his face. When Bela stared it was more like a caress.

The waiter appeared with amazing speed bringing coffee and cake.

'Go on then . . . talk,' she said, when he'd gone.

'Something terrible happened long ago and today I was forced to remember. I loved someone dearly, but I agreed to give her up for the sake of my family. I'm repeating my mistakes. I'm being selfish in seeing you. You'd be better off if we split. Not that I want to, but I can't offer you much . . . or anything come to that.'

Simon could see how shocked she was, but she was making a brave effort to conceal her feelings.

'We only have a friendship,' she said pleadingly. 'It's not much, but I need it. I thought you needed my friendship, too.'

'When someone expects love from me, I seem to let them down and this destroys them in a way. It's a recurring pattern. I can't bear to let it happen to you, yet I know that it will if we carry on. I'm married and I happen to think that my marriage vows are binding. We're not close, but Laura has never expressed a desire to leave me, despite . . . well, despite the past.' Damn! He'd almost trespassed into a no-go area.

'Silly Simon. What a strange mood you're in. I can look after myself. What brought this on?'

'Remembering. I can't give you what you want, Bela.'

'How long are you going to fight your feelings?' Bela asked, her voice low and almost harsh.

'The theory is forever.'

'No one's trying to force you to do anything. Least of all me. You came after me, remember?'

He hadn't expected an argument. If he tried to discuss emotions with Laura, there would be a quick freeze-up. Angela, on the other hand, had shed gentle tears, but the net result was the same, absolutely no communication. He'd been let off lightly, he guessed. Now that he had to argue his case, he realised he wasn't prepared.

'Listen, Bela. You're getting dangerously close to a crablike creature, squatting in a shell. My daughter told me that I'm like a hermit crab and my wife agrees with her. That should tell you something about me.'

'Yes. It tells me you've been drinking. It also tells me that you have nurtured a cruel family.'

'I've had two drinks, which is not enough to cloud my judgment.'

'Do you indulge yourself often like this, at

other people's expense, I must add?'

He could see that she no longer believed in his goodwill. Her face, paler now, was turned away, but he could still see her resentment. He felt baffled by it.

'Bela, please . . . listen to me. We can't hope to succeed with a platonic friendship. Perhaps you could, but I can't. You're a sexy, desirable woman. Laura and I . . . well . . . she won't. It's none of your business, but if we carry on with this friendship one thing will lead to another . . . and we'll become embroiled in lying and cheating, which is something I hate. You would want me to divorce my wife and I would refuse. Then you would hate me. It has happened before. Laura was pregnant at the time. Everyone was hurt and there were no winners.'

'Who was she?'

'I can't talk about her, so don't ask.'

'But you came here to talk. Isn't that what you said? So after all this time . . . what is it, seventeen years . . . ? Your wife still hasn't forgiven you, or left you. She won't make love, but you're still together. That takes some believing.'

'I wouldn't allow myself to be happy, so I threw myself into my work and so did Laura. She never forgave me.'

'Tell me about this woman you loved.'

'I'm sorry. I can't. It's a no-go area. Tonight I remembered, but I don't want to think about it again.'

'And you wanted to see me at this time of night to dump me?'

'Dump you? I could never do that. Warn you perhaps.'

'So you were warning me . . . ' She toyed with her fork, moving little pieces of cake around her plate as if unaware of her actions. When she spoke she sounded very sad. 'No. You weren't warning me, Simon. You were engaging in some pretty nifty footwork. You were trying to evade all responsibility for your future actions. You were saying: 'If it were up to me I would split now, but I can never dump you, so the ball's in your court and if we carry on, you'll end up being second-best and get hurt, but it won't be my fault because I've warned you'.

'I thought you were braver than that, Simon. Why don't you grow up and take responsibility for your actions. I'm going now and you can think about what you want . . . or don't want to do about 'us'. If you want to see me in the future, you can write, or call, or come to the door, as you did before, and we'll share the hurt and blame for whatever mess we might jointly and severally create. I'll forgive you for tonight, but only because you're drunk and you haven't thought this through properly. The truth is, I'm fond of you.'

'I'm not drunk.'

'Better for you that you were.'

Simon could feel his fury rising. 'You're deliberately misunderstanding me. I didn't want to hurt your feelings. You expect me to trot out my past like it's some kind of a soap opera, while I don't even know if you've been married or if Shah is your maiden name.'

'Why should you think I've been married?'

'I don't know. It's just a feeling. You were, weren't you?'

'Sorry. It's a no-go area.'

'D'you always have to hit back? I'm beginning to feel sorry for Mr Shah, whoever he was.'

In a lightning spurt of temper, Bela stood up and tipped her coffee over Simon's head. The coffee bar became deathly quiet except for the smash of Bela's heels on the blue and white mosaic tiles as she stalked out.

★   ★   ★

Why had she done that? Bela agonised as she hurried home. Her temper had always been her downfall. It came faster than she could think, like a flash flood, giving no warning and no time to reach safer ground. The after effects were equally destructive.

Bela seldom allowed herself to think about the past, but tonight it was a relief to retreat far away from Simon and his outraged expression as he wiped the coffee out of his eyes with his napkin.

Her life with Omar Shah began with a dream. She had only to close her eyes and she could remember how lovely the dream was . . . a few moments of respite before she faced the real world . . . but then came the awakening.

★   ★   ★

She is happy again. She is lying on the beach listening to the gentle lapping of the sea and the

173

swish of palm leaves overhead and Jason is nuzzling her neck and her shoulders. She feels tired . . . so tired: 'Not now . . . later . . . too tired,' she mutters, but the words come out like a croak through lips that are dryer than ashes. Jason thrusts himself hard over her and she tries to push him away, but his full body weight is pinning her down. He never does that. He's so gentle.

'Why?' she whispers.

She can't swallow. Her dry tongue is sticking to the roof of her mouth. All the same, a familiar stiffening is gathering force around her thighs and down her legs. Languid with pleasure, she arches her body and grips his shoulders, but then she wakes and realises that something is terribly wrong. Jason is gripping her hands, pinning them hard on the pillows and he is making love as he never has before, his legs coiled around hers, pinning them astride, while his body slithers over hers. She's in pain. Her throat is swollen and her head throbs unbearably. She pushes Jason away, but her strength is puny and it has no effect. 'Water,' she croaks. The motion intensifies, harder, faster, 'Jason, my head . . . I'm going to be sick.'

She opens her eyes and sees a stranger's dark skin so close to her eyes that she can't focus properly. Strange perfume engulfs her, black hair falls into her eyes, a gold chain is flapping against her chin. Her screams mingle with his groans as he comes with a roar.

She's in shock. The last thing she remembers is Sofia washing her, but that seems so long ago.

Then the stranger climbs off her and stands up.

'Stop screaming,' he says. 'D'you want our servants to think you enjoyed it so much? There's water.' He points to a jug full of iced water placed on a table beside the bed. Wrapping a towel around his waist, he stalks out.

Water! She pours a glass and drains it, and another, but soon nausea sets in. She must find the bathroom, but her head hurts so much she can't see straight. She crawls to an open door and throws up in the lavatory before falling asleep on the cool, tiled floor. When she next wakes she finds herself back in bed, mosquito nets draped around her, and someone has changed her nightdress. Who? That thought makes her feel sick again.

She wakes in the night and walks out onto the balcony. The moon, full and free, is rising over a tall mountain range, but Kashmir is famous for its lovely mountains and she could be anywhere. The garden is throbbing with night sounds; cicadas, night jays, an owls shriek, but she can see no sign of any guards. She returns to her room and searches through her luggage for something to wear, choosing a sari with a t-shirt and trousers. There are no shoes, but the peasant women often go barefooted. She'll try to make the nearest British Embassy, she decides.

* * *

She is pulling at the thick creeper to test the strength of its roots when someone speaks.

'Don't even think of it. Our house is

175

surrounded with a high electrified wall, not to keep you in, but to keep intruders out. There are a number of fierce dogs in the grounds at night. I'll show you round in the morning.' He spoke with a heavy Pakistani accent.

She walks slowly towards him. 'You! How dare you speak to me as if nothing has happened. You raped me while I was lying semi-conscious from drugs administered against my wishes.'

'No. You acquiesced. And why not? It was our wedding night.'

'I had no intention of marrying you, or anyone. I ran away. That's why they drugged me. You must have known.'

'I thought you'd taken tranquilisers. Why all this fuss? You once gave a talk on co-existence of Muslims in the West and the importance of retaining our traditions.'

Bela gasps. 'You were there? But why?'

'Your father invited me and I must say I was impressed. From your talk I assumed that you were a devout and loyal Muslim and that you would make a loving, dutiful wife. You are also very beautiful. I had been widowed for a year. Your father and I have financial links. He needed a cash injection, while I needed a suitable wife. One thing led to another. Now why don't you practice what you preach? Or was it all empty talk?'

Leaning forward, she peers into his eyes and steps back in shock. Voracious eyes! A plunderer's eyes. No warmth there. A gleam of derision is the only sign of emotion.

'You have nothing to fear, Bela. My lawyer will

see you tomorrow morning and explain the benefits and boundaries of being my wife. You will find you are in a privileged position. You can have whatever you want.'

Arguing or pleading would be a total waste of time, she decides. She will have to meet him on his terms. 'You speak like a civilised man.'

'Civilised? If you mean Western, then no . . . I am not a civilised man. I cling to our old traditions. As for this marriage . . . there was no other way to make you see reason.' As he gave her a brief outline of the deal the lawyers had put together she gathered that he was rich and that she had been sold in order to bolster her father's failing fortunes.

'You're in Kashmir, not England, Bela. From now on, the quality of your life depends upon my goodwill and my goodwill depends upon your behaviour. I was led to understand that you were a virgin, so we're both feeling betrayed.'

She begins to shake, her knees feel weak. She falls back into a chair and buries her face in her hands. What had it all been for, her education, her studies, her degree? All that work and expense just to end up in this medieval world. Somehow she'll escape, she comforts herself.

Eventually she had, but only at the most terrible price, and she would never forget or forgive herself.

21

Luze was returning from a few unscheduled calls on his parishioners which had left him feeling like a social reject. Only one woman let him inside the door, and that was because she needed help to shift her piano so she could set the cat on the quivering mouse cowering behind it.

He paused to sit on the bench by the fountain to think about his adopted First-World tribe and this morning's fiasco. They meant no harm, but they had no time. Back home a tribesman would feel unmanned by a rigid adherence to impossible schedules. An African man had to call his life his own and have a little choice in how he spent his time.

After three weeks in England, Luze was becoming increasingly confused about his role in the village. He longed to tell parishioners of the joy of smashing the barriers of the mind and reaching out through deeper consciousness to another perception where time stood still, a place where they could honour the here and now, but no one had time to listen. After waiting in vain for someone to stop and pass the time of day with him, Luze got up and walked home.

One person in particular obsessed Luze. He longed to help her, but despite his many trumped-up approaches she was too busy to see him. So each morning he gazed along the flagged path, fringed with lavender, and imagined

Melissa gliding towards him, her silk dress flouncing to her rhythmic walk, the sunlight shining on her red hair, her pale cheeks glowing with embarrassment. Each part of the mirage had to be painstakingly created and visualised to make it happen. He should know. Positive knowing, not positive thinking, was the essence of his former vocation.

It took a week for his vision to become reality, give or take a little English editing. It happened on Saturday morning. He'd been sitting by the fire, thinking about tomorrow's sermon while listening to African love songs, which made him feel slightly less homesick. It was raining and Melissa was doing her best to hide from prying eyes with outsize sunglasses and an ugly checked scarf over her hair, but she was here.

Barefooted, he hurried to the door.

She held out her hand. 'Good morning, Vicar. I wondered if you could spare the time to talk to me?'

'That's what I'm here for. Come in, Melissa, but please call me Matt.'

She gazed nervously around. 'Have I come at an awkward moment?'

'No. I was expecting you. You're cold. There's a fire in the sitting room. I'll hang up your raincoat.'

Her cheeks were wet and he guessed that she had come because she was feeling low and she had no one else to turn to. He reached down to switch off the CD.

'Don't . . . please . . . It's rather lovely.'

'It's a song from Zaire.' He sang the

179

translation: 'Love is like a wild bird. Don't shut it in a cage, but set it free'. Her cheeks turned scarlet with embarrassment, which was an improvement on cold white.

'How beautiful.'

'The best African music comes from Zaire.'

His wild longing startled him. He sighed himself out of reach to the other side of the room.

'Everything's changed.' She looked around. 'This room was always cold and impersonal. I hated coming here, but now it's warm and sort of homely, but I can't see what you've done. That's strange, isn't it?' She pursed her lips and turned slowly, searching for changes.

'People brings their own vibes to a house. Don't you agree?'

Hovering in the centre of the room Melissa resembled a nervous impala poised for instant flight. She caught sight of the book he'd been reading and picked it up.

'Celtic magic. A strange choice for vicar.'

'Why's that?'

'The church doesn't believe in magic.'

'People who don't believe in magic miss half the joy in life. I was reading the book to see if there were similarities with African magic.'

'And are there?'

'Yes. I've studied magic,' he said cautiously, wondering why he was telling her that.

She sat down and crossed her legs, watching him cautiously, looking cool and elegant in her sea-green woollen dress with a single onyx and diamond brooch on the lapel, her red hair smoothed back behind her ears. She leaned forward and placed the book on the table beside her.

'Oh. So you are a magician. Pulling rabbits out of a top hat and that sort of thing. For church parties, I suppose.' She was patronising and bored, already wishing she hadn't come.

'The fact that you are here is magic.'

Her green eyes opened wide. 'Is that a compliment?'

'No, but if you want compliments I can heap them on you.'

Now she was watching him warily. 'I think I should tell you why I came. I live with someone . . . ' She broke off, flinching.

Whatever David had said had hurt, Luze sensed.

'You can trust me. I'm on your side.'

'Well, here goes. The fact is he insists that I don't talk about death because it's embarrassing, but since you are a vicar I hope it's all right. You see . . . ' She licked her lips nervously. 'I'm dying.'

'Go on.'

'I have a brain tumour. The specialists told me I have six weeks to two months. That's all, and that was almost a month ago. I'm dying right now, although today it's . . . well, some days I feel all right and then . . . ' She paused. 'I was silly to come. Forgive me. I can't get used to the idea and I can't get rid of my anger . . . with David and my friends. I'm especially angry with myself. I need peace of mind. I don't want to die hating. I thought you might be able to help me.'

'Why do you want to die, Melissa? The world's a marvellous place.'

Her lovely face became set and controlled, while her eyes glowed disturbingly. She stood up and made for the door and it took Luze a couple of seconds to realise that she was angry with him, too.

He sighed and switched off the music. 'Wait.'

'No. I don't need bullshit.' Stiff with temper, her green eyes had narrowed. 'I don't want your lies. I'm not asking for miracles because I don't believe they happen. I'm a realistic person, Vicar, and I expect you to be straight with me. I need to accept this awful thing. I need to stop hating.'

'Please sit down, Melissa. If I talk straight to you, will you promise not to walk out? I meant what I said. I'm on your side. I want to help you.'

'All right.' She hovered over her chair and then sat down. 'Your sermon made me think. I don't love anyone, or anything. I used to love my work, but lately it has become a nightmare. I thought I loved David, or, rather, I was fond of him. No great passion, nothing like that, but comradeship. Then something happened. I can't talk about it. I just want to stop hating him.'

Once she began there was no stopping her. He caught glimpses of her smouldering rage, but even worse was her guilt. She had done something she regretted deeply, but he must never ask about it, she told him fiercely. She hinted at an ancient buried crime. Luze closed his eyes, pretending that he was hardly there.

She had always been a lonely sort of person, even as a child, turned in on herself, forming deep attachments to her pets. Then came her late teens when she fell deeply in love with a fellow student who dumped her for a beautiful Indian woman, leaving her bitterly disappointed. After they split, she thought he would turn to her, but he met and married someone else.

'So I ran away to Crete for a few years,' she told him.

Luze was in deep conflict with himself. He longed to heal Melissa in every possible way, physically, mentally and emotionally, but he had vowed to turn his back on those primitive talents which branded him Third World. But there sat Melissa, crying gently over lost loves, needing energy and healing and someone to care for her. What on earth was she talking about now? He gazed at her for a moment wondering how far he could take her. Maybe nowhere.

'For those pronounced incurable, there are alternative methods of healing which are sometimes successful.'

She shrugged. He was losing her.

'I don't suppose you'll find much outlet for your talents here. After all, we have the NHS and most of us have medical insurance. We're traditionalists around these parts.'

'I'm not worried about most people, I'm worried about you. No one understands the incredible power of our consciousness. What have you got to lose, Melissa?'

She caught her breath and laughed her cold, lonely laugh.

'Nothing. You really believe in this, don't you?'

He understood her obstinate refusal to

entertain hope. She was a stern, intelligent woman who could rely on her intellect, but little else. He could picture her as a fierce, precocious child, condemning fairies, angels and Father Christmas to the realm of make-believe. As an adult, immortality, God and miracles had gone the same way. She was racing towards the stone wall of extinction with lonely courage. How could he make her believe that there was something beyond it, or even that she might still defeat her illness. At that moment he longed to reach out to her, but he didn't know how to get through to her.

'Shall we get on with it?' He spoke gently, knowing she might leave.

'With what?'

'With the healing. Come and sit on the floor.'

'Oh! I should have known you would make me pray. That's what vicar's do, isn't it?'

'Please don't talk. I want to lower my vibrations.'

'Okay, I'll come along for the ride. As you said . . . what have I got to lose? I've tried everything and wasted a great deal of money.' Stiff and unbending, she sat rigidly upright without turning as he pulled up a chair and sat behind her.

He closes his eyes and draws the healing force into him, feeling it entering through the soles of his feet and rising through his body. He is a tube, nothing more. Then he wills himself into her mind. She has to play her part. Her mind and his mind.

184

Fifteen minutes later Luze leaned back feeling drained and confused.

'Melissa, listen. A festering wound must be cleaned out. Get rid of the guilt. Purge yourself by telling the truth. You can trust me with your secrets. Leave David. He's corroding you with his karma. His karma is for him alone, not for you to share, but when you sleep with him you, too, become contaminated. Stop writing about death and cruelty, it's killing you. Write about life and joy, not death. Meditate every day and see yourself getting better. Lastly, you have to take responsibility for what you did. Step one is to come clean. Let it all out. You've done something that caused a great deal of trouble.'

She turned even paler and looked afraid. 'How do you know all this?'

'Don't be afraid of me. You must have seen mediums before now. English mediums are amongst the world's best. Why are you writing about evil?'

'Psycho-thrillers are selling. Romantic fiction is dead.'

'It will come back. Write about life.'

'I must go.' She stood up. 'I shouldn't have come. I'm not sure I understand what all this is about.'

'It's about you getting better.'

'That was a very strange experience,' she said softly. 'As if an alien body moved into me. Like . . . well . . . like someone else's vibrations came creeping along every nerve and fibre of my body. I've never felt anything like it. Perhaps it was my imagination, yet it was a warm and lovely sensation.'

'It was the healing force. I don't want anyone to know that I do this. Please, Melissa.'

'Does it work?'

'We'll see. Do you have any money?'

'How much?' She smiled triumphantly. Now she was on familiar ground.

'No. Don't insult me. I'm asking if you have enough money to move out of your husband's house, into Harry's pub, for instance? If not, I have enough.'

'But why should you concern yourself? Of course I can afford to leave, but I'm not sure that I should.'

'You must. And you must come here every day. That's important.'

'For my fix.' She was smiling now.

'Exactly,' he said gravely. 'Now tell me about the past. About the sad woman in the blue sari who haunts the lake.'

'No! Don't tell me that. I don't believe in that sort of thing.'

'Believe what you like. That's your right. I think she was murdered.'

'Not according to the Coroner's verdict. Look here, Matt, it happened long ago. And it was forgotten long ago, but it still bothers me. Once I began a novel about what happened. Later, I abandoned the idea. The problem is, fact and fiction don't mix and with fact you have no leeway. Last month I sent this half-novel to the publishers and they seem interested. I regret sending it, for many reasons.'

'Write it, Meli. It will make you feel better.'

She reached out and touched his cheek with her forefinger. 'I've never touched black skin before. It feels like velvet, like a padded velvet cushion. At this moment I feel great. Alive! Thank you, Luze. I don't know whether or not I'll come back. Goodbye.'

She left hurriedly. Luze collapsed into a chair and switched the CD back on. He had over-reached himself and he was drained. He fell into a deep, revitalising sleep.

22

This time Ana had gone too far, Simon fumed, as he parked outside the Canterbury police station. He hurried inside, took a deep breath and almost gagged on the functional, hostile, dusty air of the charge office. His daughter was sitting on a bench opposite the counter looking pale, but defiant. He frowned her way while pondering on the mystery of genes. Who was this wayward girl who seemed so cocksure of herself? How was it possible one's own children could be so alien. She wore her privileges like a millstone around her neck and she was perpetually angry, but she didn't seem to know why, and neither did he. Her faded jeans, ragged trainers, an old sweater and costly diamond ear studs said all there was to say about her pseudo scruffiness.

'Ana!' He snapped her name, but she turned slowly.

'Dad! Thanks for coming.' She scowled at him, which annoyed him even more.

'Just a minute, Sir. I'm Sergeant Collins. I'd like a few words with you.' The aging sergeant led Simon through a swing door to an empty corridor.

'This won't take long, Sir,' he said in a soft Welsh accent. 'She means well, as most of them do, but public disturbances start these kids on the slippery slope to terrorism. This is not the first time we've come up against her and it could be that there's conflict at home. Take better care of her, Sir. She's a lovely girl.'

'Come now.' Simon dredged up his most officious tone. 'Ana burnt some sports shoes and a poster of President Bush. Mistakenly, I believe, but with good intentions. A lack of civil defiance amongst the nation's youth leads to a state where democracy crumbles. Then the government has more power than it should. That's how Hitler got started.' He bit back a retort closer to home, wondering why the hell he was defending his daughter?

'If that's your attitude sir, then I have no more to say, except, well, if she were mine I'd knock some sense into her before it's too late. We're charging some of the protesters, the ones that did the damage. They'll be put away for a while. Next time it could be her.'

Simon relented. 'Thanks for the warning.'

He walked back to the charge office, loping past Ana without a glance. 'Come.'

He unlocked the 4-track, climbed in and leaned across to open the door, but Ana stood frowning petulantly, making no move to climb in.

'Okay, get in the car. I said . . . get in the fucking car. I'm intensely irritated with you. For God's sake, Ana! You've gone too far this time.'

'I can make my own way home.'

'Get in, or else . . . '

Her every movement was subversive as she climbed in. 'What sort of a world would it be if no one thought about the underdog?'

'Don't talk to me about 'thinking'. You don't

know the meaning of the word. You know nothing about multinationals and I doubt you've studied the gross national product of this remote Pacific island that sparked off your demo. D'you have any idea of what happens to people when there's absolutely no work of any kind? Of course they're cheap labour. That's exactly why multinationals go there. Have you ever heard of the economics of supply and demand? Do you know what makes a man decide that any pay is better than no pay? I'll answer for you. It's watching his kids starve. Have you any idea what happens to his meagre pay packet after he spends it? It starts a spiral all on its own, a little for rice, a little for fish, a little to patch up the roof. You can use your own imagination. Finally dozens of people benefit slightly and pass on this benefit right down the line. Multiply this by a thousand workers and you've injected a bit of movement into a stagnant economy. The workers get taught a few skills, and soon they're strong enough to fight for a better deal.

'Basic intelligence, Ana. Something you know nothing about. If the multinational had to pay a US living wage, they'd stay home and employ well fed, hard working, well-educated Americans. All your campaigns are blatantly dumb and you are nothing more than an ignorant girl with a big mouth.'

She looked shocked, but still aggressive. Biting her lip, she blinked hard.

'That's Establishment claptrap. No one should work for less than a living wage. Don't blame me if I don't know about economics. You chose my so-called privileged school.'

'You were supposed to go on to higher education, but you've refused to open your mind to anything resembling common sense let alone higher learning. You and your bunch of gangsters are totally undisciplined and stupid.'

'Slow down. Let me out of here. You and I are on opposite sides of the fence. I can't stand your hypocritical world. You and Mum play lip service to things you don't believe in. You show a smiling front, but back home all you do is snipe at each other. I'm sick of the world. It sucks and there's no point in talking to you.'

'Okay. It sucks. I agree. But the youth who get to change it will know much more than you.'

Ana was far from beaten. Simon sensed the aggression that motivated her protests, but what was it really about? As they approached the village, he parked by the roadside.

'What's causing all this anger, Ana? I long to understand you.'

'It's about you lot! People are cruel and selfish and no one cares.'

'Cares about what?'

'Anything! No one cares about anything. Cruelty, torture, people starving, animal experiments. You don't cry at the death of strangers. Neither does Mum. I've never seen you protest at a damn thing. People get on with their lives. They read the papers, but they don't bloody care. Specially you. You pretend that everything's all right, but nothing is.'

'Listen Ana, you're a free-thinker. I admire that part of you. The world needs people like you, but you're no good to the world, or to yourself, if you don't know what you're talking about. I thought you told me to stop here.'

She looked away moodily, so Simon started the engine and soon they were passing the village. Ana waved her hand and grabbed her bag from the back seat.

'I'm getting off. I need to chill-out. Don't worry about me, Dad. I'll make my own life . . . and my own morality.'

'Take care and stay out of trouble,' he called after her. Ana waved without turning and after a few minutes Simon drove away.

23

Crazy to hope, Melissa thought. Her improvement was a fantasy, like a phantom pregnancy. Once, in the days when she and David tried for a child, her longing had held back her period for three months until the negative pregnancy test forced her to face the truth. Attending Matt's so-called healing sessions for fourteen consecutive days bordered on lunacy. What a laugh! Yet she was feeling and looking better, her headaches came less often and on good days she was filled with an indulgent sense of peace. What difference did it make anyway? Life was a conveyor belt hustling her inexorably from school to jobs, old age homes and inevitably the hospice and total extinction. Why should she care? But she did.

She got up to dress, taking an interest in her clothes for the first time in months, pulling on white gartered stockings with lacy tops, choosing pretty underwear and a white chiffon camisole. She rifled through the wardrobe for something special, but had to settle for a floral skirt and a white jersey. She should have packed more clothes, but how could she have guessed she would care?

It was mid-May, a perfect spring day and she decided to walk to the vicarage. Lately she needed to hang around life. Squirrels, birds, spring flowers and even the scent of grass meant so much to her.

Matt was chopping wood. His legs seemed rooted to the ground as he swung the axe, time and again. As she took in the strength of him, spasms of erotic pleasure zoomed at random and she almost cried out in surprise. It was like being born-again into the world of the living. Her libido had been the first casualty of her illness. She shivered, unable to look away as the muscles rippled under Matt's thin jersey and dark red shorts. Shapely, sinewy legs, muscled buttocks, a broad back, a long neck and an exquisite profile. Beautiful hands, too. He turned and his sensual glance startled her. He knows!

She smiled to herself, remembering David and his assurances: *He'll soon learn which side his bread is buttered on.* Silly David. Matt would always do things his way.

He straightened up, propped the axe against the tree and wiped his hands on his pants. No need for Matt to smile. His eyes did it for him. She followed him into the living room and sat down.

'You're looking great, Meli. We're winning. I squeezed some juice. Drink it. It's good for you.'

'You've given me hope. I'm not sure that you did the right thing. I'm so vulnerable now. I look at the birds and the flowers and I want to be part of this great resurrection. I want to live.' She peered through the open window at the oak tree where lilies of the valley clustered around its base beside a tangle of overgrown grass, tulips and struggling anemones. A blackbird hopped

194

around pecking at worms. Blue tits, tiny and vulnerable, were darting in the branches. So much life squeezed into each square inch. She turned to him challengingly. 'I need to feel the blood racing round my body. I need to feel passion.'

'You will . . . you're getting better. How's the writing going?'

She sighed. 'Don't ask. I hate this novel. The worst thing about writing is having to live through the scenes you create. I'm frightening myself half to death.'

'Forget psycho-thrillers. Get on with that book about the village and what happened here in '85. You have a ready-made plot. How many times must I ask you to finish it.'

'The problems is . . . there's no plot.' She spoke with feigned indifference. She should never have told Matt about the novel.

'Don't lie. Face up to your fears and guilt, Meli.'

'No. No. I won't.' She laughed. 'You look so silly with your mouth open. Doesn't anyone ever say 'no' to you back home?'

Matt recovered quickly, feigning amusement at himself rather than at her.

'You have every right to refuse. After all, this is England, not Africa. Forgive me, Meli, for imagining that you would listen to common sense. Don't you understand what I'm saying. You must purge yourself of your guilt, whatever it was. Write it out. It's part of your cure.'

'I told you, I'm busy on something else.'

Matt's black eyes burned disturbingly. 'The

healing comes from within, from your own mind. I'm only the catalyst that gets you going. Without your full co-operation the healing comes to an end.'

'Co-operation is a blatant euphemism.'

A buffalo couldn't look more dangerous as Matt lowered his head and gazed up from under his massive brows. She was snared by the brilliant white slits of his eyes and his expression, deep and dark as night.

She scowled back. 'You have no right to threaten me.'

'I think I do. If you won't let my will control you, then how can my will cure you?' His eyes defied her to argue.

'Oh God. You and your mumbo-jumbo.' She stood up angrily. 'It's all nonsense. Can't you see that? I went along with it for fun, but I won't be bullied. Goodbye, Matt. Thanks for trying.'

★   ★   ★

Red-faced and perspiring, Shirley was clipping roses in her garden by the lake, her two youngest children trailing behind her. Melissa couldn't wait to let off steam.

'Bastard. How dare he! What would you say if I told you . . . ' In dismay she listened to herself telling Shirls everything there was to know about Matt and breaking all her promises to him.

'A sangoma! My God, your life is like a novel. Why do these things happen to you? Nothing ever happens to me. Did he throw the bones? Did he sacrifice a goat? Has he made a pass?'

Melissa regretted her lapse. 'Don't get me wrong, he's a vicar, but before that he was his tribe's hereditary sangoma. Listen Shirley, I promised I wouldn't tell anyone, but I was furious. I regret . . . '

'You look so much better. D'you think he'd help me? Harry didn't come home at all last night. He pitched at seven this morning. He didn't even make excuses. I can't take it. He's trying to provoke me into a fight so he has a reason to walk out.'

Harry's infidelities had been stale news for years, but it was a relief to discuss a topic other than bossy Matt.

'Do you know what the women of the Ntuwaketse tribe do when they catch their men being unfaithful?' Shirley looked vicious as she gazed at her clippers. 'They wait until they're sleeping and they get a chopper . . . ' She broke off, sniffing loudly. A swift clip sent a rose falling to the grass, shedding its crimson petals.

'Don't look like that, Shirls.'

'For a writer you're damned squeamish. Perhaps that's your trouble.'

'Maybe. I must get back to work. I do care, it's just that I can't think of anything helpful to say. I hope Harry comes to his senses soon. He'll be a fool if he doesn't. I'm never going back to Luze, by the way. Sod him.'

★ ★ ★

Luze stood in the doorway of the vicarage watching the late afternoon sunbeams turning

197

Melissa's hair to flaming red. So here she was at last. Meli had walked out in a temper two weeks ago and it had taken him all this time to get her back again. She was proud, pampered and successful. How could he cope with such a woman? Her lips were parted, she was panting slightly and her brilliant green eyes were glinting with amusement. She was longing to be screwed. He knew all the signs, but he'd been holding back for weeks. The truth was, he was scared. There must be cultural differences, taboos he'd never even heard of. He'd never screwed a white woman. What if he committed some unbelievable blunder. What if she laughed at him. A man has to be the boss, how else can he operate? Back home every male was the boss and no one questioned that fact of life. Being a sangoma helped, too. Screwing Melissa would be like walking through a minefield, he sensed, so he had ignored her obvious invitations.

'Can I come in?' She slipped past him into the living room and shrugged off her coat. When he looked up he flinched. She had come prepared for seduction, that much was clear. Her lips were pursed like a Hollywood siren, her eyes were ringed with kohl and her frilly, see-through blouse revealed breasts that were surprisingly full. A gust of expensive perfume almost anaesthetized him.

He stepped back feeling deeply troubled by her blatant invitation.

'Would you like some coffee?'

'Let's have a drink,' she said boldly. 'I brought you some sherry.' She sat down and crossed her legs and the long split in her clinging skirt revealed smooth white thighs.

'I need some advice,' she began hesitantly. 'It's David. He wants me back, but I don't know why. It's months since we made love. He makes me feel as if I'm over the hill, but women of my age are still having babies. Well, older than me. He says my illness puts him off. How could a man say that to a woman he's lived with for over eight years? When I look in the mirror I see the same me. Maybe a bit thinner, but not much. What d'you think?'

'You're very beautiful, Melissa.'

Melissa gave him a long, searching look and began to unbutton her blouse. Acute unease tossed Luze into froth of embarrassment. He trembled as she unbuttoned each tiny pearl button and each one took an eternity.

'Melissa, stop right now. You're making a mistake.'

'Oh no! I don't think so. Your face is very expressive. Something's been holding you back. Why are you afraid of me?'

She searched his face for signs of lust as she tossed her blouse on the chair. Smiling coquettishly, she shrugged and her breasts bounced and shimmered.

The image transports him through time and space to ochre walls, crimson blood and the warm, sour stench of milk sprayed indiscriminately as the mamas haul their purple teats from toddlers' mouths. He watches the women of his father's household skinning goats, plucking chicken and making food in their beaded skirts

199

and anklets, their tiny protuberances hardly showing until the first child. By the third they are throwing their milksacs over their shoulders to toddlers strapped on their backs. The child is weaned and the empty skins hang like stretched, punctured balloons. A fact of nature, neither alluring nor disgusting.

'Come, Melissa. Button up. Don't try to seduce an African man with breasts.' Moving swiftly, he grabbed the blouse and pulled it hard together, but as he fumbled with the buttons, the fabric tore.

'Oh shit!'

'You should see your face.' She laughed as her skirt fell around her ankles. She was naked under it. Dropping to the carpet, she posed on the floor like the little mermaid. 'I'm still attractive, aren't I, Matt?'

'Oh, Meli. What are you doing?' He pulled her to her feet and tried to disentangle her arms which hung around his neck, strong as a noose. She was trying to pull his head down towards hers.

'Kissing is not an African custom, Meli.' He jerked his head away from her questing mouth.

'What the hell do you do? How come you aren't an endangered species?'

He laughed, picked her up and dumped her in the chair.

'Thanks for this . . . '

He opened the bottle and poured two glasses.

'Cheers!' he said, handing one to her. 'Sit and listen well, Meli. I'm far too proud to be someone you screw in secret. I'm not a toy boy and I'm not prepared to hide my feelings, nor get into a demeaning situation.'

'Hm! You have a fine English vocabulary.'

'Don't patronize me, Meli. I remember the first time I saw you. You were playing your favourite role . . . lady of the manor . . . and you were damned patronising.'

She crossed her legs primly and sipped her sherry. 'But Matt, being the local vicar I assume you must guard your reputation. You can't have affairs. Surely we'd have to be very careful.'

He laughed aloud. 'Is that what you think? You might be right at that, but let me tell you something . . . I don't have to be the local vicar. For you I'd make a sacrifice. There are all kinds of jobs I can do, so think before you leap into bed. I know your type. Men are your luxury and nothing is meant to last. What did you have in mind for me . . . three months? A year?'

She shrugged. 'While you're here. That would do. Why not?'

'Two years! I find that concept deeply insulting.'

'Oh, for goodness sake grow up. Yes or no?'

'Yes, but only on my terms. You decide, Meli.'

She put down her glass slowly, smiled her lady of the manor smile and stood up. That was the very last moment she was in control of herself or him, she realised later.

24

Mid-May and the hedges were white with blossom, while patches of cowslips, clover and wild angelica brightened the fallow land. The lambs, plump and skittish at two-months, were fooling around for the pure joy of being alive and Simon was humming to himself as he repaired a damaged fence. By noon he was covered in sweat, but he was pleased with a job well done.

He straightened up and out of the corner of his eye noticed Flora leading the flock down from the hills towards the lush grazing by the dam. The woods hid the river and the main road which lay beyond the farm, but at the boundary of his land he could see the road and the village, and there, like a child's toy set, came a convoy of army trucks, followed by two white vans and a police car, moving his way. He reckoned they'd taken a wrong turning to the army's shooting range. Nevertheless, he felt anxious. Picking up his tools he set off towards the homestead.

He hadn't gone far before the first truck rumbled along the farm road and swung into the yard. Inspired by a sense of impending disaster Simon began to run.

Stupid, really stupid. There's been no foot and mouth around here so far, so why worry? But they're here.

By now five trucks and the abattoir vans had parked in a neat row facing the stables and the soldiers and white coated slaughtermen were scrambling out of them.

* * *

Time switches to dead slow. Panic surges and Simon drops his tools and lurches forward. Each step takes forever as he tries to propel himself faster.

In the distance he sees Sarah arguing. One of the soldiers is pushing her away. He hears her shouts:

'Simon. Simon.'

He is running, shouting, but his voice is lost in the breeze. They neither see nor hear him. Sirens are sounding and a police car swings into the yard. A uniformed policeman gets out and approaches the officer.

Flora, the matriarch, has a well-developed sixth-sense for danger and she is leading the flock back to the hills. Unbelievably she is running and her urgent cries urge the ewes to follow. The lambs are lost and confused by this sudden flight as they search for their mothers. Simon sprints over the last hill and hurls himself around the dam and into the yard.

'What . . . ? What . . . ?' Fighting for breath, he manages to gasp: 'What's going on?'

'Calm down, Mr Shepherd. You'll be fully compensated,' one of the slaughtermen says. He is reaching for his clumsy, high captive bolt pistol.

Simon finds his voice with a roar. 'What the fuck are you talking about?'

The Lieutenant is reading, but his broad north country accent and his nervousness combine to blur his words. 'A neighbour's Large White sow . . . sent to the local abattoir . . . diagnosed F and M . . . Redhill falls into the designated quarantine area . . . all livestock to be culled herewith.'

Simon is very cold and very angry. 'Fuck you! You've made a mistake. There's no foot and mouth anywhere around this area.' Simon grabs the papers from him. *Redhill*. It's his address, too.

'There's no FMD anywhere near here.' He's shouting furiously and running out of control. 'It was never in these parts. Not one case. What the fuck's going on? Are you mad?'

'It's an offense to resist the culling, Sir,' the police sergeant is patiently explaining.

The flock are panicking. He hears their cries from the field beyond the dam. Looking around, Simon sees three soldiers waving their arms as they herd the ewes towards the yard. The lambs are scattering, lost in the turmoil. Simon is momentarily paralysed at the incredulous sight of eight slaughtermen loading powder charges into their pistols.

He screams: 'No! Stop!'

He sees Ana running between the soldiers and the flock. She's yelling at Flora, driving the flock towards the trees and Sam is with her. He seems to know what to do. She disappears from sight. Now the soldiers are calling to their sergeant who sends reinforcements. The troops run into the woods from all directions.

Simon attempts to reason with the slaughter-men. 'Listen. Let's get the vet here. He can explain. You've got the wrong place. I beg you . . . wait. I'll think of something.' The sheep emerge in twos and threes, the lambs hopelessly lost and confused, baaing piteously.

Flora stands confused, uncertain, searching in vain for a familiar face. Sunlight glints on the soldier's pistol. The report echoes round the yard as Flora's knees buckle and she crumples. She lifts her head looking puzzled and dies.

'Murderers . . . fucking murderers.' Simon is screaming at them. 'Get off my land. This is a breeding station. My best ewe. The matriarch. A gold medalist. You shot her down like a mad dog. I'll see you in court, you bastard.' He leaps towards the officer, grabs him by his lapels and smashes his fist into his face. Sobbing and punching, he's incoherent with grief and outrage.

★ ★ ★

It takes three of them to wrestle him down to the cobbles. He feels the handcuffs biting into his wrists. His face is pressed into the dung. He can't breath. It takes all his strength to turn his head against their combined strength. Unbeliev-ably, they are punching him.

'Don't try that again,' one of them mutters as they stand up.

Dazed and confused he watches his maimed and wounded flock slowly falling to the bloodstained cobbles where the killers pick them

205

off one by one. The lambs huddle behind their mother's flanks as the remaining beasts stagger around crying piteously.

He climbs to his feet, his grief so bitter he can't talk or think as he wanders amongst the prone sheep. A lamb stirs, bleats and dies.

Only two soldiers remain in the yard. They are watching Simon as if he's a rabid dog.

'Where's the police?' They point to a car. Jeff Collins, their local constable, is bent over the wheel.

'This is a terrible sight to see, Simon,' he mutters. 'Turns my stomach, I don't mind telling you.'

'Where's the key? For God's sake unlock me. Come on, Jeff. You know me well enough. Where are the rest of those murdering sods?'

Jeff takes out a key and unlocks the handcuffs. It is then that Simon hears the lowing of his prize herd of Friesian cows. As if in a nightmare, he sees them coming over the hill, driven from their luscious pasture. Now the full extent of his disaster hits home.

Candida makes a sudden bid for life. Head lowered, she batters the gate set into the low, stone cemetery wall and gallops around the old graves, lowing plaintively. The rest of the herd scatter and bolt for safety. Only three cows are herded into the yard and quickly despatched with bolts.

The chief slaughterman is yelling from the dam. 'We'll have to use high-powered rifles. We can't line up this lot. The gunshots echo around the yard.'

Up in the hills, Simon hears the dull thuds of a massive force meeting solid wood head on. Bellows of rage startle the troops. Moments later, Simon's massive champion bull, Ferdinand, bursts over the hill in a cloud of mud and dust, snorting with rage. He pauses, flicks his tail, lowers his head and charges.

The soldiers scatter, but one stands rooted to the ground as if panic-stricken and the bull is coming straight at him. From the cemetery wall, two soldiers aim their rifles and fire. A bullet hits home and Ferdinand shakes his head without slowing his charge. A soldier fires again and the bull flinches momentarily.

Simon rushes towards him and sends the soldier sprawling against the wall. Standing in front of him, he whistles at the enraged beast, waving his arms and shouting his name. He can hear his snorting breath, smell the scent of him, as two tons of savage temper bear down on him. In the split second before he lowers his head to lunge, Ferdinand veers off-course. His agonised eyes have seen the carnage and he's searching in sullen fury for those responsible. Some pristine instinct from his genetic heritage sends him galloping around the dam, away from the troops, to disappear behind the dairy.

Moments later he bursts into the yard from behind them, snorting with fury, charging straight at the soldiers who are hemmed in against the dairy wall. A barrage of rifle shots hits his chest. Now the bull is mortally wounded, but racing forward, still bellowing as his back legs fold under him. His left foreleg gives way

207

and he falls heavily. He tries to get back on his feet, snorting still as his reproachful eyes seek Simon's. Moments later his body shakes and he dies with a mighty bellow of frustrated fury.

Simon sank on the dairy steps, trembling violently as he hears the pigs squealing in an agony of fear as one by one they are killed. He sees the soldiers searching the sheds. He has two tiny calves locked in the barn behind the dairy, one bull calf is the off-spring of Ferdinand and Candida. Then he sees the soldiers searching the outhouses.

The Lieutenant hurries towards him holding a bloody handkerchief over his face.

'You broke my nose, but there'll be no charges, Sir. Not if I have any say in the matter. You saved my corporal's life and risked your own. I won't forget that in a hurry. We don't like this anymore than you do. We're only obeying orders.'

'I've heard that before somewhere. Nuremberg perhaps,' Simon mutters. The officer flushes. 'The corpses will be collected soon and removed for cremation.' He hurries to his staff car.

The troops don't look round as they climb into the trucks.

The constable gently reminds him of the quarantine. No one may leave the farm.

'Is it a home or a prison?' he wants to know.

*   *   *

Birds swooped and soared after flies buzzing around the corpses. Then Sarah came and tried

208

to persuade Simon to leave the yard, but he shook his head.

'Just go and make yourself at home. You're stuck here for the time being. Put some footbaths at the gate. There's nothing else left to do.'

'Okay. I'll take care of everything. I'll lock up the fowls later. Please Simon. Please get up and go inside. You're covered in mud and faeces and you're as white as a sheet. You'll get sick.'

He shook his head and buried his face in his hands. Once he tried to stand, but gave up. His bruises had stiffened and his legs were heavy with sorrow. Twenty years of selective breeding wiped out in a single morning. Yet that wasn't the reason for his grief. Each one of them was special. Eventually he got to his feet and wobbled across the yard to where Ferdinand lay. Gently he closed the bull's eyes and stroked his pelt and to his astonishment, felt a choking lump in his throat.

'Don't be a fool, man,' he told himself. 'You'll be compensated. It may take a few years to get back what you had, but you'll make it.'

But that wasn't it at all. He had loved every one of them. The realisation shocked him and for the first time he could ever remember he crouched on the cobbles beside the bull and cried.

Much later a new batch of men moved in with an assortment of fork-lift trucks and small cranes. They manoeuvred their vehicles close to the corpses and hoisted them like lumps of cement, packing them onto their trucks like building rubble. Simon saw Ferdinand being winched up by his back leg, his face still set in a grimace of agony.

The sun hung poised above the horizon and sank gracefully away. Purple mists moved into the valleys. The ducks waddled back from the dam in single file and the hens cackled and clucked as they were locked up for the night.

Simon tried to explain to Sarah the sheer impossibility of getting up and returning to the homestead. 'I have to see it all. You see, I chose to be a farmer. Yet I've never been near an abattoir. The truth is, I avoided them. Most of the livestock gets sold as breeding stock, those that don't . . . Well, there's just a last wave of regret as my truck leaves. Sometimes not even that. Yet this is what it's all about. All the careful selected breeding, the injections, the show rings, the rosettes and gold medals. It all comes down to killing. They're only meat when all's said and done. Prehistoric men would apologise to the game they slaughtered. They needed meat to live and pelts for warmth, but nothing was wasted. They killed only what they needed for survival and they prayed for the creature's great spirit. But between those ancient hunters and the supermarket shelves, we've lost something vital, a reverence for life. We've become contemptuous of the great life force that sustains all living creatures and we can only be diminished by this. We have forgotten how to love all living creatures. We have forgotten how to love.

'Go on now, Sarah. There's plenty of food in the kitchen. Go and make yourself supper, but feed Sam, please. Laura will be back soon. I don't know where Ana's gone.'

'Sam won't stop howling.' She sat on the step and cried gentle women's tears, but after a few minutes she got up and left.

Simon fetched a hosepipe and began to hose the cobbles. How could this happen? He thought of praying, but he could find nothing to pray to. 'God help me. I need something to hang on to.' Nothing came to him and after a while he switched off the tap, rolled up the hosepipe and made his unsteady way to the house, staggering like a drunk and feeling as dead as his livestock.

Tomorrow he would contact the department, see a lawyer and apply for his compensation. He'd get Evans to sort out this terrible mistake. He would probably sue, but tonight was for grieving. He knew nothing would ever erase the poignant sight of that massive bull thundering to the rescue of his herd.

25

Simon stumbled into the bathroom, threw off his clothes and stood under the scalding shower scrubbing himself vigorously until the blood and grime had drained away.

Wrapping a towel around him, he went outside and pushed his filthy clothes into the farm's furnace. He'd light it by and by. Yelling at Sam, who was whimpering, he poured himself a double scotch and drank it neat. He felt oddly light-headed, with a sick feeling in his craw and a sense of not being there at all. Suddenly the image of his valiant bull snorting out his last breath seemed to be right there, as if it had happened a split-second ago. More living images crowded in on him. It was shock, he realised.

Ana had not returned and Laura had left the usual message on the telephone answering service: She was working late in the village. Poor little thing. Her work was her defence against the world. It occurred to Simon that the loss of his wife's love was the most insidious of all his disasters. He needed her and surely she needed him, too. He grabbed an old pair of shorts and sweater and took the keys of his 4-track.

As he parked, he realised that he was barefooted, but it was dark so no one would notice. He hurried up the driveway to their cottage and opened the French window. Strange sounds were emerging from the bedroom: some

212

bangs, a muffled groan, then a short, sharp cry. For an awful moment he imagined the troops were culling Laura, too. Racing headlong down the passage, Ferdinand-style, he charged. The door burst open and Simon skidded to a halt.

'Oh no! No!'

It was weird. A tangle of limbs, backs twisted to breaking point and Gordon appeared to be headless. His wife and his friend collided in a heap.

'Our variation on the *blossoming* position, old man. Takes a bit of practice,' Gordon's breathless voice explained from some fleshy depths. He heaved himself away and landed on to the floor with a bump. Then Simon saw the *Kama Sutra* lying open beside the bed.

At that moment everything became very clear to Simon. No words were needed. His life was spread out over the duvet.

★ ★ ★

Laura, crimson and sweating, glanced up in horror and saw remnants of the man who cared for her draining into the floor. Intuitively she knew that Gordon's last phrase had delivered the *coup de grâce*. The Simon she knew was dying in front of her eyes. Sadness crept into his eyes and fled. Then anger. She welcomed anger, but that drained fast away. Then a slightly cynical tilt came to the side of his mouth. His quirky cynicism warded off hurt, she knew. But even that was gone in a trice leaving only a blank stare. He gave a queer sort of a nod, inclined his head slightly and said: 'Ah, so much is suddenly clear to me,' in voice of utter desolation. Then he walked out.

After a shocked moment of indecision, she scrambled to her feet and pulled on her clothes.

'I must go to him. He's hurting.'

'No. Not him. Couldn't you see how he reacted? He's not a man, he's an android. You've said that yourself enough times.'

Gordon caught hold of her arm. 'Stay here.'

'No. I must go.'

He held her wrists tightly. 'Don't go.'

'Leave me. I'll yell for help.'

'No one can hear. I told you, Simon needs to be left alone.'

'But couldn't you see? He sort of went dead on us. Right in front of our eyes. It was awful. Surely you noticed. Take your hands off me.'

She kicked his shins hard and he let her go.

★ ★ ★

There was nothing abnormal about Harry's saloon lounge. Even Harry, leaning over the bar, his face set in an expression of benign tolerance, was familiar. The brandy Harry had forced on him had reacted with several whiskies to numb his system and he was enjoying the murmur of conversation, pitched low, restrained, civilised. More than anything in the world, he never again wanted to stray outside the bounds of normality. Then Harry said:

'Heard the news. Can't say how sorry I am . . . about the culling, I mean. Are you okay,

Simon?' Normality fled.

'Sure.' He caught sight of Meli who was approaching from the restaurant. She looked excited, her eyes shining as if she were on the way to a party. This was the old Meli who'd been absent for far too long.

'You're looking great, Meli.'

'Yes, I feel great. I'm getting better and I've left David and moved in here temporarily. My house is let to Londoners. Jesus, Simon,' she went on without a pause. 'You've been putting it away. What is it with you? I've never seen you drunk before.'

'I've not seen you glowing for years either.'

She scowled at him and moved to the room behind the bar. Harry excused himself and went back stage and moments later Meli hurried out with tears in her eyes.

'Oh God! What an awful thing to happen. I had no idea. I'm so sorry, Simon. Really . . . I can't tell you how sorry I am. Will it wipe you out?'

How could he answer? Hang on to the stiff upper lip syndrome. He intended to say: 'They'll pay compensation of course,' but foreign words tumbled out of his mouth.

'I don't know who I am, Meli. I'm not in control. Life's taken a rum turn.'

'Have another brandy. That'll fix you up,' Harry said. '*Tomorrow is another day.* I had a customer used to say that.' Harry refilled his glass with neat brandy while Meli tried to stop him.

He gulped it down and seemed to hear his

wife calling: 'But where *is* Simon? I've got to find him.'

Laura seemed to have fallen out with normality, too. She looked a sight. 'Why did you come? You never come to the office,' she accosted him with unrighteous indignation, for all the world as if they weren't surrounded with interested bystanders.

'Office! Huh!' That seemed rather funny. He couldn't help laughing. 'I needed you.'

'Well, here I am.'

'I no longer need you.'

Terror flitted over her face like a moonbeam.

'Don't be spiteful. Despite . . . ' She gave up and sat down. 'I still care for you.'

'Our last Sunday lunch at home ruined any such illusions.'

'Don't talk to me like that . . . don't say that. Listen, about tonight . . . it was just one of those things, Simon. An accident. I was lonely and . . . '

Simon glanced over his shoulder. Harry had tactfully left, but Meli was nursing her fruit juice with one hand while holding a book with the other, unashamedly listening in.

'So you thought you'd try out the *Kama Sutra*. How long does it take to get on to variations?'

He saw her try to rub the tears away with her fingertips as she heard Gordon approaching.

'Are you rich?' Simon asked, as his former friend hovered by the table.

'I have a good income. Well, most months.'

'Laura likes money.'

216

'I'm not for sale, Simon.' Laura's voice was trembling.

'Well, I'm not bidding. The slaughtermen arrived with an army and police backup and destroyed everything. It took them most of the day. You should have seen Ferdinand. He broke down the gate and charged to save the herd. It took five bullets from a high powered rifle to bring him down. If he were human they'd give him the VC.'

'Oh God. I'm so sorry. What's happened to your face?'

She moved forward to touch him, but he backed away.

'I started a war and lost.'

'There'll be compensation.' Gordon was behaving as if nothing untoward had happened and probably it hadn't. Obviously they'd been screwing for years.

'Ultimately, but I doubt they'll match the value of the breeding stock.'

'Where's the 4-track? I didn't see it.'

'Nearby.'

'I'll drive back with you.' Laura looked haggard.

'No thanks. The house and the farm are in a trust, so I can't give you half, sorry. My lawyers made sure it's unbreakable back in '85. Perhaps you'd settle for half the compensation.'

'For goodness sake, Simon. These things happen. You don't have to go OTT.' Gordon's voice was calm, but he looked scared.

'Let's sort it out in private outside, Gordon,' Simon said pleasantly, as he made for the exit.

All his aggression at his tragic day went into one straight punch in Gordon's stomach. Gordon fell, doubled up, making a harsh grating noise in his chest. He wouldn't get up. Knees pulled up to his chin, his face chalk white, he was noisily sucking in air. By now they had attracted a crowd of onlookers. Simon felt cheated as he went back inside. He'd been spoiling for a fight. He beckoned to Harry for a refill.

26

By midnight Simon was feeling sick. He fought off Harry's determination to put him up for the night at the hotel, but allowed Meli to drive him home. He'd rather have driven himself, but he was too drunk.

Meli seemed to think it was her duty to cheer him.

'You've been through worse times, Simon,' she began lightly as they left the car park. 'You and Laura haven't got on for years. You'll be better off without her.'

'Are you happy with David?' Oh Simon! You certain! She's supposed to be dying. Jesus, what a night. 'I'm sorry. I shouldn't have said that. I'm very drunk.'

'I believe you. But no, I'm not particularly happy with David. In fact, I've just left him, although I'm there most days. I'm not moving out of my office for the time being.'

'Oh hell. Meli, listen. I wouldn't like this scene with Laura and Gordon to get around.'

'Then you shouldn't have had your domestic showdown in the pub.'

'Right as usual. You turn here. First left.'

'I've been here before. Remember?'

'Of course you have. Sorry.'

Meli was usually smiling and now that she wasn't, he saw signs of age and sadness around her mouth and chin. She parked and retrieved her handbag. So what was she expecting? Was he supposed to invite her in for coffee? He decided against it. Such invitations should be made when sober.

'I've often wondered why you married Laura,' she began tentatively. 'Perhaps you feel like talking about it.'

'Not particularly. You shouldn't have done this, but it was kind of you.' He climbed out of the car and attempted a theatrical bow. Unwisely, he thought as Meli leaped out of the car, ran around it and hauled him to his feet.

'Let go of me. I'm too heavy for you,' he argued, as they wobbled and swayed to the front door.

He turned the key in the lock with difficulty and switched on the light.

'Yes, it's always this cold and empty,' he said, imagining her unasked question. 'A catacomb of strangled hopes. Even the homely cushions seem like a sick joke to me.'

Meli looked stricken, he noticed. Perhaps he'd been rude. He tried to make amends. 'To answer your question . . . I married Laura because she's very beautiful and beauty is my Achilles Heel.'

There was more to it than that, of course. He reached for the scotch and offered the bottle to Meli. She shook her head, so he gulped what was left, but drink wasn't helping. Opening the fridge, he gulped cold water from the bottle. Cool drops splashed on his face and it felt good, so he poured the bottle over himself.

'I'd make you coffee if I were sober, but I don't think I'm up to it.'

'I'll make it,' she insisted.

Simon tried to hide his grimace of annoyance. 'We'll have to be quiet. Ana's sleeping and Sarah's here, too. She's not supposed to leave because of the quarantine. Neither was I.'

'Your dog's making enough noise to raise the dead.'

'So he is.' Simon staggered to the back porch and yelled at Sam who retreated to his basket and curled up whimpering.

'Is he sick?'

'Sick with guilt. He didn't save the flock and that's his job.'

'Poor dog. Surely you'll be all right? You'll be compensated. Maybe not enough, but you're young enough to start again. You'll make it.'

Simon got up shakily and poured himself another glass of water and considered the financial implications of the day. Clearly he was ruined. Probably bankrupt! Admittedly the government would pay compensation, but not nearly enough and it wouldn't come soon enough either. It had taken twenty years to create these pedigreed animals, champions from champions all the way.

He stared at Meli, wondering what to say. 'Life was so simple when the enemy could be identified,' he began, not really sure where he was going. ''Halt! Who goes there? Friend or foe? Advance friend and be recognised'. A familiar call of World War II, as my grandfather, Tom, told me often. Nowadays the enemy stalks from within and we lived in a minefield of hidden agendas: the speaker on the Party

221

Platform paying lip service to freedom while ditching democracy; the abattoir officials botching their records and destroying a life's work; the vicar seducing his choir boys; rail officials neglecting to check the lines; the smiling nurse bearing the wrong injection; my best friend fucking my wife. Well, forgive me, that's a cliché.'

And of course there was his father's treachery. He'd been well and truly sabotaged at one time or another.

'It's not the first time Redhill's fields have been laid waste, Meli. Last time it took all Tom's savings to restock the farm after my father left it derelict, but at least in those days farming paid.'

'Tell me about it, Simon,' she was saying, lolling back in the chair.

Was she some kind of a masochist? She couldn't want to know, but if he suggested she should go, he'd be alone.

'You were the one who warned me . . . well, warned us all. Don't you remember?'

He tried to explain every damn thing, but later he wasn't sure how much he'd actually told her and how much were his own indelible memories that he'd never be able to slough off.

'I was ploughing. A storm was raging overhead and it was so dark I could hardly see.' The clouds matched his mood. He'd been feeling particularly sorry for himself, he remembered, but five minutes later he had something real to worry about.

★   ★   ★

Lately he's wondering just how long he can hang in at Redhill. All his ideas to improve the land have been turned down by Father and he's forced to work as a farm labourer in order to safeguard the estate. For this he's studied long and hard. A flash of fork lightening breaks in on his gloom, lighting the figure of a woman doggedly hiking towards him through the mud and smiting rain. It's Melissa.

He climbs down. Lurching against the wind, he runs towards her. 'What is it? What's wrong?' he calls, thinking of Laura who is six months pregnant.

'Simon . . . Simon . . . You bastard. You had no right . . . ' She looks distraught.

'Hey there! What's the problem?' He pulls her to the shelter of the tractor.

'You must have heard that your father's selling Redhill.'

'Calm down. He can't.'

'Oh, you asshole. He is . . . lock, stock and barrel . . . to a consortium of foreign financiers. They're going to erect a plant to make semiconductors, plus accommodation for up to a thousand workers: highrise flats, a soccer field. We'll all be ruined. You should have known. You've got to stop him.'

'Listen. Father can't sell. Redhill is owned by a trust . . . the first male inherits. Why do you think I'm slogging my guts out as a labourer here?'

'I'm afraid he's found a way to sell,' she says in her hoarse, melodramatic voice. 'I don't know about trusts and things, but Harry heard from a

223

friend in the council that everything's settled. Re-zoning comes through in a month's time and someone called George Irving, an industrialist who heads the consortium, is flying over from Kashmir to sign the deal. We're dead meat, hopelessly over-borrowed. We'll all be ruined. For God's sake, stop him.' She mutters something under her breath and turns away without saying goodbye.

'Tell me the rest of it,' Meli said. 'I'm not leaving until you've sobered up a bit, so just talk. Would you like some more coffee?'

'Yes, please. You're a good sort Meli. Way back I had the impression you were too ambitious to be happy as a mere farmer's wife.'

Meli's eyes filled with hot tears, but that was crazy. Surely he was mistaken. He looked away quickly.

'Really? Well I don't want to hear about that. Tell me about your father. What happened that night, Simon?'

'I tackled Father and he didn't bother to deny a damn thing. I remember he said: 'You'll thank me one day, Simon. Farming is the pits. There's no money in it, my boy. A life of sheer drudgery. I tried to warn you. I told you to study for a CA, but you would study agriculture. The trust is broken. Ancient history and I'm moving to Bermuda'. He didn't seem embarrassed at being caught out, but I felt shamed by his treachery.'

He broke off. The rest was private.

'I think it's time I told you both that there's someone else,' his father had said, with a silly, bashful expression on his face. 'Someone I love.

She's out there looking for a house for us. I don't expect to see either of you again. No great loss for you.'

His mother's wails had cut short any further discussion, but between the shouts, slamming doors, bellows of rage and accusations, Simon learned that the deeds of sale weren't signed yet. They were waiting for permission from the Planning Authority, which was only a formality.

As Father half-turned, leering with triumph, Simon leaped forward and struck out, enjoying the satisfying crunch of his fists pounding flesh. Vaguely he heard Mae screaming at him. There was blood on his father's face and hands, but only because his glass had broken as he hit the wall.

Simon checked his freefall into savagery by remembering that Father was a sick man . . . and the wrong man. It was Irving who had stolen the woman he loved and who now planned to destroy his birthright. He turned away and rushed out of the house.

Dawn found him sitting on a hilltop overlooking Redhill's fields and lakes. Blackbirds were chorusing and foxes barked in the woods as they loped back to their dens. Mists were drifting in the valleys, rabbits were darting through the grass, three wild migrating swans soared overhead silhouetted against the pearl-grey sky. He watched them circle and plunge towards the calm lake. A badger plodded past making for the woods. Morning had broken.

Simon shuddered as he visualised ugly factory buildings, utilitarian, high-rise apartment blocks, mean streets and gaudy shops. Gritting his teeth, he made a vow to fight his father every inch of the way, to the death if need be. At that moment his reasons were entirely altruistic.

★   ★   ★

Meli was half asleep. She stood up and went to the kitchen to make some more coffee. 'Perhaps this isn't the best time to choose,' she said when she returned with the tray, 'but I feel I should tell you before the word gets around. I'm writing a book about the '85 incident. I started it years ago, but abandoned the project. A few weeks ago I sent the half-written manuscript to the publishers and they're interested.'

'Why would you want to do that, Meli? I don't understand.' Deep dismay was making Simon feel sick. He should never have told her about his father. It would go into her damned book.

'We all lied to the police and since then my guilt has been getting me down. I want to make a clean sweep of everything.'

Simon stood up and walked to the window where he remained staring into the dark night sky. Just how many disasters could fall on him in one day? He glanced at his watch. It was a minute to midnight, so he must have seen the last of them. He was wrong.

'I've always loved you, Simon,' he heard Meli's hoarse voice saying behind him as she came too close and wrapped her arms around his neck. 'Despite everything, I still do. So you don't have to worry about a damn thing. I'll never let on.

Never. Years back I wronged you . . . this book is my way of making amends.'

He stood rigid with shock. What on earth was she talking about? Did she think that he had . . . ? Just how far did she think he would go to save his birthright? He turned and saw that she had gathered her bag and was making for the door. Now wasn't the time to stop her. He'd ask when he was sober.

'Sleep it off,' she called. She drove off into the night leaving Simon balanced unsteadily in the doorway.

Creeping upstairs, Simon opened Ana's door and saw that her bed was empty and the pillows and duvet were missing. Now where had she gone? The probability that she had joined Laura in the village hurt badly.

He thought he heard a lamb cry. Blundering to the window he flung it open, but the fields were empty and the silence hurt his ears as he switched off the lights and lay on the bed.

There is no pain to match a father's betrayal, Simon decided, yet there were extenuating circumstances. Later, when Redhill was resuscitated and some fine pedigreed breeding animals had been purchased, he was able to think of his father without grinding his teeth. He could even remember Pat's party jokes and his amazing sense of humour, but at the time and for the next few years his father remained a poisonous blight in his mind.

27

Sam was howling again. Simon fetched a tin of dog food from the scullery and cut his thumb opening it. 'Fuck!' Sam wasn't hungry. Just scared and sad, so he shut him in the porch and returned to the couch, but as he drowsed he saw the cows coming in a wave over the hill and once again witnessed their massacre. He woke with a start to hear Sam whimpering in the porch, but there was something else. He distinctly heard a lamb bleating in the yard.

He went out to the porch and yelled. 'Come on Sam. Let's see what we can find.'

What a bloody awful night. Glancing at the clock he saw that it was four-thirty. It would soon be dawn. Crossing the yard, he passed the stable, where Daunty, shocked and lonely, stood with lowered head. Quickening his step and averting his eyes, Simon passed the empty dairy and the abandoned cowsheds until he reached the barn, where he flung open the door.

There was an intruder in the barn. He could hear rustles in the straw.

'Okay, out you come or I'll set the dog on you.'

Ana climbed to her feet, muttering something that he didn't catch, as Sam flung himself on her, knocking her back into the straw and licking her face.

'Have you been here all night, Ana?'

'Yes,' she mumbled. 'Mother phoned. She said she's moving out. She's collecting her things later. She said . . . ' She broke off and began nervously picking at a piece of straw. 'She also said you know.'

'Know what?'

'Oh, Dad, you know what you know.' She gave a long, loud sniff.

'Knowledge was forced upon me, I promise you that. I didn't want to know.'

'Typical.' She turned on him looking savage. When Ana frowned her brows knitted, her eyes turned sloe-black and her mouth looked mean.

'Listen. Look here.'

She heaved at a heap of straw bales and Simon saw a huddle of six lambs and two calves nestling in the straw. He knew exactly who and what his daughter had saved, the best of Redhill.

Unable to control his emotions, he turned his back on her. Through the open doorway he could see the sky turning crimson over the Channel. When he'd got his upperlip under control and he wasn't going to weep, or shout for joy, or indulge in other un-English pursuits in front of his daughter, he said: 'That's my girl. You hid them in the woods.'

'Yes.'

'Bit smarter than a punch-up.'

She shrugged.

'Ferdinand's calf. And Candida's new-born, and the rest. I'll be blowed.'

'They've probably caught colds.'

'They'll be all right. You've saved Redhill's pedigrees with these little creatures. We'll have to keep them hidden until this mistake is cleared up. Perhaps you'll make a farmer after all. How can I ever thank you, Ana?'

★   ★   ★

Watching her father trying to control his emotions as he gently fondled the little creatures, Ana had a moment of misgiving. She was about to deliver the final thrust and she felt bad about it. Dad was laid low and she was well aware of her advantage. Well, here goes!

'By letting me go, Dad. Without a fight. I was leaving anyway. And now . . . well, I might as well tell you that mother wants Sam and me. She can have Sam, but not me. I'm not getting embroiled in a custody battle, not when I'm about to turn eighteen. I've always loved Mum, but sometimes she's hard to understand. She doesn't love Gordon anymore than she loves you, but she's always been great with me. She's an artist, neurotic as hell, still trying to find herself.'

'She's had a lot to put up with. Things you don't know about.'

'You've never been human, so don't start now. In fact, now would be the worst time possible.' She scuffed away her tears with the back of her hands. 'I was about to leave home, but I hadn't got round to telling you. I'm getting a job and a room. Past tense would be more accurate.'

'But that's madness. You must study.'

'Listen, Dad, it's like there are two Englands. You live in one, but I want to live in the other.'

230

Her father took a deep breath and she sensed he was trying to think of something that might get through to her.

'Privilege and corruption are not synonymous,' he said pompously.

She sighed and stared stonily at him. He'd failed again. She wanted to hit him. 'Why are you so damned complacent, so cock-sure your ways are best? You won't look life straight in the eyes.'

'What on earth are you talking about?'

'Mum, for instance. Everyone knew about Mum's affair, even Mae kept hinting, but you won't look at what you don't want to know. That's why I'm getting out of this fairy story where everything's so right, so good, so special and we all live in a state of denial and look the other way.'

Dad got up looking as if she'd lashed him across the face. Ana longed to take back her words, but the time-polyp crept past recording her shame, every last nuance of it, bonding with the split-second before, and the one after, to build life's towering coral cliffs in the karmic ocean.

'I'm sorry, Dad. I shouldn't have said that, but you can't stop me from leaving. I've made up my mind.'

'I can stop you, but I won't. Instead I'm proposing a bargain. Go to University and study for a degree and I won't stand in your way. Of course, you'll need an income,' Dad said with immense and obvious restraint. 'I'll get it organised.'

'Only after my gap year. I want to earn my keep for a year. That way I'll know I've earned the right to my opinions.'

'Ana. That night . . . I spoke in anger . . . I longed to take it back.'

'It's not because of what you said. Wish me luck, Dad.' She held out her hand, unwilling to get drawn into an argument that might weaken her cause.

'Luck! I wish you every possible good fortune that fate could ever devise.' He grabbed at her clumsily, unused to hugging her, holding her so tightly that she gasped. He let go abruptly and she tripped back into the straw.

'Ouch!'

'Just go! Go! By morning you might find yourself locked in here.'

'I'll be in touch.' How forlorn he looked. How bloody typical. She'd just been hugged for the first time in her life because she was leaving.

*   *   *

Simon sat in the barn hoping his daughter might still change her mind. She spent about an hour in the house, packing, he assumed, and then he heard her car moving down the driveway to the main road. Unbelievable how his disasters had faded into insignificance compared with Ana's decision to leave home prematurely. But still he hoped to hear a car brake suddenly, a U-turn clumsily manoeuvred, footsteps running across the courtyard, but all he heard was silence.

Simon remained in the barn, comforting the

little orphans and mixing their feed, stroking them and wishing he could understand himself. He felt strangely humble. It was something to do with a curious surge of empathy that was spilling out of him from some inner generator. It was that strong! Even stronger than that, and it seemed to comfort these mewing bundles of life. He'd felt the same strange sensation when he had begged Ana to stay. Had it taken the destruction of his livestock, the bravery of that magnificent bull and the premature desertion of his daughter to teach him what love was all about?

*   *   *

Dawn breaks softly, a gentle glow that slowly turns to gold. A warm south-west wind sweeps through the farm shaking the new emerald leaves and raising dust devils over the land, bringing a promise of warmth, Simon soaks in the morning, sensing that there will be no carefree summer days. There will be only a sifting and turning of the chaff as he searches for that elusive kernel that holds the essence of his being.

PART 3

Summer, June 21 – September 21.

Blood-red poppies,
Blooming in the empty fields,
Speak so eloquently.

28

Shoulders hunched, Simon stood in the killing yard in blighting gloom, while massed clouds wept enough for two of them and gulls wheeled and soared, hurling their anger at their hostile world. Ten long and tedious days had passed since the culling. Busy days as Simon plagued the Union and the relevant departments for written acknowledgements of the mistake made, the lifting of the quarantine and a promise of eventual compensation. Despite his final success Simon was beginning to acknowledge the disintegration of his sense of self. He was no longer a farmer, nor lord and master of his own squat, since the troops dug his nose into the dung and beat him near senseless. He wasn't a husband, nor a father, nor a Christian, nor a patriot. So what the fuck was he? A loser, perhaps, since losers lose things. By and by he'd lose himself, if he stood here waiting long enough, he reckoned. The thought cheered him enough to walk to the dam where he wondered what on earth to do between now and doomsday.

Sarah had been and gone. She'd fed what little livestock was left and scrubbed out the dairy, but it was Sunday, he seemed to recall. He had to walk down to the gate and retrieve the newspaper out of the box before he could believe that it really was Sunday, Sarah's only day off, yet she'd come to help him. She'd coped like a star during their quarantine period. He felt cheered by her kindness. It was Sunday and he should have called Mae, but he hadn't and wouldn't. Presumably she'd heard the gossip since she hadn't called him.

Lunch consisted of a ham and pickle sandwich, a beer and the blissful absence of Laura and her guests, and that included Mae. He was washing his plate when a shadow fell across the doorway. Expecting Laura, Simon looked up and saw Bela. He turned away, hoping that she hadn't seen his astonishment that she would invade his home, or his joy that she was still talking to him and that she had come.

She looked so desirable and as he stared at her, he saw her nipples hardening under her silk blouse. Primal urges were zooming through his bloodstream, quickening his energy for the fray, but guilt strutted and crowed in his gut. Guilt ruled his psyche. Guilt made him cringe when he ought to argue. Guilt was cock of the roost and it took on allcomers, particularly lust which was pecked and clawed into the dust. So he stepped back and smiled sadly.

How lovely she was. Her hair was scraped back into a thick braid and she wore jeans, sandals and a blue T-shirt. She wasn't built for jeans. Her waist was too small and her hips too full. He frowned, thinking that she resembled a comic-strip sex symbol, with her curvaceous figure and her huge eyes and long lashes. She examined him, standing too close and looking concerned, before running her finger over the partially healed black eye and his numerous cuts.

'I heard you took on the army single-handed.'

'A five-second rebellion. It's not serious. The cuts have almost healed.'

She glanced around the kitchen. 'I heard much more than that. Are you alone?'

'Completely. Laura even took my dog. You should have waited. I would have called you. You must know that.' His voice was hoarse. He cleared his throat. 'I was only waiting for a decent interval to elapse.'

'Let's be indecent. I couldn't wait any longer. Am I welcome?'

'Please! Feel at home here. Help yourself to coffee, or whatever you want.'

'This is what I came for.'

She wound her arms around his neck and placed her lips passionately on his and for a few blissful moments Simon existed in the here and now. Then he pushed her away.

'Bela, I'm forty-six,' he said sternly.

'So who's perfect?' She giggled like a schoolgirl. 'I also came to say I'm sorry. So very sorry. The slaughter of your stock is the scandal of the district. And all because of an error. People say Laura left you because you're broke.'

'So the tom-tom drums have been beating overtime. It isn't true, of course, but it will do.' He couldn't help wondering where that story had originated.

'So why did she leave?'

'None of your business, Bela.'

She frowned and hesitated. 'I know anyway. Everyone knows about that, too. Harry has a big mouth.'

'I was very drunk, otherwise I wouldn't have spoken in his hearing.'

'But surely you should have suspected . . . I mean . . . after having no sex for seventeen years.'

'Well, that was a slight exaggeration, but lately that's exactly how it's been.'

'I want you to make love to me,' she began firmly. 'Because . . . well, because it's been too long for me, too. Because I need you . . . and because I want sex to become a joy again. Once, very briefly it was a joy, but then I was obliged, not once, but many times, night after night, when I was married . . . ' She broke off when she saw his shock. 'It was an arranged marriage. I was trapped into it. You don't know anything about my past, Simon. I need to erase those memories by giving myself freely to someone whom I desire. I desire you madly. I need you to make love to me. Right now.'

'Wow! That sounded so rehearsed.'

'It was . . . all the way here. Does that matter?'

'No. It's just that I'm not sure . . . ' He was flushing. 'Just like that, unexpectedly, in the middle of Sunday morning.' He caught her around the waist and pulled her hard against him. She felt so soft and pliable that he wondered if he were hurting her, so he loosened his grip.

'How about dinner and dancing and nightcaps . . . the accepted mating ritual? Then I'm sure there'd be no problem. Every morning I wake with such a hard-on, it hurts.'

She shook her head and moved her hips

against his and Simon flushed, but couldn't move away.

'Don't talk, just love me,' she murmured. 'Let's get it over and done with.'

'You mean, like your marriage. Close your eyes and pretend you're somewhere else.'

How could she be so unromantic? Was this how young women carried on? *Young* had suddenly joined the battalion of chilling words, like abattoir, culling, rejected, middle-aged. Words that could hurt like hell. When Bela was ten, he was leading his first prize ewe around the arena, proudly clutching his rosette. When he was gaining his degree, she wasn't even born. Such thoughts were best avoided.

'I mean like breaking a barrier, forging a bond, taking it from there,' she fought back.

She was determined enough for the two of them. He couldn't believe that she was undoing the buttons of his shirt and gently removing it. Then she tackled his shorts. Feeling obliged to participate, he pulled off her T-shirt and saw that she was bra-less under it. How beautiful her breasts were, as perfect as a Grecian statue, and again the word *young* came to mind as he ran his hands over her smooth and radiant skin.

'Now what have you done?' He pulled her close and grinned shyly as he unwittingly smeared lubricant over her perfectly sexy, but stretch-marked belly.

'Oh Simon, don't talk. Just fuck me.'

★   ★   ★

'See what I mean about breaking the ice.' She smirked knowingly.

'Breaking it. My God, we pulverized it, vaporized it, smashed the rocks and spawned every fish in the sea.'

It was four hours later, and Simon felt as if he'd run a marathon. They were lying on the double bed in the spare bedroom, although he had no clear idea of how they'd got there. He vaguely remembered hearing a car, grabbing Bela and mounting the stairs two at a time. She wasn't much heavier than a wheat sack, he reckoned, as she squealed protestingly. Whoever it was had left after ringing the doorbell twice.

Inwardly exalting that a decade of meagre sex had in no way diminished his performance, Simon ran his lips over her stomach, kissing the rough surface of the stretch marks.

'So now you can tell me about these marks. Where is your child . . . or children?'

She sat up abruptly. 'I don't want to talk about her.'

'Her! Just the one . . . ?'

'Please! How about tea? Would you like some tea? I'm going to shower first.'

Without waiting for a reply she rushed to the door and found it locked. She looked round questioningly as she turned the key.

'Obviously my daughter has the front door key, and my wife hasn't given hers back yet. There's a shower through that door.' He pointed across the room. 'Laura redesigned this old house and all the bedrooms are en suite.'

She fled, leaving the door open, and he heard

the shower running.

Bruised and humiliated, Bela cowered in the shower as scalding water blasted her. It must be hotter. Blazing hot. As hot as she can stand, to wash away her guilt.

Screwing her eyes shut, she endured the blast, but it wasn't enough, nowhere near strong enough, to wash away her insidious past that would never be banished. Simon's question had opened the floodgates she'd kept locked for so long. She slithered to the floor of the shower, wrapped her arms around her knees, and tried to fight off the images falling about her.

★　★　★

At dawn a servant tiptoes into her room bearing a jug of iced fruit juice, fruit and biscuits, but she can't eat, she feels too sick. In the centre of the tray, an ornate silver lid covers a silver platter. Lifting the lid she finds a costly emerald necklace. Leaving it there, she swallows two aspirins, takes the ice out of the juice and wraps it in a cloth. She lies on the bed, holding the cool cloth on her forehead. Amazingly, by lunchtime, she feels better and even slightly hungry.

'Why don't you make the best of the situation?' Omar says days later, when he shows her around his acres of amazing gardens. 'You are rich. You have a lovely home here and extensive properties and investments all over the world. You can have anything you want . . . anything in the world.'

'Except my freedom.'

'That will come. Be patient.'

As soon as Omar learns that she is pregnant the nightly visits cease and she assumes that it was the child that he wanted.

As the days pass she feels increasingly repelled by the alien that has invaded her womb. She imagines a tiny Omar, complete with a gold tooth, a long nose and greasy hair, curled up within her. She does her best to starve this monstrosity by starving herself. At times she contemplates suicide. The alien seems to sense that it's unwelcome, and it causes the minimum of trouble. No morning sickness, no cravings and the only discomfort she feels is constant back pain as her pregnancy advances.

After nine hours of labour, the alien emerges at dawn, opens its mouth and screams.

'I hate you,' Bela mutters, as she falls into an exhausted sleep.

All that day and most of the night, the doctors and the nurses wait for Bela to accept her child. Her breasts are so swollen the pain is almost unbearable, but she refuses to feed or even to touch the baby. Eventually they give up and the doctor sends a servant to the pharmacist for a bottle and formula. The baby is allergic to milk and it throws up after every feed. Feverish mutterings and whisperings take place on the balcony outside her bedroom. Omar has called in another specialist.

In the night Bela wakes to frenetic wails. The baby has been placed in a cot beside her bed. The nerve-wracking cries go on and on until she thinks she'll go mad. Eventually she runs to the servants' quarters and is appalled to hear that her nurses have been sacked.

'The master wanted a boy. He's not interested in a girl,' the housekeeper tells her.

A girl! She can't get to grips with this unexpected situation. Hurrying back to the bedroom, she picks up the tiny bundle of white linen. How silly of them to wrap a baby so tightly. She unwinds the linen until a tiny, ivory body is revealed. How perfect she is. Bela gasps at the minute fingernails, the long eyelashes, and the soft black hair. When the baby opens her eyes, she sees her mother's eyes, huge and amber like a newborn doe. She is so beautiful and so vulnerable. As she presses the tiny mouth to her nipple, the baby begins to suck vigorously and she feels bonded forever to this tiny infant. Her daughter! Her very own! Hers to cherish.

Omar isn't a cruel man, she learns, but he is unable to step outside the mores and traditions of his culture. He can't understand her. Perhaps if he could, they might reach out to each other. For the sake of her child, she decides to try.

★   ★   ★

Simon was day-dreaming as he waited for Bela. Suddenly she emerged and stood naked and aggressive in the doorway.

'My daughter died and it was my fault. It's the worse thing that ever happened to me. It's

245

something I have to live with. Maybe one day I'll tell you, but right now I never want to talk about it again. That was why I left Kashmir.'

Simon, who had never known she'd been to Kashmir, had the sense to keep quiet.

29

Gratefully astonished that someone like Bela could love him, Simon moved into a kind of living that was like nothing he had ever encountered. His weekdays were more like Kafka nightmares than real life as he battled for hours with robot telephone connections and finally, in desperation, tramped all over London, to the Union, to his lawyer, and another lawyer for a second opinion to find out whether or not he should sue, to the Minister of Agriculture, to his MP and finally to the callous desks of innumerable civil servants, only to return to an empty and depressing home.

By contrast, his weekends were enchantingly unreal. Bela usually arrived on a Friday afternoon and stayed until late on Sunday night and the two of them hid from the real world and guarded their happiness as ferociously as Cerberus guarded Hades. Yet no amount of persuasion could induce her to see him on weekdays. She worked all hours, she explained. Likewise, she never spoke about her family. He knew nothing about her working life, or her childhood and marriage, and she was so secretive about her past. When he pressed her, she fobbed him off by telling him she was a very private person. And so the weeks passed, bringing an ever-deepening sense of unreality to Simon's world which had changed irrevocably.

'Are you winning?' Bela asked, when she arrived one lovely evening late in June.

'Of course,' he lied. 'But I've come to the conclusion that civil servants are spawned by aliens from a hostile planet. They aim to destroy our race and replace us with their merciless androids ... reared on red tape and pro- grammed to drive mere humans utterly crazy.'

'Then I'm an android?'

'You have feelings. You're the aberration that could defeat their entire crusade.'

'And you ... what are you?'

'I'm a middle-aged man searching for passion, longing for another chance at youth and hurting because I was unable to make my wife happy.'

'Do you still love your wife?'

'Yes, but I never truly lusted after her. That was the problem. It was unfair of me to marry her. At the time, my feelings were tied up with someone who had left me. Now that really is a no-go area, so don't ask.'

'Ancient secrets! You're a walking mausoleum. Let them out. It's better for you.'

'Who's talking? One day perhaps.'

Later that night, Simon grilled steak while Bela made a salad and they sat by the blazing wood fire listening to music and drinking wine, but Simon unwittingly drifted into a state of melancholy. His world had fallen about his ears and he found himself in a strange and unfamiliar place where none of his values applied. Traditions were being trashed as rapidly and scornfully as the Royals dumped their gifts.

Momentarily Bela's lips drifted over his and he pulled himself together. Foolish to be sad. The truth was, fate was giving him another chance.

Time speeded up when Bela was here. Hardly had she arrived, than it was time for her to leave. Once again he was standing on the porch watching her car . . . a flash of red between the trees . . . zoom along the main road towards the village. He longed to put a stop to this. Bela should move in. They'd both be happier, but he was waiting for her to broach the subject.

★   ★   ★

Bela was enduring her Sunday night willies as she drove home. As usual, the house was dark and quiet when she got back. The Puris were tucked up together in their queen-sized bed, and she was alone and missing Simon. Tonight she felt particularly desolate for there was no one to help her bear her memories. Earlier that afternoon, Simon had mentioned marriage and she'd had to hide her expression of utter desolation. It was unbelievable how this one word had the power to open her own personal can of worms.

If only she had given in and made the most of the marriage her father had arranged for her. But Bela was honest enough to realise that she never could have allowed her daughter to experience the same abuse.

Of course, Omar had tricked her. The new

doctor was a psychiatrist and his ploy had worked. From that time on, the nannies called her 'Tiger Mother', for they never got to hold her baby, whom she had named Salma, meaning peaceful. The cot remained where they had placed it, right beside her bed. It was a joy to wake each morning to the sound of Salma gurgling and cooing. She seldom cried and she was so beautiful.

Eventually Bela gave up trying to sleep and switched on the light. She pulled out the old, forbidden photo album, which she kept hidden in a locked suitcase. This was madness, she told herself, but she couldn't resist opening it.

Never was there a lovelier baby. There was Salma taking her first bath and her first trip into the garden in her expensive English pram. She recalled how she had fought Omar to get her child out of the long, embroidered silk gowns and shawls and into rompers. When Omar tried to hold Salma, she snatched her away.

'She's my daughter, too,' he had said, looking miserable.

'Wait a bit. She's too vulnerable. You don't know how to hold her properly,' she snapped at him.

Omar bought the most expensive camera he could obtain and took hundreds of pictures, scanning them onto his computer and sending them to everyone he knew. Album after album were filled, labelled and filed. Omar couldn't do enough for his daughter.

By the time Salma reached her first birthday, Bela was free to come and go as she liked. For her child's sake, she had decided to make the best of her life. She tried to make a friend of Omar and on the whole she succeeded. They entertained, took holidays, made mutual friends and Bela began to study by correspondence for her Master's degree. A governess was employed to teach Salma basic skills because Omar could not allow his daughter to attend the local primary school. Only the nights were dreaded because Bela could never overcome her abhorrence at having sex with a man whom she neither loved nor found attractive. The truth was Omar repulsed her, perhaps because he was obsessed with his own well-being. He always had to have his own way ... which led to their most damaging confrontation.

There was a heatwave, fans and air-conditioning were blasting cool air at them, but Omar seemed distracted during lunch. He snapped at Salma for singing at the table, which seemed unfair to Bela.

'Why did you do that?' she demanded, when Salma had been led sobbing to the nursery by Nanny.

'We have relatives coming to stay. They're arriving next month and I want Salma's manners to be absolutely perfect.' He looked a little guilty, she thought.

'At four?'

'Of course, at four. They will be bringing their son, Adam, who is six, so Salma will have someone to play with. Their family are very wealthy and they have excellent government connections.' He shot a calculating glance her

251

way. 'Salma and Adam are to be betrothed. It will be a most advantageous match for both families.'

Bela had gone very cold and very quiet. So this was the price of apathy. Her daughter was to go through the same grief and pain that she had endured.

'I don't think so,' she said in a cold, hard voice. 'I shall do all that I can to prevent this betrothal.'

'Don't waste your time,' Omar said, with a sarcastic gleam in his eyes.

★　★　★

The following afternoon, Bela instructed her driver to take her to Srinagar for shopping. She took time off to visit the British Embassy with her daughter.

Mrs Ogilvie-Newton, who ran passport control, was sympathetic but firm.

She sighed. 'I help so many British-born women trapped here to escape and return to Britain, but I can only do this before they are married. In your case, particularly with your child, it's out of the question. You probably noticed that your surveillance was lifted after your child was born.'

'Well, yes.'

'For the simple reason that you can't get your daughter on to your passport without your husband's written permission.'

'A letter?' Bela asked hopefully.

'If it were signed by him in front of a

magistrate . . . ' She gazed compassionately at Bela. 'So while I am able to replace your passport, I cannot put your daughter on it. That's the law here. I'm so sorry.'

So she'd have to find another way, Bela decided as they hurried back to the car.

★   ★   ★

There was no limit to the amount Bela could spend, but she never had any cash. She paid for her purchases with a credit card which enabled her to cash small sums only. She began to buy expensive jewellery, which she sold, hiding the money, while she made discreet inquiries about entering Britain with a forged passport. It didn't take long to find the right contacts.

The night before Salma was to be betrothed, Bela packed a suitcase of travel requirements and mother and daughter left their home while Omar was out. They spent the night in hiding in the poor quarter of the neighbouring town of Mendhar, in their guide's house. That night they were driven by car across the border into Pakistan, to Rawalpindi, and from there they climbed the steep, winding road to the Kyber Pass and into Afghanistan, a journey of frustrating delays and breakdowns which took them four days. By the time they reached Kabul, Salma was running a high temperature and refusing to eat. Bela called the doctor who called the ambulance and Salma was rushed to an isolation ward in the fever hospital. 'Cholera and yellow fever,' the doctor told her. 'It will take weeks for her to recover.' By evening Salma was in a coma.

The child woke in the morning and cried for her father, so Bela put aside her fears and pride and called Omar who flew over. For the next seven days, Omar hardly left his daughter's bedside. Top specialists were called in as Omar impressed on the hospital staff that money was no object.

Eventually the cholera was defeated, but the yellow fever was a new mutation and highly resistant to antibiotics. Salma died in hospital a week later and on the same day, Omar informed Bela that their marriage was over. He never wanted to see her again.

She considered herself fortunate to obtain a post at Kabul University teaching English until it became too dangerous for foreigners to remain there. She had never once stopped grieving and she knew she never would.

Hugging her album, Bela whispered to her daughter: 'You're so beautiful, my darling. I miss you so much.' Then she curled up under the duvet and tried to sleep.

30

Greed is a wobble of fat. Greed is an incurable virus that turns Homo Sapiens into Homo Degradatus. Greed can crash the stock market, declare war, demolish forests, kill the whales and vaporize the ozone. Greed had got under her skin, Ana realised, as she raced sullenly among the six tables in her care, balancing plates of spaghetti, noodles, rissoles, roasts, salads, and watching her clientele putting it away with horrendous speed and total lack of finesse.

One couple, in particular, made her feel squeamish. The woman, squat and coarse-featured, flashed her showy jewellery. Her black satin coat, flung over the back of her chair, sported a fur collar of unknown origin. She and her hard-eyed, over-weight companion, had moved through the menu: oysters, *foie gras*, from a force-fed goose, a large fillet of endangered cod, veal (the poor creature, deprived of sunlight and movement and soon of life itself), and now these guzzlers were well into their second helping of fresh strawberries and their third bottle of wine.

This was no job for a vegetarian, Ana decided. She'd have to leave.

Just what was that fur? Hurrying to them with a glass of iced water, she leaned over the coat. Just as she'd thought, it was dog fur. A sheep-dog by the look of things. She was

255

overcome with remorse. How could mankind slaughter their best friends? She tripped and the water shot over the woman's companion, running down his face and arms, dribbling into his strawberries and cream.

'You clumsy bitch. What's the matter with you?' He mopped up with a serviette. 'Every time I look up you're staring at us. It's like being in the bloody zoo.'

'You act like you're in the bloody zoo,' she screamed in total silence.

'Bring another . . . oh . . . and more cream. And while you're at it, bring the coffee.'

She rushed to the back and stood shuddering, with her hands over her face, feeling totally humiliated because she and they shared the same species.

'What's the matter?' the manager asked.

'People. That's what's the matter. I'd better take them their coffee and cream.'

She hurried back, but they had left without paying. Running outside, she saw that the curbside was empty. A black car had been parked there only moments ago? *Table Six*, she told the manager. 'They ate for six and left in a hurry. I was getting their coffee at the time. You saw me there.'

'You know rules. Their bill comes off your wages. Better keep a look out next time.'

Sod them and sod you! 'I quit,' she said.

It was that simple. No more waiting until past midnight for clients to finish gobbling, no more swollen feet, no more leftovers to scrape into the bin. And why? Because she could always depend on Dad to help her out. Other girls weren't so lucky, were they. But she still had her dismal room with the lumpy bed where the smell of baked beans wafted in passageways and kids snivelled their endless laments. Par for the course!

She went home, took out her PC and wrote a piece about the couple. It wasn't as funny as she'd intended. Funny and she were not on the same wavelength, it seemed. The following morning she took her article to the editor of the local rag and asked for a job. Her luck was in, the editor, with his earnest, cocker spaniel eyes, large ears and balding pate, took a shine to her.

'No. Can't use this,' he said. 'It's not interesting and the fall guys are our readers. Pick on someone interesting. There's a new vicar in Temple Minnis. I've heard the locals call him the *Wicca*. There might be something there. Be as scathing as you like. You got folks to stay with, Ana?'

'Sort of . . . '

'What sort of an answer is that?'

She shrugged.

'You need a degree for this profession, else you'll always be on the outside, like me. I don't care. I own this rag, but you should aim for something better.'

Ana came to a sudden decision. 'I have a place at London University, starting next month, but I'm not sure I'll take it up. I need to earn cash writing the odd article.'

'If your stuff's any good you'll find I'm a steady buyer.'

'Listen. My Dad's going through a bad patch. They culled all his livestock. He'll be compensated, of course, but it won't be enough. Not near enough. I had this place offered me, but I reckoned I'd be a burden to Dad. I haven't been able to make up my mind.'

'Make him proud. Take up the place. You can always pay him back later.'

It was beginning to look like she'd do that after all. Ana was on a high as she went to tell Dad.

31

Summer wouldn't win any rosettes this time round, Simon reckoned. June had been cold, damp and disappointing and so far July had been almost as bad. The crops and the grass grew tall and strong in the intermittent drizzle and warm haze and without livestock grazing over the land, masses of wild flowers were taking over.

On Saturday the weather cleared and temperatures rose to the late twenties, so Bela and Simon swam in the dam and climbed up to the higher woods where the big cat still lurked and later picnicked in the orchard. They made love under the trees and slept in each other's arms, waking in time to fetch the young animals from the field. Bela mixed the feed for the calves and laughed as she tried to give each their fair share, hauling the stronger calf back, her arms around his neck, her feet dug into the cobbles.

'Wow! Ferdinand junior is as strong as an ox. Oops! What have I said?' She slipped and landed on her back and the calf dived into the bucket. 'Is there a difference between an ox and a bull?' she asked when she'd picked herself up and got a firm hold on him.

'Testicles.'

She looked stricken.

'Ferdinand is keeping his.'

'I'm glad. I love yours. I love to cradle them in my hand when you're sleeping. I've never loved like this before. My mind, my body and my emotions have become completely intertwined because each part of me loves you in its own way.'

Simon watched and wondered. He seemed to have undergone a personality change. Now he was lovable, whereas before he had been hateful, he was brimful of bright ideas, but before he'd been boring, he was sexy and virile, but before he'd been a well-trained eunuch. He loved what he had, but he wasn't quite sure how to hang in there.

★   ★   ★

At the stroke of six o'clock, Bela stopped whatever she was doing, put on an apron and prepared dinner in Redhill's gorgeous kitchen. This was happy time. Suddenly she was all-woman, scouring pots, putting flowers in a vase on the windowsill, making pastry, grilling steak, or cooking some exotic Kashmiri curry which he loved.

This kitchen . . . it's just amazing . . . Laura must miss it so badly,' she said.

'Other than creating it, she seldom came here.'

'What a shame. I'm so sorry, Simon.'

'The funny thing is,' he said, folding her in his arms. 'You mean it. You truly are sorry, and if you could, you would make it all come right for me, even with Laura.'

'It stands to reason that if I love you, I want you to be happy, which is just as well, because she'll want to come back.'

'I saw my lawyer on Wednesday. He's started divorce proceedings. I'll tell Laura when she next visits. She's in Paris.'

'So it's over? Really finished? Are you sure?'

'Yes, I'm sure. It's not only for my sake. I've been thinking a good deal about . . . well, what happened. Laura must have been very unhappy. She's insecure, otherwise she would have left long ago. I have to think about us, too. We have to get out more together. How about dinner at Harry's Place? I'll introduce you to my friends. It's time they realised we're a unit.'

'Are we?'

'I'm pretty sure that we are? How do you feel?'

'I'm very happy, but I'm not a child anymore. I know that there are good times and bad times. This is one of the highs of my life. You're all that I ever longed for . . . sensitive, kind, clever, but sexy, too. But no one can expect permanence? Take what comes, grasp the happiness, endure the sadness. Nothing ever lasts and it's best to be prepared.'

Simon hugged her with unusual force. 'This is going to last.' His voice was stern and uncompromising, as if he could hold back change with the power of his will.

★ ★ ★

It should have been a perfect evening. It had all the trappings to make it so. Bela had rushed home to change and returned looking amazingly lovely in a light grey silk designer dress, a pearl necklace, matching drop earrings, and silver

261

strap sandals. Her eyes sparkled and her dark hair shone in the light as it fell about her shoulders. She was brimful of happy anticipation, like a kid at a party, but her mood crumpled at the stir she caused when she walked in. Heads turned, two perfect strangers, both male, called out to her and the women's eyes glinted with malice.

'What's upset you, Bela,' Simon grumbled as they sat down.

'Those people. Couldn't you just sense their hostility? Vibes like daggers. My God, they looked as if they'd like to kill me.'

'Quite honestly you look superb and it's not just the dress. Surely you know that you're a very attractive woman, Bela, and you look classy. And clever,' he added as an afterthought. 'I don't know what the hell you're doing with me, and right now those leering men are probably saying much the same. If you don't want to cause a stir, plait your hair, wear jeans which make your bum stick out, and absolutely no makeup. If you set out to look attractive, don't moan when you attract. It's that simple. That dress . . . tell me . . . did you rob a bank or something?'

She began to laugh quietly. 'To you, everything's simple. It's an old dress. I told you I was married, but I didn't mention that my husband was immensely wealthy.'

'And you left him?'

'So you think money's important?'

'Specially to those who don't have any.'

He had reserved a candlelit table in an alcove overlooking the lake. The evening scene was idyllic, birds were swooping and twittering as they took up their nightly roosts, bats were whirling after gnats, swans glided over the still water.

The mood was shattered as Harry's new Latin-American band started to play. Why hadn't the bastard warned him?

'Oh good,' Bela said. 'I love dancing.'

Simon's stomach lurched. At least he could samba, although he hadn't tried since his bachelor days. Harry arrived and introduced himself, his brown eyes glinting with curiosity, as he took their order. Then he hung about relating the latest gossip.

'So where are you from, Bela? What's your nationality?' he pressed her, with as much finesse as a soccer hooligan.

'I'm English,' she said, clearly nettled.

'But I mean, what are your roots?'

'English,' she said in a cold, hard voice. 'What is this . . . some kind of an inquisition, Harry? Lay off.'

Harry was as thick-skinned as a buffalo. 'You could be Spanish,' he said. 'Or Portuguese, or possibly Iranian. And then, of course, South American is another strong possibility.'

'Buzz off, Harry,' Simon said good-naturedly, determined that none of his friends would get him down. 'We're about to dance. Come on Bela.'

They threaded their way through the tables to the dance floor, but at that moment, the music changed to something distinctly Arabian with its haunting minor chords and rhythmic beat. Bela began to writhe, subtly and tastefully, which made her all the more provocative, while her hands shimmered and coiled and behaved like angry cobras. How the hell did he get into this fix? Perhaps if he jigged around? Bela could dance all night, that was obvious, and he wasn't aiming to be the first to quit. After an hour, every step made him whimper. Thankful that Bela couldn't hear his rasping breath above the racket the band was making, he gyrated on and on, wondering if his hips were dislocated?

Eventually Bela noticed his misery and they returned to the table, but his relief was soon shattered.

David arrived, pulled out a chair and sat, waiting to be introduced.

'Jesus, how d'you do it, Simon. An old farmhand like you. You go for beauty and you get them, too. That's what's so amazing. Even when we were students. What was her name? Anabelle . . . ? Agnes . . . ? Angela . . . ? She belonged in Hollywood.'

'Shut up, David. You're being offensive.'

He turned to Bela for support. 'Am I?'

'Not at all,' she said, pale-faced and icy.

'You should see his wife . . . Oh Lord! Now I have put my foot into it.'

'What exactly are you trying to do, David? Warn Bela off? Laura and I . . . well . . . we've split and Bela knows that. Bela and I . . . ' He'd been about to say we're just good friends, but she reached across the table and clasped David's hand.

'Tell me about Angela,' she said.

264

That seemed to stun David. Suddenly serious, he stood up. 'Simon's a great guy. Good luck.' Then he had the sense to leave.

'Don't worry about him. He's drunk,' Simon said. 'He means no harm.'

Meli drifted by and hovered until Simon, who was trying to keep a cool head, introduced the two women.

'My God, you fucked up with the dancing,' she muttered to Simon. 'I sweated for you.'

'I can samba, but the bastards switched their music just as we got there.'

'He's out of practice,' Bela said stoutly.

'Three down, three to go,' Meli said slyly. 'And then, of course, there's Ana. Enjoy yourselves!'

After that they were left in peace, but the evening was spoilt. Bela was moody and unresponsive. They left right after dinner.

32

They went to sleep without making love and that was unusual enough to worry Simon. Little wonder Bela was depressed by his friends' incredible lack of tact, he reasoned. Of course, it was deliberate on their part. Analysing the evening, it seemed to be David who had caused the most damage. Bela had been happy until he joined them. She had shrugged off Harry's insidious probing, and she seemed to like Meli and Shirley, but David had tossed her into a deep depression. Perhaps she felt put out by David's reference to the past. He was a silly bugger who didn't understand women at all. No wonder Meli had left him. What a fool to tell Bela how lovely Angela had been. Could she be jealous? Surely not. It had ended so long ago. Another woman might have asked: 'Whom do you love the most?' But not Bela. She was far too introverted to reveal such an obvious insecurity.

The truth was, he loved Bela most of all, yet he had never stopped loving Angela. But his memories had faded, so that nowadays his feelings for Bela were mingled with memories of Angela, as if the two women in his life were rolled into one.

This was foolish, Simon decided. He had only one photograph of Angela which was hidden in an album of snaps from his student days. He got up quietly, went back to the bedroom he had shared with Laura, and switched on the bedside light to retrieve the album from under his shirts. He'd been right, he decided, studying her youthful features. There was no resemblance between the two women.

At nineteen Angela had been outstandingly lovely . . . tall, willowy and graceful, with a lovely smile and huge, slanting eyes. He'd been obsessed with her and jealous to the point of madness. In those days, inter-racial affairs were frowned upon and both of them had endured a good deal of flack from their friends and family, although, as far as he knew, Angela's relatives were in Kashmir.

Her name wasn't Angela at all, but Anjana, a lovely name which he preferred, but Angela had been so intent on anglicising herself. They had planned to marry, but Father had threatened to break the trust and disinherit him if he brought an Indian bride to Redhill. He never told Angela this, merely that he couldn't afford to marry until he took over the farm. So they waited, and then she simply left. He had only given up searching for her when the Missing Persons' Agency traced her to her wedding, in Kashmir. He was left with unbearable grief, his loss and a massive bill to pay off by working nights.

An image of Angela's face, so calm and lovely floated out of the night of its own volition. Her sari was torn revealing her lustrous skin, now pallid and almost grey, with blue and purple patches starting up like weals on her bare breasts and shoulders. He had tried to fight off the ambulance men who were intent on closing her eyes and carrying her away. Then Harry and David dragged him weeping back to the hotel. But why was he punishing himself? Thrusting the album under his clothes, Simon blundered back to bed.

In the night, Bela stirred and cried out in a foreign language, waking him. It was cold despite the day's heat. He pulled the duvet over her naked breasts, tucking it around her shoulders. Unable to sleep, he watched the moving patterns of moonlight on the wall and thought about the evening, remembering Melissa and her blanched disapproval. Harry's eyebrows had taken off like startled ravens. Even Shirley had looked devastated when she saw how young Bela was.

'You bastards are all the same,' she had muttered, when he paid at the bar. It was common knowledge that Harry was screwing his PA and Shirls was turning into a caricature of a dumped wife.

Simon was acutely aware that he'd blundered against the invisible silken web that maintained the social order of the middleclass locals. He might even have broken a few strands, but what the hell did it matter?

* * *

'It's Sunday,' Simon said grudgingly, early the following morning. 'Sarah's off, so I must feed the fowls. There's a few other things to attend to.'

'I'll help you.'

'Best not,' he said 'You'll get wet and muddy.'

268

'My boots are here.'

They walked down the farm road in the mist towards the yard. A low, whitewashed wall lined the gravel track and beyond stood a thick, old hedge of hawthorn and dogwood. Behind the yard, the fields were bright with oxeye daisies, thistles, marigolds, goldenrod and wild mignonette. The yard was clean and empty and silence hung around them like a shroud. Then his mare stamped and whinnied, waking the lambs who set up a chorus for their next feed and the calves joined in.

'Daunty hasn't been ridden much lately. It's time I got back into a routine.' Empty words, he thought, since he knew that he could not. At least, not yet.

'How long will it take before you receive compensation?' Bela asked, as he fed Daunty.

'Not long now. The problem is, I don't feel like starting again. It happened once before and it took me years to recover.'

'I share your life, I feel I have a right to know.'

'It's a boring story.'

'How shall I get to know you with all these hidden secrets?'

Simon refilled the water trough and squatted in the straw beside Bela. With a good deal of prompting he produced the bare bones of their ancient trauma.

'Father hated farming, so without telling me, or anyone, he persuaded the trustees to let him sell the estate to an industrialist who wanted to manufacture semiconductors. I got hold of a good lawyer, but nothing seemed to be able to save us.'

'Us?'

'Basically the locals.'

'So who were they?'

'What does it matter?'

She scowled at him.

'David, of course. Harry and Shirley, David and Meli, who weren't together in those days, Gordon and I. And of course every new householder in Temple Minnis. We all faced financial loss and possible ruin.' He tried, but failed, to keep the anger out of his voice. 'We roped in students and wild life experts. To my surprise they found five endangered species breeding on Redhill. Then we brought in the British Heritage who tried to prevent our listed homestead from being destroyed. Petitions were signed, meetings were held, the media came out on our side. Finally it seemed that we had won, but we were wrong. Politics scored.'

'And then?'

'The Council gave the go-ahead, the papers were ready to sign, but at the eleventh hour I managed to persuade Father to come to his senses and sell Redhill to me. Father was in a hurry to leave, so he accepted fifty per cent of the value of the land. We applied for a mortgage and Redhill was transferred into my name. But meantime Father, on the expectation of selling the entire estate, had sold the farming implements and sent all of our stock to the abattoirs. He pocketed that cash, too. My mother was in hospital suffering from shock and Ana was about to be born. I couldn't think how to survive. Then Tom, my grandfather, who had lived on the farm with Pat and Mae, handed over his savings. His cash enabled me to restock. That's the story.'

But that wasn't all of it. He fell silent. Lost in the past, he had almost forgotten Bela was there.

'Were you talking about George Irving?' Bela asked.

He was surprised that she knew of him.

'Yes, that's right. Irving managed to buy land being sold off by the Church, beyond the railway line, so finally he went ahead with his semiconductor plant, and his housing estate, but it was sufficiently far away not to damage local property prices and of course it didn't affect Redhill at all.'

'And who was this beautiful woman David mentioned. This Anabelle . . . Agnes . . . or Angela . . . What was her name?'

'Someone who died.'

'You must tell me about her.'

'No. Don't ask. Don't be cruel.'

Bela, who was strangely silent for the rest of the day, left much earlier than usual, and Simon, who was missing her badly, wondered where he'd gone wrong. What could have upset Bela so badly? She'd been silent and thoughtful for most of the day. He'd loved only three women in his life. Bela was the third and he knew that he loved her the most.

He felt he was cursed with an inability to make the women in his life happy. With difficulty he restrained himself from going after her.

271

As Bela drove home she was remembering the night she returned from Europe with the rescued children hidden in her camper. She was taking a short cut to the motorway when she began to nod over the wheel. She'd never make Manchester, she realised with a jolt. She had to find somewhere to sleep. It was then that she saw an open gate and a track leading into a wood. It looked safe and private, so she pulled off the road and drove until the track reached a river. There was a glade, a rushing river and a pile of rotting wood for a fire. She decided to camp there for the night and feed the children with something better than the sandwiches they'd had to make do with on their long journey from Kabul.

How shocked she had been when Simon had told her his name.

She'd always treasured his name, ever since that awful night when Mama died, for it was Simon who had tried to save her mother, she realised later. No one had noticed the eight-year-old girl getting in the way. Simon had been her hero ever since. Yet lately an idea had taken hold . . . a terrible suspicion that someone had wanted to kill her father, but Mother had died instead.

Not Simon. Surely not Simon. The woman Simon had loved all those years ago couldn't possibly have been her mother. She thought about it while she parked her car outside the Puri's house.

Mother was always at home. She had no interests other than her family. Every morning she drove Bela to school. Lunchtime she was waiting to fetch her home. Mama spent her afternoons helping her with her homework and later they would go out for a walk or go shopping together. Nights were usually spent at home, but if they went out, they usually took Bela with them. No, she was being absurd. Her mother was devoted to her family and they were so happy until she died. And after all, she wasn't the only woman who died in 1985.

Had Simon ever met her mother, she wondered. And if not, what heroic impulse had led him to plunge into icy, dark water and risk his life for a stranger? But Simon was like that. She wondered what he would say if he knew that she was the daughter of the woman he had tried to save, and that he had always been her hero.

33

Bela spent a restless, confused night, dozing occasionally only to dream of snow and ice and black water closing over their car and her mother's face, as white as the snow, as they lifted her out of the boat and covered her with a blanket.

At four a.m. she sat up and switched on her bedside light. 'Walk away from it,' she said aloud. 'You've had enough sorrow. It's so simple. You just walk away.'

But it wasn't that easy. When she got up to make a cup of tea, her mind was so full of muddled facts and images that she burned herself with boiling water.

David had said: 'What was her name . . . Anabelle . . . Agnes . . . Angela? She belonged in Hollywood.' Her mother had been beautiful, too. The implications frightened her. She was unwilling to delve further into her mother's secrets. But how could she possibly face Simon again?

All this horror and sadness had been dead and buried in the recesses of her mind for years. It was Simon's fault, she reasoned. He had opened her own personal can of worms. Once again her mind was veering away from the real problem . . . there was something wrong. She'd always known that. Something vital that she had missed, yet she couldn't put her finger on. It was something that she had to remember.

* ★ ★ ★

Childhood memories are always tainted by imagination and after so many years, it was hard to distinguish between real and imagined events, but Bela had to know what happened the evening her mother died. After a restless night spent trying to unravel her confused images, she took time off from her studies to drive to the editorial offices of their local newspaper and go through their files. She found what she was looking for on page three, dated December 12, 1985.

Police are investigating the tragic death of Mrs Anjana Irving who drowned when the car she was driving crashed through ice into a lake beside a Temple Minnis hotel, known as Harry's Place.

George Irving, an industrialist, accompanied by his wife and daughter, were visiting Temple Minnis in order to finalise the purchase of Redhill Farm. This estate has recently been re-zoned to enable a consortium of foreign investors to erect a plant to manufacture semiconductors, plus high-density living accommodation for up to 1,000 employees. The deal was cancelled following the death of Mrs Irving.

Local hero, Simon Shepherd, who farms at Redhill, saw the car moving on to the ice and raced towards the driver shouting a warning, but was unable to make himself heard. When the car plunged through the ice, he dived into the water and was able to force the door open. He brought the unconscious woman to the bank, where mouth-to-mouth resuscitation failed to revive her. She was pronounced dead on arrival at the hospital.

Mr Shepherd is in hospital recuperating from pneumonia and shock.

After all these years, Bela could still smell her mother's perfume and the swanky leather of her father's new Jaguar. She was trembling with anticipation at accompanying her parents for her first formal dinner wearing her new blue dress with frills and a beautiful, white fun-fur coat with a hood. She felt like a princess.

It had snowed for days and the streetlights, reflecting on fields and trees, transformed the world to a strange, snowy twilight, although the sky was dark.

Papa, who was driving, was cursing softly because they were late. Mama, as lovely as ever in her blue silk sari and ermine coat, reached out and squeezed his hand.

'They need us more than we need them, George. Relax. It's a bad night and they'll understand.'

Bela leaned forward to touch Mama's hair that shone and sparkled in the lights as it hung over her shoulders.

'Sit back and fasten your seat belt like a good girl,' Father said.

She obeyed sulkily, feeling excluded. Fumbling around for her new puppet, she fitted it on her hand and wiggled her fingers. Soon she was lost in a world of make-believe.

There was a sudden sharp bend in the road. The car skidded and landed in a bank of snow with a dull thump. Father reversed, but the wheels skidded on black ice.

'Damn!'

Bela opened the door, but shut it quickly when Mama shouted at her. She watched her father get out and try to push the car out of the snow. There was a muffled exclamation. He gripped his back and leaned over the bonnet.

'Shit! My back's gone again.' He straightened up, groaning, as Mama helped him into the car.

'I'd better walk back to that house we passed and ask to use their phone,' her mother said. 'The AA will be here in no time. Will you be all right? Should we cancel the meeting?'

'No. Of course not.'

'Give me your card. They'll want the number.'

'I want to come, Mama,' Bela pestered her mother repeatedly.

'All right, but don't fall. It's slippery.'

Mama always gave in.

They reached the farmhouse, where an old woman gave her sweets and admired her dress while her mother called the AA. Then she'd made another call to say that they'd be late. 'My husband has hurt his back trying to push the car out of a snow drift,' she heard Mama explaining. 'I'll be driving, which will take a little longer.'

They hurried back to the car. The AA arrived and towed them out of the snow and soon they were driving past the village shops towards the hotel.

'What a pretty place,' her mother said. 'We must come here sometimes, Bela.' She drove up the hill and braked in the hotel driveway.

Her father sat up groaning.

'My damned back has never come right since the skiing,' he muttered as he got out of the car. 'I'll go and apologise while you park. Come along, Bela.'

Bela scrambled out of the back and glanced around. It was so cold. Snow covered the driveway, the hedges and weighed down the branches of the trees. The U-shaped road curved around a large white expanse ringed with trees, past the hotel, which was glittering with fairy lights. The parking sign, standing tall at the edge of a flat, snowy field, was painted white with black letters and it pointed straight ahead.

Several men were waiting on the steps. Gripping her hand, her father hurried towards them. Bela dawdled, gazing over her shoulder, watching her mother drive slowly forward. The snow seemed to crackle and groan. Couldn't Mama hear it? She started to tug her father's hand as the car slithered and skidded in the strangest manner. Cracks like gunshots echoed around.

And then . . .

Everything seemed to be happened at once. Her father let go of her hand and limped down the driveway calling: 'Anjana, Anjana' over and over. People were running out of the hotel. There were shouts. A woman screamed. People were pushing against her. She fell and when she picked herself up she saw that her knee was bleeding and her coat was covered in mud and snow. Papa would be cross. Slowly she followed the crowd to the field, which wasn't a field at all, for there was a large jagged tear in the snow. She could see black water rippling as it reflected the coloured fairy lights. Their car was nowhere to be seen.

She needed to find her mother who always took her side, so she found a shadowy corner under a bush and stood there waiting. She saw a dark shape loom up through the water. A man waved and shouted. He was holding her mother's coat, but that, too, was dirty and wet. Someone was pushing a small boat out over the ice. They helped him lift the coat and topple it into the boat. The man was hauled in, too. They had to break the ice, to get back to the shore.

Minute by minute her mind recorded every detail. The man who had found Mama's coat was crouched beside the boat crying. She stared at him. She'd never seen a man crying before. The ambulance arrived and parked beside the lake. A policeman caught hold of her hand and tried to pull her away, but she tugged free. She stared in dismay at the blue sari, the long, black hair and the bedraggled fur, as the men picked up her mother and laid her on the stretcher. They covered her with a white plastic sheet.

Then she knew.

That was how the nightmare began and sometimes it seemed that it would never end.

34

'It's your agent on the line, Ms Marlowe. Will you take the call?' The housekeeper sounded anxious.

Melissa's stomach flipped. Two weeks ago she'd given Tracy the first half of the manuscript of the story of Angela Irving's death. So while she'd said no calls, this was one she could never dodge. Tracy seldom phoned nowadays and when she did it was usually bad news.

'Thanks. I'll take it.' Steeling herself, she grabbed the receiver. 'Hello there,' she called bravely.

'Oh hi! Tracy here.'

Even the sound of her agent's voice sent her stomach into a series of acrobatics. They used to be friends, probably still were, but her plummeting career had turned Tracy into a bogeyman. I should have her garroted as a bearer of bad tidings, Meli thought peevishly.

'The publishers have been in touch.' At this point Meli's stomach excelled itself with a double back flip and a lurch into nowhere.

'You there, Melissa?'

'Oh, sure! Fire away.' You're killing me, but who cares.

'Good news. They love it,' she said, in a tone for delivering bad news.

'Oh!' Meli breathed her relief into the receiver. So why aren't you shouting with joy? Don't you know how I've slogged? But that wasn't Tracy's style.

'How much?' Meli was aware that she'd be screwed after having been off the market for so long.

'They said they'll make a good offer, whatever that is.' Tracy sounded doubtful. 'They need time to consider their forward planning and of course we have to remember you've been off the market for a while. They'll come back to us in a week to ten days if things go well.' An impersonal click terminated the conversation.

★ ★ ★

The following Saturday, the drenched and dismal August transformed itself in time for the local cricket match. Most of Temple Minnis turned up at the sports club to enjoy the sunshine, swop gossip, get the low-down on David, take bets on whether or not he knew Meli was screwing that weirdo vicar, see if Laura, just back from Paris, had the guts to show her face and incidentally support their cricket team, too.

David was anxious to squash the rumours. Ignoring the villagers' curious stares, he was stretched out in the long grass, eyes half-closed, propped on his elbow watching Meli, who was sitting cross-legged under a nearby oak tree, gazing intently at her laptop.

'You need some sunshine,' he called loud enough to be heard. 'Come and sit here, darling.'

'You know I can't see the screen in the sun.'

When she flashed a brief smile, it was like

going back a decade, to a younger, sparkling Meli who never caught colds and hadn't seen a doctor since mumps at school. She sat up and stretched, rolling her shoulders in a circular shrug, tossing her hair back, beaming a conspiratorial smile his way before shrinking back to the screen. She'd changed. A new vitality surrounded her. She glowed like a young girl in love. Had she? Or hadn't she? And how could he be sure? Could any spouse ever be sure unless he caught them in *flagrante delicto?* The question had tormented him for days as he tried to trap her into spilling the odd, unwary word.

'Of course I'm in love,' she'd answered evasively when he'd questioned her yesterday. 'In love with life. Who wouldn't be in my position?'

Bitch! It was strange how the cancer had improved when Meli was at death's door. Had the vicar's caducean cock propelled her into submission and remission? A week ago she'd had a film offer for one of her earlier books, written in the days when she was on top. It came out of the blue, but she hadn't asked him to check the contract, or offered him the cash. Lately she only thought about herself.

He flung himself beside her in the shade. 'Still frightening yourself to death?' He fondled her neck, just to show he was on her side nowadays. 'Did you nail the serial killer?'

'I didn't finish that one. I need to do some research. Meantime, I'm on an old novel . . . the one I told you about.'

Meli's words felt like a kick from a mule. He had thought she'd given up on that idea. Would she dare to blurt out a secret which had been successfully hidden for seventeen years?

'How can you make a novel out of that silly business?'

'Well . . . there's an ancient murder and the entire village is affected by it in one way or another. Everyone had a motive. We were all involved. We all lied like crazy, resulting in a verdict of Accidental Death. I'm quite sure that in the dark hours, some of us shiver and shake. As a matter of fact the publishers have accepted it.'

* * *

Unwilling to show his anger, David leaned back in the grass, pretending to snooze. Five minutes later he got up for a pee and ambled back to Gordon. He slid his hip flask out of his pocket and slurped a double tot of badly needed scotch. An enduring state of outrage was keeping every nerve-end working overtime, but he was well aware of the need to display a picture of lazy insouciance as he listened to the occasional thud of bat against ball, the drone of bees around the poppies, distant laughter from the club house, and nearer a hum of conversation from drowsy spectators sprawled around the grassy verge. Except for the magpies' chatter, the sounds were distinctly English.

'Lovely afternoon. Just like old times,' he said.

'Not quite. We own this club nowadays, and much more, but for how long?'

David sat up warily. 'Can't I have a day off

from bloody business, you bastard?'

'I can't, so why should you? Tell me about the Taffies. Did they give you more time?'

'I paid over the cash. Thanks for the loan. The new deadline is November 15, so I have almost three months.'

Gordon was a tight-fisted sod. He'd amassed a fortune built on kick-backs skillfully gleaned from the company, four percent here, six percent there, hidden in the Cayman Islands, David suspected, but except for a couple of instances, he'd been unable to prove it. He fumbled for his flask. He was working up a major sweat again.

'Relax, David. You're as taut as a winch. I've found a way out for you. I need to do a bit more research before I tell you about it. Hang in there and don't look so damned worried. It's bad for business.'

'Tell me more . . . is it short-term or long-term relief?'

'It will haul you clean out of the shit. I'll be in touch as soon as I've gathered all the facts. Everything's going to be all right. Trust me.'

There was a sound of clapping and a boo from Harry as his son was run out.

'Your turn to bat.' Gordon picked up his drink and raised it. 'Good luck!'

'I'm getting past it,' David grumbled, ambling onto the field. As if to prove his point, he was caught out by the first ball.

He wandered back to Gordon.

'Listen, my mate. I've just found out that Meli was dead serious about that damned book she's been taunting us with for years. She's been very

284

sneaky, but evidently it's half finished and the publishers have accepted it.'

'Is she hinting at murder?' Gordon asked, his voice deep and functional. Only his eyes betrayed his rage.

'She won't say. She's damned secretive about it.' David passed his hand over his face in a gesture of anxiety.

'Get hold of it. Let's have a look at it. She might be lying.'

'D'you think I haven't tried. She works on a PC and she's got a password. I can't find out what it is.'

'I'll speak to her. If that fails, I've some equipment that can get around the lack of a password, but it takes time. Tell your house-keeper that I'm designing an extension to the conservatory. Then take Meli out somewhere. I need a few hours.'

'She's going to see her London specialist on Monday. She usually spends the day in London.'

'Good. I'll copy her work onto a disc and print it out at my office. She'll be none the wiser and at least we'll know the worst.'

*   *   *

As soon as Gordon left, David's anxieties returned, so he strolled to the clubhouse and settled on a stool at the bar. Despite Gordon's reassurances, his living nightmare zoomed back. The miners' deadline loomed over him like a death sentence. His latest scam wasn't the whole story, far from it, and the resulting investigation would reveal the short cuts he and Gordon had resorted to when they had to raise cash, back in '85. Meli was opening a can of worms.

You're going to win through, David, he consoled himself. Everything's going to be all right. Trust Gordon. He's always saved you!

He ordered a refill and another. Soon his disaster seemed trivial, but he needed to talk to someone.

'A lesser man might shoot himself with the troubles I've got now, but I trust in my luck. It's never failed me. Never,' he explained to the barman. 'Meli and her damned novel are small fry, compared with the Great Whites that are slowly circling.'

'No kidding! So what's Meli's novel about?' the barman asked.

'Fill it up and I'll tell you the story. It's all about straws. We drew straws you see, and no one ever knew who picked the short straw. To this day, I swear even I don't know, but one of us is a real mean, sneaky bastard. Just listen to this.'

★　★　★

The news that Melissa Marlowe's novel had been accepted by her publishers spread rapidly. David denied telling anyone, but Melissa knew she only had herself to blame since she should have kept her mouth shut. Resentment flashed and crackled like summer lightning through the village, so Meli walled herself up in her office and used her housekeeper as a fire screen.

Gordon was first to breach her firewall. He

bamboozled his way in by telling the old battle-axe that Melissa had called him to measure the proposed extensions to her conservatory.

Melissa was caught off balance, sprawled on a settee, feet up, coffee mug in hand, gazing dreamily at the squirrels in the branches outside the window. She knew that Gordon didn't like her, but the ferocity in his eyes astonished her.

'You're not working. What's going on? Are you ill again?'

'I'm off the social round until the book's finished. How did you get in, Gordon?'

'Silly, arty-crafty nonsense.' Gordon neatly evaded the question. 'From what I hear there's no planning to be done, since you're writing from memory.'

'You've been listening to David.' She matched him scowl for scowl.

'There's a rumour going round that you're writing about Angela's death. I hope you're not.'

'What's it got to do with you?'

'Well are you?'

'Actually, yes.'

Meli met Gordon's gaze unflinchingly and for a few fraught moments they glared at each other.

'So you're claiming that Angela's death wasn't an accident!'

'You'll have to wait and see, like everyone else.'

'You're an arrogant bitch at the best of times, but right now you're being downright silly. Give it up.'

'Good try.' She smiled in the face of his fury

and watching naked dislike gleam in his strange, slanting eyes.

'What if your silly guesses cause a scandal that brings our shares crashing? Do you want to ruin us all? Is that your game?'

'You're boring me, Gordon.'

He swiftly changed tack. 'Murder presupposes a murderer and if you're right, then he'll come after you. So why are you doing this? For Angela? She brought Irving here and she ruined Simon's marriage.'

'Oh, I think you had a hand in that, Gordon.'

White-faced, eyes glittering, Gordon seemed to have turned to stone. Several scary seconds later he moved towards the door. 'You won't get away with this,' he muttered through taut lips. 'Whoever killed Angela Irving will have to stop you from publishing.'

'Are you threatening me? Well, you're the first. Congratulations!' Melissa burst out laughing. 'You should see your face, Gordon. You look like a Japanese mask. Pure fury! Suits you better than that damned silly Peter Pan expression you put on.'

She was still laughing as Gordon ran out of the room.

Humour is just another form of aggression, Meli knew. The tables were turned and she was getting her own back. Not one of those bastards had cared when she was dying, but destruction came in many disguises, she told herself contentedly.

35

Early the following morning, Melissa waved goodbye to Shirley at reception and walked down to the lake. Leaning over a bench, she gazed at nature's magnificent rebirth without regret for once. The day had squirmed out of its cocoon and was flaunting itself in the warm, moist air. All too soon it would take flight, but she was here to stay. To convince herself that it was true, she once again relived Monday's triumph.

Three specialists, looking so serious that her heart missed a beat, were examining the charts and X-rays. Eventually her doctor broke the silence.

'Melissa, my dear. Hm! Well . . . it's a little unusual but the tumour has shrunk. I can't understand this, but you appear to be recovering.' He seemed unwilling to say the words. Strange that he'd had no difficulty pronouncing her death sentence. Unexpectedly he smiled.

'How far has it shrunk?'

'It's disappeared. If you'll look there.' He pointed with his pencil. 'And this is how it was two months ago.'

She frowned as the monstrous shadow that had threatened her life.

'It's unusual to say the least. We've checked and double-checked all previous scans. It was there and growing fast, and now . . . But, my dear, you are looking a picture of health. That should prove something.'

'You seem so shocked.' She wondered if his patients ever got better.

'Well, you had not responded to treatment . . . ' His voice tailed away. He glanced at the others as if for confirmation. 'I don't want to give you false hopes, Melissa, but clearly your cancer is in remission. Of course you must come here for tests at regular intervals. It could remain dormant for years or for the rest of your natural life, or it could return. I can't explain why this has happened.'

'I've been seeing a faith healer.'

The three men gazed pityingly at her. 'The unknown power of the mind,' one of them muttered.

She had returned to the hotel in a state of shock and told no one, in case it was only a dream. Even the sight of Bela dancing with Simon could not diminish her happiness, although it had hurt. Since then she'd been filled with a sense of lasting joy.

She turned and hurried downhill to the village with a jaunty spring to her step.

'Hello, Mr Jennings,' she called to the newsagent.

'Why, Ms Marlowe. It's good to see you looking so well.'

'I'm better.'

'Well I never. What a relief. Mr Fergus must be so happy.'

'So happy,' she echoed.

David didn't know yet because she hadn't told

him. He'd be over the moon, she thought generously.

Benson, the grocer, dropped the box he was carrying onto the pavement and stood plucking his braces like guitar strings. 'You look a treat, Melissa. Just like the old days.'

'I'm better, that's why.'

Time seemed to last a little longer as every villager and his dog passed the time of day.

'The power of prayer, Ms Marlowe,' the grocer's wife called out. 'We've watched you going to church every morning. Just shows, miracles still happen.'

'Yes, indeed.' Melissa giggled when she had hurried past.

She rushed into the church, her usual route, and since it was empty, went straight out through the back door, passing a copse of ash trees to the vicarage.

She rang the bell, but there was no answer. The curtains were still drawn. Clearly the lazy sod was still sleeping.

★　★　★

The doorbell rang. Luze stirred and groaned. He had become prey to aching bones, a stiff neck, creaking joints and sneezing fits. Unused to the damp cold, he liked to sleep naked in bed with the windows open. At night the duvet usually landed on the floor. As he lay there, as unprotected as a newborn baby, the sneaky mist would creep through the window like a fat snake and freeze his bone marrow. He usually woke

291

groaning with pain at the effort of climbing out of bed to recover the duvet. Why didn't he shut the windows? The answer was a mixture of claustrophobia and sheer cussedness.

He glanced at his clock. Eight a.m., who could be ringing his bell at this time of the morning? He was tired, having meditated for half the night. He stretched out to haul the duvet from the floor and rolled himself into it. A dismal drizzle had lasted all day yesterday. It was still misty, but from where he lay he could see the sun trying to break through the clouds. He shrank down into his tube of polyester, feeling reluctant to face his world. Then steel-tipped heels, Meli's heels, pounded their way towards the church. Luze thrashed around, but the duvet held him fast. By the time he'd managed to unroll himself, Meli's footsteps had passed through the grove. Damn! Meli in bed was exactly what he needed to lighten a dismal morning.

He waved his shirt out of the window and to his delight saw her stop and turn. Smiling happily, he hauled on his tracksuit bottoms and padded downstairs.

'It's so gloomy,' he grumbled. 'And it's July. I guess it isn't going to get any better than this.'

'We had a good April. Be grateful for that. Listen, listen!' She caught hold of his shoulders and spun him round. 'You did it. You did it! The tumour has vanished. You should have seen their faces . . . all those silly specialists. They couldn't understand it, but they looked so embarrassed when I told them I'd been seeing a faith healer.'

'It was magic.'

'Whatever you did worked.' She wound her arms around his waist and hugged him.

'I'd like to take all the credit, Meli, but let's just say I brought you into contact with an all-powerful force. You were very receptive.'

She giggled. 'I'm still receptive. Try me.'

Matt's eyes narrowed. As he moved closer, desire stunned her like an electric shock. It was something about his ebony skin against the whites of his eyes. Or was it his lustful, predatory expression? Or his dominant pristine maleness? Or something truly basic like his dick pushing against his tracksuit bottoms? She gasped and felt his rock hard body pushing her back towards the wall. Lust exploded like the swollen waters in a flooded dam. She lost her balance and was swept away, feeling his hands thrusting her clothes aside. 'Hurry, hurry, hurry!'

★   ★   ★

Lying in his arms, Meli wished she could hold back time. The moment was precious. She adored the musky smell of him, his beautifully shaped hands, the velvet touch of his skin. Most of all, she was intrigued by his mind. She had never met anyone like him. His strange psychic spells astounded her. The week before last he'd said: 'Why do you never visit your aunt's grave? It makes her sad. She'd like some flowers from time to time.'

'You're talking nonsense.'

But of course he wasn't and he'd shown her

293

the tombstone, even though her aunt's married name was Welsh. So she'd reluctantly cleaned up the grave and bought some flowers. The man was a regular weirdo.

'Oh, Matt, listen! I've good news. The publishers accepted that novel you've been nagging me to write. I didn't tell you, but the fact is, I began it years ago, so I sent several chapters . . . about half . . . and the synopsis, and they were interested. Now I've almost finished it and they've accepted it. I'll be the village pariah.'

'You'll survive. I'm overjoyed. But listen, I miss you Meli. Why don't you shack up with me? We could move somewhere else if you like.'

'I don't know.' She paused, feeling tempted, but moments later she was shuddering with real fear. My God! Just imagine! She'd almost said 'yes'. Her fright wouldn't go away. She wondered if he knew that her feelings for him were way out of line. Ridiculous! As if she could shack up with a six-foot-three witchdoctor and his spooky mind. Yet she'd love nothing better. Matt was so damned good and he was good in the sack, too. The best. She wasn't in love with him. Early on she'd learned she was a one-man woman.

Sometimes she wondered what her past life would have been like if she'd married Simon. Rather dull, she decided there and then. Instead, with no commitment to anyone, she'd compartmentalised her life into a series of adventures, choosing men that made good heroes . . . or villains . . . and her life became the skeleton of her next novel. Pity psycho-thrillers were 'in'. She didn't fancy a mass-murderer or a copper.

She smiled and then pulled herself together. Daydreaming wouldn't get her manuscript delivered on time. She'd have to be brutal with Matt, she decided.

'I'm moving back to the manor today. Wish me luck.'

His obvious hurt made her flinch. 'You must be mad,' he growled as he swung his legs out of bed and pulled on his clothes.

'Don't do it, Meli. Who's going to cure you if the headaches strike again?' That was a body blow unworthy of him, she thought, but understandable.

'Who else can make you come six times in a row? Who loves you like I do?' Love! That was her problem, too. It was fears that she might do exactly what he had asked which was prompting her swift return to David.

'Love!' She laughed. 'Grow up, Matt, and join the real world.' She glanced at her costly, gold watch. 'I have exactly twenty minutes. Think you can make it again? Then I must go, but I'll be back this afternoon.'

★   ★   ★

Later that evening, lingering and regretful, Matt walked Meli back to the hotel.

'If you don't want to live with me, why don't you get your own place? If you're short I could manage the rent.' He understood the social pressures that she feared.

She didn't answer and once again Luze sensed that he was losing her, yet there was no need to ask if she loved him. Her body told him that.

She paused by the entrance. 'You have made me feel desirable again.'

'You were always desirable.' He touched her softly, reassuringly and watched her go.

36

It was almost eleven p.m. when Luze emerged from the pub and plodded home, treading gently past the hopes and fears of the locals, whom nowadays he knew as well as he'd known his tribesmen. Poor Mrs Rose, longing for her youth, was recovering from painful plastic surgery in her lonely bedroom. Silhouetted against the blinds, Bernard was crouched over his laptop, trying to make a fortune on the Internet. Luze trod softly past their dreams. Strains of Prokofiev hung in the night air. Barbara Beeston, who danced at Covent Garden, had broken three toes, so now she lay pining for what might have been. And little Julie Atkins, nine, hoping that her Dad would one day love her, came top in everything at school. Newly wed, Vera, with buckteeth, was praying for her husband to survive his car smash. Old Mr Jones had just learned he had Parkinson's disease. Jessica Long, widowed these five years, was listening for her teenage daughter's footsteps.

He loved them all. They led good lives, made joy go a long way and hung on to their dreams. They were so vulnerable and so different to the arrogant colonials he'd known back home, with their ranches, pools, tennis courts and splendid lives. The locals hadn't had a lot of joy. Hardly any of them came to church. Over half of them didn't believe in God or their own immortality and this troubled him. The Church had failed them, yet strangely there was no lack of morality here. Quite the reverse. He was amazed at a people who chose goodness without promise of reward, nor threat of punishment. People here were good and kind for no better reason than they wanted to be. A few fell by the wayside, but with a little help they got back on their feet. Sometimes he thought that the strangely mixed-up people of this overcrowded island were leading the world in secular morality.

He walked on slowly, considering his own problems. He'd sworn to put the past behind him, but Melissa's tragedy had touched him and he'd used the ancient skills of his tribe to bring about her recovery. One thing had led to another and he had over a dozen 'regulars' who came to his faith healing sessions to be cured of their aches and pains, mainly arthritis, but each one was special.

He was almost home when he bumped into Joe Thomson, the blacksmith's son, crying bitterly as he jogged along the street. Joe was an abused boy who took black-eyes and bullying in his stride. Joe denied being beaten, so other than contacting their local welfare office, there was little else Luze could do.

'What are you doing out so late, Joe? Surely it's past your bedtime.'

Joe backed away from him looking wary. Clergymen and pederasts seemed to be synonymous in the eyes of the local kids.

'Lost my dog, Sir,' he sobbed from a safe distance. 'My Dad'll have something to say about that. It was for my birthday. Reckon it'll starve, or get run-over. It's just a pup.'

'Okay, let's try to find it. How did it happen?'

'I took off its collar to put on the name tag I'd bought and another dog went for it. So it took off, didn't it.'

'Hey, that's tough. Can I hold its collar?'

The boy handed a bright yellow leather strip to him. 'Hush a minute, Joe. Just let me listen.' Luze sat on a low wall, closed his eyes and let his mind go blank while he lowered his vibrations.

'I'd better get home, Sir.'

'Hang on. We're getting somewhere.' The collar was vibrating in his hand. 'I can feel his fear. He's afraid of the dark.'

'He is, Sir. That's right.'

'Sh!'

He can hear sheep crying, and the sound of a train racing past him. It sounds very close and the ground is vibrating around him. So he is near the railway line. Someone is singing — a tenor in a strange, warbling minor key that reminds him of Tanga. Ah! Of course! He's hiding in a field, by the mosque near the railway line in Newtown.

'I know where he is, Joe. Let's hurry.'

The two were united, Joe was happy, and Luze went home feeling great.

★　★　★

Joe's mother, Mrs Thomson, arrived at the vicarage the following morning carrying a bunch of wilting roses. She was a large, but crumpled woman with sagging breasts, frizzy, ginger hair and the complexion of a corpse. Her shifty blue eyes glanced every way except at him.

'It's like this, Vicar,' she whined. 'We've got trouble at home and I thought you might help me.'

'I've noticed Joe is always badly bruised,' he began helpfully.

'He's accident prone,' she snarled.

Luze shuddered. 'Can you truthfully tell me he's not beaten?'

'He asks for it. Little sod! I need to raise a thousand pounds and I just can't lay my hands on the cash. Bill, my husband, has been gambling. Now these thugs say that if he doesn't pay them they'll break his hands. That'll be his living gone, so what will become of us?'

'You'd like me to accompany you to the police station.'

'No. Nothing like that.'

'What then?'

There was a long pause while she gazed at her fingertips 'Use your magic. Why don't you? Let's have the lottery numbers for Saturday's draw.'

He could only gape at her. A bucket of iced water couldn't have shocked him more. He recognised the threat before it was uttered. This was seriously damaging. He was astonished by her hard, brassy attitude and he felt his temper running away from him as he struggled to stay calm.

'I can't imagine what led you to think that I could possibly know such a thing. What magic are you talking about? If I knew that, d'you suppose I wouldn't win a little for myself. God

300

knows the church needs money badly. Ask the bank to help you. I'm a vicar. Is there anything else?'

'Fucking right there is. Ms Marlowe comes here every day.' She spoke with studied indifference, but she was stoked up with fury. 'Anyone can see she's getting better and last night you found our pup. Joe told us how you used your black magic.'

'Ms Marlowe is getting better because she prays with me every day. Finding your dog was sheer chance.' Deeply exasperated, he could only allow himself to scowl at her.

'Oh, really! You want to watch out, Luze. A word from me to the bishop could send you packing. I need to win. Okay?' She flounced out.

⋆ ⋆ ⋆

On Saturday, Joe's mother won two thousand pounds with five correct numbers. The buzz went round the village and Luze's phone began to ring until he pulled the plug out. Hot sorrow became physical as tears coursed down his cheeks. It was pure chance, he knew. Not even he could manipulate chance, he assured himself modestly. But the villagers would think he did it and that would bring endless trouble.

After all I wanted a full church. He pursed his lips. But not this way. They'll come for the wrong reasons. Greed instead of love.

He could not face going to the pub, instead he played African music all the evening and went late to bed feeling lonesome.

37

Simon loathed mobile phones, but lately he was never without his, as he waited for Bela's call. It rang repeatedly, but it was usually from his lawyer, or the Union, or the Department, as they haggled over his compensation. Never from Bela. Matt phoned from time to time. He'd taken Simon up on his offer to study ancient Celtic fields and waterways and the two of them sometimes tramped over the hills and woods and usually ended up dining in Harry's pub. The days dragged by. Eventually Simon wrote the closest he would ever get to a love letter.

I'm missing you. Ferdinand is lonely, too. As for Candida, her eyes shed outsize tears as she peers over the orchard wall. Where are you?

After three weeks had passed without a word from Bela, Simon sadly gave up hope of ever seeing her again. Why was his life running in a groove which always led to the same ending? Why was he incapable of making the women he loved happy? He could find no reason for Bela's sudden alienation. It had been the same with Angela. Twice in one life-time was more than a tragedy, it was a disgrace.

Painstakingly, Simon set out to trace the source of the barriers he had erected. He found a small boy standing by the school gates, willing

302

himself never to feel again. Step by step he traced the incidents that lead him to create his inviolate alter ego. Willfully he dissected this stiff-upper-lip, square-shouldered, Christian, patriotic, well-bred, back-bone-of-the-nation, land-owning, clone. When he'd finished, the wreckage was impressive. Was there any part of him that he could truly call his own?

* * *

It was noon. Simon wiped his forehead with a cloth and blinked his stinging eyes clear of sweat. A heat wave had hung around for the past week with temperatures hitting 30 degrees in the afternoon. The somnolent farm was drowsing, birds perched motionless in shady branches, beaks open, wings hanging. Swollen with heat, Simon worked lethargically as he replaced the straw in the barn.

He heard a car pull up in the yard and a few minutes later, a movement at the side of his vision caught his attention. He turned and dropped the pitchfork, screwing his eyes against the glare, watching a moving shape shimmer through heat waves from the baking cobbles. Was it Bela, or a mirage caused by his overheated mind and his longing? Just what sort of a game did she think she was playing? He leaned against the bales of straw, frowning at her. Watching her graceful approach, his anger surfaced.

'Simon, are you there?'

She took off her sunglasses and peered into gloomy recesses between the bales of straw. Then she saw him and seemed delighted, but her smile soon faded when she looked into his eyes.

'Is this your idea of a joke, Bela? Why did you run away?'

'I needed to be alone.' Petulance lingered. Her shoulders sagged despondently and her mouth was downturned, but Simon couldn't control his exasperation. Gripping her shoulders, he pulled her hard against him.

'You're hurting me and you're all sweaty,' she grumbled.

'D'you think I wasn't hurt.'

He pushed his thighs hard against hers, pinning her against the barn wall and heard her gasp.

'I've tried so hard to keep away, but I can't,' she whispered. 'I love you too much. Love me, Simon. Make it seem right again. I need you.'

'Show me,' he murmured.

★ ★ ★

She lay in his arms, her eyes closed, criss-cross straw marks on her naked back and shoulders, a silly smile playing around her lips. Her hair shone with bronze strands in the sunlight. He tried to imagine what had kept her away from him. She was a secretive, introverted woman and most times he had the sense not to intrude.

Why had she chosen a man from another generation? She could have anyone. And would he be able to cope with the burden of being the older man?'

At forty-six, he'd never before felt old, but

nowadays his anticipated lifespan appeared to be so fleeting. Time was relative and no doubt the evanescent romp of the Mayfly seemed like an eternity to those tiny creatures. Yet he felt that there was some other forgotten experience against which he measured his meagre allotment.

Bela's sleepy voice brought him back to reality.

'I kept hoping you would come and save me from my doubts.' Bela was physically spent, hot and half-asleep. She closed her eyes and shuddered as he ran his fingers over her smooth, ivory skin.

'I called several times. Thrust letters onto that Puri fellow. You didn't even return my telephone calls.'

'He didn't tell me. They don't approve of us.'

'It's none of their business.'

There was no answer. She was sound asleep in the straw, her head on his shoulder.

'In World War II, my grandfather, Tom, a salvage diver, was sent down into bombed ships to assess the cost of recovering the vessel and its cargo and to decide whether or not it was worthwhile,' Simon murmured. Glancing at Bela, he saw that her eyes were closed and she didn't stir when he stroked her check.

'Like him, I've plumbed the depths of this ship and found it to be a worthless hulk without a cargo. So why bother to refloat?'

'You didn't look properly. Come here.' She wound her arms around his neck pulling him closer. 'Dive in again.'

He laughed to hide his embarrassment. 'I

305

thought you were asleep.'

Was Bela completely unscathed by their differences? he wondered when they had made love and promised never again to part. Or was that why she'd tried to split?'

He folded Bela in his arms. There was only one way to be sure.

'Move in here with me and as soon as my divorce comes through we'll marry. You can study as well here as at the Puri's.'

She sat up looking anxiously at him.

'I feel I should explain that I'm not sure if I'll carry on farming, Bela. Ana's not keen either, so I might sell this place. Do something completely different. Would that make a difference?'

'Of course not. I wouldn't mind, but you've always loved farming. You're good at it.'

'I can't even face restocking.'

She looked upset. 'Did they pay the compensation yet?'

'Most of the cash is languishing in the bank. I'm expecting more, but I can't bring myself . . . not yet. Maybe never.'

'Let's talk about it.'

He managed a grin. 'A few short months ago I had no such worries. I thought I knew exactly who I was and what I was doing with my life. We come from a long line of achievers and our family roots go deep into history. Some of our ancestors fought with the Crusades. One of them was a court advisor to Good Queen Bess, another died with his men in the Charge of the Light Brigade. A Shepherd was decorated for gallantry in the Boer War, another made a fortune with tea in Madagascar although his grandson gambled most of his fortune away. Redhill remained in our hands because the family produced at least one good farmer every generation. So I was happy with my lot. Almost happy,' Simon corrected himself.

'Knotty problems of running the country I left to the government, because my responsibility began and ended with casting my vote. Bringing up Ana was left to Laura. As for religion, I left that to the churchmen. It was enough that I ran the farm well.'

'Plenty of people have much less than you.'

Simon frowned. 'I suppose so. Farming has become a fool's game. But that's not it either, Bela. I lost my self-respect when the troops ground my face into the dung on my own land. I no longer feel that this is my home.'

For the first time Bela had a glimmer of understanding of just what the culling had done to Simon. Torn between pity and horror she struggled to find a way to comfort him. Words would never help, so she cradled his face in her hands and kissed him long and passionately.

'I love you, Simon. That's a start, isn't it.'

'It's all I want. I've reached a watershed and I have to work it out for myself. But these are my problems, so if you don't care whether or not I'm a farmer, or where we live, then why don't you move in?'

She frowned and looked away.

He said: 'I think it's time you told me what's wrong.'

'Something worries me. I can't talk about it

307

yet. Maybe soon, but not now. There's something I have to find out.'

A jolt of *déjà vu* seemed to mock him. *Angela's words!* The self-same words! What kind of trick was fate playing on him? He sat up and wiped the sweat off his forehead with the back of his hand, remembering.

★ ★ ★

It was February, 1976, and they'd been going steady for several months, but inexplicably Angela had been moody and unresponsive for almost a month and eventually he had taxed her with her strangely, prolonged bad mood. And she had said: 'Something worries me. I can't talk about it yet. Maybe soon . . . ' And the rest of it, or words to that effect.

They had been clutching each other in her single bed in her dowdy Cambridge digs, the steel edge of the springs cutting into his buttocks. He had wanted sex, but she had refused. That, too, was unusual.

She had sat up in bed and gazed wildly at him.

Noticing her swollen nipples he'd imagined she wanted to screw. So why was she holding back? Was she using sex to control him? His suspicions were strengthened when she'd said:

'Where is all this love leading us, Simon? Are we going anywhere? What exactly are your intentions towards me?'

'What do you mean?'

'You know what I mean.'

The sun moved behind the clouds and the

room suddenly darkened. For the first time he saw how squalid it was. It had always been transformed by the reflected glow of her beauty, but lately her face was puffy, there were deep brown rings under her eyes and her skin had lost its lustre.

'I love you,' he had said, making an effort not to lose his temper, 'but I don't want to be manipulated.'

She'd shuddered and murmured: 'That goes without saying.'

'My father would never understand, but when he retires I'll be free. He's not well. We'll have to wait until I qualify and run the estate, or we might lose out. It won't be long. It's as much for you as for me.'

She'd turned her back on him, facing the wall, which was more expressive than any words, he reckoned. When he spoke to her, she wouldn't answer. After a while he had dressed and driven home.

★ ★ ★

'I need time, Simon,' Bela said. 'I love you, but there's something I must do first. It's a private matter. Can we turn back the clock and carry on where we left off? I just need a little while longer.'

Foolishly, he wondered if she was waiting for her divorce to come through.

'Home is where you are happy, so this is my home. This farm. Here is my only reality. Our weekends are my life. The rest is like a dream.

Do you feel this way?' Her eyes burned like a fever.

For an answer he had lifted her arm and pressed his lips on the soft, smooth skin, brushing his mouth over her palms, wondering how such delicate fingers could have so much strength as she pulled him to her.

38

The sound of Angus barking tossed David from his scotch-inspired coma into the anxiety zone. August was passing rapidly, leaving him that much nearer to the miners' deadline. After weeks of scheming he had no idea how to raise the cash he needed and Gordon remained elusive and close-mouthed. 'Trust me', was all he could get out of him. He heard the housekeeper stamp her way to the front door, and then Gordon's deep voice echoing in the hall, bringing a sense of relief.

'Hello stranger,' David clapped him on the back and tried out a grin that failed dismally. 'I could do with some company. Meli's always working and I sit here drinking alone and getting bloody gloomy. Things have come to a pretty pass when you can't raise half a million.' He broke off and blew his nose violently into a large white handkerchief. 'What'll it be?'

'The usual . . . with soda water.'

'You should take it neat. I've told you before. Soda ruins the scotch.'

Gordon shrugged and sat by the fire.

'How is Melissa?'

'Blooming, but she's left me again,' David said, looking even gloomier. He caught sight of himself in the mirror above the fireplace. His features had become dough-like and puffy, a clear sign that he was drinking too much.

'Been riding lately?'

So it showed. David shrugged. 'Tension's a killer.'

'I have a plan. Let's see what you think of it.'

'Not before bloody time.' David tried to disguise how badly his hands shook as he took a cigar, bit off the end and lit it. He was on the verge of cracking up and he knew it.

'Listen to this!' Gordon's eyes twinkled and his lips curled in a mischievous smile as he raised one eyebrow.

'I'll buy it, whatever it is. Come on, Gordon.'

'As you know I have friends at the council. It seems that George Irving's consortium have bought the rights to a new process.'

'They have to do something,' David interrupted him. 'Irving's in shit. His shares are still dropping daily.'

'Yes! Everyone knows that, but listen carefully. They've bought a new, improved, patented method to incinerate old tyres in order to recover the steel from them.'

'Let me get this straight. This is your so-called good news.'

'Bear with me. Irving will deny it when he's questioned, just as he did in '85 when rumours circulated that he was buying Redhill to put up his damned plant. Remember?'

'I'll never forget.'

'Right! So this time no one will believe him when he denies our allegations. Incinerating tyres is a messy business producing continual heavy smoke emission and soot, a revolting smell of burning rubber and masses of toxic waste.'

David looked worried, Gordon noticed with amusement.

'And guess where he's planning to erect the incinerator? Right on our doorstep. He's negotiating to buy those fields below the church. They adjoin the most expensive houses in the village.'

'Come off it. That's my land.'

'No. Here's the story. You sold it to Joe Bloggs years back, who bought it under a nominee, who's hiding behind an off-shore company somewhere in the Caribbean. The truth is, you haven't the faintest idea who owns that land.'

David gulped, leaped up and paced the carpet. 'For heaven's sake get to the point.'

'Naturally we're obliged to inform the Temple Minnis Home Owners' Association of Irving's plans. After all, their property values are at stake. If the plant goes into production they won't be able to give away their homes and they'll be stuck with mortgages far in excess of their house values. They'd be ruined and so would the shops and businesses hereabouts. It would be like the 1985 debacle, all over again.'

David glanced worriedly at Gordon. 'This news, even though it's fiction, would put the lid on future sales.'

'Only temporarily. Meantime everyone will be galvanized into action to protect their homes, their kids' health, their investments and their way of life. First, they'll try to make Irving see reason on ethical grounds, but he'll deny all knowledge of it. That's his style and for once he'll be telling the truth.'

'Jesus, Gordon. I see a glimmer at the end of the tunnel. Keep going, man.'

'We'll help them fight Irving tooth and nail, as we did in '85. We'll call meetings, contact the council and so on. Eventually we'll locate Joe Bloggs?'

'Are you sure about that?'

'Okay, perhaps we'll locate his nominee, a lawyer. After all, Bloggs is a fugitive from British justice living in . . . ' He paused.

'Pakistan.' David offered. 'No extradition treaty.'

'Perfect. We'll find that the sale hasn't gone through yet and Bloggs' lawyer is prepared to take the best offer. Alas, our company doesn't have the ready cash to bid for the land, but we'll do all that we can to help the home owners, Finally the locals will have to come to the conclusion that the only way to stop this smelly, revolting, life-threatening monstrosity from landing on their doorsteps and choking their kids, is to outbid Irving for Joe Bloggs' land. They'll have to pay up, jointly and severally, perhaps by taking out second mortgages, but they'll own the fields and at some time in the future they'll be able to sell off the plots. They might even make a profit if they wait long enough.'

'Hm!' David watched him with ironic humour 'Thanks, Gordon. I think you've saved the day. Not for the first time either.'

'So finally you'll get the million you need for your acres.'

David leapt to his feet and grabbed the whisky bottle. 'You're a clever bastard. You've always been damned devious. I like it. Yes, I really do. You were a bit slow in starting, but you've come up trumps at the eleventh hour. Wait a minute, though, there's a snag. I lose the land.'

'You greedy bugger! You'll be paid handsomely for it, enabling you to settle up with the miners. If we play our cards right, we might even land up owning a portion of the new property company as our management fee, so you'll still own part of it.'

'That's bloody brilliant. You're wasted as an architect, Gordon.' He gave a smug smile. For a few minutes the two of them grinned at each other. Then David looked depressed again.

'There's still a snag. I've only got six weeks to find the cash. We can't get this scam moving in time and the banks don't want to know my troubles.'

'I've thought of that,' Gordon said. 'Have you heard that in Africa they're using derelict mines to bury toxic waste. Why not in Wales?'

'We'd never get away with it.'

'Eventually, not, I agree, but the rumour would frighten the shit out of the Taffies. Perhaps long enough to encourage them to give you time . . . say a year to find the cash if, in return, you promise to shelve your plans for the mine.'

'They'll kiss my ass I'm damned sure.' He leaped up with a holler of pure joy. 'Saved, you bastard. Saved again. How many times hasn't that clever, devious mind of yours come up with the answer to our problems? Saved at the eleventh hour.' He grabbed the whisky bottle and

315

liberally splashed the liquor over two glasses and the sideboard.

'This is going to work, David. It's all a matter of the right spin. I'll spread the word and get my secretary busy. I have my contacts and there's Ana's, who's stringing for the local newspaper, or so I heard. There'll be some paper shuffling to do. Who owns the land, you personally?'

'No, my Grenada company.'

'We'll have to make sure that's watertight. I'd better go.' Gordon glanced at his watch.

'Thanks Gordon. I could never face a prison sentence.'

'Try living with Laura.' Gordon regretted the words at once, but David hadn't heard. He was frowning as his fingers stabbed his calculator.

'See you tomorrow,' Gordon said with a smile. 'I'll let myself out.'

39

Gordon drove home smiling to himself. It was true, he was a genius. David, on the other hand, was an arrogant sod who took people for granted. Everyone was his bloody serf, but not forever, he promised himself. He hummed an old Elvis tune as he put his foot down hard.

Gordon was a fashionable person and naturally his home reflected the sharp edge of his painstakingly honed good taste. There was nothing superfluous or out of place, except for *La Bitch* who lately filled him with violent disgust. He had never actually invited her into his wooded hilltop eerie. She'd sort of drifted in, like a musty smell, hardly noticeable at first, but soon to become quite sickening and once in, hard to eradicate. His belly quailed at the prospect of another confrontation.

As he opened the front door, the fierce lustre in his brown eyes flared momentarily, but with fury rather than joy. Sam had left a white sheen of hair over his exquisite blue, handmade Chinese carpet. The damned dog wouldn't keep off it and it was starting to stink. He caught sight of the dog's tail as it dived under the sideboard. The smell of fried fish wafted around the hall ruining the ambiance and then he heard *La Bitch* calling from the kitchen.

'Gordon, have you been hitting Sam?'
'No.'

317

'Or scolding him?'

'Of course not. Come here, Sam.' He clicked his fingers, but the dog squeezed closer to the wall.

'So why is he frightened of you?' She emerged from the kitchen, her eyes flicking malice.

'Is he? Perhaps he thinks I stole him from the farm.' Was it really the same dog? This moping, moulting mongrel was a shadow of the former, boisterous Sam.

'I'm going to take him back.' Lines of vexation appeared on Laura's face.

'Yes. Do the dog a favour. But why don't I take him?'

'That won't be necessary. Sorry to disappoint you.'

She was brimful of spite and wry amusement. She knew perfectly well he was looking for an excuse to go and make his peace with Simon. He missed those carefree days on the farm, riding Daunty before lunch with Sam bringing up the rear and evening sundowners at the pub with the gang. Most of all he missed Simon. Women were always jealous of the staunch bond between men, suspecting ulterior motives that didn't exist. Simon must be missing him as much as he was missing Simon, but how to break the ice was a problem and *La Bitch* wasn't helping.

'You're late! Dinner's been ready for over an hour.'

'So what!' He stalked into the dining room, but one glance at her expression diminished his courage.

'Okay, Sorry. I had to see David. A problem's

318

cropped up. I'll explain it to you tomorrow. Meantime I have to dig up a few more facts. I'll be working all evening.'

'Again! It's bloody lonely when you shut your office door. It wouldn't be so bad if you didn't play Elvis Presley all the time. It blasts out and I can't play the music I like, or watch TV.'

You could if you went home, he mouthed. 'Helps me to relax.'

She plonked two plates of soup on the table, canteen-style, and collapsed into a chair. 'My feet are killing me. I'm not used to standing all day. Maybe I should get a stool for the easel.'

Laura was over the hill. Why hadn't he noticed? Gordon watched her sidelong as she wolfed down her soup. Had she always made such a noise when she swallowed? He felt utterly revolted. She had seemed so desirable when she was Simon's, but he had dumped her fast enough. No pleading or begging her to reconsider. Not on your life. Just a quick, clean cut-off. Was it possible that he'd always had that luscious olive-skinned girl lurking in the background? What was her name? Bela? Well-named, he had to accede. He made a reluctant foray on his soup. A couple of weeks back they'd run out of conversation. Now every mealtime was an ordeal. He'd started making notes of subjects they could talk about. Ah yes. Of course. Ana!

'How's Ana getting along?' he asked.

'Fine, as usual. Why?'

'Still working at the restaurant?'

'She quit.'

319

'We ought to take her to lunch. See how she's getting along. Maybe tomorrow. Phone her. I'll book.'

Laura smiled tremulously and doubtfully, as if she couldn't quite believe her ears. 'That's so sweet of you, Gordon. Let's do that.'

Her hand slid over the table towards his, but he managed to move his to safety.

Laura got up and came back with the sad, overheated fish. Laura's cooking was a disgrace, like everything else. She had no idea how to run a home. She'd wanted to hang on to her housekeeper, but Mrs Watson wasn't keen. She was retiring, she'd said. Laura wasn't exactly over-worked and lately she spent most of her time creating dreadful textile designs in the messy outhouse she'd turned into a temporary studio.

'I'm sorry. I'm just not hungry.'

Leaving his plate, he went into the bathroom to floss and clean his teeth, taking care with each space, twisting and turning the floss and then brushing again for a good five minutes before rinsing with mouthwash. When he reached for the towels he got a handful of stockings which he flung in the shower. Women's paraphernalia disgusted him. The heated towel-rails weren't for drying underwear. Hurrying to his office, he locked the door, leaned back in his adjustable leather chair and grabbed his calculator. Toting up his marvellous opulence was one of the few pastimes that brought Gordon genuine joy. It was amazing how the two, three and even ten percent takes on purchases the company made

320

had grown into a fortune over the years. It was all carefully tucked away in Swiss bank accounts, held in the name of a dozen off-shore companies.

Shortly afterwards he heard Laura go into the bathroom and exclaim with annoyance before slamming the door.

'Bastard!' As the echo floated down, he switched on Elvis loud and clear and gazed out of the window at the gulls swooping and soaring on thermals. A few minutes later he saw Laura leading Sam to the car. One down, one to go!

★　★　★

'I blame myself,' Simon heard himself saying to Laura as if in a dream. 'I screwed my way into hell, and it wouldn't have been so bad if I hadn't dragged the women I love with me . . . you, Angela and ultimately Ana, too.'

'Don't kid yourself. You don't love me and you certainly don't love Ana.'

'You're wrong, Laura, but I don't blame you for thinking that. Back in '85 it was a question of love versus lust. I was running out of control, but it's not like me to be trite. Can we change the subject?'

'I'll tell you my good news. A French textile house who took most of my designs recently, have invited me to join them as an in-house designer. They're offering a very attractive package deal.'

'Sounds great. Congratulations. So when are you leaving?'

'I'm not sure. I've agreed to spend a month there on a trial basis. My real ties are here.'

Not me, surely, Simon wondered uneasily. He said: 'Thanks for bringing Sam back. I've missed him badly.'

'I felt he wasn't safe with Gordon. Besides he obviously misses the farm.'

'Of course! Just look at him!'

Through the window he watched Sam rolling in manure. He had reinforced his scent around the fences, bullied the fowls and lambs and nuzzled Daunty. Happiness was brimming out of him.

'He's loving that.' He frowned at Laura. 'Has Sam been to the pet parlour?'

''Fraid so.'

'Shame on you. He's a working dog.'

'I had no choice. D'you remember how Gordon used to play with Sam for hours. It was Gordon who taught Sam to play hide and seek and once he'd learned, he could never get enough of it. Well, the strange thing is, Gordon hates Sam. He hates the smell of him and his hairs on the carpet and just the fact that he exists. Sam crawls under the nearest table when Gordon comes home. Clearly he's kicked the dog. He's a bastard. It's not like Sam to be cowed, so I brought him home.'

'Have you seen Ana lately?'

'I called round at her frightful digs. She's lost weight and she looks scruffy.'

Laura looked disarmed and defeated. If nothing else, she'd always been a caring mother. 'I'm so worried about her.' Laura described their brief encounter while she clattered around making coffee.

'Good God, who's been poking around here? Just look at these ugly mugs. Where are the ones I bought?' She picked up the fructose jar and shook it. 'What's this?' She dug her index finger into the jar and licked it. 'This is sugar, not fructose. Your girlfriend's not very concerned about your diet, I notice. Damn! There's no proper coffee left.'

'The jar of Instant is over there, next to the kettle.'

'Instant! Oh hell! And all my copper pans are missing. Just look at these dreadful black replacements.'

'Your kitchen equipment is packed in the attic. It was all for show. These are for use. You don't live here anymore, Laura,' he reminded her brutally. 'Bela's a marvellous cook.'

She flinched and for a moment Simon was overcome with guilt.

'Ah! So you've gone for bed and board have you,' she said. 'Cheap at half the price.'

'It's not like that at all. Bela is a highly intelligent young woman.'

'Well you're a fool, so perhaps you'll learn from her.'

Having delivered that salvo, she gave a long, loud sniff, collapsed on a chair and burst into tears. Through nineteen years of marriage Simon had never seen Laura cry.

'The place smells like an Indian bazaar. I suppose you like all that weird, spicy food.' She took out a tissue and dried her eyes. 'And she spends hours driving to London and back every day. She has an evening job and she freelances for the newspaper weekends. Her studies must be suffering.'

She was back on Ana again, Simon realised, after a moment's confusion.

'Laura, listen to me. Ana is savouring life. She has promised to stay on the pill, so she can't come to too much harm. As for Gordon. I want to tell you a story.'

He tried to describe the Gordon he used to know: skinny, scared and skint. Being the only scholarship boy in a public school was tough and Simon, who hated bullying, stepped to rescue him occasionally. One evening, when Simon returned from a late rugby practice to take a shower, he'd found Gordon sobbing hysterically as he was pinned naked over a bench in the locker room. His first impression was the disgusting smell. God knows how the boys had acquired a douche-can to administer an enema of soapy suds. They were punishing Gordon for farting in the dormitory, they told him gleefully. Their sadism sent Simon skidding dangerously into a fury he'd never known he possessed. All eight boys had to be patched up in the sickbay later. Nursing his badly bruised knuckles, Simon was sent to detention for refusing to talk, but after Gordon blabbed, the headmaster decided to bury the matter.

'From then on Gordon developed an unhealthy dependence on me. Whatever I did, my shadow copied and whatever I had, Gordon

324

wanted. After a few more silly incidents, Gordon took to trailing along wherever I was, which was irritating, but normal, I suppose, since I could fight and he couldn't.'

Brilliant memories of school days, Simon thought grimly as he forced the images away.

'Since then he's longed to be like me and have what I have. You made the mistake of becoming his, so now you're tarnished with his own self-image and Gordon doesn't like himself much. I tried to tell you this years ago when you were intent on giving him one of those pups from the litter Sam fathered. You wouldn't listen, so I found other homes. You were cross at the time.'

'I thought you were jealous.'

'Perhaps I should have been, but you know what they say about ignorance.'

Laura opened her mouth to argue, but he put his index finger on her lips.

'Forget the past. We've enough on our plates coping with the present.

'As to Ana's studies: she's clever and this is only the start of the year. She has the cash to pay for her residence in London, so it's her choice. Leave her be.'

'Why can't you force her to come home? She's only just turned eighteen,' she wailed.

'Surely you know your own daughter better than that. When she finds herself perhaps she'll come home.'

'I want to come home.'

'I'm sorry, Laura. I want a divorce. My lawyer has worked out a generous settlement.'

A slight implosion of sound was Laura's only answer as she grabbed her bag and fled. Simon, who was glad to see her go, suffered a painful flare of guilt that stayed with him for days.

40

David was into his morning workout when his mobile rang. He glanced at his watch. Seven a.m.! Now who on earth . . . ? It was Gordon.

'There were only two chapters on the PC . . . the first two . . . ' He sounded peeved. 'Where the hell is the rest of it?'

'God knows. It was first planned in the late eighties. Meli had an ancient laptop in those days. She dug up the MS recently and sent what she'd done to the publishers, so it's probably on a disc in her safe.'

'But why the early chapters?'

'She's rewriting. She has to transpose the chapters to the PC she's using now.'

'D'you have a key to her safe?'

'Actually, no. She's ultra secretive about her work, but I'll try to find it.'

'I'll drop these round, but make sure the housekeeper doesn't hand them to Meli.'

'Ring me when you get near. I'll meet you at the door.'

By the time David got round to opening the envelope, he'd showered, dressed, gobbled his kippers, and he was in his office where the housekeeper had placed his second pot of coffee.

Digging Up the Past, by Melissa Marlowe. His eyes skimmed over the dateline: Saturday, June 14, 1975. Was that when it all began? They were so young and they were all in first year at university, except Simon, who was studying agriculture at a Cambridge college. Meli was right, David decided. She'd pinpointed the precise time and date when they first planned to turn their dreams into reality. He began to read:

England is warm again. Fields and flowers drag themselves out of hibernation, white-limbed, pale-faced creatures crawl out of tweeds and woollies. Wild flowers wave their flaglike petals, incited by the sun, while insects hum around aimlessly, drunk with joy. It is a moist and somnolent afternoon, temperature in the eighties, the air heavy with moisture, the sun torpid and hazy, winking away behind misty clouds.

Oh God! That took him back to days where there was pleasure and wonder in almost everything, when the crackle of dried leaves underfoot brought spasms of joy, when kippers tasted like kippers, and eggs like eggs, and every moment of every day was meaningful, when a glance from a girl could send you to heaven, when the delicious touch of flesh against flesh was like entering the Garden of Eden and when other people's pain was your own. His emotional skin had hardened . . . or solidified. That's what survival was all about, he reckoned. But joy was lost, too. He felt cheated. Momentarily, he longed to feel anything . . . anything other than bloody panic. So many times he'd had to take life's blows on the chin. He'd hauled on his armour plating so often it had become part of him.'

Meli and her bloody book! No good would come of it. He returned to the manuscript.

A low mumble of conversation comes from groups lolling on the grassy banks, and sitting in style on the clubhouse verandah. Every now and then we manage an outburst of lazy clapping. Temple Minnis is playing a Cambridge team away from home and David is batting. We watch and gossip and lie around in the grass, soaking up summer.

David blinked hard and put down the pages, overcome with nostalgia. He remembered the occasion so well, mainly because he'd batted a century. He relived the triumph with a satisfied smirk and turned back to the pages, reading half-heartedly, his mind on those youthful days.

At eighteen, I'm frothing with frustration. The object of my desire is Simon Shepherd, who's studying agriculture at a nearby College, while I take English in the hope of becoming a writer. Both from Temple Minnis, we've known each other for years, so it was only natural that we should gravitate together when we first arrived here a year ago. We had a few one-night stands, no commitment, no promises, but I've fallen deeply in love.

David jumped to attention with a start. The bitch! The sly, secretive bitch. Why hadn't Simon told him? He'd never guessed. Not once, in all these years. David sighed and poured another cup of coffee, pacing the room for a few moments before carrying on.

Six months into our first year, I was devastated when Simon fell in love with Angela, as she likes to be called. Her real name is Anjana and she's British-born of Kashmiri roots, a girl of sultry sexuality who is studying librarianship. She's also rich, spoiled and well-travelled. The pain of watching them together is unendurable, but I can't keep away.

Just look at Simon, his green eyes fixed moodily on Angela, sensual lips pouting, blue-black hair glinting in sunlight. He makes a swift, compulsive lurch across the clearing and flings himself down beside her. Circling one arm around her waist, he leans forward to press his lips fleetingly on her bare shoulder, a male gesture designed to mark his territory. Why don't you piss on her and be done with it, you idiot?

Cries of disappointment echo around the field as David, who has just scored a century, is caught out. Gordon gets up to bat. He's both available and good-looking, but for me there will only ever be Simon.

Sweaty and crimson, David flings himself on the grass and fumbles in the icebox for a cold beer.

'Phew! Whose are these? May I?'

'Harry brought them for everyone. Help

yourself,' Shirley calls in her soft Inverness accent. Shirls is studying art at the RAC. She has real talent, but she's thinking of dropping out to please Harry who is in a hurry to get married.

Three local farmer's sons, who have just come down from Cambridge, saunter over to join us. Gordon, a mediocre sportsman is soon bowled out and Harry takes his place. There's a chorus of good-natured boos when he, too, is run out on his first try.

'Come on, Harry, you can do better than that,' David grumbles as Harry returns dragging his bat behind him.

Harry grins good-naturedly and flings himself on the grass. 'You lazy bastards get to enjoy your weekends, but I'll be working until midnight tonight and flat out all weekend. I haven't had a day off since father died.'

'My heart bleeds for you,' David says dryly. 'Poor sod, running your own show, with no one to answer to, planning how to make a mint.'

It's no secret that David and his father, who owns most of the land around Temple Minnis, are at loggerheads over running the estate.

'We've a sudden rush of bookings,' Harry says. 'The railways are cutting the train times to and from London to less than an hour soon. Lo and behold, this green and luscious village is joining the commuter belt. It will be ruined.'

'Not necessarily.' David jumps up looking furious. 'In the right hands, this place could be turned into an up-market professional's dream. We used to own those stables. Father sold them for a song. There's plenty of land being re-zoned

331

and the jackals are moving in. Temple Minnis has reached it's watershed: exclusive, or high-density homes? It all depends on which property developer gets in first. Father's selling out to the wrong people. Why should he care? He's on the way out with Parkinson's, but that damned disease takes forever. By the time I take over it'll be too late.'

'Don't talk like that, David,' Angela scolds, in her sing-song accent.

'Why not? Between us, we'd have enough clout to call the shots if we could only get going in time. We need to tie up the tenants with options while we get our act together. Gordon's got some amazing ideas. Why don't you tell them, Gordon?'

'What's the point?' Gordon returns to his book. David shrugs, gets to his feet and ambles to a clump of stinging nettles to pee.

For the first time I sense that Gordon's shy. He hides it well. He's studying architecture on scholarship, and cashing in on his appearance by modelling to cover his living expenses. He always looks extraordinary with his Greek mother's dark eyes, black hair and olive skin. His square jaw, blunt nose and broad brow come from his Scottish father.

David returns and sprawls on the grass. For while he sits moodily picking at daisies. Then he says: 'Listen, you ignorant lot. This is how we'll do it.'

I lean back in the grass and plan my proposed first novel. After a while I hear my name and frown. David is listing my assets, which include an inheritance from my great aunt and a cottage left to me by my mother.

'Where d'you get that info from, David?'

He shrugs. 'You are going to join the group, aren't you?'

Appalled by David's sneaky probing, I can't help snapping back: 'I'll think about it when the time comes.'

While Jeff explores the assets of each member of our gang, I gather my things together. I'm still feeling furious.

'Hang on a bit, Meli,' David calls. 'We're about to hear how we can raise cash on our current assets, to say nothing of future expectations, to launch our own property company. The bank will back us with a generous overdraft and we might even be able to go public.' One of the newcomers grabs his notes.

I plead a fictitious date and leave.

This is when I first encounter rising entrepreneurship (to be polite) amongst myself and my nearest and dearest. Even Simon is contaminated.

'Saint Bloody Simon,' David mutters. He drains his cup and picks up the pages with a sigh.

Everyone I know scans the business pages daily. We all scrimp and save to buy shares, or buy them on credit. Paintings are taken down to make room for graphs and statistics as the world's bourses shoot up or down on rumours.

(NB Unbeknown to all of us at the time, we

were about to help create the greedy Eighties. I sensed the mood and wrote a rags to riches novel which launched my career, but I've run a bit ahead of myself. I'll end off this section with some words of wisdom and move on to the end of the year. Maybe I should start a new chapter here.

December: The door bell is ringing and that's too bad, for I'm checking the page-proofs of my first novel. Never having seen my words in print before, I'm over the moon and really don't want to be interrupted. My Cambridge digs consist of a tiny room beside the front door close to the street. Anyone outside can see in, so I've installed Venetian blinds. Peering through them, I see Angela standing in the porch, but there's no sign of Simon. That's strange! She's trying to smooth her wind-blown hair with her fingers. I'd like to pretend I'm out, but she might have heard my footsteps. Reluctantly I open the door.

'You look as if you're freezing. Come in.'

'Sorry to intrude, Melissa. Can you spare a few minutes?'

Her voice is low-pitched and lately she seems to have lost most of her amusing Indian drawl. Presumably she's been working at it. For Angela's benefit, east and west have defied convention to meet and merge and create perfect symmetry. I hate to say it, but I must . . . she's incredibly beautiful and consequently men behave like savages when she's around. Beauty is the world's most longed for commodity. Ask the bees, ask the peahens, ask a Hollywood film

334

tycoon. *Angela has it and I don't.*

'Don't be so damned self-effacing, Meli,' David whispered irritably. He'd never found Angela the least bit attractive. He preferred his women a bit more classy. Years back, Meli, with her fine reddish hair, her wide green eyes, her pure white skin and gorgeous English features, was exactly what he wanted, but he'd never scored with her, at least not until she returned from Crete, and now he could see why.

Today, maybe Angela doesn't have so much of 'it'. There's something wrong. I can't help noticing that she looks sick and nervous. She tries out a smile that fails miserably.

'I'm leaving and I wanted to say goodbye,' she says.

Why me, I wonder as I lead her into the living room? We've hardly spoken and surely she must realise that I don't like her. Nothing personal, of course. It's just that I love Simon.

'Well, that's a surprise, Angela. Where are you going?'

'To London.'

I try to conceal my elation. 'I thought that you and Simon . . . '

'There's a problem . . . I'm pregnant, you see.'

She breaks off and places the palms of her hands softly on her belly, a subconscious desire to protect her child perhaps. There's something so vulnerable about her which always turns men on.

'Does Simon know?'

'No. I mentioned marriage to him, sort of

335

casually, and he nearly flipped. Poor Simon! He's scared of what his parents will think. His family and Redhill are very important to him. He wants to wait until his father retires and he takes over before we marry, but that could be forever and as it is . . . ' She gazes shyly at the carpet and when she next speaks her voice is soft and diffident.

'I've tried to tell him, but each time I chicken out. I want you to tell him. You're a good person and you care for Simon.'

Me! Is she that stupid? With an effort I accept the implied fiction that I also care for her, since the two of them are together.

'This is not something you can pass off, Angela.'

'But don't you see . . . if you tell him he won't feel under pressure. He's free to make his choice without embarrassment. I love Simon and I don't want to harm him. I'll be staying with my cousin in London. Tell him I'll wait there until the end of the month. I hope and pray he'll come.'

She thrusts an envelope into my hands.

'And if he doesn't come?'

'I have an old friend who wants to marry me. I shall accept his offer.'

She sits around and wastes more time discussing the weather, of all things, as if she can't bring herself to leave. I have little to say. What on earth can you say to someone you're about to sabotage? After that visit, I didn't see Angela for years and when I did I wished I had never set eyes on her.

But I'm running ahead of myself again. Right now, we have to wait for David, the catalyst, who can make it all happen. Sometimes we meet and waste time agonising in case we miss our big chance. We long for the wealth that is within our grasp, but it's not only wealth. We truly care for this corner of England we call home and we fear that the dreaded, high-density suburban sprawl might spread our way. So we plot and plan and squirm with impatience.

Simon is spending a fortune searching for Angela and daily my guilt grows heavier. Surely he can't love her that much. Oh Simon, tell me it isn't true.

David locked the manuscript in his briefcase and went outside for some badly needed fresh air. The lousy bitch! He began to jog around the lake. He could smell autumn, although he was never sure just what autumn smelled like. It wasn't so much the temperature, but rather a certain tang in the air, or just a feeling, yet it was still August. He wondered what Simon would say when the book was published, if it ever was. Had Simon known how Melissa felt? He'd probably feel like killing her. No wonder she kept talking about guilt and coming clean. This entire fiasco sat fair and square upon her shoulders. Jesus! This so-called novel read more like a diary. What exactly did she hope to achieve by washing her dirty linen in public . . . absolution? Or revenge? And was this all of it, or were there other, more deadly daggers in her sheath?

41

Gordon telephoned later that day. It was seven p.m. and David was pouring his third scotch. 'Have you read it?' he demanded.

'I've read the first chapter.'

'For God's sake. It's not long. Get on with it. Have you found the key?'

'No.'

'It seems to me Meli's sticking to the facts.'

'Verbatim,' David agreed.

'Call me when you've read it. We'll have to make a plan to find the rest of it.'

'Sure.'

David replaced the receiver with a sinking feeling. The truth was, he'd read the first sentence and then put it aside. He didn't want to think about his father's death. It made him feel ashamed. He sighed. He'd better get on with it.

First draft of Chapter 2, by M Marlowe. Temple Minnis, Monday, February 11, 1981, David read reluctantly. Moments later he was lost the past.

David was a man in a hurry. He called a company meeting on the day of his father's funeral and the first thing I knew about it was when he cornered me in the bar. 'Gotcha! I've been searching all over. Aren't you eating, Meli?

338

Don't you like the food? Harry did us proud I thought.'

'He did indeed, but I've lost my appetite.'

David wasn't listening. At twenty-five he was a huge man with shoulders like an ox, which served him well in rugby. His frizzy blond hair gleamed in the electric light. Today there was something new: a glint of triumph, a ready smile, an aggressive posture. Arrogance was all about him and it was only going to get worse. Beguiled by his new-found power, he was about to be devoured by his own ego.

David put down the manuscript, stood up and very deliberately walked to the nearest mirror. He stared at his reflection for a long time, but he could see no trace of arrogance.

'Bloody bitch,' he muttered, returning to the manuscript.

'Can you round up the gang and herd them into my study?'

'Whatever for?'

'Ah ha! A surprise meeting.'

I winced. 'Let me get this straight. We've just buried your father. Well, he's in the grave, but I doubt he's buried yet. And you're calling a business meeting?'

'Time's running short.' His shrewd grey eyes gazed questioningly at me. David needed to be surrounded with willing helpers. He'd been testing me for some weeks, phoning with petty requests, but I was resisting.

'Why don't you call them yourself?'

'Because I'm the host and I have to hang around until the last possible minute,' he growled, looking sulky.

'Okay, will do. Where's your study?'

'Third on the right down the hall.' He pointed vaguely southwards. 'Gordon's there setting out the brochures. Meeting starts at two. I'll circulate amongst the guests until the last possible minute and then fade away. Come on, Meli. Lighten up. One drink won't hurt you.'

He pushed a glass of wine towards me and picked up his glass. 'To future profits.'

'I'll drink to your father. He was a good man who never harmed anyone.' Enduring David's anger, I drained my glass. I'd made a point, but at what cost! I'm allergic to wine and now I could feel it surging into my bloodstream, while my nose twitched and burned and my eyes began to weep.

What a bloody awful day. Naturally the gang had attended the 10 a.m. service in the old Temple Minnis church. Later we had stood shivering in our thin, dark suits that were quite inadequate for a bad December, unwilling to wear anoraks, keeping slightly apart from the hundreds of affluent relatives and business associates in their furs and cashmere overcoats who had gathered for final prayers at the graveside. Afterwards six of us piled into David's new BMW for the short trip to the manor where the family wake was being held.

Looking back, I find it fitting that we wore mourning for our first company meeting, but at the time I'd felt furious.

I found Harry and Shirley scanning the buffet spread with anxious eyes, trying to work out what the guests weren't choosing. This was their first outside catering job for which they'd received a modest fee.

'You guys won't believe this,' I told them. 'David wants a business meeting at two sharp in his study. That's the third door on the right, down the hall from the entrance.'

'I believe it.' Harry gave a wry grin. 'From now on there'll be no stopping the bastard.' He gave his great booming laugh which didn't match his beanpole silhouette. Shirley's flowing black dress showed off her ash-blonde hair and concealed her bulge. Shirley was a short, compact, energetic girl and the life-force of her budding child radiated through her transmitting a glow of sensual vitality. Lately Shirley was either nursing a child or expecting another. Was it her second or third pregnancy? I felt bad because I couldn't remember, and envious because I, too, longed for a child. I was starting to consider single parenthood.

'He might have warned us,' Shirls grumbled. 'I'll have to supervise the twin's lunch and check with the babysitter.' She glanced at her watch. 'I'm sure I'll make it, but if not, Harry will be there.'

Harry's eyes beamed with tenderness. Analyse his face and he'd be ugly, but his caring eyes dwarfed his ugly features. When he bent to kiss Shirley I had to look away. I, too, longed to be loved like that.

As usual, Simon, was surrounded with a tight

knit group of discontented local farmers. Today it was the powerful supermarket groups who were under fire. I pushed my way through the throng and bumped into Laura, Simon's wife.

'God, but they're boring,' Laura drawled. A few heads turned our way. After Angela left, I'd hoped I might score with Simon, but this wasn't to be. Eventually he'd met Laura and proposed shortly afterwards, but I could never understand why he had fallen for her. Admittedly she was beautiful in a doll-like way, if you liked cold and fragile elegance. She was always well-dressed, she knew the right people, and she could trace her family roots back to the twelfth century. She was also a neurotic bitch, which was what Simon deserved for grabbing a pedigree. I passed on the message.

To hell with David. I decided to skip the rest of his friends.

David swore under his breath. So that was what went on behind Meli's sweet demeanor. He remembered that she had endless deadlines to meet and was never available when he wanted her. She'd always been a mystery to him. He was beginning to see why.

Looking delightfully Art Deco from the lake, David's mansion underwent a metamorphosis inside with long, dark corridors hung with ancient portraits. Dust enzymes attacked as I hurried past, sending me reeling and sneezing, eyes streaming, fumbling for absent tissues and swearing softly under my breath. I bumped blindly into the door, flung it open and found myself on deep Persian pile. Another no-go area. Damn! I exploded in a sneeze fit to blow my head off. Dust rose from the bookshelves bringing more tears. I was only vaguely aware of Gordon guiding me to a chair and handing me a large white handkerchief.

'Thanks, Gordon.'

Gordon was quiet and very, very private. If he had a sex life no one knew. He was always fashionably dressed, since most of his clothes were handouts from his modelling. There was nothing wrong with working his way through his studies, but why did he always look as if he were poised on the catwalk?

I rubbed my eyes and blinked feeling awed by the rich decor, the leather-bound books, the sheen on the long ebony table. David was such an arrogant sod and little wonder with a background like this. Ten places were laid around a long oak table, with glasses of sherry, name-tabs, notebooks, pens and brochures. David's name tab was at the head of the table. David Fergus: Chairman Temco. No round table for our David!

* * *

David swore and wiped a tear away. Fuck the book. And fuck Meli. He really didn't want to know how the rest of the world saw him.

'I'm glad you're first, Melissa.' Gordon looked nervous. 'I'd like your views.'

343

I took the brochure he offered and fingered the pages wonderingly. All our ideas, tossed out during informal meetings at Harry's pub, looked shockingly real in full colour on glossy paper, as if the converted homes, shopping arcades, club house, trout hatchery, stables, tennis courts and golf course already existed.

Gordon spoke first. 'I did the artwork.'

'Well done, Gordon.' I meant it. 'It's unbelievable . . . I mean . . . everything looks so established.'

'Exactly.'

I glanced up and scowled as Simon and Laura arrived, followed by Harry. David, newly pompous as lord of the manor and local squire, sailed in with three friends in tow. He launched into a formal speech about saving the environment, protecting our forests and keeping the hoi polloi out of this English paradise. 'We shall hold back change,' he thundered. A veritable St George against the sprawling urban dragon.

'Give over, David,' Harry called after five minute of tacky rhetoric. 'We're going to turn this village into a goldmine and that's the long and short of it.'

We all had something to barter for shares in the company and we handed over what we owned . . . or hoped to own . . . lock, stock and barrel. I was bartering my cottage and an inheritance from a great-aunt for ten per cent of the action. Simon was penniless, but his family farm adjourned David's land. He agreed that eventually he would provide a portion of his grazing land for a golf course in return for ten

344

per cent of the company. We all promised to pledge our shares to our banks for loans and lend the cash to Temco, which was the name David had chosen for our joint property development company. One way or other we had bargained all we would ever own and got ourselves deeply into debt as well. It was make or break for all of us, but we couldn't imagine how anything could possibly go wrong.

Halfway through the meeting, Shirley arrived wrapped in a roomy fur coat which hid her bulge.

'Heavens, Shirley, did Harry rob a bank?' David called.

Shirley flushed with pride. 'It's a present for being pregnant.'

'What is it?'

'American Cony. From the Rockies.'

Cony! Rabbit is my worst and Shirls made a point of sitting next to me. I love Shirley and at any other time I would have been pleased.

'Feel how soft it is.' Shirley caught hold of my wrist and ran my hand over the fur. My palm began to burn and itch. 'I've never seen a cony,' she was saying. 'Harry says they're quite rare. To tell the truth I feel a bit sorry for them.'

'Don't! They're evil-minded creatures,' David called out.

'It's a kind of furry bat with blood-sucking properties,' Gordon added.

Shirls shivered and Harry flushed. 'Shut up you lot.'

We did.

The meeting went off without a hitch and eventually turned into a celebration. We were all drunk . . . with dreams of future riches or alcohol . . . when we left at 2 a.m. Simon and Laura lived in a village cottage near mine so they offered me a lift home. Laura was laughing to herself as we came down the hill. 'Listen to this,' she giggled.

'The blood-sucking, evil-eyed cony, digs its lair in a mountain that's stony. It's claimed to be rare, so you'd better take care, that you don't let Shirls know it's a phony.'

'For goodness sake don't be so cruel,' Simon grumbled. 'How much have you drunk?'

'Enough to make you seem bearable.'

An uneasy silence made us all feel uncomfortable. I was glad to get out at the next corner. Prickles of glee were running over my skin. If that was married bliss, I could do without it.

And she had, David thought, putting the manuscript down to rub his eyes. He'd always fancied her. In the pre-cancer days, he'd done his best to legalise their relationship, but Meli would have none of it, comparing marriage to a mousetrap.

He sighed and carried on. Seeing himself through Meli's eyes was a humbling experience.

Over the next four years, dozens of homes were modernised and sold profitably to friends from university, most of whom had taken out 95 percent mortgages. Plans had been passed for the first shopping arcade and the building materials had been purchased. The construction of the various sports facilities was in progress and the club house was nearly finished. We took to wandering around the new sites dazed with optimism.

It was when we were up to our ears in debt, having hocked all we would ever own, that the blow fell. George Irving, a Scottish industrialist, whose family had run an international trading house in Kashmir and India for three generations, together with a consortium of Indian investors, were negotiating to buy Simon's family farm, Redhill, part of which ran alongside the main street of the village. They planned to erect a semiconductor plant. Factory buildings would extend over five acres. Highrise apartments for a thousand semiskilled and unskilled workers and their families, plus the infrastructure to create a high-density workers' village, including sports facilities and a Muslim cemetery, would sprawl over the land right next to our upmarket homes. The deal had been kept under wraps until it was almost too late to fight.

Disaster faced us. Once the news leaked to the media, property and share values would plummet overnight. The banks would call in our overdrafts which we couldn't begin to pay. We'd all be ruined, our inheritances lost and we would never sell another cottage. Existing homebuyers, who were our friends, would probably sue us, since their mortgages would far exceed the value of their homes.

'Jointly and severally, we and our company owed several million pounds. Gordon and David

347

had cut too many corners and would undoubtedly face fraud charges. We'd taken a gamble and lost.

As for Temple Minnis. I cried when I thought about all the losses that could never be calculated. Could you buy or sell the mist wafting through the woods, or put a price on the otters in the lakes, or the river where the trout swam? Could you set a figure for the village green, or the wetlands where endangered snipe and reed warblers nested? Temple Minnis was more than just a village, it was a way of life, something worth fighting for, a part of old England.

42

A widow gains her peers' respect. Her hard-earned place in the social pecking order is only slightly impaired by the lack of a male, but find yourself relegated to Number Two and it's quite another story. You find yourself ridiculed, while the 'other woman' is secretly admired. Shirley couldn't stop mulling over the injustice of her catastrophe as she chose a seat at the end of a row near the exit of their conference centre. Harry's Place was the venue for the Rate Payers meeting and David, in his position as chairman of Temple Minnis Property Company, was about to address local homeowners on ways and means to combat Irving's proposed tyre-incinerating plant.

It was a warm evening in mid-September and the French windows had been opened wide. From where she sat, Shirley could see the unruffled surface of the dark lake where bats were darting after insects. She was determined to show Harry just what he was discarding. Earlier that afternoon she'd taken time off to visit the beautician and the hairdresser. With her hair restored to its former blonde, her face brilliantly made-up and her body starved and pummeled into shape, she looked about as good as she could get. At the back of Shirley's mind was the hope that she could win back her husband. It shouldn't be necessary after giving him five kids, running his hotel and sharing his bed for twenty-six years, but she still loved him. Her stomach growled ominously and embarrassingly. Shirley grated her chair over the floor to hide the sound and considered her prospects.

A few weeks ago she had intuitively suspected that something was going on between Harry and his blasted personal assistant. Why did he need the woman? Hadn't she always done everything? But Harry had become big stuff since he became Chairman of the local Hotel Association. After some nagging, Meli had finally confirmed the truth and it hurt unbearably.

The seats were filling up well before time. She could hear Gordon's voice booming at reception. She half-rose but decided that rushing outside would be a tactical error.

Gordon walked into the hall, waved to a few people and mounted the steps to the platform where Shirley had arranged the table and chairs with glasses of water, notebooks and pencils. He caught sight of her and nodded.

A few minutes later, Shirley was surprised to see Ana standing in the doorway. How lovely she looked in her tailored black trouser suit, with her curly black hair hanging loose over her shoulders. She ached at the thought of all those hundreds of thousands of teenagers, emerging daily from their chrysalises, so soft and seductive, fresh and naive, with pouting lips and dewy eyes, wasp waists, breasts that had never been milksacs. She imagined them swarming into her world like flying ants on a summer's night, fluttering on every male and all those men who had fouled their nests, or fallen off their pedestals, were magically transformed into shining knights in the eyes of these näive nymphs.

Gordon whispered to Ana and she turned abruptly and saw Shirley. Her warm brown eyes lit up with a smile as she hurried towards her.

'Oh, Aunt Shirley! I've just arrived. You don't look well. What's wrong?'

Shirley licked her dry lips. 'I've been dieting . . . well, starving . . . and suddenly I feel sick. Come and sit with me, love. Why are you here? I wouldn't have thought this would interest you.'

'Guess what? I'm stringing for the local rag and I'm loving it. Look here's my press badge. See here.' She flipped it out of her bag and waved it in front of Shirley's face.

'Hold it back a bit, love. I can't see without my glasses. Have you had anything published?'

'My first story . . . about our vicar . . . will be out tomorrow.'

'Well done. So you're going to write about this tyre-incinerating problem.'

'I cheated, Shirls. Gordon mentioned this to Mum when they took me to lunch and I listened in. I've already outlined it to my editor and he's very interested.'

Shirley fixed her troubled eyes on the doorway and saw Harry walk in and glance around the room. He saw her, nodded curtly, and stepped back into the hall. If he'd struck her with a cow prod, she couldn't have felt more stunned.

'We've never even had a fight,' she whispered through dry lips. 'Yet lately he seems to hate me.

351

Did you see the way he looked at me?'

'I expect he's in a bad mood. Men often are, it seems to me.'

Ana reached for her hand and squeezed it and it was strangely comforting.

Shirley's hopes of reconciliation fast faded when Harry returned closely followed by his PA who seemed to have been reborn. She, who fitted unobtrusively into a corner of his office, skillfully camouflaged in a dark grey trouser suit, with glasses and her hair scraped back in a bun, was now revealed as an exotic, costly vamp. She had everything and she made sure everyone knew it. Her red silk trouser suit clung to a voluptuous, but perfectly slender figure, her long black hair tumbled around her shoulders, her profile was perfect and when she turned to the audience, Shirley saw that her eyes were large and deep blue. Her plunging neckline reached to her delicate waist revealing that she was bra-less and that her breasts were full, perfectly moulded and mainly visible. She mounted the platform, sat beside Harry and crossed her legs, revealing a gold ankle chain clasped around a shapely, tanned ankle. The shroud of hurt and despair settling over Shirley almost choked her.

'Fuck her! Why would someone like her want my Harry?'

'Maybe she doesn't,' Ana whispered. 'She's absolutely stunning.'

'It's the money,' Shirley snarled.

Harry, in his new poncey suit and shirt, was eloquently avoiding her eyes as he introduced

Gordon and David, whom everyone knew. Silly bugger!

Shirley couldn't take another moment of humiliation. What did he want her to do . . . lie down and die? She felt shamed and inadequate, like an old coat flung out with the garbage.

'I'll walk outside and sit by the lake. I need to be alone, Ana.'

'Will you be all right?'

'Of course I will.'

* * *

Taking advantage of a storm of applause, Shirley left via the French window and walked slowly down to the shore. She sat on a bench, muttering and swearing between her rasping sobs as she gazed wildly across the lake and tried to ignore the uproar in the hall. Harry was addressing the meeting and his voice, reminiscent of past happiness and blighted hopes, hung in the misty air. For how long would she manage to hang in here?

Last week, when she'd taxed Harry with what Meli had told her. Harry had offered her a lump sum to get out of the hotel. It wasn't enough. Not nearly enough. Money could never repay her twenty-six years of solid toil, to say nothing of all that wasted love. Oh no! She'd built him and she could destroy him. She bent her head on to her knees and sobbed out her misery. Her mascara was running into her eyes and stinging like mad, her shoes were wet with dew, her feet frozen and she couldn't stop shivering, but she couldn't bring herself to move.

Footsteps were approaching and for a happy moment she imagined that Harry was coming to comfort her, but it was only Ana.

'Don't be sad, Shirley. What can I do to help?' She crouched beside her.

'You don't understand. Half the time I think I'm in shock. For twenty-six years he's been a wonderful husband and father. He loved me so dearly . . . and the kids. Now he seems to be possessed. It's like she's put a spell on him . . . a sex spell, of course. Harry was almost impotent, but somehow she gets it up for him. She probably puts Viagra in his coffee. My kids are broken-hearted. Harry is besotted with her and no one else counts.'

'I didn't know.' Ana bit her lip as she watched Shirley crying. She grabbed a tissue and handed it to her. The minutes passed as Shirley fought for self-control.

'I suppose you know that my mum and dad have split. Mum was talking to me the other day. She said that nothing lasts. The trick is to enjoy happiness while it's yours and to know when to let go. Move on . . . look elsewhere for happiness. Well, that's what Mum said. Old style romance is out. 'New Romance' is in and it's often only short term, so make sure you have a good career and enjoy love while you have it.'

'Did Laura say that? I didn't know she could be so cynical.'

'Maybe she was being realistic. You and Uncle Harry were the only couple we knew who were still together.'

'I'm spoiling your story, Ana. You should be inside getting the news.'

'The locals are queuing for shares in the new property company, about to be formed. They've pledged themselves to raise the cash, so it's all over. You're more important than any silly story. Harry will come crawling back. You'll see.'

'Are you serious about this journalism?'

'Of course I am.'

'Then I'll tell you something that will interest you. I don't believe David ever sold those fields he's trying to flog to the local homeowners. I'll tell you why. One of my bedroom windows overlooks that area and I often see David checking out the fences. He's been doing it for years. Prods in the bushes with a stick to make sure no one's dumping rubbish. I haven't seen him there for a month now, but I don't believe that anyone would check out a couple of fields regularly if he'd sold them years ago. Doesn't make sense. Specially David. And he needs money badly.'

'Hm!' Ana sat silently contemplating her lack of financial know-how. Dad was right. She was an ignorant girl with a big mouth.

'You must follow it up, Ana. And there's something else you might like to look into. Has anyone told you about the 1985 incident here in the lake? I was present when the directors of the property company drew straws to decide who would bump off Irving. They faced ruin, you see. You can look up the cuttings in your newspaper library.'

Riveted with shock and excitement, Ana could

355

hardy think straight. She'd read the brochure she'd been given at the door. The directors listed were Harry, Shirley, Meli, David, and Gordon. Could one of them murder?

'Ask around. Follow it up. Melissa knows a lot about it. She's supposed to be writing about it.'

'Wow! Thanks, Shirley. You're a star.'

'Be careful. You'll have to check things out very carefully.'

'Of course. Anything else you've got tucked up your sleeve?'

'Maybe for later. Look, people are leaving. It didn't take long to sign them up. You should go now.'

'But will you be all right? Don't stay out here. Promise!'

'Only for a while.'

Deep in thought, Shirley hardly noticed the hall lights being switched off. Ana wouldn't miss a scoop like that. But would the police take it seriously enough to reopen the case? And would the scandal be rough enough to get rid of Harry's precious PA? It had to be Harry who moved the signpost. She'd always known that. The others had never realised how much Harry had borrowed to rebuild the hotel. The night before the accident, he was up all night, pacing his office and with good reason. Who'd want to visit a plush conference centre standing the shadows of a five-acre factory and surrounded with a high-density workers' village? They would have lost everything.

Besides Harry, who else was there? Gordon would never have the guts. Or would he? She'd never been sure. David always delegated, but could you delegate murder? Everyone thought it was Simon, but she knew that it wasn't. He'd called in at the hotel before leaving and asked her to pop in on Laura around midday. She was threatening a miscarriage. Lunchtime, Shirley had gone around the lake, searching for a lost swan and she'd made a point of checking out the parking sign. So someone had moved it after Simon left for London. That left Meli, who was writing a book about it. Would she do that if she were the guilty one? Perhaps. But she'd put her money on Harry. He was a ruthless bastard. How could they have coped with three kids and another on the way, what with all those debts and an empty hotel?

As she reached the steps, Gordon and David walked out of the hotel. Lingering in the doorway, she heard Gordon say: 'Let's take a turn around the lake before we leave, David. I want to tell you something confidential.'

'Bit chilly isn't it?'

'But secure . . . ' David shrugged and the two of them disappeared into the shadows as Shirley walked inside.

Glancing at his friend, David saw that Gordon's eyes were radiant with secret amusement. Like Puck on crack. He had a mind full of dirty tricks which had saved them on many occasions.

'A Japanese consortium are about to take over Irving's plant,' Gordon said. 'Irving's played out because he can't market enough units, but the Japs can. There's still a growth market in the

357

East for mobile phones and the rest of it. They're going to let Irving keep ten per cent of the action if he hangs in there for a couple of years. It's up to us to grab all the shares we can while trying to keep the price fairly constant. I have a full time PR girl spinning out bearish reports. I suggest you spread your purchases over a number of brokers and buy in small lots under nominees. We don't want anyone to get wind of a takeover.' His lips were quivering and twisting into a smirk.

David frowned. 'Anything could go wrong and we'd be stuck with a load of useless shares. We don't know enough about it.'

'Well, as a matter of fact, we do. You see, I'm in on the deal.'

David swore. 'You've been moonlighting, you bastard.'

'No, it was sheer luck. I was contacted by a head hunter with a short-term commission, which was to design an extension to . . . wait for it . . . Irving's plant.'

'You've got to be kidding.'

'That's what I thought until I investigated. Naturally I jumped at the job just to get in on the action. Big profits are there for the picking if we plan this one properly.'

'I haven't seen a sign of anyone vaguely Japanese around Temple Minnis,' David complained.

'That was my idea so that no one gets wind of any takeover. In confidence, the company's called Tohara Trading. They're multinational traders and manufacturers who are moving into

England for the first time. They have a firm of international finance experts scouting around. You wouldn't know them if you saw them.'

'Why here, of all places?'

'It'll be a back door to the EU for other goods marketed by Tohara's group. The truth is, it'll be more like an assembly plant for various items whose parts have been made by various Far East bases. That's why they need an extension for a massive stockroom.'

'Shrewd buggers. They probably won't do much more than stamp 'made in England' on every item. Well, at least that's something,' David grumbled. 'The way things are going, that sign will soon be rarer than a black parrot. Everything from cars to shoe makers are pushing offshore. I don't know what England's coming to. Local endeavour can't even support our steel industry. We're following Japan's footsteps and look what happened to them.'

'Not our problem,' Gordon said lightly.

That was his theme song, David often thought.

'I have an appointment with the bank first thing in the morning,' Gordon went on. 'I need bridging finance. I already have a parcel of Irving shares in my portfolio, but I want much more. Currently they're down to one pound fifty from twelve pounds, a year ago, but they'll hit twenty when news of the deal breaks.'

'This needs careful planning or we'll be bidding against each other. What's our ceiling? Keep me posted on what you're paying.'

'We'll have to play it by ear. We don't want to

bid against each other, but the point is . . . we want them.'

Gordon rapidly concealed his resentment. David took him for granted. He always saw him as some kind of personal assistant, ever ready to do his bidding, even on personal matters, like getting even with Luze. He longed to put him straight, but now would be the worst possible time.

'You in, or out, David?'

'What do you think?'

David's eyes were gleaming as he reached in his pocket for his calculator. Making and spending money never failed to put him on a high. He hardly spoke on the way back to the car. Every jab of the keys meant another small fortune falling like manna from heaven.

43

Brakes squealing, Ana came off the motorway in a squall of rain and sped towards George Irving's factory. She felt exhilarated. Shirley's idea about David's possible scam had intrigued the editor. 'If you get a lead story, I'll double your rate,' he'd promised. 'Your best bet would be to beard the lion in his den.' He'd called his secretary to make her an appointment and here she was, fired with enough aggression to blast Irving with questions.

She could hear shouts and whistles. She put her foot down on the brakes and skidded round the corner. An angry crowd, pressing hard against the barred iron gates to the factory yard, jostled and yelled. Behind the gates security guards nervously fingered their batons. Excitement flared as Ana grabbed her camera and stepped out of the car, taking shot after shot. Further up the street a column of demonstrators waved their placards while chanting: '*No to tyre incinerating.*' '*Don't pollute our planet.*' '*No to pollution.*' Chaos reigned.

Two policemen walked towards her. 'Press?'
'Yes.'
'If you value your car, Miss, you'd best park somewhere else,' one of them called.
'Thanks. That makes sense.' She drove to the end of the block, parked and ran back.
'Press,' she called to the security guard,

showing her card. 'I have an appointment with George Irving.'

He called through on his mobile before turning back to Ana. 'First floor, fourth door on the left.'

Emerging from the lift on the first floor, Ana was on a high as she hurried past glass-enclosed cubicles to reach the MD's office. Irving was standing at the window, rubbing his hands together nervously. He frowned at the sight of her.

'Rather young for this assignment, aren't you. This is an important story.'

'Don't worry. I'll get you front page headlines,' she quipped. 'So what's going on? Why does everyone think you're polluting the planet?'

He stood up and walked to the window and stood there cracking his knuckles, which jarred her nerves.

'Believe me, I don't know the first thing about a tyre-incinerating plant. I've handed out a statement, but the truth doesn't seem to make much difference to this mob. They're mainly students and not from these parts. Professional hooligans by the look of them. Someone's organised this demo, and I think I know who.'

Returning to his desk, he sat down, shook his head and sat drumming his fingers on the highly-polished surface before sliding a sheet of typed paper, on a company letterhead, towards her.

'You can take a copy.'

She read:

'*There is absolutely no truth in recent allegations that George Irving Consolidated are planning to erect a plant to incinerate used tyres. We have not applied for a license to use the new patents for steel recovery and no member of our holding consortium has attempted to purchase land for any expansion of existing production or for a new endeavour. The entire story is utter fabrication. We are currently in the process of consolidation. Signed: G Irving.*'

Ana placed her tape recorder on the desk and switched on.

'I can only assume that certain people . . . ' Irving broke off and sat staring at the tape recorder as if it would bite him. 'What was I saying?'

'That certain people . . . '

'Certain people are spreading rumours against me. It's beginning to feel exactly like the winter of '85. However, this time I've called in expert financial investigators. They're London-based with offices all over the world and they're very costly, but it's a necessary expense.'

'Is this the only reason for the demonstration?' She gestured towards the road.

'As far as I know, but retrenchments are yet another problem that have stirred up discontent.'

'If there's no truth in the rumour, why are you so harassed by it? Sooner or later the truth will emerge.'

'Our shares are falling. I don't need this adverse publicity and there's another reason. Local homeowners being duped into parting with big investments. Many Newtown residents have already applied for second mortgages to launch a property company to purchase . . . '

'I know about that . . . the field by the church. The one you're supposed to be buying. I went to the meeting yesterday.'

'Would it help to give you my word that I'm not involved?'

She smiled. 'I believe you, but that won't help either of us. We need something tangible to go on.'

'D'you want some coffee, young lady?'

'Mm, yes. That would be nice.'

There was a light knock and Irving's secretary came in and handed him a fax.

He peered at it and stood up looking agitated. 'Please wait here. I have to talk to you. I won't be long. My secretary will bring you some coffee.' He left, closing the door behind him.

Irving was gone for ten minutes. The coffee came and Ana helped herself. When, at last, Irving returned he was looking happier. Locking the door behind him, he picked up the telephone receiver, growling: 'Hold all calls.'

For a while he sat silently doodling on his pad. 'I'll begin at the beginning. Back in '85,' he began eventually. 'At my late wife's insistence . . . I decided to site our proposed semiconductor plant in or around Temple Minnis. Several industrial property developers were scouring the district for suitable land and it so happened that a local farm was offered. It was ideally placed and I decided to go ahead.

'At the time I had no idea that I would come

up against a certain local property developer and his partners who had been converting old labourers' cottages into up-market homes and selling them at exorbitant prices. In particular, David Fergus was intent on turning the area into an upmarket zone. Fergus had masses more land to sell at a price, as and when he succeeded in creating the need for expansion. It so happens that David Fergus is facing bankruptcy and fraud charges right now.'

Ana sat up with a jolt. Fraud charges against Uncle David. Wow!

'This business about tyre incinerating cropped up first a couple days ago, which is when I called in a top company of investigative economists. They're fast workers. This morning I received a fax from them stating that the land which Fergus claims is destined to house a recycling plant, was once owned by him. It's a scam, I'm sure of that, and these investigators will soon get to the bottom of it. I've just called them and arranged for them to see you. Make sure you get all the facts, but whatever you write must be checked with me first. Here's their address. I'll be seeing you soon, I assume.'

'Sure thing.'

For most of her journey home, Ana agonised over the morality of exposing her father's friend. Just where did her allegiance lie? Being a journalist wasn't quite as straightforward as she had imagined. For the first time in her short writing career she was faced with a question of loyalty versus a scoop.

Part 4

Autumn, September 22 – December 20.

Softly, the north wind
Flutters the autumn leaves.
It is but a warning.

44

Luze stood at the gate in the blustering wind clutching the note Simon's assistant, Sarah, had thrust into his hands.

'*David wrote to the bishop accusing you of heresy. He seems anxious to get rid of you. I wonder why??? An agent will be in the congregation taking notes, so toe the church line for once. Simon.*'

Ah, he thought. Simon is a good friend. Joy brought a lump to his throat. The knowledge that he was being spied on was insignificant compared with this discovery. David was a Neanderthal cretin, a body bag chockful of puss, yet Meli had gone back to him like a deranged torture victim. If he meditated for weeks he still wouldn't understand how she could have done this.

He walked back to the vicarage worrying if his sore throat would affect his sermon. How would he cope with an English winter? September was supposed to be autumn. Winter only started in December, yet he hadn't seen the sun for a fortnight. His mind veered back to Simon's note. The bishop's agent! Yeah, yeah! That made sense.

Glancing in the hall mirror, he caught sight of his eyes throbbing like red warning lights. He'd been up most of the night preparing a sermon on consciousness. It combined his total studies and years of meditation. He passionately longed to tell the world what he knew and to share the joy of his close encounters with the amazing cosmic force.

So why should he stick to Church dogma, since the churches were mostly empty? The Church had had its chance for two centuries, but it had failed the people. Half the population of Britain didn't even believe in their own immortality.

There must be a way to repackage the age-old message. The way ahead, Luze truly believed, was to mix and match, taking the best from all the world's teachers: combining Zen's freedom and intellectualism with Buddhist, Hindu and Christian teaching. These three rivers sprang from the self-same spring, only parted by different cultures and dogmas. But the bishop's agent would be there, he reminded himself, so perhaps he should keep his precious sermon until later. Regretfully he pushed the pages into the desk drawer and rifled through a file of back-up sermons for something truly innocuous, hating himself as he did so. There was always another Sunday.

Are you sure? a small voice squeaked at the back of his mind. 'Phew!' Luze exhaled noisily. Tell them the truth, for heaven's sake. Why else are you here?

He sat cross-legged to meditate, but a sudden image of Meli sitting in the bath, as she had looked yesterday, seared his mind. She was naked and her white skin glistened as she squeezed the sponge over her shoulders. She turned and smiled at him, green eyes glinting with satisfaction. Her thick red hair was fluffed out like a chow's. I could have that woman forever. I have only to use my mind . . . perks of my former profession. But she had to be his of her own volition, or not at all. He made an effort to free himself from cloying thoughts.

A loud ring at the doorbell brought Luze back to the present. He swore as he scrambled to his feet and hurried to the front door. The wind raced gleefully down the passage, spiralled, blew down his neck, puffed in his sore ear and curled around his cold feet. He couldn't stop shivering.

Cunning eyes blinked up at him from a round, simian face. The bishop's agent looked wrinkled, sly, merciless and obsessed with money. That's his weakness, Luze decided. Clearly he wasn't expecting someone as big or muscular as Luze, but he disguised his fear with a simpering smile.

'I'm from the bishop's office. Name's Aubrey St John-Brown. Can I come in?'

He raised one limp, white paw and pushed past Luze, walking straight to the living room. He'd been there before, that was clear. His hips were all wrong, Luze noticed, for he walked with bent knees and toes pointing outwards which increased his anthropoid appearance.

Reached the center of the living room, he turned and glowered at Luze. 'I'm a lawyer by profession, not a cleric, so I don't make decisions. I listen and record. You're skating on thin ice, Luze, but you've got one thing in your favour, you're the token black in this area, so no one wants to see you go. You get my meaning. I'm here to warn you that we've heard strange reports about you.'

'Please sit down.'

'No. I'm not staying. Too warm for my liking. Does the Church pay for the heating?'

'A local property company covers services.' Luze bridled with resentment at his impertinence.

'That's something. Pretty nice here. You've got yourself a comfy billet, Luze. I don't mind admitting, I'd like something like it. You've been very silly. What's this I hear about magical cures, finding lost dogs and something weird about a certain lottery win?'

'The power of prayer, my friend.' Something you will never experience, you puffed up toad.

St John-Brown gave a snickering sneer. 'The bishop might fall for that, but I certainly won't. Just lay off the cons. Do we understand each other?'

'I understand you perfectly.' This guy had no business in a spiritual realm since there wasn't an ounce of love in him. Luze smothered an urge to pick him up and fling him out.

'I'll be seeing you again. Be warned.' The agent turned, gathered his dignity like a cloak, and fled.

★　★　★

Was he going to run from the likes of St John-Brown? Was he hell? He picked up his precious sermon and smoothed his long fingers over the ruffled pages. Standing in the presbytery later, he stared in amazement at dozens of flower arrangements which had suddenly appeared, filling the church with fragrance. Mrs Montrose was already seated at the piano and the young choirgirls from Newtown were moistening their incredible throats with the barley water he provided and giggling at their jokes. He frowned. Each one of them was his own personal discovery, but he should have included a token white. When he listened to their voices he experienced pride such as Livingstone must have felt when he caught sight of the Falls. Pride turned to shock as the pews filled to capacity. He noticed so many new faces and the newcomers came from both sides of the railway line. All races, all ages, all incomes and religions were out there, by the look of things, like a microcosm of the Isles. On the right was a mass of crimson fezzes bobbing around like poppies in the wind and it was still ten minutes before deadline. Incredible! The verger was staggering in with spare folding chairs and already a group of youngsters were sitting cross-legged in the aisles. As Luze listened to the low rumble of muttered prayers, the pianist's asthmatic breathing and the crunch of footsteps on the gravel driveway, he had a strong impression of being the accused in a sensational trial, but what was the charge and was he guilty or innocent?

The sight of David with his arm around Meli brought a painful stab of jealousy. Joe was with his mum, Mrs Thomson, she of the big mouth, who had caused him so much trouble, but filled his church. They had all come to grasp luck by the scruff of its neck and he feared their eager eyes and acquisitive faces.

He strode to the pulpit, greeted them all and stood feeling dazed through the first hymn, hardly noticing the brilliant voices soaring with joy. Would he succeed in digesting his lifetime's quest into one brief sermon? The hymn was drawing to a close. He squared his shoulders. Expectant faces gazed eagerly towards him. He and they knew what they were really waiting for, but they had to listen.

* * *

Sitting in the pews, notebook and pencil poised expectantly, Ana could see what a stew Matt was getting himself into. He mopped his brow a couple of times and gazed anxiously around as if trying to find the courage to begin. He began with a roar, which made her jump and she could see the folks around were startled, too.

'My friends, we must look within for that which we seek,' his deep voice bellowed. 'We are too evolved, too sophisticated, too clever to be spoon-fed our beliefs. Besides, it's too important for each of us. I guess you all manage your own financial transactions, don't you?' He gazed earnestly at them and his congregation were persuaded to make a couple of hoarse assents. 'So how much more important is it to find your own spirituality? Each one of you must take responsibility for finding the way and attaining your own enlightenment. No one else can do it for you.'

Ana sat up and shivered. That was exactly what she'd always felt.

'Through meditation you can achieve enlightenment. Through enlightenment you will discover who you really are. Wisdom exists deep within our minds and wells up like a spring, because we share with God one nature, or one mind.

'All of us, everywhere, together with the Infinite, are one. God created consciousness so that He can go with us, think with us, hurt with us, from birth to rebirth, until eventually we rejoin this Cosmic force of love. God shares our lives, feels our pain, hopes our hopes. In other words, our consciousness is God's consciousness, or Buddha nature. Imagine a beehive and we, the worker bees, eventually return bearing our uniquely gathered nectar of love, integrity and moral responsibility.'

He paused and crossed his arms. 'How can I convince you unless you find out for yourselves,' he said in a deep growl.

Matt's confidence seemed inversely linked to his congregation's fidgeting. Looking round, Ana saw anxiety and embarrassment, but that was mainly the wrinklies. Most of the guys around her age were listening intently.

'This oneness is not a new idea. On the contrary, it has been known for generations by all manner of people. 1 Corinthians chapter 3 verse 16, reads: *'Do you not know that you are* the temple of God and that the Spirit of God dwells in you?' 'All is One and One is All,' is taught by all the schools of Buddhism.

'The great Buddhist master, Rinzai Lin-chi, who died in 867, and who launched the school of Zen, said: 'When you cease to search outside yourself, you will find that you are one with God and all living creatures'.' A restless rustling, like the wind seemed to take hold in the congregation. Matt put down his notes and glared at them all.

'Everyone shares the cosmic mind, or God's nature, or to put it another way: Buddha-nature lies deep inside you. So it stands to reason that you are good, loving, compassionate and wise, and all deviations are only caused by a loss of faith in yourselves. Sometimes we fall by the wayside, but God, picks us up. We come from God, we go back to God and our inner power is always there. So use it.'

Those last three words were delivered like gunshots. Ana dropped her head and drew in a deep breath. She could see the trickles of sweat running down Matt's back and his neck. Tension she guessed. He looked so disappointed.

★　★　★

That was it, Luze decided, twenty minutes later. He'd had enough for one day, although there was plenty more where that came from. Why couldn't they understand what an exciting adventure life was? They would all be around forever. They would never be destroyed.

376

A hand shot up. Luze frowned. This wasn't school.

'Tell us about magic,' a gruff voice called from the back of the church. His words were taken up by the congregation like echoes bouncing from the walls: 'How d'you fix the lottery, Matt?' Pandemonium reigned.

Luze felt an overwhelming need to escape into the open air and be alone for a while, but that was impossible. He waited impatiently for quiet.

'All right, if that's what you want, but you might be disappointed. Magic is the power to make things happen against all logic and reason. It can be very important and powerful for us all if it is in the right hands. You might ask what it can do? The correct answer would be 'anything'. It is not wrong as long as it is used for good. Say, for instance, you were to concentrate on fame and fortune. That would be okay as long as no one else was harmed. Good luck is often the same thing as magic, or positive knowing.

'Visualising and positive knowing (rather than thinking) makes things happen. That is because we share that infinite, all-powerful nature, limited only by the extent of our brains and intellect.'

Luze leaned over the pulpit, in a state of numb anxiety, remembering that odious St John-Brown. 'I don't suppose many of us here have an inkling of the power of our minds, but this power must only be used for good. Those who use this power wrongly discover that return to sender takes on a new and deadly meaning.'

An eerie silence fell around the congregation.

For a few moments you could hear Ajax plodding his weary way over the flowerbeds. Luze sensed their fears. He felt overwhelmed by his responsibility. Sometimes he thought there were as many views as there were people in this over-populated island. That's why Zen suited their characters so well.

'I'll read from the New Testament: Jesus said: '*Therefore I say unto you, what things soever ye desire, when ye pray, believing, ye shall receive*'.'

He glanced at his watch. 'I'll get something organised at another venue and then you can ask all the questions you wish.'

'But Matt . . . '

'I'm sorry. This is neither the time nor the place for questions and answers, although I feel it should be.'

As Luze searched the congregation, his lips pursed with disappointment. They'd forgotten his sermon. All they wanted was magic. Something for nothing. Had he got through to anyone, he wondered? The bishop's agent would report back to the bishop and that would be that. He had a few more days, Luze reckoned, but not many.

45

Rashid Puri had been laid low, and it wasn't only by his months on the dole. Since the horror of 9/11 he had stumbled through his idle hours, wild-eyed and anxious, hardly noticing if any member his busy family bothered to address him, but at least in the local coffee house he could voice his concerns. A strong scent of roasting coffee beans and Turkish tobacco filled the warm café cheering Puri, when he arrived at ten a.m. to meet his friends and discuss news and views.

His friend, Tariq, the local baker, motioned him over to join his table before continuing his sentence. 'As I was saying, from now on, each one of us will be viewed as a potential terrorist.'

A sadness seemed to wash over Puri as Tariq uttered these words. The rest of the café's clientele looked gloomy, too. They had all experienced a sense of loss with this terrible catastrophe. Like most of his friends, Puri could fill a book with his predictions of doom for the Brits' way of life, but he loved the people for their instant acceptance of the many foreigners, cultures and religions that had arrived in their midst. They judged each comer for what he was, not where he came from and generally-speaking, they adopted a live-and-let-live attitude. God forbid this terrible deed would change their perceptions.

'I was very relieved when I arrived from Pakistan,' he said. 'I simply sank into the day-to-day fabric of British life, like a purple thread woven through a multi-green tweed cloth. Just like the rest of us, I blended in, enhancing the fabric, becoming part of the whole.'

'So what's wrong in that,' Fouad, who owned a bookshop, interrupted, drawing deeply on his long-stemmed pipe and wishing Puri weren't quite so fanciful with words.

'It's their acceptance that threatens our traditions.' Tariq took up the challenge. 'It's too easy to absorb the culture here. Our youngsters are becoming more individualistic as they compromise and adapt. We must always remember that our faith requires that we love for the sake of God and hate for the sake of God.'

'I can't stop worrying about our position here,' Puri said, without much hope of being understood. 'In my opinion, Islam was the true casualty of 9/11. Right now Muslim terrorists hold the world in their terrified grip. We've spent so many years trying to bring about an understanding of our culture, but now we will see our progress destroyed by a single action . . . an action born of this hatred you're talking about. It's a tragedy for us all.'

'That's true, my friend,' Fouad interrupted him.

Puri hurried on. 'So far the British are more protective towards their minorities than any other nation in the world and I love them for this. We need to hang on to the *status quo*.'

'Perhaps you love them too much. We need to

380

cast out the traitors amongst us,' Ahmed said fiercely.

Puri fought back deftly. 'Everyone is searching for Nirvana, there are various perceptions of it by all mankind, not just Muslims, but possibly we are short-sighted in restricting our love to members of our own faith.'

There was a sudden silence as his friends glared accusingly at him.

'One can go too far,' Ahmed retorted. He bent his head to whisper in Puri's ear. 'Are you aware that Bela Shah was seen drinking in a public house last weekend? She's often seen with Simon Shepherd, a local farmer.'

Puri, an intelligent, honest trader, felt a sense of great sadness. He thought of Bela as a daughter. Perhaps Ahmed was wrong, he wondered without too much confidence. From then on he sat mourning silently, listening to the others, but not participating.

⋆   ⋆   ⋆

Bela parked at the supermarket on her way home to buy some groceries which she planned to slip into the kitchen when Mr Puri wasn't looking. The way he'd been laid off so suddenly by her father, after so many years of work, was an injustice that troubled Bela. No one knew that George Irving was her father, but she still felt like a traitor. And that wasn't all of her guilt. She had joined the Muslim community and the Puri's household because she had chosen to go back to her roots and be true to her mother's

381

faith and culture, but now that she'd fallen in love with Simon she felt like an imposter.

It was late September and already there was a chill in the dusk air and Bela was looking forward to getting home. She opened the front door and hurried along the passage, enjoying the homely odours of steaming, spiced food.

The Puri's living room was crowded, as usual, as their extended family tried to squeeze around the ornate, dark oak table, standing beside a carved sideboard, a cupboard and a warmer. The other half of the room was full of velvet sofas, with tasseled cushions, gathered around an old Persian carpet in front of the hearth. Shasta, who had been rushing from the kitchen to the table with dishes of rice and steaming vegetables, took out a tissue to mop her face. Everyone was there, Shireen, the Puri's eldest daughter, with her husband, Hassan, the ugly sisters and a neighbour.

Bela dumped her shopping in the kitchen and hurried in to sit down, but stopped short when she realised that everyone was watching her accusingly.

She took a deep breath and hung on to the chair. 'So where's the rack? And the thumb-screws? And the knotted whips?' she quipped, but there were no answering smiles.

She turned to Mrs Puri, silently begging her for help. 'What's wrong?'

'We've had disquieting news, Bela,' Mr Puri began, aggrieved and accusing.

'Bela, dear,' Mrs Puri interrupted him. 'I know that you've come from a very different cultural background and it can't be easy for you to return to your mother's faith, but we have to speak up.'

'We're not spying on you,' Mr Puri stammered, 'but certain information has been forced upon us by just about everyone in this street and the next. In fact, it's all over the village and even the Imam called round this afternoon.'

'It seems you spent last Saturday evening drinking in a pub with a crowd of rowdy men.' Shasta whispered from behind.

She laughed with relief. 'Is that it? It's all right. I was with Simon. You met him, remember? He ordered wine and I must admit I drank some, too.' Maddeningly, her voice was faltering. Pulling out a chair, she sat down, just to show she wasn't scared of them jointly or severally, and smiled around the table at their wooden faces. 'So what's the problem?' she flung at Mr Puri.

'Since you live here we're expecting a certain decorum in your behaviour. Muslims don't drink alcohol. You know that. Of course, some do in private, but the point is they should not. My dear Bela, you must make up your mind. If you want to be one of us, you must obey the rules.'

Oh God! That accent! She wanted to laugh and cry at the same time.

'Bela.' Mrs Puri took over. 'I'm sure you have a reasonable explanation.'

'Simon is a very close friend. When in Rome . . . ' Whatever made me think I would fit in here? She felt frantic. 'Look, I think I'll go to bed. I'm tired. I've had a long day.'

From Mrs Puri's expression it seemed that a

profound tragedy had struck her family.

'You've shamed us all with this friendship of yours. An infidel, and still married,' Mr Puri said. 'We understand how difficult this must be for you, but give us some ammunition to fight back.'

'To fight whom . . . the neighbours?'

'The Imam. He called. He wanted to speak to you, but I told him you were working.'

'I have nothing to say. Simon is my friend and if I wish to see him, I will, although not in this house, out of respect for your ways.'

'You call that respect?' Mrs Puri sniffed.

'Great,' she said. 'Just great. I'll go and pack. I'll leave as soon as I can. My rent is paid up until Friday and I need time to find a place to stay.' Her voice died away as she stood up.

Mr Puri frowned at her. 'You don't have to go. Think first, Bela. You must make up your mind what you want and just who you are. You never mention your father . . . '

'I hate my father, that's why.' She blasted unblinking fury at Mr Puri, who looked embarrassed.

'Hate is too strong a word, surely.'

'He betrayed me, just as he betrayed you.' Oh God! What had she said?

Mr Puri kept a grubby handkerchief in a top pocket of his shirt. He took it out and rubbed his wet forehead. 'You surely can't mean . . . that woman's daughter?' The words were flung with infinite menace. He broke off looking embarrassed.

'What do you mean? Why did you say *that*

woman? You must tell me.' Now her voice was reduced to a whisper.

No one would look at her. 'Please keep out of pubs, Bela, for whatever reason. We live here and we don't want to lose all our friends.' With that, Puri turned away sadly and sat down.

Bela hesitated in the doorway. 'I'm fond of you all and I've been happy here, so thank you,' she said.

★ ★ ★

Bela spent a restless night. The way Mr Puri had said ' . . . that woman's daughter . . . ' had hurt. What did he mean? What had Mother done to anger the Muslim community? Was it because she had married her father?

She rose at dawn to pack. When she carried her first load to the car she found flowers outside her a room and a note that read: 'It's not too late. We hope you make the right choice and remain here with us. We all love you.'

Where on earth could she stay at short notice? With Simon, obviously. Perhaps this was fate pushing her into making a decision. She could never love anyone as she loved Simon and she wanted nothing more than to live with him for the rest of her life. Such a slight and silly suspicion kept them apart. It was the fear that Simon might have been involved in her mother's death. But that was absurd.

Mrs Puri's eyes turned glacial when she saw Bela carrying her overnight bag to the front door.

'Wait right there, Bela,' she called, rushing to block the way while she sent Shasta to fetch her husband, who was in the back garden talking to Hassan.

'Well, that's great,' Bela muttered. 'Just great! I couldn't get luckier.'

Mr Puri put his hand on her shoulder and stared into her eyes. There was no anger there, only sorrow.

Mrs Puri had tears in her eyes. 'Bela, dear child, you must reconsider. Forgiveness and tolerance is part of our creed. We all love you, Bela. Say something, Rashid,' she ordered her husband.

'Listen Bela, however bad our disagreement may seem to you, it will pass. I'm sure you'll understand how we feel. You had a bad start, but you said you want to get back to your Muslim roots. Don't run away. Perhaps we were too harsh. We're all fond of you and we don't want you to make silly mistakes.'

At that moment Hassan came in from the garden. 'You don't stay with Muslim relatives every weekend like you said, do you, Bela?' Hassan sneered. 'You stay at that farm, Redhill and you sleep with Simon Shepherd.'

How had he found out? She had never intended to tell them. She could never do that to Mrs Puri, but faced with a direct challenge she couldn't lie. Instead she clamped her lips together and picked up her suitcase.

'Simon has asked me to marry him.'

'I've heard that he's married,' Hassan put in.

'His divorce is in progress.'

'But how can you consider marriage when he's not a Muslim?' Aunt Dohra ventured.

'I love him. We haven't discussed religion yet.'

Mr Puri stood up and walked out, but the look he gave her in passing showed how much he despised her.

'You must leave here,' Mrs Puri was white with fury. 'We don't condone this kind of loose behaviour. And he's not even Muslim.'

'I'll come back and pack on Friday when my rent runs out,' Bela muttered. She was in tears by the time she reached her car.

'I don't blame them,' she whispered, as she drove half-blinded by tears. 'I should have moved out when I fell for Simon.'

She pulled over and sobbed out her misery. How could anyone ever understand what it was like to be half and half? Half of her longed to be Muslim, to carry on her mother's traditions and to be closer to her and her memory, but there was this other part that simply wanted to be free. 'If it weren't for my hard-headed, stubborn British half, I could have been so happy as a Muslim,' she muttered. Then she dried her tears and drove on towards the village.

46

Simon was walking back to the house after locking the barns for the night when he saw Bela's car driving up from the road. Bela's arrival at four p.m. each Friday was so predictable you could set your clock by it. He waited impatiently to find out what had brought her here on a Monday evening.

'Welcome home. This is a marvellous surprise. I was missing you like crazy.' Bela climbed out of her car looking as if she'd been crying, but what or who did she have to cry about? He decided not to ask what had gone wrong in her very private world, as he led her into the house. 'Have you had supper?'

'Thanks. I'm not hungry.'

'I'm starving. I must be psychic, there's a couple of unopened cheese pizzas in the fridge and some homegrown salad . . . washed and ready for you. How about making one of your superb Indian salads?' He followed her to the kitchen.

'All that I feared, happened. It's so stupid, but so predictable. I'm a fool to have thought it might work,' she explained as she bustled around in the kitchen. 'I feel much better already. It's amazing how relaxing it is to potter around doing something familiar.'

Her story poured out . . . pitiful and shabby and she told it with disheartening intensity.

'I'm still trying to decide, so don't try to influence me,' she said when she'd put the salad on the table and warmed the pizzas. 'You don't understand how I feel about being Muslim. How could you? My mother gave up her birthright when she married my father and in some strange way, that I don't really understand, I'm doing it for her, but it's difficult.'

'Maybe I understand more than you think,' he said gently. 'Freedom costs, Bela. If you are prepared to obey the rules and lose yourself in the well-being of the group, you can find contentment in selflessness. The English are all loners at heart. We don't impose so many rules. Everyone muddles through and somehow we hang on to personal initiative and individuality, but the point is, we have to go it alone. In a Muslim community there's the support of the wider family to help out, but this also controls you. What we call liberty they . . . or you . . . call licence. My own view is that your leaders don't trust people enough to make the right choices, but that's just my humble opinion. It's not the English way and you've been brought up English, or at least in an English school. Weren't you?'

'Yes, but don't pry.'

Holding back a sigh, Simon opened the wine.

'This is nice. I'm feeling better already. I love this old house.'

'I guess you realise that you've reached a watershed. For my part, your religion is your own, private affair, but I could never live by other people's rules. You'd have to go it alone.'

Bela picked at her food. The truth was, she was feeling sick. Lately she had a sense of foreboding about the future, although she wasn't sure why. Simon loved her, she knew that, but up until now, theirs was a strange sort of a love affair conducted mainly at weekends. Bela worked all hours Monday to Friday. In the evenings she was too tired to do anything but sleep, so she stayed at home. Her weekends were for Simon when they lived out the lie that their domesticity was real and enduring. Occasionally they ate out at Harry's Place, but mainly they liked their own company. She knew they had settled into a highly unsatisfactory groove, but to commit herself for life frightened her, perhaps because she'd felt so trapped last time round. She longed to talk about her fears. Perhaps there would never be a better time than this moment, she decided, with a twinge of doubt.

'How do you feel about something less final?' she asked.

'Which is..?' Simon looked surprised.

'Shacking up to see how it goes. You see, last time I was trapped. I think you feel the same way as I do, too. After all, you seldom talk about our future. Only today I've brought things to a head . . . or the Puris did . . . and that's not really fair on you.'

'Is that a fact, or your own theory?'

She ignored the question.

'Bela, listen to me. If I've been backward in defining our relationship, the fault lies with doubts about myself, not about my feelings for you. What can I offer you? Do I want children?

390

Am I still a farmer? Am I going to stay here at Redhill? I didn't have the answer to these questions, but lately I've been feeling more enthusiastic.' He reached over to refill her glass. 'Can we talk about it later? It's chilly tonight. I thought I'd light a fire. We could sit by the hearth and open the bottle of pure malt whisky I recently acquired and talk all we want.'

Which they did, to the crackle of wooden logs exploding and the strains of *Goyescas* in the background.

'Farming has changed irrevocably and Britain will be the poorer for it.' Simon looked glum as he refilled his glass. 'Most of my neighbours have converted sections of their homes, and their old barns into letting accommodation, so they can subsidise their meagre farm income.'

'You could do that.'

'*We* could. Believe me, that's our last option, but it may still come to that. I'm losing up to eight pounds an acre on producing wheat. I can't carry on indefinitely producing grain at a loss, at the same time I'm loathe to apply for agricultural hand-outs. If I restock, will the troops come here again.' He shuddered.

'Aren't you exaggerating?'

'Not at all. At times I'm tempted to turn part of the land into a nature reserve, but I have to live and pay my taxes. So am I to once again restock and marry and kid myself that what I have here is permanent, only to find that it has gone?'

'You might as well say, we'll soon be dead, so why live? Nothing's permanent. Nothing ever

391

stands still. Change is the only thing we can be sure of, except our love for each other. I believe that our love survives death.'

★ ★ ★

That night Simon made love with a tenderness Bela had never before experienced, but later he lay quietly staring at the ceiling.

'Can't you sleep?'

'No.'

'What the matter?'

He turned over. 'I don't want you to go. I want you to live here. The spare room downstairs would make an adequate office for you, and it's big enough for your furniture. After all, it's not so far from Newtown. Please stay. If you were happy . . . in a few weeks, or whenever the divorce is finalised, we could marry, if that's what you want. How do you see your future . . . marriage, children, giving up work, or something less conventional?'

'Simon, come here. Turn over.' She caught hold of his shoulder and hauled him on to his back. Putting her head on his shoulder and throwing her leg over his hips she gently pulled his face towards her. 'Yes, yes, and yes and if there are any more questions, yes. I want everything, but not necessarily in a hurry. The ball's in your court. Whatever you feel you can cope with is okay by me. Don't feel obliged, or trapped, or even rushed. My feelings aren't going to change in a hurry, whatever we do, or don't do. Of course I'll stay, if that's what you want.'

'Yet it took the Puris to get you to move. That tells me something that I don't want to hear.'

'I have a few problems of my own to sort out, too.'

'Want to talk about them?'

'Maybe soon. Meantime, let's stay together and see how we go.'

'Yes, and we'll be happy, I promise you.'

★　★　★

Why is it that I can't share my world with Simon? Bela was thinking. And what are my roots when all's said done? I'm a hybrid, I've always been a hybrid, a citizen of nowhere, part Muslim, part Christian, part nothing. But once I was delighted with the prospect of marrying Jason. I was braver then. My mother had the strength to break away from her roots, so why shouldn't I? Besides, I was hardly brought up Muslim. Mother's hurried catechisms when Father was out, and weekly visits to the mosque, did not denote a Muslim background. At least, not until Fatima took over the household. But I badly want to believe in something and belong to something, bigger than me . . . a creed to make life meaningful . . . a place where I belong. Simon offers me love and kindness, a beautiful home and future happiness, but would that bring fulfillment? Shouldn't there be something in my life that I would be prepared to die for?

Bela fell asleep, but woke in the night and lay awake worrying about her secretiveness. Of course, Simon was so right, but he didn't know half of it. Her inheritance was carefully invested by lawyers until she made a decision on how best to use Omar's wealth. She would certainly never touch a penny of it, but an Imam in Sopur was begging her to set up a trust fund for orphaned and abused children. She had just about made up her mind to do this and to appoint lawyers to oversee the fund, but sometimes she was tempted to return to Kashmir and handle the project herself.

She loved Simon dearly and she could wish for nothing more than to settle here and start a family, but her past exerted a strong pull. It was so full of mistakes and misery. She wanted to make it right . . . turn disaster into a triumph. To make amends. In the night, snuggled against Simon's back, she remembered Salma, her beautiful daughter and her eyes burned.

47

Ana had fallen in love with London, with the busy, cosmopolitan crowds, the fast pace, the dazzling neon lights that gave every evening a party atmosphere, the ever-changing shop windows where no expense was spared, all of which lent a sense of surging prosperity. She loved the local's quick wit and generous spirit, and the sense of being right at the crest of a new world order, where every conceivable race, culture and creed rubbed shoulders, happy and secure, as if unaware of their differences.

Ana's life was taking on new shape and meaning. She studied hard from Monday to Friday, worked as a waitress most evenings and freelanced for the local newspaper weekends. She usually managed one or two articles a week. These latest two were dynamite and had to be checked with Dad, since he might once have been involved with David and his henchmen. So she was driving to Redhill to meet Bela and face a traumatic Sunday lunch.

She glanced at her watch. It was midday and she had almost reached the Canterbury turn-off, so she was early. It wouldn't do to be late for her first meeting with Bela. She arrived and parked, but only Sam greeted her. He glanced up, saw her and flung himself at her. Ana sprawled on the floor of the porch, hugging him and enduring his sloppy tongue over her face and neck.

Where was everyone? She stood up and tried to brush the hairs off her trousers. Returning to her battered car, Ana opened the boot, took out the pot of chrysanthemums and set off for Grandpa's grave, with Sam racing around happily. She had promised to do this for Mae and she'd left it far too long. Mae had been in hospital for a week, something hush-hush. Then she had moved on to friends in Scotland to recuperate, refusing visits or sympathy.

Ana planted the flowers with the rusty old spade they kept behind the headstone and pulled out a few weeds. She walked back slowly and paused to sit by the dam. It was so still. Nothing moved. She could imagine herself in a painting entitled: *Noon in Redhill*. It was mid-October, but an unexpected Indian summer had painted the farm in Van Gogh's colours: ochre and saffron fields, dark purple forests and emerald shoots around the dam. To Ana, the impression was heightened by the unbearable silence: no sheep lowed in the hills, no lambs cried, even the air was hushed. She guessed that the lambs and calves she had saved were shut in the orchard. Dad was neurotic about them getting hurt.

She glanced at her watch. She'd have to go in. A twinge of fear twisted her belly, or was it regret? Sunday lunch with a stranger sitting in her mother's place was going to be painful.

The house had changed, she noticed as she walked inside. For starters, the doors and windows were all open. Then Sam rushed in ahead of her and sprawled on the rug. From the look of the hairs on it, he liked that spot. Arabian music ebbed and flowed like the tide and the scent of herbs and spices hung around. Sam was getting fat. Clearly Bela didn't believe in a cup of dog biscuits daily. Then she thought maybe she ought to ring the doorbell, so she went outside again and rang.

'In the kitchen,' she heard Bela calling.

Something was wrong. Surely this woman couldn't be Bela. She looked nervous as she twisted round from the stove and dredged up an anxious smile. Ana thought back to last Wednesday when she'd ducked her studies to spend the afternoon with Dad. 'She's immensely beautiful and clever,' Dad had claimed. 'She's also a linguist doing research for her Ph.D. in Middle Eastern languages and she works as a part-time translator.

'How dull,' she'd said spitefully, but Dad had laughed at her.

Bela's face was unusual: dark eyebrows soared like crows wings and under them her large eyes glowed like light shining through amber. Her nose was small and shapely, but she looked vulnerable and bruised. Not beautiful. No, never beautiful. She could be my sister, Ana thought. Her hair was plaited and she was wearing shorts and a T-shirt and standing barefooted on the kitchen tiles.

'Whoops! Mind the sauce,' Ana exclaimed. Bela grabbed the pan and lifted it from the hotplate just in time as it bubbled up.

'Oh, thanks. Dearest Ana,' she said, still looking over her shoulder as she stirred the simmering sauce. 'I've been longing to meet you.

You must never again ring the bell. Promise me. This is your home. I'm so glad you're here. If I neglect this sauce for one split-second it will curdle. Your father misses you so much. Did you know that? He's gone to fetch Mae, by the way. He won't be long.'

'Oh, really. So she's back. Have you met her?'

'No. I'm terrified.'

She pushed the saucepan from the hot plate and hugged Ana. 'Welcome home, Ana. I'm worried about you. You're so thin and pale. Is that normal, or aren't you eating properly?'

'I work hard,' Ana said, fobbing her off.

'Could you stir while I lay the table?' Bela asked. 'When it thickens, take it off fast. Where do you sit?' she called through the hatch.

'Down the end, near the window. You probably haven't made enough for me, but don't worry, I'm not very hungry.'

'I've cooked for you every Sunday, just in case. It was never wasted. Simon finishes the leftovers on Monday. I hope you'll eat properly.'

The sauce thickened. 'I think it's done,' Ana called. Bela rushed back and poured it over an exotic dish of pot-roasted lamb with aniseed and an aubergine bake for Ana.

'Wow! That smells good, Bela. Will you give me some lessons?'

'I'd love to.' She turned impulsively and hugged Ana. Together they pushed the food through the hatch onto the warmer and walked through the doorway into the high-ceilinged dining room. When Sam followed, no one yelled at him to go outside.

'Ah Sam. I almost forgot you. Come.'

Looking hopeful, the dog followed Bela to the kitchen. Watching curiously through the hatch, Ana saw him take a meaty leg bone gently from her and trot outside with it. Clearly this was routine on Sundays. Sam's never had it so good, Ana thought with a sense of deep contentment. She began to unwind.

★   ★   ★

The front door slammed and she heard Dad's footsteps coming from the kitchen garden to the kitchen. He walked in and caught Bela in a bear hug, rocking her too and fro, nuzzling his lips in her hair. Ana wanted to look away, but she couldn't. Their shared desire enveloped them both like an invisible aura. For the first time in her life Ana saw her father as a man, rather than a father and she was surprised to find that he was still attractive, with his blue-black hair, his sensuous lips and the way his eyes lit up when he laughed.

'There's Ana,' Bela tried to free herself as she pointed through the hatch.

Dad looked up, half-smiling, and waved his arm before clamping it back around Bela's waist.

'So you've met. I should have been here to introduce you both. Glad you came at last, Ana. I hope we'll see you often now.'

Ana was conscious of being an outsider. The orphan kid at a family party. Dad let Bela go and gave her a self-conscious wink before washing his hands at the kitchen sink. Strange how she'd always seen her father as a loser . . . it was as if she'd seen him through her mother's eyes. Now she saw a sexy, vibrant, handsome man. How could she have been such a fool?

There's a whole lot here that Mum wouldn't have tolerated, Ana thought nervously, but it seems to work better. Dad walked into the room smiling self-consciously.

'You're happy. I can see that.'

His eyes met hers and he smiled. 'Come here.' He put his arm around her shoulder and hugged. 'I never used to hug you enough. I'm worried about you, Ana. You look so tired and thin. Why is that?'

'I'm fine. So where's Mae?' she asked, avoiding the question.

'Tidying up. She's in a bit of a tizz.'

'Why?'

He shrugged. 'Women never cease to amaze me.'

Bela came hurrying in to serve the pot-roast. It had always been Dad's job. She began to ask questions in her low, seductive voice.

'So tell us about your day, Ana. I was in your college. I loved every minute of it. What are you studying?'

'Economics and allied subjects. Lately I've been thinking of switching to law and eventually specialising in human rights, but I need economics, too.'

'And you work all the time?'

'Some afternoons I walk to St James' Park and share my sandwiches with the ornamental ducks and geese. It's lovely there, especially when the lake and the trees blur with mist.

She broke off, remembering last Sunday when a military band, splendid in red and gold, marched from the Wellington barracks towards the palace, playing *Men of Harlech* while the tourists' cameras flashed. She had sat there unobtrusively watching the passing crowd of all nationalities and colours. London was her city and here lay her destiny, she was sure, but it was way off in the future. She wanted to make a difference, somehow, one day.

Mae came into the room looking extraordinarily nervous and self-conscious, tucking a chiffon scarf tied around her hairline. Her hair was blonde, most of her wrinkles had miraculously disappeared, her skin was smooth and the folds that used to spoil her eyes had vanished. Her neck was as taut as a young girl's and for the first time Ana realised that she must have been extraordinarily pretty when she was young. Ana looked away to hide her smirk.

'The holiday's done you good, Mae,' she said as she kissed her grandmother on her cheek. You look so young and . . . different.'

'That's what I said.' Dad winked at her.

'I can't return the compliment, Ana. What on earth have you been doing with yourself? You look tired out and so thin. Are you working nights?' Mae frowned at her.

Ana flushed and nodded.

'And weekends.' Bela added.

'I'm all right, Mae . . . Bela . . . Dad.'

The family plagued her with questions about

her life while they ate and she did her best to answer them.

'You were right, Dad. I need to study. Sometimes I'm scared I'll never know enough, never get there, but listen to this. I have the next front page lead in our local newspaper. I've unmasked a hoax. Of course I was given the lead, but I can't reveal my sources.'

'Spoken like a true journalist.' Dad beamed with pride.

'I'm sorry I can't tell you about it, but it'll be out in next Thursday. Right now it's being checked out by their lawyers. Well, maybe I can tell you just a little. There is no tyre-incinerating plant scheduled to be built. There never was. George Irving has called in a top London firm of investigative economists and they gave me their report. The editor's checking it out with them, too.'

Dad looked upset and she felt stricken. Dad and David were complete opposites and she'd never understood their friendship. She hurried on. 'There's another article I want you to check, Dad, when you have time. I'm not handing it to the editor until you give me the go-ahead.'

'Does it affect me?'

'No. Of course not. But still . . . maybe in some way that I don't know about. That's why I want you to check it out.'

'I'm worried about David. He'll be in trouble. It's not your fault, Ana. Irving would have given the report to the editor. It's probably with the police by now.'

'The editor said David will claim that he

believed the rumour. He reckons no one will ever find out who really owns that field. That's what the economists' report says, too.'

'Fair enough. Perhaps it's what he needs to pull himself together now. He's always cut too many corners. He burned his fingers badly, but he's out of the mess he was in. I hope he knuckles down to hard work instead wheeling and dealing and thinking up scams.

'If you believe that you'll believe anything,' Mae said ferociously. So far she'd been on her best behavior, but Bela kept refilling Mae's glass . . . no one had warned her . . . and as the alcohol entered her blood-stream, Mae became more aggressive.

'So how did you meet my son,' Mae said, smiling sugar sweet as she watched Bela refilling her plate.

'I camped in his woods almost a year ago. He thought someone had started a fire and he came to investigate.'

'And you left your shoe.'

Bela looked startled. 'How did you know that?'

'Laura teased Simon about the shoe he was polishing.'

Mae turned to them all with an apologetic shrug. 'He was looking for love. He always has. I neglected him as a child. I'm afraid I'm not at all maternal. The truth is, I hate children, but I've never known a better adult. I'm proud to call him my son. You look after him, Bela. He's vulnerable, but he's all right.'

For a split second Dad looked astonished. He jumped up and took his plate to the sideboard.

'But Mae,' he said over his shoulder. 'What did you ever learn about family life? Nothing! You were pushed around from pillar to post. You never had a home. Tom was always on the move.' He turned swiftly. 'You have nothing to feel sad about,' he said, putting one hand on her shoulder. 'Everything's fine. We're all okay. Even Laura. She's fallen for a young French designer and she's over the moon.' He glanced apologetically towards Ana.

'I knew that, Dad. Mother wrote to me about him.'

She began to giggle like she used to when she was a kid, and once she'd started she couldn't stop.

'I'm sorry,' she spluttered eventually. 'But don't you see . . . this is like a musical comedy, where everyone comes on stage for the happy finale, singing and dancing.' No one seemed to be laughing

Ana began to tell them about her studies, since no one else had anything to say.

'You'll all have to excuse me,' Dad said later. 'I must finish fixing the tractor. I have to start raking tomorrow.'

That was when Mae stood up and demanded to be taken home at once. She dabbed her eyes with a tissue and made a big show out of hugging them all, before coyly explaining that she needed a rest because she had a date that evening.

'Let's go, Mae,' Ana said, after she'd hugged Bela and Sam. I'll see you soon, Bela. Thanks for a lovely lunch. Please ask Dad to check this out.'

She passed her a few typed pages folded into a proof copy of Meli's book. Catching hold of Mae's arm, she walked her firmly to her car. She helped her in, clipped on her seat belt and set off down the farm road. Sam raced after them, but he soon gave up and trotted back. Peering through the rear view mirror, Ana saw him jumping up against Bela and for a moment she felt hot with jealousy, but it didn't take long to convince herself that she had never felt any such thing.

48

Simon had located the fault and almost finished repairing the tractor. Through the door he could hear Bela, Mae and Ana chattering in the yard. Ana shouted, 'Bye Dad,' her car door slammed and he heard her drive away. Sunday lunches should always be like this, he thought happily. He hummed as he finished his work, tightening the last screw and pushing his tools out from under the tractor. Raising himself on his elbow, he hit his head and swore.

He crawled out and wiped his tools on an old cloth saturated with turps before putting them away. The familiar smell was part of his life, like the odour of wool at sheering time, the scent of the dairy, and the keen stench of manure. This was his world.

I'll restock, he decided there and then. Start again! There's a good auction coming up at Maidstone. Yes. It's time. More than time. Whistling softly he walked down to the dam, feeling unnerved by the golden softness of the mist that hung around the hilltops under the ardent sky. The hills, over-brilliant with patches of yellow Oxtongue, pink Meadow Saffron, red clover, and the last of the Martagon Lilies, looked unreal, like a backdrop to a pantomime. How had the fecund seeds survived twenty years of ruthless nibbling? The sun was baking the land, the dew had dried on the grass, bees were making late forays into the flowers, and Daunty was munching contentedly. It had been one lovely day after the next, for the past ten days, and it seemed that this gloriously unexpected Indian summer would never end, but of course it would. It was mid-October and a cold front was moving in across the Atlantic, the weather forecast had predicted.

Gazing at the woods, radiant with bronze, copper and shining yellow leaves, a bitter-sweet longing stole through him and he vowed he would turn back the clock. Once he had valued every clod of earth, but lately he had lost that passionate involvement. For months he had worried that he would never recover; that a lethal nuclear fall-out from his blitzed world had wasted his passion, leaving only indifference, but something inside him whispered that this wasn't true.

Hearing Bela's footsteps hurrying towards him, he turned abruptly. She looked upset.

'Ana left this for us.' She thrust a plain paperbound book into his hands. Two newspaper clippings were folded into it and a note from Ana was clipped on the cover.

'Hi Dad. This is a proof copy of Meli's novel. I've finished with it and the editor likes my piece (enclosed), but you (and I) won't like what Meli said about the death of someone called Angela Irving back in '85. Meli seems to think that Mae's father, Tom, was responsible. See page 200 . . .'

He fumbled for page 200 and read:

'It was 2 a.m. Apart from the security lights, Harry's hotel was in darkness. The police, the ambulance and grieving guests had all left, but the hotel's Christmas lights had been left on and they lit the snow in macabre shades of red, yellow and mauve. There was something strangely familiar about the white-haired figure I could see by the lake, twisting the signpost around. When he looked up, I recognised Tom Shepherd and I could see that he was turning the signpost away from the lake to point towards the car park.'

'Absurd, don't you think,' his daughter's note continued. 'I didn't mention that in my article. I came to discuss it with you, but didn't want to spoil the happy mood. It was a great get-together and a fabulous meal and I'll see you guys again soon. I'm driving back to London this afternoon. Classes start early tomorrow, so we won't have another opportunity to talk until next weekend.

Love, Ana.'

Bela confronted him, her white face set and controlled, her tragic eyes conveying her mood. He tried to embrace her, but she backed away and turned to the house ahead of him.

'Bela, stop. What's the matter? What's wrong with you?' He hurried after her.

While he walked, his eyes skimmed through his daughter's newspaper cutting. Suddenly, he

408

stopped dead, feeling shocked, trying to control his hurt and sense of betrayal as he read Ana's crit' of Melissa Marlowe's forthcoming book: *A Shadow on the Snow*. But Ana didn't know, did she? She wasn't even born. It wasn't her fault.

He read: 'On December 18, 1985, at 9 p.m. five men and two women, directors of a property company in upmarket Temple Minnis, met in a private room at a local hotel. They agreed that George Irving, an industrialist from Kashmir, who planned to erect a five-acre industrial plant adjourning the most costly area of the village, must be got rid of by any means. They faced financial ruin if the deal went through, but all their efforts to prevent re-zoning had failed. They agreed to draw straws. The one who drew the short straw would be responsible for ensuring that Irving never signed. If necessary he, or she, must go all the way. Complete secrecy would be maintained amongst them, they would back each other to the hilt, and never reveal which of them was guilty.*

*   'It was cold and snowing when Irving drove his family to a meeting at a Temple Minnis hotel, but disaster met them on the way. Rounding a bend, George Irving skidded into a deep snowdrift. He got out, cursing, and tried to push the car, while his wife, Angela, reversed. A sudden painful wrench told him that his back, once injured in a skiing accident, had gone again. So with his wife driving, they arrived in the dark to find a parking sign directing them across the frozen, snowy lake, which exactly*

409

resembled a parking lot. While George Irving hurried up the steps to greet the dignitaries gathered there, his wife drove to her death in the icy water under the splintered ice.

'The deal was never signed and two years later, Irving set up his plant on a convenient site to the south of the village, well away from the residents, but rumours persist to this day that the coroner's verdict of Accidental Death was incorrect and that Angela Irving's ghost haunts the shores around the lake.'

There was so much more and Simon read every last word several times before remembering how shocked Bela had been. He couldn't imagine what possible interest this report could have for her. He walked heavily back to the house.

★ ★ ★

Bela was standing in the porch beside her two packed suitcases dangling her car keys in her hand. She said: 'There's something you should know, George Irving is my father. My mother drowned in the lake and I was there, witnessing everything. I saw you running after the car shouting to her. I saw you scrambling over the ice on your hands and knees and diving into the black hole. I saw you carry her out of the boat and later, I saw you crying because you couldn't revive her.

'You could cry, but I couldn't. I was frozen with terror and horror. Since then you were always my hero. But now I learn that you were

410

there at that terrible meeting. You were, weren't you? You were one of those bastards who drew a straw to see who would kill my father. All these past months you kept secret about it. You never told me. You had no right to do that.'

Simon could hardly believe what she said. Angela's daughter. Oh, God! Oh no. Tiredness was settled in on him like a dose of pre-med. His refound lust for life looked like a sick joke. He would never escape from the past. He tried to hang on to his composure.

'Why couldn't you tell me who your parents were? That would have made more sense. Be reasonable. I don't possess a crystal ball. You knew who I was. Now that I come to think of it, I remember your strange expression when I told you my name the very first time we met.'

Simon felt fired with righteous indignation. Bela's deviousness was to blame. His voice strengthened. 'And why didn't you confide in me? What is it that makes you so damned secretive? Are you ashamed of your parents? Or did you come here to spy on me?'

Suddenly conscious that he was overreacting, Simon made an effort to calm himself. He tried to think of something cutting and reserved to say, but Bela got in first.

'I'll ask the questions, Simon. You have some explaining to do, so ditch your righteous indignation because it's a futile exercise. What a lie you and your friends told the police. What a magnificent, combined, falsification of the truth. The entire village, all of you, stuck to the story that Father's factory would be welcome and

411

bring income to the village. The police and the Coroner were convinced that you told the truth. You tried for months to get rid of him and finally you . . . all of you . . . came to the conclusion that the only way to rid yourselves of the factory was to kill my father. That's the truth, isn't it?'

'For a brief, insane, absurd moment, yes. That was true.'

When he looked up from his earnest examination of his shoes he noticed tears trickling down her cheeks. He longed to embrace her, but her eyes dared him to try.

'So which one of you bastards drew the short straw?'

'I did.'

'You?' The word emerged like a bleat, chock-full of misery.

How could she jump to these shabby conclusions? Didn't she know him at all? She met his eyes and flinched.

'Do you think I'm a murderer, Bela?'

She looked surprised at his bitter tone.

'The facts speak for themselves.'

'I'm guilty of plotting to save my heritage and of drawing a straw, but that's all. The coroner's verdict came as a reprieve. To this day I've believed your mother's death was an accident.' Until Luze arrived, he thought uneasily. 'If you'll let me explain in my own way, I'll tell you what happened. Come on. Put the keys down. I'll make some tea and we can sit down and talk. I'll tell you everything I know. Come on, do.' Taking her arm, he led the way.

How could he explain the inexorable wheel of

destiny which had driven them to that terrible point of no return? So much had happened. They had found themselves faced with a stark and grotesque deed and all because they'd been greedy. That was their only crime. Fate had let them blunder along, cutting corners, taking chances, nothing too serious, and then . . . when the time was ripe . . . they found they had walked into a trap.

'I'm waiting.' Bela's voice shocked him. It rang with false authority. She'd appointed herself judge, jury and executioner.

'Give me time!' he said as he put the kettle on. 'It's hard to know where to start. Most nights we met in a back room in Harry's pub after the bar closed. It was private. There was even an outside door which led in from the lake shore. We did all our planning there away from curious eyes. I can never explain what the past few weeks of high-tension had done to all of us. We'd lost weight and we looked sick and half of us were anyway. There was a bad flu going round that winter. As winters go, it was the pits.'

★　★　★

He can feel the cold freezing his ears, smell the fir branches crackling and spitting in the grate, a strangely acrid, comforting smell. He can see the flames flaring, then falling and dying, until one of them throws another log on, then flames and sparks shoot high into the granite chimney. He can hear the loud ticking of the grandfather clock and taste the softly seductive pure malt

413

Harry always provides. The six of them
. . . Harry, Shirley, David, Meli, Gordon and he
. . . are toasting in front and freezing behind, for
the fire's warmth hardly penetrates the large
room with its glass doors and ultra-high ceiling.
It is snowing outside, and they can hear the wind
howling. When the curtains blow up in a sudden
blast, they can see the snowy hillside sloping
down to the frozen lake.

'How's Laura?' David asks.

'Battling to cope. She's enduring a difficult
pregnancy. No one seems to be able to work out
why. There's still a month to go.'

'I'm sorry. Well, let's get on with it.'

They are trying to find a way to avert disaster
at the eleventh hour. No one holds much store
by Simon's efforts, since he has nothing concrete
to report.

'But listen! I'm telling you guys, it's going to
work out.' He implores them to believe him.
'Father will accept my offer just as soon as the
mortgage comes through. He's said as much.'

'Well, that's on hand, then.' David dismisses
his claims politely.

'I went to see George Irving,' Gordon admits.
'I spilled the beans . . . told him about our plans
and the cash we'd spent, and the borrowings.
Everything! I told him that Simon's father had
broken the family trust and that we had no
doubt Simon's lawyers would prevent his father
from selling. I promised to find him a better site
for his factory. There are plenty of places far
more suitable, as I explained. I even offered him
a share of our company, but the bastard laughed

414

at me. For some obscure reason he wants Redhill specifically. I couldn't get through to him.'

'It's him or us,' David announces crudely. 'We stand to lose everything we own, quite apart from the disgrace. It's quite certain that Gordon and I will be charged with fraud. We pledged the same security to two different banks, mainly because we needed to get the golf course and clubhouse in progress in order to step up sales. We only need a couple more months to pay off both loans. This couldn't have come at a worse time.'

He is pacing the floor beside the table, as he usually does, explaining as reasonably as if he were planning a business project.

'I think we all know what has to be done and one of us has to do it. This is no time for getting squeamish. We have to go all the way. You know what I mean. Out of consideration for Simon, I suggest we concentrate on Irving. He cannot be allowed to sign. Anyone disagree?'

Simon does not move. Fear and guilt are eviscerating his moral sensibility. He is hurling integrity into fate's bottomless pond and the ripples will never be stilled. Like him, no one stirs a finger. They sit in catatonic immobility yet their silence is a kind of protest as they fight their inner conflicts and barter their souls.

What happened next seemed as appalling now as it did then, eighteen years ago, Simon remembered.

'We'll draw straws,' Harry insists.

Gordon frowns. 'Okay. The one who takes the short straw gets rid of Irving. How he does it is

415

his business. It's best if the others don't know which one of us it is. You don't have to draw, Meli, but you have to help with the alibis.'

'I'll draw,' she says grimly.

'We must all agree to provide an alibi for each other and full backup,' David adds.

'That goes without saying,' Harry agrees.

Simon listens in a state of dread. He wants to object, but the consequences of the sale going through are too terrible to contemplate. He cannot bear to lose Redhill or Angela.

Harry goes out and returns five minutes later with a cigar tin. Five straws protrude from the perforated lid. They pass the tin around. Simon is suffused with a sense of unreality as he reaches out . . . *and draws the short straw.*

★   ★   ★

'I decided to play things my way and that's the truth of it,' he told Bela after he had tried to explain how it happened. He stood up and rubbed his aching head and felt blood on his fingers. He hadn't realised he'd torn the skin when he bumped his head under the tractor. That seemed a long time ago.

'My father had cancer and he couldn't be sure how long he would live. His girlfriend was waiting for him in Bermuda, so when the lawyer convinced Father that we could delay the sale for years, he gave in, but he still struck a hard bargain. He wanted half the value of the estate and I had to agree. It has taken me seventeen years, plus my inheritance from my grandfather,

Tom, to pay off the mortgage we took out to pay him.

'So there I was . . . waiting on the steps of the conference centre for your father to arrive. He was late. So late, in fact, we'd just about given up expecting him when his car came through the gates.'

Bela's eyes blazed. 'No, that's another lie. Mother telephoned you. She spoke to you. I was with her. We had to walk down the road to the nearest house to call the AA.'

'No. I was waiting at the centre. I'd driven there straight from Heathrow after seeing my father off. You must believe me. I've always believed that your mother's death was an accident, but I felt guilty, too. My guilt stems from agreeing to draw a straw.

'After all, it's not the sort of murder strategy that anyone would envisage,' Simon argued. 'Such a plan would depend upon seizing the moment. The signpost had been hammered into the turf years before to prevent clients from parking around the lake and spoiling the grass. It pointed right across the hotel towards the parking lot and . . . '

'I can't believe that the time will ever come when I don't despise you.'

'My poor darling.' Simon leaned over Bela and tried to pull her close to him, but she lashed out.

'Leave me. Leave me alone. Don't ever touch me.' There was more than a touch of hysteria in her voice.

'I didn't move the signpost, Bela. Please believe me.'

'Perhaps there's someone else who didn't believe that you would succeed,' Bela said softly. 'So he did the deed for you.' She spoke slowly and clearly as if he were an idiot while her cheeks flared with temper. 'Go and find out who it was.'

* * *

Why had she been so secretive about her parents? Simon wondered as he carried Bela's suitcases to the car. If only he'd known, he would have told her about Angela, but then he would never have embarked upon their affair in the first place, said a small, stern voice at the back of his mind. There was something obscene about loving the mother and the daughter. He felt disgusted with himself. Perhaps he should have guessed. All those familiar mannerisms and that strange sense of *déjà vu* the first time he saw Bela, were explained.

Tragedy had touched his life and not for the first time, he considered as he watched Bela drive away. He knew he would never forget her wild, dark eyes and the love she was unable to entirely hide.

49

It was Sunday. Sarah was off and there were numerous tasks to be done before nightfall. Feeling shocked and distressed by Bela's sad departure, Simon moved restlessly around the yard checking the stable and the barns before returning to the house. Too miserable to eat, he poured a neat brandy and sat by the gas fire considering the past. In his mind, he could hear Tom's voice, recounting one of his many living testaments. As a boy he'd listened wide-eyed with awe to eyewitness accounts of the burning of Smyrna, or the bid to rescue Russian refugees from Odessa before the Bolsheviks found them, or the Battle for the Dardanelles and later how Tom had laid the oil pipelines under the Persian Gulf. He had made history come alive.

'In the Battle of Jutland we had over 6,000 dead in one day, my boy,' he said in his soft, clear voice, with the faintest tinge of an Irish accent from his late father. 'As I gazed into the crimson sea, some instinct deep in my soul told me that we had sinned . . . against God, against nature and against ourselves.'

Tom, at seventeen, had made up his mind never to take part in killing for whatever reason. After his release from hospital, he took the only honourable route out of naval service by becoming a deep-sea salvage diver, which in those days was a highly hazardous career. From

419

then on he travelled the world to mend and refloat wrecked ships.

So why would Tom put the signpost back? It presupposed that he had moved it in the first place, but somehow Simon didn't think so. Besides, Meli would have seen him. Tom would never kill, so he must have been covering up for someone. But who? It had to be someone close to Tom.

As Simon remembered Bela's account of the night her mother died he felt overwhelmed by the sadness of it. An image of Bela's tragic eyes seared his memory and for a moment he was lost in the past.

He pulled himself together sharply. The facts, Simon . . . stick to the facts! Fact one, their car had skidded into a snowdrift; fact two, Angela had called the AA; fact three, she had made a second call and told an unknown person to pass on the message that they were late and she would be driving.

This opened up new possibilities. What if someone had wanted to kill Angela, not Irving? Someone who knew she would be driving?

Naturally Angela would have tried to call him at the cottage in the village where he and Laura lived, or at Redhill where he worked, while he was racing from London to the conference centre. Would she have spoken to Tom at Redhill? Or Laura at the cottage?

Looking back, he remembered how his anguish had become almost unendurable. He had taken too many chances and been caught out first by Tom and then by Laura, who had threatened a divorce. Tension was wrecking his health, but still he couldn't bear to give up Angela.

'You can't expect to get away with this kind of behaviour, Simon,' Tom had told him. 'Laura and her child need you.'

Simon was overwhelmed by a sudden image of Laura begging him to give up his mistress for the sake of their child. He remembered her lovely face, set and controlled, her eyes brave and watchful, her lips trembling as she pleaded with him. Finally he had agreed to leave Angela and he knew he would keep his promise. How he would do it God only knew, but somehow he would, for the sake of his family, but his good intentions, born out of guilt and sorrow, had been meaningless, for Angela, whom he loved more than his own life, had died a day later.

Suddenly it all fell into place and Simon began to tremble. He had to try to relax so he could reason it out again. His headache was worsening. He struggled to concentrate. It wasn't murder in the true sense of the word, more of a chance taken, a wayward move that left the execution of the deed to chance. Could a heavily pregnant woman move the signpost? Probably. And would she have gone to Redhill and told Tom what she had done? Well, she'd told him everything else, so why not? Would Tom cover for her? Of course, since she was about to give birth to his great grandchild.

Laura had returned from Paris three days ago, but she was leaving again soon to take up her new position. He picked up the receiver and dialled her number, but there was no reply. After trying several more times he decided to see her in the morning.

★　★　★

It was almost eight a.m. when he rang the bell and walked through the open front door into the cottage. The decor had changed since he was last here. The living room looked larger. A bowl of white roses on the table was the only sign that someone actually lived there. Then came the scent of Laura's perfume and he called out.

Laura looked relaxed and it suited her. She'd shed ten years and she seemed carefree and happy and as usual she was perfectly groomed. Suddenly he felt grimy and out of place in his oil-stained overalls. She didn't seem to notice. She chatted happily about the French textile house and her colleagues while she made coffee.

Eventually he found the courage to say: 'I've been thinking about Angela's death. Last night it all clicked into place. Laura, my dear, I'm so very sorry. All the blame belongs to me.' He saw her cheeks blanch. She looked shocked and miserable. He said: 'I came to tell you exactly how it happened.'

'Don't tell Ana. It's best to keep this quiet,' she whispered through dry lips.

'Ana will never know. She wouldn't be able to live with it. It was all my fault, Laura. I'm more sorry than I can ever tell you.'

Laura looked bewildered as he explained how

Angela had called that night to say she would be late.

'How could you possibly know that?'

He shrugged.

Laura bit her lip. 'Anyway, it's true. Angela called. She wanted to speak to you,' Laura admitted bitterly. 'How could she call you at our home. She was a real bitch. She only thought about herself. I hated her. It was Angela who persuaded Irving to move to Temple Minnis, so she would be closer to you. It was she who encouraged him to buy Redhill. She told me this. She wanted to hit back at you for something you did once.'

'But when did you see her?' Simon asked with morbid intensity.

'I was eight months pregnant. I went to her with my belly sticking out and I begged her to leave you alone.' She stood up, clutching her hands nervously. 'You didn't know that. Only Tom knew. Angela told me that you had always been hers and that you'd married me on the rebound because you couldn't find her. She said you two were going away together.' She scowled at him with frightening intensity.

'Something died inside me that day. I thought it was my child, but thank God it wasn't Ana.'

Simon wanted to be kind, but he was filled with violent disgust as Laura gazed at him, evil-eyed and still vindictive, after all these years. He wanted to reassure her:

'I swear I will never tell anyone. We both have to accept that the guilt is mine. I drove you to do this. I'm so very sorry, Laura. I want you to

423

know that I was going to keep my promise to you.'

She looked bewildered, but slowly her expression changed to anger.

'Me? You think I murdered Angela? Oh, but this is farcical. Is that what you've worked out? Well, that's neat. I thought you meant *you*. I always thought that you had planned to kill Irving. You weren't to know that Angela would be driving.'

For a moment Simon felt deranged and his stomach turned. Was she lying? Somehow he didn't think so.

'I admit that I hated the bitch,' Laura was saying as she paced the carpet again, but I wouldn't have bothered to kill her. Why should I? You see, while I was talking to your bloody mistress, my love for you drained away entirely. Did you really think you were worth killing for, Simon?'

A profundity of suspicion held them both in its sway. For a while they sat in silence. Laura spoke first.

'D'you want to hear the truth? Gordon always thought it was you, and that Tom moved back the signpost to cover for you. I told Tom that you drew the short straw. You see, Gordon heard you gasp when you drew the straw. Until today, I, too, thought it was you. With Irving gone you'd get the farm and Angela. That's what you wanted.'

Simon bit back the retort that came to mind. He had to think, but this was difficult. The headache which had been threatening since dawn broke through with a sledgehammer blow to his right temple. His little flush of compassion for Laura had entirely drained away in the face of this new shock, but he believed her.

Perhaps Gordon had taken on the responsibility of getting rid of Irving, just as he'd rushed to complete so many of Simon's school chores in the days when he'd openly adored him, much to Simon's acute embarrassment. Somehow Simon didn't think he'd have the guts.

He got up and blundered out without saying goodbye. Reaching his truck, he sat with his head in his hands feeling dissociated and unreal.

Something was worrying him. Something that Melissa had said the night she drove him home. She loved him, she'd blurted out, but surely it wasn't that, he asked himself feverishly. He forced himself to go through her conversation, word by painful word. And then it came to him. 'Years back I wronged you . . . this was my way of making amends.' Was that emotional statement connected to this terrible business?

* * *

Starting the engine, he drove uphill to Harry's Place, thinking that he might as well try there first, since it was on the way to the manor. Melissa seemed to hop from home to hotel almost daily.

Approaching the entrance, he caught sight of Meli jogging through the grass around the lake wearing trainers and a tracksuit. He ran after her.

425

'Oh, it's you, Simon. Do you believe in ghosts?' she asked as he caught up with her.

'No.'

'Neither do I. Yet Matt has a knack of describing people accurately. People that he's never even seen.'

'He once told me that he's a medium.'

Simon described the night Luze had seen the lake as a field of snow, with a parking sign pointing across it. 'He told me Angela was wearing a blue sari with a white fur coat. How could he possibly have known that?'

'She can't rest until those who wronged her have been punished.' Meli whispered, looking stricken.

He stopped short. 'Slow down, Meli. D'you really believe this superstitious nonsense?'

'I'm not sure, but Matt does, so just in case I'm setting the record straight . . . with the novel, of course. I assume you haven't read the proof copy.'

Meli was out of breath. She stopped jogging and bent over, her hands on her knees, as she tried to get her breath back.

'You look dreadful,' she said when she stood up at last.

'I have a headache and I've been talking to Laura. So all these years everyone thought it was me who moved the signpost.'

'By everyone I assume you mean the old gang.'

'Yes.'

'Well, I can't speak for the others, but I did.'

'It didn't seem to worry anyone much.'

'We were only too glad it was all over.' She reached out and caught hold of his hand. He didn't remember her doing that before and he felt unfairly imposed upon.

'Well, you were all wrong,' he said stiffly. 'I have to know who it was.'

'Simon. I'm so very sorry. My jealousy caused everything.'

'What are you saying, Meli?' Was it her? He felt frightened and inadequate to cope.

'No, not that. My crime was much earlier and the ramifications went on and on. They're still going on now.'

'What are you talking about?'

'Listen . . .'

Simon grew cold with dread as Meli related her story of Angela coming to see her and revealing her pregnancy.

'And then?' Simon asked, hoping against hope that she would say something to save him.

'And then nothing. I never saw her again until you lifted her out of the boat. You were crying and her daughter was watching. I'll never forget the look on her face. I wanted to kill myself.'

He had a vague feeling that he would kill Meli later. At the moment he had to contend with waves of intensely physical self-disgust, each one worse than the one before. It was as if his flesh had putrefied and was falling away in decaying strips. He was a vile and decadent person. He had broken mankind's oldest morality code, the pristine law against incest, planted deep into the psyche of males for millions of years. Meli's eyes were wide with shock and he guessed she had realised from his reaction who Bela was. He stumbled behind some bushes and threw up.

When he staggered back to the lake, Meli had gone He felt dizzy and light-headed and his nausea persisted. Later he couldn't remember how he drove back to Redhill.

★   ★   ★

Simon has no idea how long he's been shut up alone in the house. Time has ceased to exist. Only pain exists. A jumble of images plague him. Are they real? He has no way of knowing. Some are vaguely remembered. All are tragic. He knows he is teetering along the edge of reason.

The telephone is ringing. It has been ringing on and off for days. It goes on and on. Eventually he picks up the receiver. It is Bela and her voice is like a dagger thrust.

'Simon, I had to ring. I'm sorry. I had no right to be so unkind. The fact is I'm going through hell. I want you to know that I miss you. I love you, Simon.'

The long silence bothers him. What should he say?

'Are you there, Simon?'

'Forget me,' he growls. 'Forget you ever met me.'

He hears a sound like a gasp or a sigh.

'Are you ill?'

'No.'

'But you don't love me?'

'It's all a terrible mistake. Don't phone again.'

'Something's wrong. You can't mean it. What

are you talking about? Is this something to do with Melissa? What did she say?'

'Leave me alone, Bela. I don't want to see . . . '

An impersonal click terminates the conversation.

His days pass in a blur of misery. Alone at home, Simon is sometimes aware of his tormenting guilt, but then his physical symptoms of pain and nausea drive the guilt away again. Reality comes in spasms, out of context with time or place. That's the worst . . . a harsh reminder of who and what he is.

50

Falling leaves, a misty morning, birdsong and the lake like a sheet of burnished steel. Melissa breathed in deeply feeling grateful for her life. It was seven months since her reprieve, but still every moment was precious, despite the turmoil in the village.

'Come on, Angus.' She whistled and saw David's fat old Alsatian, who had lagged behind, prick up his ears and gallop towards her. Reluctantly she returned to the house.

David's housekeeper met her in the porch. Lips drawn to a fine line, eyes glinting with fury, she let rip.

'I never thought I'd live to see the day ... not in this house ... now old Mr Fergus ... he was a real gentleman ... none of this wheeling and dealing. Four policemen, mind you ... it took four of them. He was dragged away at dawn yesterday like a common criminal. Things have come to a pretty pass ... come the month's end I'll be handing in my notice, Ms Marlowe.'

Her footsteps beat a disdainful tattoo as she hurried away.

The story had done the rounds yesterday and Melissa had called David's lawyer to see what she could do to help.

'They've got nothing on him, Meli. He'll be home tomorrow, you'll see. Unless, of course, he's stupid enough to confess, but I don't think he'd do that, do you?'

'No.'

She decided to move back until David returned, but she kept her room at the hotel.

★   ★   ★

It was noon when Melissa heard the sound of David's tyres skidding on the gravel driveway. Looking up, she saw their automatic gates close behind him leaving a queue of cars to park outside. Eyes wide with shock, panting heavily, his hair damp with perspiration, David resembled one of his hunted foxes as he bolted up the steps and slammed the front door behind him.

'Tally Ho,' she muttered under her breath as she hurried into the hall.

David stood leaning against the door, flapping his arms, eyes wide and distraught. He looked hugely offended and lost, like a small child after his first smack. She steeled herself against a rising tide of compassion.

'Bloody media . . . followed me from the station . . . fuck the lot of them . . . got to have a drink.' He was still panting as he lurched into the lounge and downed a glass of Scotch neat. Then he fell back into his chair. 'Fuck!' He broke off and drew a deep breath.

'Fuck . . . fuck . . . fuck . . . ' He ran his hands through his hair and blew his nose loudly.

'Oh fuck! What are you doing here?'

'Holding the fort and waiting for you. I

phoned your lawyer, he said you'd be back today.'

'Don't go, Meli. Stay here. Give up your room at Harry's and stay home with me.'

She walked up to him and put her hand on his shoulder. 'I can't even though I'd like to. You see, David, I saw your expression when I told you that I only had a month. Your eyes . . . oh David . . . they gave you away. Pure relief. It was then that I remembered the insurance policy we took out on my life years ago, when I was the only one of us earning. Sadly for you, I didn't die.'

'No, not sad. Never sad. You're talking rot. Besides, I don't need the cash. I'm out of debt.'

'Only because you and Gordon cooked up a massive fraud. You have no scruples. Everything revolves around money.'

'You can't prove it and neither can the police. They just said so. I've seen the last of that lot.' He gave a shaky laugh.

David was like a rubber ball, Meli realised. The harder the knock the higher he bounced.

'They admitted they didn't have a leg to stand on. I'm through with that nightmare, thanks to Gordon. If it weren't for the bloody media I'd be laughing.'

'But what if it hadn't worked?'

'Bloody women with their ifs and buts.'

'Stop wiggling.'

'Okay, Meli, I'll give it to you straight. I might have thought that since you were dying anyway, thank heavens for the insurance, but that's the worst you can pin on me. Put it down to the

432

feverish imaginings of a mind half-crazed with panic.'

Meli decided to drop it. Words wouldn't change anything and David was getting that hunted look again.

'You're far from blameless, Meli,' he said so softly he might have been talking to himself. 'How about Luze . . . and you . . . not once . . . dozens of times. Have you any idea how hurt and humiliated I felt. I love you. I always have done.'

Meli tried to hide her shock. 'That's hard to believe, since you never wanted me near you,' she retorted, trying to work out how much he really knew.

'There's more to love than sex. I admit I didn't fancy you. Not towards the end . . . well, it wasn't the end, thank God. You should never have made me look at the X-rays. Finally all I could see was that damned mushroom in your head. I'm sorry, but I desire you now that you're better.'

'About Luze,' she began uncomfortably. 'You've always had a vivid imagination. Luze spent hours each day meditating on my cure.'

'Don't . . . please . . . Shirley told Harry . . . everything . . . and Harry told me. I'll get the bastard back, you'll see. He won't be here for long.'

Melissa couldn't speak. Shirley's treachery was something she couldn't begin to accept or understand.

'Well, I can't say I'm leaving, David, because I've already left. I'm keeping an eye on the house and Angus. Don't try to read more into my daily visits.'

Unbelievably David's eyes were shiny with tears. He blinked hard, drained his glass and turned away.

'Well go then. What are you hanging around for?' His hoarse voice and hunched shoulders were dead giveaways.

'Are you likely to be charged?'

'No. Do you care one way or the other?'

'Yes,' she said truthfully. She felt several things at once, relieved, almost happy, but irritated because he always got away with everything.

'Come here, Meli.'

He grabbed hold of her clumsily and they toppled back on the couch. Angus, who had always been Melissa's protector, bounded forward and caught hold of his arm.

'Down, boy, down! Jesus! This is just like old times. Remember how he used to go for me if I so much as touched you. Oh, Meli, those were the days. I've missed you like crazy.' Leaning closer he began to kiss the tears from her cheeks. 'Listen. Don't be upset. Everything's going to be all right.'

David was the world's biggest optimist, Melissa thought, as the tears rolled faster. Now wasn't the best time to tell him that life would never be all right again. At least, not for the two of them.

'What about the Welsh miners and their depleted pension fund?'

He sighed. 'Believe it or not, I hate intrigue and cutting corners, but I had no choice. The

434

story is that my late uncle (in the Cayman Islands) left some cash in a Swiss Bank, a million actually, and I used this to buy back the miners' near-defunct shares at the price the pension fund paid for them.'

'So you're out of the woods, but life at the sports club will never be the same again.'

Melissa felt grossly contaminated by David's shady deals. She left early the next morning, although she had intended to stay until the weekend.

★   ★   ★

By the time Gordon arrived late the following afternoon, David had bounced back to normal and convinced himself that they were winning.

'The usual?' David asked, moving towards the bar.

'Thanks.'

'Listen Gordon. I'm skint, so I had to call a halt to buying Irving's shares. At first investors were throwing them away, but they quickly rose in price. Currently they're reaching six-fifty.'

'You can safely go to ten. I told you that. They'll hit twenty in six months time, but we'll be selling instead of buying. Trouble is, the word's got out, so be careful. Quote your ceiling every time you buy. I'm out of it. I've exhausted my funds and my credit . . . everywhere.'

'I need some proof. If this should fail . . . ' David's fears hung around them like heady incense.

'There's no profit without risk, but I can't see

how it can fail. Both sides have agreed. Members of the Japanese consortium have just confirmed that they are flying over. They're scheduled to arrive on Friday evening. I've been press-ganged into joining the welcoming committee at Heathrow. The deal's laid out here.' Gordon went on, patting his briefcase. 'If you like I'll leave you the documents, but David, you must keep them locked in the safe and whatever you do, don't look cheerful near Harry. He's become the town crier. We'll make a killing with this deal. How d'you fancy moving into property development in the States from an offshore base?'

'Oh, I don't know.' David stood up and gazed out of the window.

Watching him, Gordon, always sensitive to his moods, understood that for David there would never be anywhere better than his home. He loved to travel, but as the squire of Temple Minnis. This was his image and here lay all that he loved. David could have sold his home to get out of the crap months ago, but he could never bring himself to do that. Gordon, who had no family to speak of, no roots and no background to boast about, had always managed to conceal his fury that he had never acquired the aplomb that money brings. All this, he thought, gazing through the window towards the stables, is only money. It's not tradition, or culture, or trees, or horses, or a well-stocked cellar that counts, it's money. When I have enough I'll buy this, or something better.

★ ★ ★

436

Friday came at last. Sitting on his balcony overlooking the lake, David Fergus sipped his coffee, inhaled the aroma of his ten-year old, pure malt scotch and smoked his cigar, while a smile curled around his fleshy lips. He had recovered from his fear and every part of his body tingled with a sense of excitement. It was a sunny winter day, warm enough to sit outside, if you were dressed in a fur-lined, waterproof anorak with a Paisley cashmere scarf. Life was good. He loved the scent of autumn: burning logs in the living room, the sour tang of the still lake, rotting leaves and wet grass as the dew rose. He loved wheeling and dealing, too. He was about to make an extraordinary coup. His prospects were suddenly reversed, thanks to Gordon's genius. On the table beside him was his mobile phone to keep in constant contact with his brokers, who were engaged in last minute mopping-up operations of Irving's shares. Pom-tiddly-om-pom went his musical call. David grabbed the phone.

'Fergus.'

'A batch of two thousand's just come on offer at six-fifty each,' the broker said.

'Buy!'

'Very good, Sir.'

The line went dead.

'Hah!' he said aloud. Gordon was right. When news of the takeover hit the press, they'd shoot up to twenty. He and Gordon would make such a killing they'd never have to worry about money again.

He grabbed his calculator and stabbed away at

437

the keys. Finally, with Gordon's assurances that they were on to a good thing, he had made a courageous decision to hock his home, his land and every asset he could muster in order to buy Irving's shares.

David glanced at his watch. At this moment the Japanese industrialists were going through customs at Heathrow where Gordon was waiting to drive them to the Newtown semiconductor plant. Understanding his fears, Gordon had just called to reassure him that the plane had landed safely. A plane crash would have ruined him.

At six p.m. precisely they would meet in Irving's boardroom to sign the deal. The Japs would own controlling interest, but he and Gordon between them controlled most of the listed shares which they would sell slowly and carefully as the price soared over the next six months.

Gordon had big plans for them in the States, but David knew he could never quit England forever. This was where he would live out his days, hopefully with Meli, when she came to her senses. His roots were here. His friends were here, and he enjoyed being a big fish in a small pond. Okay, so he'd been through a bad patch, but he was about to score big time.

As darkness fell around the lake, the ducks returned to their willow-strewn island and David retired to the roaring fire in his living room to await Gordon's call.

He was still waiting at midnight.

When he could no longer stand the tension, he drove to Irving's factory, but a night watchman was the only sign of life there. Gordon wasn't at home either, he learned when he raced there to find him. So where the hell was he? Perhaps at Irving's house, but apart from a security light above the porch the house was in darkness, he found when he arrived, panting and trembling.

He called Irving from his mobile, but when the man answered, David cut the call. 'Of course he'd lie. He'd think it was the media on his trail.'

Feeling desperate, he drove to Gordon's deserted house and parked in the driveway to wait for him. Doubts zoomed in like summer gnats, but staunchly he squashed them all. At dawn he fell into an exhausted sleep, only to wake at sunrise to the sound of hammering. It was the estate agent putting up a For Sale sign.

⋆   ⋆   ⋆

By nine a.m. the sports club was ablaze with rumours. Gordon had done a moonlight flit and the local estate agent was charged with selling his household effects and putting the house on the market. Irving's shares had been delisted at ten that morning when liquidators closed the plant. Most of Newtown were now unemployed.

Strangely, there had been a surge of buying of Irving's shares for the past month that had sent prices sky high, the local broker told them. Gordon, who had bought them for next to nothing months ago, had unloaded all he had purchased and made a mint.

Melissa, who had a shrewd idea of what

Gordon had done, drove round to David to make sure that he was coping.

The housekeeper didn't answer her ring, but the door was ajar, so she walked inside. She found David crouched on a monk's bench in the hall, unshaven and dishevelled. He looked like a man enduring the worst that fate could deal him.

'The rumour in Temple Minnis is that Gordon's done a moonlight flit.' Melissa said.

'He's ruined me. Totally! I fell for one of his scams. I can't believe the bastard could turn his evil genius on to me. I'm still in shock. This house, the estate, even the horses . . . everything was hocked to the bank for the cash to buy Irving's shares. He told me . . . he said that . . . Oh God!' He leaned against the bookcase and stared wildly at the wall opposite.

'I'll get some lunch,' she said. 'You need to eat. I'll stick around for a month or so while you sort out the mess.' When she came back with the food, David was still sitting there. He seemed incapable of hearing or seeing her, so she called an ambulance.

Gordon had always been bent, Meli thought. She had blamed him for dragging David into his get-rich-quick schemes. Creative, restless, filled to overflowing with grandiose schemes and very convincing, he was the perfect con artist. There was always a fall guy who lost out badly and David had never cared who it was or what happened to them. Meli was reminded of an old African saying: *he who feeds the crocodiles gets eaten last*.

51

Simon emerged from two weeks of drinking and remorse to a sense of deep shame. A vile taste of stale liquor was contaminating his mouth and his head ached abominably. Yet his biological clock, shock-proof and enduring, which was more than he was, had sounded the milking alarm, although no cows were left. Was that why he felt like weeping? Then he remembered. 'Bela! Oh God! Bela!' He heard himself groan. The culmination of all the hurts he had ever inflicted in his lifetime had zoomed back like homing pigeons.

He showered, shaved, cut himself, rifled through the medical cabinet for sticking plaster, and stumbled downstairs to make strong black coffee.

When he walked outside, daylight struck his eyes like a missile strike.

Sarah took one look at him and groaned.

'Isn't it Sunday? Why are you here?'

'Because you've turned into a drunk.' She turned away.

Simon checked around the yard and stables which was a waste of time since Sarah was super-efficient. Unable to endure Sarah's contempt, Simon got into his van and drove to Harry's Place.

'Jesus, Simon. Just look at you. Pull yourself together,' Harry grumbled. He reached for the phone. 'Breakfast for my friend, Simon,' he called into it. 'Eggs . . . ' He looked up. 'Could you face sausage and eggs?'

'No, thanks. Dry toast is more like it.'

'Plenty of coffee and toast, scrambled eggs, honey. A big pot of honey. See if you can find a couple of strong headache pills. Bring the coffee and pills right away, we have an emergency here by the look of things.' He hooked the phone back on the wall. 'There's nothing like honey for hangovers, Simon. For me it's the only thing that works. We can't all go to pieces like David.'

Simon shrugged and waited for Harry to enlighten him.

'Didn't you hear the news? David's had a nervous breakdown. Gordon fleeced him of every last cent, including his home and estate, before taking off for foreign shores. A very neat con. An ambulance took David to a mental hospital five days ago.'

By the time Simon had swallowed two aspirins and drunk three cups of coffee heavily laced with honey, he felt well enough to worry about his friend. He'd go and see him later that day, he decided.

'Surely you're not taking Meli's ramblings seriously?' Harry asked. 'Tom was eighty-six, for Christ's sake, and dying of cancer. No one believes it was Tom. He was about the only person in the village who didn't have a motive. From what I hear, most folks think the tumour has affected Meli's sanity. Two detectives were here yesterday. They consider Meli's story to be a publicity stunt. The case will remain closed, according to them.'

Simon began to relax and soon his indefatigable sense of denial was flooding into his psyche, smoothing away the trauma and making him feel heaps better.

How could it be true? Things like that didn't happen to people like him. Meli might have been lying about Angela's visit. Or perhaps the tumour had affected her sanity. Surely Angela would have told him if Bela were his child when they met up in the village eight years later. Of course she would. So his thoughts ran on, pondering, weighing up his chances, while he listened to Harry and put in the odd comment now and then.

Enjoying his role as town crier, Harry talked about Luze for while. He'd been sacked and turned out of the vicarage. He was lodging at the hotel and preaching in the village square.

'Hundreds of kids come from all over to listen to him. It's good for business, but only in the short term,' Harry told him. 'He's leaving soon . . . going home. He's been offered a top job by an American pharmaceutical firm, to set up and manage a research station in the heart of Africa, to identify the herbs that sangomas use.'

More coffee came and Simon began to feel human again. The room began to fill and Harry was busy serving most of the time, so when Simon heard a loudspeaker coming from the direction of the village square, he left the bar and went to investigate.

★　★　★

Over five hundred young people were wedged into the square, many of whom were strangers to these parts. Londoners by the look of them. Matt, in a track suit and trainers, his hair brushed up like some mad jungle growth, rings and chains glinting in the brassy autumn sun, was standing on the steps of the main hall holding a microphone. He caught sight of Simon, smiled broadly and waved. Simon nodded back and watched Matt adjust the microphone, square his shoulders and speak to the crowd.

'God is not dead, my friends,' his melodious voice echoed around the buildings, sending a flock of pigeons soaring to the trees. 'He's alive and well and right now he is staring at me through plus-minus five hundred pairs of eyes. Yes, you! Christ is born in every one of you.

'If you were to take away the Godliness in each one of you (supposing that it were possible to do this) there would be nothing left, I promise you. We and God share consciousness . . . our minds are one . . . and when we feel that truth in our hearts, the sky's the limit.

'You . . . everyone of you . . . have always existed in some form or other. You always will. Your consciousness survives the death of your body, the death of the planet and the death of the universe. There is only one reality one mind or nature, one consciousness. We share it with God. And loving is what God is all about.'

Was this the normal Church line, Simon wondered? It didn't sound familiar.

Matt paused and scanned the crowd. Because

444

of the poor acoustics, he had to wait for the echoes to die down between each sentence, so his sermon began to sound like punches flung into the air.

'Mankind's entire spiritual search is available to you in all its scriptures. Study them all. That's my advice to all of you. Zen offers you the chance to take responsibility for your own spiritual quest through meditation and enlightenment. Christianity offers the devotional path. Choose the way that is meaningful to you. Meditate to seek your own enlightenment. No words can match personal experience. With words you learn and believe. With experience, you know.'

No wonder he got flung out of the church, Simon thought, suddenly seeing a side of Matt that he had never known existed. Just look at the man, head thrown back as he roared at the crowd, trying to push them into experiencing his fervour.

'This cosmic force, which is your total nature, is forever striving to make itself known to every one of you. Start your quest for your true selves today.'

Simon stirred restlessly. At least half of the crowd seemed spell-bound and the rest were glued to the vicar's words. Simon felt that he was missing out badly and he felt deprived.

'Spiritually speaking,' Matt was saying, 'we face a hazardous future. As Church influence declines no one is left to teach morality to our youth. So each of you must take up the responsibility.

'You can be sure that God is helping you. Even now as we speak, a revolution is spreading throughout the world. It comes through our young people. It's reaching across the boundaries of nationality, language, religion and culture. Enlightenment is emerging through the unconscious of many millions of people worldwide, bringing a surge of spiritual awareness.'

Simon's headache was intensifying and he felt very cold. He got up, waved and walked away. Matt's words faded as he neared the lake.

''*Who knows God, becomes God*'. This quote comes from the ancient *Mundaka Upanishad*. Thousands of years ago . . . '

His voice was lost in the wind as Simon walked back to Harry's Place. Who or what was Matthew Luze, Simon wondered?

★   ★   ★

Simon looked as if he had taken as much as he could of life's up and downs, Luze reckoned, as he saw him walk away. He was deeply introverted man who presented himself as an extrovert. He offered the ready-smile, the outstretched hand, the firm grip, but behind the English charm lurked a hidden personality. Had he created any part of himself? Or was he merely a clone of an Englishman, hammered and tempered in the harsh forge of English culture. Luze made up his mind to find him when his sermon was done.

It was noon by the time Luze left the square. He felt exhausted. There was nothing he wanted more than a hot shower and his lunch, but

Simon was his friend. He found him sitting by the window in Harry's lounge, soaking up the dazzling sunlight. His eyes burned disturbingly and he was hunched over the table like a drunk over a bar, nursing a cup of black coffee. He looked exhausted and dejected. Luze wondered how he could penetrate the invisible shield of Englishness, which to Luze often seemed like a bulletproof glass barrier.

He held out his hand and received the usual firm grip and frank smile.

'Harry said I'd find you here. I want to talk to you and this time you can't walk away.'

Simon raised his eyebrows. Red eyes flashed a warning. 'It's not necessary, Matt, but thanks. I'm on the mend.'

'No, you're not . . . that's just it. Listen to me, Simon. All our identity comes from our past. That's all we know about ourselves. But who are we really? Our false identity compels us to try to put the past right and make the future better for ourselves and for others. So we bust a gut trying harder and harder, but those darned events just keep on getting worse. It seems that there is no escape. Until, one day, in a flash of insight, we realise that our ego is an illusion. When that happens, guilt and desires no longer bug us, so we can simply step off the treadmill.'

★　★　★

Simon frowned and looked around surreptitiously, but there was a large space surrounding

447

them and he doubted anyone had heard. He was always acutely embarrassed to talk about religion, or God, or anything like that. To his mind, the vicar was talking poppycock. Matt was peering intently at him and his huge black pupils and the whiter-than-white surrounds seemed to be beaming a message.

'Can't you talk plain English, Matt? But keep your voice down, please.'

'We are punished *by* our sins, Simon, not *for* them. Try to understand what karma's all about. Think of it as a kind of levelling. No one fully understands the karmic law, but we know that it works to adjust all imbalances, such as right and wrong.'

'Really.' Simon said politely, draining his cup for a quick exit.

'All that is happening to you, must happen. You pushed the pendulum aside and it must fall back. Nothing can prevent it from doing so, except you, the real you. D'you understand?'

'Perhaps I should get a book on it,' Simon muttered. 'Thank you, Matt. You're a great guy. You really care. I hope things work out for you. Good luck with the new job.'

He stood up and shook hands firmly, trying to ignore the disappointment in Matt's eyes and the ache in his gut.

'Okay, you win, Simon. But go and see George Irving. He has all the answers you need.'

Simon stepped back in shock. For a moment he almost punched Matt. He could well do without his crazy, psychic visions. To hell with him. Let him find someone else to preach to, but

448

he didn't say any of this because he hated to be unkind.

* * *

Late that afternoon, Simon was taken aback when Melissa arrived at the farm with a large, tatty German shepherd.

'My God, is that Angus? He's got old fast. Hello Angus,' he said, stroking the dog's head. 'But what's this?' he asked, as Meli handed him the leash. 'Surely you aren't . . . '

'He's a marvellous watchdog and he needs a good home. I've finished my novel and I'm selling up here.'

Simon tried not to show his shock. 'He looks like a nice dog.'

'Thank you Simon. I knew I could rely on you,' she said. 'Technically-speaking Angus belongs to David, but I've always looked after him.'

'How's David? I was planning to visit him later.'

'No visitors for two more weeks. He'll be out soon. Believe it or not, he's planning to join Gordon in the Cayman Islands.'

'More fool him. Does he never learn? Aren't you coming inside?'

'No time. Someone's coming to value my cottage.'

'But where are you going?'

'Wherever I find a story. I thought I might start off with Matt's life. He's leaving next week and I'll be joining him in Tanzania.'

449

'Have you thought this out carefully, Meli? You're going on safari with someone you scarcely know into one of the few untouched areas of the planet. Who will help you if you run into trouble?'

'Matt will, of course. If it weren't for him I'd be dead.'

'I've never heard such a load of superstitious rubbish. You just got better.'

'If you say so,' she said with a silly, superior smile on her face.

'I'm not leaving yet,' Meli told him as they walked towards her car. 'It may take a while to sort out David's things and make sure he's all right, but I'll have no place for Angus. So thanks, Simon.' She stepped into the driving seat.

Then she looked up, suddenly serious, her eyes searching his. 'Simon, there's something I have to ask you. If I return, could you and I . . . ?'

He put one finger gently to her lips. 'Sh! Take care of yourself, Meli.'

Then she was gone without saying goodbye to her dog.

'That's life for you, Angus,' he said, trying to console the whining beast. 'The women you love play hard to get and the ones you don't, hang around forever.'

52

Irving's house was built well back from the road behind a low wall and clumps of trees and shrubs. It might once have been a farmhouse, for it was set amongst acres of arable fields at the end of a leafy, muddy *cul de sac*, which led off unobtrusively from the road. The garden was neglected, the woodwork needed renovating and there was a For Sale sign near the gate. Security guards hung around the entrance and Simon guessed they were there to defend Irving against his sacked workers.

Having explained that he had an appointment, that he had no identification on him and seldom carried any, the guard grudgingly let him drive past. He parked near the front door and an Indian manservant let him in immediately. The interior was in better condition, the oak panelling newly polished, gleaming oak floors were covered with numerous Persian carpets and a bowl of fresh flowers stood on an antique table.

Simon glanced around curiously. At the other end of the hall an open door led to a large, old-fashioned conservatory. Angela had once mentioned that this was her favourite place and he moved towards it, noticing the over-stuffed silk-covered sofas, the gaudy cushions and ornate furniture. Not Angela's choice surely. He had to acknowledge that he had never learned much about her background. For a moment he was lost in useless regrets. Then, hearing footsteps behind him, he spun around.

Simon had only seen Irving on the night Angela died, so he had only a vague idea of what he looked like. He saw a powerful man in his late fifties, built like a nightclub bouncer, whose eyes glittered like ice under deeply hooded lids. Sharp Scottish features, a pointed nose and a shock of white hair reminded Simon of school textbook pictures of Scrooge. He could see no resemblance at all between him and Bela and at this observation his spirit quaked.

A brief nod was the only welcome Simon received. Irving led the way in silence to his panelled, book-lined office and sat behind a large ebony desk, indicating that Simon should sit opposite. The room was full of Indian souvenirs and a massive tapestry of a Kashmiri lake and mountain backdrop dominated the wall behind the desk. Contrived and kitsch, Simon decided.

He didn't like Irving and he wished he hadn't come. Damn Matt and his silly ideas. The thought of his soft and gentle Angela in this man's arms was ludicrous. The hostile silence was unnerving him and he couldn't imagine how to get the answers to his two vital questions . . . where was Bela and which of them was her father?

'Let's get one thing straight,' he began tentatively. 'We got off on the wrong foot years ago when you wanted to purchase the Redhill estate. You were not to know that it was held in trust for the family, or that I had always believed

452

it to be my birthright.'

There was no answer. Irving's face remained impassive and Simon was beginning to feel intensely irritated with the man. 'Of course my father was wrong to try to sell Redhill to you, but there were extenuating circumstances. He was dying of cancer and he wished to live out his days in a sunny climate.'

Irving's only sign of interest was a deep sigh as he gazed blandly at Simon.

Nevertheless, Simon leaned back feeling that he'd made a good start and cleared the tension. Perhaps he should ask a question and involve the man in the conversation.

'I don't know if you knew that my father was dying of cancer. Did he mention this?'

'Extenuating circumstances can be taken only so far,' Irving began, his watchful expression scarcely disguising his obvious malice.

Simon had never heard the man speak before. His voice was a curious mixture of an Indian intonation grafted on to a Scottish accent.

'Your father was an immoral man,' Irving said with sardonic amusement. 'Like you, he took what he wanted and never lived up to his responsibilities. The man was a liar and a cheat and so are you. And now . . . what is it that you want?' He clasped his hands together and gazed out of the window as if bored with the whole procedure.

'Hold it! Wait a minute. You have no right . . . '

★   ★   ★

453

Simon had never experienced a conversation where social conventions were so swiftly and ruthlessly abandoned. Irving was deliberately insulting him, but to get up and leave would be to admit failure.

'You have your facts wrong, Irving,' he went on calmly. 'You can't back that statement.' But of course he could. Simon realised that he had blundered, forgetting his own role in the drama.

Irving leaned back looking thoughtful. 'You cheated and lied to your pregnant wife. You pursued an adulterous relationship with another man's wife. I'd say that makes you a liar and a cheat. As for your father . . . I think I'd rather keep that to myself.'

Keep calm, Simon told himself, resisting the pressure of his unspoken question. There must be a reason why he has agreed to see me. Perhaps he wants to voice his rage after all these years. Taunt him until he loses his temper. That's my best bet. My guess is that his dour attitude covers a vile nature. He's on a short fuse and he might let something slip.

'Look here,' Simon began. 'Our friendship went back a long way. Back to 1975 when Angela and I . . . '

He broke off. How do you tell a man whose wife has died that she and you were an item long before he came on the scene? What appalling bad manners to ask if he were the father of his own child? Simon knew he should have stayed away, but he hadn't been able to bear the uncertainty. He had to know one way or the other.

Irving was toying with his ruler. 'Anjana and

you. I see. Well, carry on. You had a reason for coming to see me, I assume.' His ruler began to beat the ebony desk, so lightly . . . so softly, like the seconds of a clock ticking by.

Simon felt as if he'd gatecrashed the world chess championships without learning the moves. Somehow, he had to ask his question, but how could he?

'Angela was always mine,' he blundered on. 'We met when we were nineteen and we fell in love. She loved me from then on. Before she married you, she left a message telling me that she was pregnant and asking me to marry her. I received that message only last week, but how could she have known that? She ran away and married you on the rebound.'

He'd got through to the bastard at last. Two icy blue eyes glittered with loathing.

'She had no right . . . ' He got up and paced the floor. 'She came from a strict Muslim family. She wasn't free . . . she was never free. Anjana was betrothed to me when she was twelve. This was arranged between our two families . . . her father, who was my business partner in some ventures, and myself. She begged permission to study in Britain before she married. Foolishly, her father gave his assent, but she betrayed us both. So when you say she was always yours, you were wrong. I had watched her growing up and loved her long before she went to Europe.'

'At twelve! You're a bloody paedophile, Irving.'

Irving's face had undergone a transformation from his former stoic expression to a mask of fury. His mouth twisted and opened as if he wanted to argue, but couldn't find the words.

'You're British, Irving. You took advantage of a cruel, foreign tradition. Angela had every right to choose her husband. It wasn't a case of screwing your wife,' he said spitefully. 'She was promised to me of her own volition. When she disappeared, I spent all the cash I had trying to trace her. I only stopped searching for her when I learned that she had married. When we met up again, eight years later, it was like turning back the clock. Nothing had changed. We loved each other as much as ever before.'

Irving sneered at him. 'You and Anjana would have done well together . . . the same trusting innocence, the same naiveté. Like you, she thought that loving allowed you both to ignore responsibilities and vows. I knew everything . . . when you met, and for how long, and on what dates, in that absurd and scruffy cottage you hired. She didn't know that I knew. When I first suspected something was going on, I sent home for an experienced detective who joined my family as a driver.' Irving was gazing at him with savage triumph.

★   ★   ★

Good God! Simon tried to hide his shock. They had been like babes in the jungle, quietly enjoying their passion and fondly imagining that Irving had no idea what was going on. Simon had spent weeks persuading Angela to go away with him, but she'd never believed in him.

'Your wife will win because she's pregnant,'

456

she had told him time and again.

Duty or love? He agonised nightly. She was right. In the end duty won.

Keeping his eyes down, Simon waited for Irving to let it all out. It was coming . . . all the spite, all the disappointment, all the pent-up rage and the information that he needed so badly. The man was chock-full of hatred and revenge, but Simon saw no sign of grief.

'Were you aware that Angela was pregnant when you married her?' Now for the explosion.

Irving ignored his question. 'Anjana was unhappy in Kashmir,' he said softly. 'She'd had a taste of the West and she liked it . . . or that was what I believed at the time. For years she pestered me to take her back to England. She never let up. The Kashmiri climate was too harsh for her, she missed her mother, she wanted our daughter to be brought up English. Finally she left and joined her mother in Finchley, knowing that I would follow her. She pestered me to set up the plant in the South East. She wanted to be close to you, I suppose. When I heard that Redhill was on the market I decided to buy it. Of course that was wrong, too.'

Irving had a thin sneer of sadism hanging around his lips and touching his eyes. 'Finally she begged. Can you believe that? On her knees. It was very touching. She promised never to see you again if I would give up my idea of buying your farm. She's probably the only person in the world who ever cared for you, Simon. Your parents certainly didn't.'

Irving was into his stride, doing what he loved

457

best, hurting like hell.

'Let's go back to the week before my wife died,' he was saying. 'Anjana told me that you and your friends had sat around a table at Harry's Place and plotted how best to kill me. It was you who drew the short straw . . . need I say more?'

'I had no wish to kill you. I fought you fair and square, Irving. My lawyer prevented my father from selling and the deal fell through. We fought tooth and nail, but legally, and I won. It's that simple.'

'Is that what you thought . . . that you'd won? Is that what you still believe? You fool! An alternative site came on the market at a good price. It was closer to the railway station, larger and flatter, so I decided to buy it.'

'You're lying.'

'Am I? Your father took it badly. He insisted that I should reconsider. He even mentioned coming down in price, so we met for lunch at Harry's Place. He seemed anxious to ensure that his wife and father-in-law didn't see me. I remember how shocked he was when I wouldn't budge. I thought he'd pass out. Eventually he admitted that he was having trouble his end. He said that you and your lawyer had come up with an alternative plan. You were in London trying to raise the cash to try to pay him out. He begged me not to tell you that I was no longer in the market for Redhill. He even persuaded me not to tell my wife. Don't you think that's strange? That was when I realised that everyone knew you were screwing Anjana.'

Simon pushed himself half out of the chair and then fell back into it. *Harry's Place*. The bastard had been there only days before. He'd had lunch overlooking the lake.

★   ★   ★

Irving had lost his impassive pose. He was leering at him and there was a mad look in his eyes. His need to hurt was overtaking his commonsense. 'Ah! I see the penny's dropped. It was you who was getting screwed for a change.' Irving seemed delighted with his sick joke.

Simon flinched, but tried not to show how disturbed he felt. Nothing made sense. If Irving had changed his mind about buying Redhill, then why attend the meeting at the conference centre? Why did he drive over for a formal dinner to say nothing of the speeches? Even the mayor was going to be present. And why, for heaven's sake, bring his family? Bela had told him that she saw the signpost pointing towards the snowy field and that her father had taken her hand and hurried to the lobby, gesturing to show his wife where to park the car. Yet a day or two before Irving claimed to have met his father in the restaurant for lunch. The restaurant was built around the lake and in daylight it looked exactly what it was, a lake covered in ice, with a sprinkling of snow scattered over it. Harry kept the ice broken immediately below the restaurant for the ducks and swans.

'So you were coming to dinner, dressed up to the nines, to inform everyone that the deal was off. Have I got this right?' Simon asked slowly.

For the first time Irving looked uncertain. 'It was merely a change of venue, and a short delay. Nothing else changed.' He sat up abruptly. 'It's getting late and I have another appointment. Why don't you come out with your question, Simon? You want to know if you, like Oedipus, must put out your eyes. Is that it? Or is incest permitted in your world?'

Dominated by the need to know, and feeling frustrated and helpless, Simon felt his anger run like shafts of electricity along his skin. He longed to batter Irving, but what would that prove?

'I'll tell you what you want to know,' Irving went on in a conciliatory tone. 'Anjana had a miscarriage two weeks before we married. I think it was induced, although she never admitted to that. Three months later she became pregnant again. Bela was born at the end of December. The new coat she was wearing to dinner was her birthday present.'

Relief coursed through Simon in waves of uncontrollable shudders.

'Now you've got what you came for, please leave.'

He shook his head. 'Not yet. We're not finished yet. Nothing like. You were a fool to tell me about my father's deceit, but you couldn't resist. You wanted to hurt and God knows, you succeeded. Of course you knew there was a lake below the restaurant. You couldn't have lunch there without seeing it. Only I don't understand when you found the opportunity to move the signpost? After lunch? In broad daylight? I don't think so. Harry was already talking about putting up a fence. He was aware of the danger, but one thing I know . . . you killed Angela, you murdering bastard.'

Irving paled, yet there was a glimmer of satisfaction in his eyes.

'No, you killed her, Simon, not me. Anjana was sentenced to death the moment she committed adultery. Under Sharia law she would have been buried to the neck and stoned to death. I had thought of sending her home to face her punishment, but I balked at the publicity. Where I come from there are many willing executioners. I hired one of them. The signpost was twisted around while we were driving to the hotel. It might not have worked, but one way or another Angela would have died, I promise you that.'

All notions of self-preservation fled in the face of his anger. Simon lurched across the desk and grabbed Irving's left wrist, pulling him towards him. He drew back his fist to smash it into the face of the man he had hated for so long.

'Bastard! You bastard!'

Irving's hand slid into the drawer and a split second later Simon found himself staring into the muzzle of a handgun.

'Pull the trigger. Why don't you? Then you'll have killed both of us. Or can't you face a second killing?'

Minutes passed. Then Irving dropped the gun on his desk. 'We're behaving like fools.' He sat back shaking.

Lunging forward, Simon grabbed the gun and

pointed it at him. He ached to kill pull the trigger, but he knew he never would.

'She said she was leaving me,' Irving was muttering hoarsely. 'I could never allow her to go. She belonged to me.' Tears cut a crooked course down his cheeks.

The gun was vibrating in Simon's hand. As he saw it, both of them were guilty. So were the rest of his friends who had drawn straws and vowed to get rid of Irving and provide each other with alibis. And they were still covering up, not knowing which of them had done the deed.

Irving appeared to be waiting for something. His eyes were closed, his hands clasped together as if in prayer. Did Irving think he would do his dirty work for him?

Simon put the gun down carefully.

'If you want to die, do it yourself. By the way, I've been taping the conversation,' he lied, as he walked out. It was only when he reached the gate that he heard a shot and saw the guards run inside. A woman screamed. Simon shuddered and turned back.

53

Ten days later, Simon received a text on his mobile which read: '*Dear Simon, I have returned from Kashmir for my father's funeral. I need to see you. Could I call round on Saturday in the late morning? Bela.*'

Joy came on strongly like a punch in the guts. She was back! She was here! But she might be leaving again. Nevertheless, she was coming to see him . . . that must mean something. Hands shaking, he made three bad starts as he dialled back his okay. He should have guessed that Bela would return for her father's funeral, but the news that she was nearby kept him panting with hope.

Hoping to entice Bela to stay for lunch, Simon drove to the village and bought a roast chicken, a French loaf, a ready made salad, a jar of olives and freshly squeezed orange juice. Then he tried to keep calm as seven thousand seconds dawdled by. When, at last, her car approached, Simon fell victim to a dozen conflicting emotions, but when she stepped out and smiled, joy took over. To Simon she had never looked so lovely. Her gamine charm had fled and a sophisticated woman walked towards him in a classic black trouser suit with a white blouse and a single row of pearls. Her hair was swept up in a roll at the back of her head and fastened with a black Japanese comb that sparkled in the light. She had lost weight and it suited her. Deep black shadows under her eyes only heightened her appeal.

'Well, Bela, this is a surprise,' Simon said, trying to act as if nothing were wrong between them. 'I've missed you.'

When she bit her lip and didn't reply, Simon realised that his joy had been entirely misplaced. He had to search around for small talk.

'So what's this I hear about your father's factory being sold?'

She frowned at him. 'I sold it to a Japanese consortium. The new MD is a pretty shrewd operator. I think he'll make a go of it. Mr Puri has been put in charge of in-staff training. He's learning Japanese.'

Suddenly she giggled and he caught a glimpse of the old Bela.

'The company are looking for village homes for the new executives and their families,' she went on, as if glad to have something to say. 'Fifty skilled workers from the company's Nigerian plant are on the way here to teach the Brits how it's done.'

'Never mind that. Tell me about you. How are you keeping?'

'I'm very busy. There's not enough time each day. I've created a trust fund for orphaned children in Kashmir. We're building a home and a school. The Salma Shah Children's Trust. Salma was my daughter's name. It means peaceful. It's a lovely name, don't you think? I hope that it will bring peace and happiness to the waifs we rescue. I'm supervising everything and loving every minute of it. I've quit the West. I'm devoting myself to Muslim duties.'

She was always astonishing him, but this time his anger got the upper hand. 'What the fuck are Muslim duties?'

She looked startled at his churlishness. 'Good works, religious ritual, preparing special foods. All kinds of things. As a matter of fact, I usually wear a burkha at home.'

Home! That hurt! Hope dimmed like a power failure. But even power failures come to an end, he consoled himself.

She walked inside and took his hand. Glancing up at him, she smiled gravely and he felt a rush of love.

'I thought we might go for a walk before lunch,' he said bravely.

'The garden looks desolate.' She peered doubtfully out of the door.

'Of course, it's November, but the sun's shining and it's always warmer in the orchard.'

'Let's sit in the back porch. It's pretty there.'

'Yes. That's dead right. Let's.'

'I'm not hungry, Simon,' she told him, as he put a cloth on the table. 'But I'm thirsty.'

She sat down formally at the garden table, ignoring the couch. Mutual apprehension seemed to have put a stop to their small talk. Mouth pursed, she looked grave and he was tense with disappointment.

'Orange juice?'

'That's perfect. She began to tell him about her life in Kashmir. She no longer drank alcohol and there was little entertainment where she lived, but she loved gardening and she studied a great deal. He gathered that she had become very devout and serious, under the guidance of the local Imam, and he yearned for his sexy, fun-loving Bela.

'Why don't you have some wine?'

'You know why.'

She was slipping away from him again.

'Listen, Bela. Nothing's changed,' he said, feeling desperate. 'My feelings haven't changed.'

'No. You're wrong. Everything has changed,' she said. 'I was right to go away. We could never . . . '

'I love you, Bela,' he said, reaching across the table and grabbing her hands tightly. 'We can work it out.'

A flicker of doubt crossed her face. 'Can't you see that we could never again be normal with each other.'

'I don't believe that. When I found out who you were I went through hell because I thought I was . . . I thought I might be . . . That's the only reason why I was so damned rude on the phone. I had to find out before I could bear to talk to you.'

She gaped at him for a moment, not understanding, but then her hand flew to her mouth.

'I always suspected you . . . with my mother. You see, I saw you weeping when she died.'

'I loved her dearly.'

'She wasn't yours to love,' she whispered.

'Of course she was, because she loved me, too. Think back to when you were forcibly

466

married against your will.'

'You didn't marry my mother.'

'We were only nineteen. I was waiting until I earned enough to marry.' That was part of the reason, but now was not the time to bring up his father's racist views and his very real fears of losing his birthright.

'So how could you possibly have thought . . . ?'

Her eyes were dark with fear when he repeated all that Meli had told him about Angela's pregnancy. He knew he would never tell her what he had learned from Irving. Such a trauma would blight her life.

'So who caused my mother's death? Who moved the signpost? You promised that you would find out.'

'I've come to the conclusion that it was an accident, perhaps children playing, or the gardening service. Who knows? The coroner was right.'

'Is that what Melissa thinks?'

'I don't know,' he said uneasily.

'You're lying. I can see by your eyes. You have no talent for lying.'

'Melissa thinks it was me, but she's wrong, as usual. She tried to blame it on my grandfather, 'to protect me', she said. Her suspicions are absurd. Surely you know that I couldn't kill anyone.'

Hot sorrow burned in her eyes.

'I asked you to meet me because I want to know what happened when you saw my father. Immediately after you left he shot himself. You must tell me what you were talking about. That's why I'm came to see you. You must know what prompted my father to do this awful thing.'

Surprised and badly hurt, Simon had no answer. He needed to talk about 'them', not her father and his mad jealousy. Bela looked so vulnerable that he hardened his resolve. She must never find out.

'It was obvious that your father was depressed about his business.'

'He's had business failures before. He bounces back. Fatima heard you both shouting. Your chair was knocked over. My father kept a gun in his drawer. It was illegal, but he'd been threatened once or twice. Strangely, it had your fingerprints on it, as well as his. The police . . . and I . . . think he pulled his gun on you.'

'The police questioned me about that, too,' Simon admitted, 'but I was getting into my car when I heard the shot. There were witnesses.'

'I know, but why did he threaten you?'

'We were arguing . . . shouting at each other. I grabbed the gun. It wasn't difficult. I don't think he was serious about shooting me. Then I put the gun on his desk and left.'

'Yet he shot himself only minutes after you left.'

Simon sighed. There had to be a good reason. She wouldn't take any old lies. He stared at her for a long time, trying to impress her image on his memory while he searched for something that was both relevant and believable.

'I proved to him that I had no reason to kill him, nor Angela, since the sale of Redhill had fallen through. I told him, too, that Angela had promised to leave him and live with me.'

'Is that it?'

'Yes. He was hurt and angry.'

'So he tried to maintain his family's honour by shooting you . . . that was his duty under Sharia . . . and when he failed, because he never had the killer instinct, he was so ashamed, he turned the gun on himself.'

Simon kept quiet, afraid that he might let some vital fact slip out and she would pounce on it.

'Leave it, Bela,' he warned. 'Just let go. I won't discuss it further.'

'I know that you drew the short straw, so in thought, if not in deed, you helped to kill my mother,' she murmured.

'Oh, this is farcical. What's happened to you Bela? You were never like this.'

'And then you dishonoured my family with this adulterous relationship with my mother.'

'We loved, as you and I loved. Was that wrong?'

She wasn't prepared to listen as she talked over his voice. 'And in some small way you are killing me, too, because our love was very dear to me.'

Bela stared at him as if seeing him for the first time. She stood up and walked out of the room. He heard her footsteps in the hall. Then she hesitated and came back. For a moment of incredible optimism he thought that she had changed her mind and forgiven him.

'I've told you how it was,' he said with a catch in his voice. 'Now we must move on.'

469

Tears streamed down Bela's face. 'I must honour my father's responsibilities. It is my duty.'

A deep sadness fell about him, for Bela as well as for himself. For a moment he almost lost his resolve. He longed to fold her in his arms, but if he did, he would weaken. Give her time, he thought, watching the tears roll down her cheeks. Eventually she would come to terms with what he had told her and she would forgive him.

She fumbled in her bag while Simon sat there, loving the sight of her. Moments later he was amazed to see that she was holding a revolver. She looked so absurd that he wanted to laugh. Perhaps he did. He half-rose, dazed with disbelief as the muzzle swung towards him.

'No! Bela! For God's sake!'

He seemed incapable of movement as he watched her finger tighten on the trigger. He felt no pain as he spun around, only a total loss of balance. The report exploded in his ear as he fell.

As if in a dream he saw Bela leaning over him and felt her tears splashing his face. The gun was pointing towards him, her mouth was open, but her eyes were closed. She fired again . . . and again. His mind wandered. He seemed to be watching himself and Bela from a great distance.

* * *

Simon woke to tremendous pressure and pain in his shoulder. He groaned and opened his eyes to see the pale face of Sarah, eyes wide, mouth open, bending over him.

'Call an ambulance.'

'I have. I have. Ten minutes ago. They're on the way. The dogs fetched me. Can you believe it . . . I was collecting mushrooms in the woods when Angus and Sam came whining and barking. They were so distressed, so I ran back after them.'

'How badly hurt am I?'

'You've been shot in the shoulder. Who did this awful thing?'

'Only one shot?' he gasped.

'I can't tell, there's so much blood. But there are two bullet holes in the floor near your head.'

He struggled to stay conscious. 'Pull a rug over them. I tripped and the gun went off.'

'What are you talking about? There's no gun here.' She was shaking violently.

'I was in the woods. I managed to get back. I don't remember how.'

Cold with terror, Sarah hung on to his hand. 'Don't talk. Lie still. You've lost a lot of blood. I'll back you, if that's what you want. Don't worry about a thing, Simon. I'll move into the house and stay here until you get home. But just . . . just be careful now. Don't talk. Lie still. Ana's on the way. I persuaded her to come by train and not to drive. Hang on. Don't let go, Simon.'

He passed out again.

Part 5

Winter's end, Early March, 2002

Joy returns blinking,
Like a hedgehog
From its winter hibernation.

54

Three months after he returned home from hospital, Simon received a letter with a Kashmiri stamp. He opened the envelope with shaking fingers and as the fluttering airmail sheets unfolded, it seemed that the paper carried the scent of the woman he loved, but perhaps he only imagined it. He read the letter quickly and then burned it, but the words were gouged in his memory.

Dear Simon,

Matthew Luze came here to see me. Can you believe that? He told me what happened to you. He said that the police questioned you in hospital several times, but you stuck to your story of the hunting accident and eventually they gave up.

Despite what I did, you lied to protect me. Thank you, Simon.

I want you to know that I took our first orphan, a girl of only nine years, recently rescued from a carpet workshop, on an outing to a nearby lake to feed the ornamental ducks. She looked so happy that I was transported back to the day when I was taken by my father to a hotel in Temple Minnis. My mother was ill and Father had to meet a town planner there.

For the first time in years I had a crystal clear

recall of that day. I remembered how I sat waiting by a roaring fire with my fruit juice and cake. Later my father took me outside to feed the ducks and swans.

No wonder I could never look back on my mother's death without trauma. I used to adore my father and I guess that my conscious mind could never accept the awful truth . . . that my father knew there was a lake under the snow. I feel sure that it was his mad jealousy that led him to direct my mother to drive across the ice to her death on that bitter night.

I now know why you lied about your conversation with my father. I'm sure that you trapped him into admitting his crime. Perhaps you threatened to tell the police. Then you tried to protect me from learning the truth.

I am very confused about morality nowadays. I still feel a hybrid, but on my mother's behalf, I am determined to be a good Muslim, which is why I had to avenge my family's honour, which is my duty under Sharia. Yet another part of me knows that it is wrong to kill, for whatever reason.

You must forget me now, Simon. Think of me as having taken orders as a nun. I work hard, live simply and the trust I have set up (but do not control) pays me a small wage for the work that I do. I want no more than this out of my inheritance. I thank Allah that you did not die and I love you, as before. No, much more.

Bela.

55

It was mid-March, nearing full moon and during the evening the wind had swung to the north-west. The sky was clear and Simon reckoned that this was about as good as it was going to get. At 4 a.m. he got up and dressed in his warmest farm clothes. Leaving the dogs locked in the porch, he set off towards the extreme south-east boundary of his land. Taking his rifle, a thermos of strong, sweet coffee, a torch and binoculars, he soon built up a sweat as he slogged uphill over fields and hills until he entered the woods, where he slowed to pick his way through the dense bushes.

Reaching the stream, he flicked his torch along the muddy slopes and sure enough saw the puma's spoor. From the look of it, the beast often drank there. After a twenty-minute slog uphill through the thicket, Simon emerged into a barren, sandy area, fit only for spasmodic grazing, but even that was dangerous for the land sloped steeply to a pebbled beach where the surf raged in at high tide.

Keeping up a punishing pace, he neared his goal: a rocky outcrop perched near the edge of the beach, where neighbouring farmers had reportedly seen the big cat heading. If they were right, it had found an ideal place to hang out, he decided grudgingly. The piles of boulders were unmovable without a crane, and the crevices between them made an ideal lair for a marauding predator. Nearby, fresh water flowed through a near-impenetrable wood and there were plenty of rabbits around.

For all he knew, the cat could be watching him. Well, that was a chance he'd have to take, but he was counting on the puma leaving its lair by night and hunting over the neighbouring farms. When it returned he would be waiting.

Having scouted the area in daylight, he knew exactly where he would hide, in a convenient cleft in the rocks near to where he hoped the puma would pass. The ground was damp, temperatures were only slightly above freezing and the keen wind brought a chill factor of minus four degrees, or thereabouts, he judged. Sighing, he pressed his body into the crevice.

He waited. The wind dropped and moonlight lit the scene with a strange, ethereal glow. An hour passed and then another. Simon's feet numbed inside his boots, he felt he was freezing half to death and he had the unwelcome feeling that when he saw the big cat, he might suddenly sneeze and frighten it away. Could he pull the trigger with his numb hands? Trying to keep quiet, he flexed his fingers and placed them carefully around the barrel of his rifle, one finger gently touching the trigger.

Half-dazed with hypothermia, his mind wandered to Bela, as it so often did when he was feeling vulnerable. It had taken weeks of misery before he had realised that he would never have to stop loving Bela. There was no law against loving. His memories would never fade. From time to time he would take them out and air them. It was enough to know that she was happy.

Sometime later he switched to full alert without knowing why. It was as if a subconscious alarm had triggered him back to the here and now. Something had moved at the periphery of his vision. The great lake of shadow that surrounded the woods had undulated, stretched, and flowed into another shape, like a globule of fat on water and it was silently coming his way.

As the shadow approached in short bursts of speed, Simon thrilled with excitement and trembled with anticipation. Moments later, he saw the puma clearly as it slunk over the ground, a rabbit carcass hanging from its mouth. It looked emaciated and patches of white shone on its back and mouth. It was limping, favouring the left hind leg. As it neared, Simon saw that it had been wounded with a shotgun and the fur had turned white around the shiny scars.

The wind was carrying Simon's scent out to sea. Unaware of the danger, the beast passed close by, almost near enough to touch. Then some sixth sense signalled danger. It stopped short and spun around to face Simon. Flattening itself on the ground, snarling, the puma inched slowly backwards until it paused, as if sensing that there was no escape. Facing death, it stilled and stared into the barrel of the gun. Despair shone in its eyes and then its gaze turned to Simon.

Simon stared at the puma as if mesmerised and the creature stared back. Time slowed and stood still as they remained locked in an unlikely clash of wills. He felt drawn to the beast with grudging admiration. How could he kill it when he was filled with understanding? He felt the puma's pain and its desperate fight for survival. Loosed as a cub into an alien world, the beast had reached back to pristine instincts to find the means to survive.

Simon lowered the gun gently, but remained still as he stared into the puma's blazing yellow eyes. A fleeting interchange seemed to be passing between them, recognition of something shared. He felt a sense of deep compassion as the boundaries between them melted away. All at once, he was the puma and the puma was him. He was the trees and the rocks, he was the grass and the swooping owl. He was part of consciousness and consciousness was all. He had merged with a force of overwhelming, intense love and he had lost himself entirely, as time stood still. How and why it happened, he never understood. He knew only that he had slipped out of the self-made shell that was Simon Shepherd and merged with another reality.

The spell was broken as the puma, scared and maimed, but never beaten, backed away, yet its eyes never left Simon's. It seemed to know that it was not going to be shot. Not today, at least. It leapt up and limped to a crevice in the rocks, leaving its prey behind.

Stiff with cold, and strangely moved, Simon struggled out of the hole and tried to rub his limbs back to life. Something had touched him. He understood that he had received a gift. A certain recognition had come to him. But why me? He wondered.

Turning, he saw the puma crouched on the rocks watching him intently. He stooped and flung the rabbit carcass towards it. Was it a plea for life that had shone in those blazing yellow eyes? More than this, surely. Simon picked up his gear feeling puzzled.

Later, he could never find words to describe his experience, even to himself, although he tried. Whichever way he put it, words fell far short of the reality.

$$\star \quad \star \quad \star$$

In a sudden flicker of painful acknowledgment he realised that in some indefinable way he and all life were one. There had been intimacy; too. He had encountered and merged with a force of intense love. But why say encountered when it was always there . . . or here? He gave up trying to find the right words to describe something that was indescribable.

As he plodded home, he began to think about the life force that had led the puma to endure such pain and hunger in its bid for survival. He was amazed by the beast's courage, its indomitable spirit and its quest to understand its world. Life . . . all life . . . was not quite as he had thought it was.

At that moment Simon knew that he had taken the first step on a long journey. As he saw it there was the delusion and the reality. The trick was to know which was which. His life would carry on just as before. He had the farm to run. Nothing was changed. Yet everything was changed.

★ ★ ★

After the long night's vigil, Simon was ravenous, which was strange. He couldn't remember when last he felt so hungry. After he'd fed the dogs, he took a fresh loaf of wholewheat bread from the freezer and defrosted it in the microwave. Each movement was familiar and it seemed to bring him peace. When had he last bothered to make fresh coffee, he wondered. The idea appealed to him, but as soon as the aroma of fresh coffee filled the homely kitchen he was suffused with bitter-sweet memories. But that was the past, he decided. He let go of it gently, as if releasing a butterfly. Taking out a side of smoked ham, he cut thick chunks, which he placed between slices of buttered bread and smothered it with homemade mustard.

I'll soon be making my own butter again, he decided.

The wind had veered to the south-west and the temperature was fast rising as the sun warmed the land. He decided to sit on the bench in the vegetable patch, as Tom used to, so he carried out his plate of sandwiches and a mug of coffee.

It takes a long, harsh winter to appreciate spring and to Simon, every daisy, primrose and snowdrop looked delightful. The dazzling sun was rising over the hill and the grass and wild flowers sparkled with dew. Leaving his empty plate on the bench he went down to the yard where Sarah was cleaning the dairy. She looked sulky and sad. No doubt she would tell him what was wrong. Sarah's big mouth was a source of endless embarrassment.

'I miss the cows and Flora,' she grumbled.

'There'll be others. We're restocking,' Simon told her. 'You're settled here, aren't you, Sarah?'

'Yes.'

'You'd best come along to the auctions with me. Start learning the business properly. I'll teach you,' he told the startled woman.

Saddling Daunty, he set off over the land with Sam and Angus loping behind. He could smell the grass and damp earth, a blackbird was singing, crows were cawing and innumerable small birds were chirping away in the hedgerows, while in the distance he could hear the faint sound of a siren floating over the downs from the Newtown plant, which had been resurrected by the Japanese consortium.

The land had lain fallow since the previous June, so Ana's ewes and rams and Candida and Ferdinand were up to their bellies in dense grass and wild flowers as they wandered from one luscious patch to the next.

A strange sensation set Simon quivering with warmth and reassurance. He'd had this feeling long ago, but he couldn't remember when. After a while he realised it was joy. Like ripples on a pond, the past year's traumas had been played out and debts had been paid, although Simon had to admit some were taking longer than others. Most of the locals had returned to their usual frenetic chase after profits and happiness, while Newtown residents were fully employed and planning strikes for higher wages. As Daunty trotted on, he thought about the women who were lost to him, but whom he would always love.

Cresting the hill, he paused and dismounted to gaze at the village far below: the church steeple, the main square, the tumble of shops and houses and further up the hill, the lake, the manor and Harry's Place, a picture postcard view, so calm, so still.

But who was the watcher? That was what he longed to know.

We do hope that you have enjoyed reading this large print book.

Did you know that all of our titles are available for purchase?

We publish a wide range of high quality large print books including:
Romances, Mysteries, Classics
General Fiction
Non Fiction and Westerns

Special interest titles available in large print are:
The Little Oxford Dictionary
Music Book
Song Book
Hymn Book
Service Book

Also available from us courtesy of Oxford University Press:
Young Readers' Dictionary
(large print edition)
Young Readers' Thesaurus
(large print edition)

For further information or a free brochure, please contact us at:
Ulverscroft Large Print Books Ltd.,
The Green, Bradgate Road, Anstey,
Leicester, LE7 7FU, England.
Tel: (00 44) **0116 236 4325**
Fax: (00 44) **0116 234 0205**

Other titles published by
The House of Ulverscroft:

TWISTED THINGS

Madge Swindells

Rescued after hours in the freezing water clinging onto the wreckage of her yacht, Clara Conner wakes up in Dover hospital. Patrick, her husband, is missing, presumably killed by the explosion that tore the *Connemara* apart. Clara becomes convinced that Patrick was murdered and that she was attacked. As she sorts through Patrick's business affairs, she realises that her husband had led a double life. He was involved with criminals and owed someone a lot of money. So when a mysterious man appears to be following Clara's every move, her fears for her safety grow — and that of her twelve-year-old son. Could this man be the attacker, and does he want to finish the job?

WINNERS AND LOSERS

Madge Swindells

It isn't until her grandfather's accident that Samantha Rosslyn realises that Woodlands, the family-owned brewery, is in deep trouble. To raise cash, Sam decides to sell an ancient family title, but the proposed sale attracts a young American historian, whose presence brings unexpected complications. As Sam struggles to pull the company round, her sister becomes involved with a campaign to publicise the plight of animals kept in battery conditions, her grandfather teams up with some wartime comrades to fight off a threat to the brewery from organised crime, and Sam's best friend is desperately trying to avoid an arranged marriage.

SUNSTROKE

Madge Swindells

A fund manager for a London merchant bank, Nina Ogilvie vowed that love would struggle to have a place in her life. She has reaped the rewards and become one of the City's most brilliant — and most heartless — operators. When her firm decides a sojourn in South Africa is just the break she needs, Nina finds the Cape's beauty piercing her professional defences. Caught up in a romantic whirlwind with Wolf Moller, a wealthy German, she becomes pregnant and sacrifices her career for a man she deeply loves — but barely knows. Two years later, Wolf disappears with her beloved son, Nicky, exposing the reality of a man wanted by both Interpol and the CIA . . .

SNAKES AND LADDERS

Madge Swindells

Marjorie Hardy has brains, courage and beauty - but these assets aren't nearly enough when she falls in love with Robert MacLaren, heir to a Scottish whisky empire. Her family is poor and her accent and upbringing are totally wrong for Robert's calculating step-mother. Finding herself alone and pregnant, Marjorie makes up her mind to keep her baby and fight for her daughter's rightful inheritance. Her dream sets her off on a long, tough road of business. She reaches the top, becoming co-owner of a highly successful publishing company — but now she must choose between ambition and love.

THE PALACE TIGER

Barbara Cleverly

India, 1922. A tiger has turned man-eater and is terrorizing the northern villages of the Princely State of Ranipur. Governor Sir George Jardine dispatches Joe Sandilands, war hero and Scotland Yard detective, to join in a hunt for the beast as the guest of the maharajah. But the weaponry with which Joe is issued rouses his suspicions about the true nature of his trip. The maharajah, an ally of the British, is dying, and the succession is unclear. The first heir to the throne has already died in a panther-wrestling incident. A second violent death occurs as Joe approaches the city. Misadventure? Or is a killer prowling the corridors of the palace of Ranipur?